Walking on Air

Catherine Anderson

A Valance Family Novel

Walking on Air

A SIGNET BOOK

SIGNET
Published by the Penguin Group
Penguin Group (USA) LLC, 375 Hudson Street,
New York, New York 10014

USA | Canada | UK | Ireland | Australia | New Zealand | India | South Africa | China
A Penguin Random House Company

First published by Signet, an imprint of New American Library,
a division of Penguin Group (USA) LLC

First Printing, February 2014

ISBN 978-1-61129-151-3

Printed in the United States of America

This book is dedicated to my three grandsons, Joshua Anderson, Liam Anderson, and Jonas Anderson. Each of you has, in your own way, filled my life with gladness, and I consider it a privilege to be your nana.

Chapter One

Random, Colorado, 1880

Gazing at the woman he'd just bedded, Gabriel Valance strapped on his double-holster gun belt, tested
each Colt .45 to be sure it slipped easily from the leather,
and then tied the thongs that kept both weapons firmly
seated low on his hips.

Grinning sleepily up at him, the young but experienced prostitute murmured, "Merry Christmas, gunslinger. It was nice to have a true gentleman pay me a
visit for once."

When was the last time anyone had referred to him
as a gentleman? Gabe couldn't remember. He glanced
at her again, feeling a familiar compassion. This woman
lacked the hard edge he'd seen in most working girls.
If she considered him to be cut from fine cloth, Gabe
shuddered to think what caliber of man she normally
entertained.

"Yeah," he said. "I guess it is Christmas Day, isn't it?
Merry Christmas."

She nodded. "I can remember better ones. But
thanks." She sat up, letting the sheet fall from her small,
well-formed breasts. She reached up to push her brown
hair out of her eyes, and for an instant he thought he
saw the glint of tears. He wondered how life had

turned her down the path of selling herself and con-
demned her to spending Christmas in a shabby room
that smelled of a succession of men she didn't love.

Ambivalence rose within Gabe at the thought of
Christmas and all the traditions of worship associated
with the holiday. In a vague way, he believed in God,
but as a kid, he'd never been taken to church or even
taught to pray. The celebration of Christ's birthday
each year had barely made an impression on his hard-
scrabble existence. Christmas was a time for people
with homes, families, and faith. Gabe, born to a prostitute who'd died young and sired by a gambler who
had acknowledged him only after death, had grown
into adulthood as a street orphan, stealing garments
from clotheslines to stay warm, sleeping in hidey-holes
to remain dry, and scavenging for food to keep from
starving. In his experience, only other folks lived in
regular homes with families who cared, and did things
like celebrate Christmas.

For some reason, the whore's wishing him a merry
Christmas triggered a queer sense of something lost.
Well, he'd learned long ago not to dwell on might-
have-beens. He knew that people exchanged gifts at
Christmas, and he could at least make one person
happy today. The girl had asked him for two dollars, a
high rate even in cities. He slid a hand into his pocket,
brought out a five-dollar gold piece, and handed it to
her. As she thanked him, her voice tight with some emotion he couldn't identify, he fished out two gold eagles
and casually laid his hand on the top of her dresser to
release the coins. She'd find them later, after he'd gone.
Maybe she'd get herself a new dress. Better yet, maybe
she'd purchase a stage ticket and get out of this hellhole
town in search of a better life.

Not that other towns would necessarily offer better.
In his younger days Gabe had believed that something

sweeter existed just beyond the next bend in the trail, but after thirty-three years of disappointments, he'd finally come to accept that it was a grim old world, and a goodly number of folks who walked the earth with him were as hard put to find happiness as he was.

He didn't look back as he left the shabby enclosure and stepped out onto the landing, which was sheltered by only a shingled roof that connected the brothel rooms to the tavern next door. A nice bit of civility, Gabe thought with a grimace. The fine gents of Random, Colorado, could frequent the bar, have a few social drinks, and then sneak like thieves in the night to the upstairs rooms, where all semblance of respectability vanished as they unbuckled their belts. Then, of course, to avoid explaining the expenditure to their wives, a lot of them tried to cheat the whores out of their fees when it came time to pay. That was a fine gentleman for you, long on looks and short on honor. Now that Gabe came to think of it, he didn't take it as a compliment to be compared to one of the bastards.

He stood on the landing, staring at the snow falling just beyond the boardwalk. The flakes melted the instant they landed on the packed-dirt street, but judging by the thickness of the downfall, Gabe guessed the ground would be white within a couple of hours. The upstanding citizens of Random would be pleased to get snow on Christmas. Personally, Gabe thought snow was about as much fun as chiggers in his boot socks, but then, he'd never really celebrated Christmas properly. He'd glimpsed the festivities only through windows, and the way his life was playing out, that was how it would stay. No decorated tree, no wonderful smells coming from an oven, no gaily wrapped gifts. Gunslingers didn't get to enjoy things like that, and he'd learned long ago to curl his lip at all the folderol and pretend he wanted no part of it.

As he started down the steps, he heard a whisper of rushed movement under the stairwell. Stopping dead, he hovered his hands over the butts of his Colts before he continued down the steps. As he neared the board-walk, he grasped the railing to vault over it and drop to the ground beside the staircase. On edge, he leaned low to peer into the deep shadows not yet illuminated by light of day, still an hour or so away. Narrowing his eyes, Gabe quickly made out a huddled form on the ground—a ragamuffin boy who sat with his thin back pressed into the corner created by the two exterior walls of the tavern and the brothel. The child clutched his arms around his knees in a pitiful search for warmth.

Memories blackened Gabe's mind, for he'd spent many a cold night as a small child under the stairwell that led up to his mother's room—a room where she'd been nice to the gentlemen, frequently abused for her trouble, and, more times than not, had earned too little to feed her child, let alone herself. To this day, Gabe had no idea what kind of sickness had taken her. He'd been—what?—five or six when she died. Much too young to understand death without some adult to ex-plain it to him. A man in a black frock coat had tromped up the stairs, followed by two male helpers, and they had carted Gabe's mother away on a board, her body covered by a sheet, one of her arms dangling. Gabe could remember yelling out, "Where are you taking my mama?" And the man in black, whom Gabe now real-ized had been the undertaker, turned to say, "She's gone, boy." Gone? Gabe could still see his mother, her slender arm and delicate hand swinging like a wet rag. What did *gone* mean? How could she be gone when Gabe could still see her, plain as day?

Nobody had visited Gabe's shadowy, damp hiding place below his mother's room to explain that his mother had died. Over the next few days, an older prostitute named Priss had occasionally tossed him a hunk of bread, saving Gabe from starvation, until he'd finally come to understand that *gone* meant his mother wasn't going to return. She would never again wait until all the men stopped knocking at her door and then sneak him upstairs into her room. Her gentle arms would never again hug him close. The endlessly long, cold nights would never again end in her bed, which had been dry and warm even though it reeked of the countless men who'd lain between the sheets. There would be no more bits of food to make his belly stop gnawing. No loving hands to brush his black hair from his eyes. Gabe's world had ended as if someone had obliterated it with a stick of dynamite.

Maybe it was those memories that prompted Gabe to bend at the waist to get under the stairwell. The boy cowered against the wall, shrinking inside his tattered clothing. Even in the dimness, Gabe could see that the kid's oversize wool jacket was so full of holes that only a few threads held it together. Gabe crouched a distance away, recalling all too clearly how much he'd come to fear adults when he'd been a kid on the street.

"Hey," he said, trying to smooth the gruffness from his voice. "What're you doing down here?"

"Nuthin'."

Nuthin' made sense to Gabe. Long ago, he would have answered the same way. "Where's your mother?"

The boy had dark, dirty hair that fell over his face in oily hanks. With a jerk of his head, he indicated the upstairs rooms. "She used to work up there. Then she went off with some cowpoke, sayin' she'd come back for me. I'm still waitin'."

Gabe had a bad feeling that the kid's mama was gone coon, a cowboy's way of saying gone forever. Maybe the mother had taken sick. Or maybe she'd hooked up with some bastard who'd injured her so badly she couldn't return. In the end, the woman's fate didn't matter. She'd left a child behind, and Gabe understood just what that meant for this boy. The hell of it was, Gabe was powerless to intervene. He couldn't take on a kid to raise, even though the idea had some appeal. Because of his father's belated sense of responsibility as he lay dying, Gabe had been left a heap of money back in Kansas City, enough that, after selling all of his sire's fancy gambling houses, he could live in high cotton for the rest of his life. Sadly, circumstances had never allowed him that luxury. For one, he didn't know how to live fancy, and second, his reputation as a gunslinger kept him on the trail, trying to avoid upstarts who wanted to make a name for themselves. All Gabe had at any given moment was his horse, a saddle, two trail blankets, a little dry food in his bags, and enough coin in his pocket to lie over in some out-of-the-way town until he got the itchy feeling that always told him it was time to move on. Then, if he was lucky—and he wasn't always—he could slip away, ride the trail hard, and spend some time in another town before some man, young or old, called him out into the street. That was no life for a kid. Gabe's existence could end abruptly, and then what would happen to the youngster? Besides, Gabe didn't want this boy's death on his conscience, if the child got between him and a bullet.

The thought made Gabe shudder. He'd been in Random for only a month, but he was already getting that itchy feeling. Tomorrow, with Christmas over and the shops in most towns along the trail open for business again, he'd be moving on. It didn't matter to him that it was the dead of winter, or that he had only the brim of his Stetson to keep the snow from slipping under the collar of his coat. But a boy couldn't endure such harsh conditions.

Still, Gabe couldn't bring himself to walk away. He considered his options. There weren't many. The kid was too young for Gabe to give him a bunch of money. He'd piddle it away or lose it, or it'd be stolen, and in the end, he'd end up under the stairwell again. Maybe, Gabe decided, he could stay over an extra day, guarding his back every second, and talk with the local preacher. Surely there was a family in town who'd be willing to take in a kid and raise him properly—if Gabe offered enough money to make it worthwhile. Money talked. He'd sure learned that. And he'd learned, too, that few people could do such a deed out of the goodness of their hearts. This boy would be an extra mouth to feed, bottom line, and folks with smallish incomes would be unable to say yes unless the boy came with a generous monthly stipend attached.

Yes, Gabe decided, he'd stay an extra day and see if he couldn't get this kid settled somewhere. At present, though, it was a hair before dawn on Christmas morning, when the preacher and his flock would be celebrating the birth of Christ. Nobody would have the time or interest to consider the fate of an orphaned boy until the holiday passed.

Gabe drew a third gold eagle from his trouser pocket and, with the ease of long practice, gave it a toss. The coin landed on its edge and rolled to the gouged and holey tips of the boy's boots, which appeared to be several sizes too small, judging by the protrusion of one toe extending well beyond the sole. Gabe's excellent aim, much to his shame, came from frequently following in his father's footsteps, elbows braced on a poker table in some gaudy saloon. The one and only good thing Gabe could say that he'd inherited from his dad was a gift for playing cards. Learning how to spin a coin on its edge across green felt had served him well over the years. It kept his hands free to go for his guns if some cocky asshole decided to call him a cheat. More than one man had lost his life over a poker game. Gabe had made it a point not to become one of them.

"Boy," he said softly, "there's ten dollars to get yourself some decent clothes. You can't buy any today. It's Christmas and all the shops are closed. But you can get some tomorrow."

The kid snatched at the coin, closed his fingers around it, and stuck a grubby fist into his pocket. The twist of his lips that passed for a smile was clearly visible to Gabe in the charcoal gloom. "Mister, my belly's emptier than a beggar's pocket. Ain't clothes I'll buy."

Gabe lifted his hands. "No need to buy food. I plan to mosey next door for a couple of whiskeys to wet my throat, but afterward I'll take you out for a big breakfast, and you can roll all the leftovers up in a napkin to hold you for the rest of the day."

The kid's unchildlike gaze locked with Gabe's. "Yeah? After a couple of jiggers you're gonna feed me? Hell, mister, thanks for the money, but I know better than that."

Gabe recognized that snort. He'd made it himself more than a few times—mostly as a disillusioned youngster. He stared hard at the kid for a long moment. "I said I'll be back to take you to breakfast. The hotel restaurant stays open for guests. We'll have ourselves a feast. But first, I got a gnaw in my gut for a little whiskey."

The boy nodded indifferently. Obviously, he didn't believe Gabe would return. "You a drunk?"

Gabe nearly smiled. He tipped a glass now and again, but he wasn't dependent upon alcohol. He simply had an inner clock that told him it was still way too early for the hotel to be serving breakfast, and, God help him, one of the few pleasures in his life was a good belt of booze after being with a woman.

"No, not a drunk." Gabe backed out from under the stairs and straightened. "Keep your appetite sharp. I'll be back in a few minutes."

As Gabe turned toward the tavern, he realized how lonely and utterly empty he felt. He wanted so much more out of life, but the good stuff, like taking that boy under his wing, always seemed just beyond his reach. A quiet hopelessness welled up inside him, bringing unaccustomed and unwelcome pain. Things were never going to change. He was never going to change. And the hell of it was, he wasn't really sure he wanted to go on living if this was how it would always be, day after meaningless day blending into equally meaningless nights. Dodging bullets because some punk wanted to be known throughout the West as the fastest draw. What was the point?

A few steps took Gabe to the bat-wing doors of the saloon. He pushed them open, scanned the few men sitting at tables wreathed in smoke, and then walked over to stand at the bar. Behind him, the room fell silent. Well, he was used to that. His formidable reputation with a gun made him fearsome to a lot of folks. "A bottle of your best whiskey and one glass," he told the barkeep.

Bald pate gleaming in the lamplight, the plump older man slung a white towel over his shoulder, pulled the cork on a bottle, and then set it and a glass in front of Gabe. "Merry Christmas."

Gabe nodded as he poured a two-finger measure of amber liquid into the tumbler. After one gulp followed by a whistle through his teeth, Gabe barely suppressed a shiver. Even so, he sloshed another measure of alcohol into the glass, downing it quickly so he'd get the burn over with fast. Though he didn't often overindulge, he knew that drinking rotgut liquor most of the time because nothing better was available meant he'd probably die with yellow skin from liver disease, just like his father. At the thought, Gabe poured another jigger. Why not? It wasn't as if he had one damned thing to live for.

The barkeep moved to the far end of the counter to serve another man, a seedy-looking fellow in a rumpled gray suit. The doctor, maybe? In the month that Gabe had been in Random, he'd kept pretty much to himself and still couldn't recognize all of the town's residents on sight. He studied the man in the mirror that lined the opposite wall, which, by power of reflection, made the establishment's liquor stock look a lot more ample than it was. The fellow had a thin, haggard countenance, a large nose to support his wire-framed spectacles, and a prominent Adam's apple that bobbed with nervousness above his dingy white shirt collar, which sported a limp, off-kilter red necktie, the loops escaping from a tarnished stickpin. His blue gaze locked with Gabe's in the mirror. Recalling his manners, of which he had few, Gabe looked away and found himself staring at his own reflection.

Christ on crutches. He looked like the very devil, his attire all black from his Stetson on down. His jet hair needed a trim, the shaggy ends shining in the light where they curled over his collar. His eyes, the color of thrice-boiled coffee, glittered like polished stones in his sun-darkened, sharply chiseled face. No wonder ladies veered off the boardwalk to avoid encounters with him, and people fell silent when he entered a building. He had the look of a coldhearted killer.

Well, that was fitting. He was a killer, though he'd never set out to be—or had a choice. Some people believed they were in control of their lives, but Gabe had learned the hard way, and at a young age, that fate was as fickle and inconstant with her favors as a dance-hall girl.

Remembering his breakfast date with the ragged, hungry boy, Gabe corked his bottle, asked the barkeep to put his name on it, tossed a coin on the bar, and left the saloon. As he pushed through the doors onto the boardwalk, he saw signs that people were awakening to celebrate Christmas. Scattered ribbons of chimney smoke canted upward into the gunmetal gray sky. He fleetingly imagined the interiors of the homes from which the smoke came. Sleepy children staggering downstairs to stare in wonder at the gifts left for them under the Christmas tree. Cheerful fires crackling on brick hearths. Gaily decorated stockings stuffed with sweets. Women stoking their stoves to roast stuffed turkeys. Was that really what Christmas was like?

In comparison to the cozy pictures in his mind, Main Street looked funereal, the windows of the shops dark and bleak, snow drifting listlessly through the gloom. Only one spot of brightness shimmered in the dreariness, the windows of the milliner's shop a half block away. Candles flickered on the interior sills, warm beacons to a lonely man. Gabe bypassed the stairwell where the boy waited, thinking he'd come right back, and strode slowly toward the light, yearning to catch just one brief glimpse of Christmas before it turned daylight and he'd be caught staring through windows.

Several yards before he reached his destination, Gabe heard a man call his name. The hairs on his nape prickled. He had lived through this same scene too many times not to know how it always unfolded. Hand hovering over his six-shooter, he whirled to face the danger. He glimpsed movement in the shadows of a building. Then he heard a shot ring out and knew that whoever was lurking in the folds of darkness meant to kill him in an unfair exchange of lead.

For an instant, Gabe welcomed the thought and didn't go for his weapon. But then his instinct to survive took over. He slapped leather and fired at the black blur of a man . . . and felt a slug of lead plow into his chest with such stunning force that he was knocked backward and off his feet before he heard the second report of his opponent's gun.

Lying motionless on the frozen ground and staring stupidly at the still-dark sky, he felt no pain, just an odd heaviness and an awful coldness.

"I got him!" a man shouted. "I shot Gabriel Valance! Me! Pete Raintree!"

Gabe managed to turn his head slightly and saw a thin young man staggering toward him, crimson already staining the front of his jacket. The youth's legs gave out just before he reached Gabe. He fell to his knees with a bewildered expression in his eyes and then touched the blood on his jacket as if he couldn't quite believe it was there.

"Dammit, you went and kilt me, mister."

The younger man no sooner uttered the words than he pitched face-first into the frozen mud, dead before he ever hit the ground. Gabe tried to sit up, but his limbs wouldn't work and there was no air.

This is it, Gabe thought, and returned his gaze to the sky. The air around him smelled faintly of gun smoke, whiskey, and the metallic sweetness of blood. A fitting end. The chill of Gabe's gun butt lay against his palm, his fingers limp around it. He regretted that he'd ever pulled the damn thing from its holster. The dead youth beside him was barely old enough to be dry behind the ears, yet Gabe had snuffed out his life. And all for what? So he could lie in the street and die with snow pelting him in the face?

It hit Gabe then that no one would mourn his passing, not even the boy for whom he'd promised to buy breakfast. As the fog of death closed in around him, as the effort to breathe became exhausting, he felt a clawing regret. He wished that just one person would cry for him, that just one person might miss him. Just one. But in all his miserable life, not once since his mother had died, had he known or earned that kind of sentiment. He'd caused plenty of tears, he guessed, but none of them had been shed for him.

His world was growing colder and darker. Why couldn't things have been different? Why, despite all his efforts and good intentions, had he been unable to change? *It's Christmas, dammit. People shouldn't die on Christmas.* His unsteady gaze searched for the brightly illuminated windows of the hatmaker's shop. In the moment of brilliant clarity that comes right before death, he managed to focus. Candlelight beamed in the window, casting a cheerful amber glow over the artfully draped fir boughs that framed the glass. The greenery outlined the face of a woman, her solemn gaze fixed on Gabe, her blond hair shimmering like a halo. She was so beautiful Gabe wondered if he wasn't already dead and seeing an angel.

Dark spots dotted his vision. Her sweet countenance began to swim in and out, clear one moment, gone the next. With every ounce of his remaining strength, Gabe tried to keep his eyes open, but the blackness grew thicker until it settled over him like a blanket, wiping out everything, even awareness.

Chapter Two

Gabe jerked back to fuzzy consciousness, then blinked, startled half out of his wits to find himself standing outside a wooden shack with a closed rickety door hanging slightly awry from rusty hinges. He clamped a hand over his chest, expecting to find blood, but felt only the front of his shirt and firm, unwounded flesh under the cloth. *I'm dead*, he thought. *Only this isn't how it's supposed to be. Where the hell are the pearly gates?* Maybe better people got pearls and streets paved in gold, while others, like him, were sent to the back entrance. Just deserts. After the life he'd lived, he couldn't expect a grand reception. Not that he'd ever believed in, or even heard much about, the pearly gates. His lack of faith undoubtedly accounted for the fact that the door was closed, barring his entrance.

So now what? Where was he supposed to go? He turned, glanced down, and felt his heart skip a beat when he saw that his boots rested on what looked like a wispy cloud. He stepped sideways, but there wasn't any earth. Jumpin' Jehoshaphat. What was holding him up? He felt his chest again, to reassure himself that he still had a body.

Suddenly two men appeared outside the shack. They wore long, flowing white robes and had rope sandals on their feet. One blond, the other brunette, they each sported long hair falling to just below the shoulder. Gabe assumed they were some sort of entrance attendants—only, the entrance to where? Given that he'd killed a young man only moments before dying himself, he didn't care to explore the possibilities. He wasn't all that sure heaven even existed, but he knew from personal experience that hell certainly did, even though the hell he'd lived in since early childhood had been on earth.

Without a word, the two men—were they angels who'd forgotten their wings?—entered the structure and gestured for Gabe to follow them. Gabe wasn't real sure he wanted to. What was in there, a yawning hole that led to an eternity of fire and brimstone? But he couldn't spend eternity standing outside a stupid shack that looked like a good sneeze would blow it over. Feeling shaky, which was unusual for him, he stepped inside but left the door hanging open behind him, just in case he needed to make a quick escape. His boots made no sound on the floor, and Gabe, bewildered by the lack of noise, looked down to discover that he still stood on clouds, not wooden planks, as he'd expected.

The men had taken seats behind a paper-strewn table that looked highly unorganized, and then they proceeded to quarrel heatedly over Gabe's identity, one of them convinced Gabe was someone named Abe Van Horn, the other insisting he was Pete Raintree, the boy Gabe had just shot. Trying to look as if he didn't resent being talked about as if he weren't there, Gabe averted his gaze and found himself staring stupidly at the men's bare knees and lower legs, revealed beneath the table. Apparently they'd hitched up their robes to get more comfortable.

Holding up a hand, Gabe forced himself to look them in the eye and said, "Hold it! My name's Gabriel Valance. I'm guessing you two are angels. Right? But where the hell are your wings? Do you dress different to greet newcomers or something? And am I at the wrong entrance or is this the back way into hell?"

Gabe had never pictured male angels with bony knees and hairy legs. Now that he thought about it, he'd always had a vague idea that angels were female. And he wasn't any too sure he wanted into heaven if it meant he'd have to wear one of those girlish-looking robes. Not that he was likely to get an engraved invitation, anyway.

The two men began shuffling a little frantically through their papers. Their eyes widened as they scanned Gabe's life history. With an appalled expression on his face, the blond angel glanced up and asked how a man with a respectable name like Gabriel could have led such a deplorable life. Gabe suspected he was face-to-face with the archangel Gabriel—a biblical figure almost everyone had heard of, even if they didn't go to church. Apparently the angel was none too pleased that one of his namesakes had been such a miserable sinner.

Still, delivered by an angel or not, such a sweeping condemnation seemed uncalled-for. Gabe felt a little indignant. "Come on," he said. "I haven't lived *that* bad a life. Aside from killing a few people, of course. But that was in self-defense, and I never really had a choice. It was shoot back or die myself. You going to hold that against me?"

The two men assumed stern expressions, making Gabe feel like a boy about to be dressed down by the schoolmaster, not that he'd ever been fortunate enough to experience that dubious pleasure. Even so, he wasn't far off the mark. From out of the clouds surrounding the shack, Gabe suddenly heard voices. After listening a moment, he realized they belonged to people from his past, a recounting of conversations they'd once had about him. In nearly every exchange, he was either cursed or greatly feared by the speakers. Only a couple of old ladies who knew him as a boy had anything good to say, and that was more pitying than anything else. *Poor little Gabriel Valance. That boy doesn't stand a chance.*

Gabe figured that just about covered his life story, and since he was clearly dead, his chance to make amends was gone. Never a man to put off the inevitable, he asked, "Where is hell? Sounds to me like I may as well make tracks in that direction. As you two have pointed out, I've killed fourteen men, counting the one this morning. Why bother reading the rest of my history? I don't want to wear a damned robe, anyway."

The two men regarded Gabe with saddened expressions, and in a flash, the clouds around Gabe's ankles turned to flame.

"Ow! Holy hell, that's hot!" He lifted his feet, trying in vain to escape the heat. "This isn't fair. I shouldn't have to go through this until I actually get there!"

Before Gabe felt any real sting, the angels waved away the flames. "Do you still have an aversion to wearing a robe?" the blond asked.

"Rather than roast like a bird on a spit, I'd wear just about anything, petticoats included," snapped Gabe, belatedly tacking on a respectful, "sir." Relieved that the flames were gone, however temporarily, Gabe added, more to himself than to the angels, "I can't believe hellfire actually exists. How can God call Himself merciful and yet sentence sinners to burn for eternity? I've got a hell of a lot of faults, but I wouldn't be that cruel to a dog."

The dark-haired man studied Gabe with solemn brown eyes. "It is indeed a very harsh punishment, but it isn't of God's making. The flames are Satan's creation, which is why Gabriel and I—Michael is my name, by the way—are assigned to heaven's gates. It's our job to save everyone we can, even men like you."

Gabe gave a bitter laugh and gestured at the shack. "Gates? What gates?"

Michael shrugged. "It's also our job to make every new arrival feel comfortable, and because you don't truly believe in the existence of ornate gates to heaven, we felt a shack might be less intimidating."

Gabe didn't like the fact that these two fellows seemed to know what he believed in and what he didn't, but he was relieved to hear that they were there to save him. Hey, if anyone needed saving, it was definitely him. He wasn't about to say so, though, and he sure as shootin' wasn't going to act cowed. "So, if your job is to save everyone you can, what do you have in mind for me?"

The two angels resumed their perusal of Gabe's life history, shaking their heads and clucking their tongues. The angel Gabriel glanced up. "Do you realize you have intimately consorted with one hundred and fifty-six women, all without benefit of matrimony or any feelings of genuine affection?"

That couldn't be right. Now they were insulting his manhood. Gabe grabbed the paper from the angel's hand and scanned it. "This isn't correct," he said indignantly. "You left off a bunch of names. And for your information, I was damn good at it." He ran his gaze down the list, then slapped the record with the backs of his fingers. "There, you see! You forgot to list the gal I made love to last night, proof that you might have left out others."

Michael's dark brows snapped together. "We haven't had time to add the name of the woman last night." His expression grew accusing. "So we'll make it a hundred and fifty-seven, and ask you again what you have to say for yourself. This isn't something you should be bragging about, Mr. Valance. Your flagrant disregard of nearly all of the Ten Commandments is shocking."

Gabe couldn't understand what they were so het up about. "I wasn't bragging. I was being accurate. And I never touched a married woman in my whole life. No adultery. You can't pin that one on me."

The angels sadly shook their heads. The golden-haired Gabriel took over the exchange. "Did no one ever explain to you that the seventh commandment encompasses far more than just adultery? Sexual inter-course with prostitutes falls under that rule, not to mention countless other things."

"Holy hell," Gabe replied. "Next thing I know, you'll be outlawing booze. Just because a man has the good sense never to get married, that doesn't mean he wants to live his entire adult life without getting a little now and again."

The angel Gabriel sighed. "You are a challenging case indeed." He turned another page of Gabe's life history and once again did a head waggle. "Have you done nothing with your life to commend yourself?" he asked. "Did you perform no acts of kindness?"

"Oh, hey, I'm good on that one," Gabe said. He felt on firmer ground now. "Take the whores, now. I always paid double their rates, even if the service was bad. You two probably don't have any experience with working girls, but that was definitely unusual, you know? A lot of men fasten their flies, bolt out the door, and don't even pay the tab." On a roll, Gabe stabbed a finger in their direction. "And let me tell you, that isn't all they do! Most whores get knocked around more times than not, and even then the bastards who're fond of beating on women don't pay for the privilege. I not only paid that last gal's fee, but I gave her twenty-three bucks extra. That's a lot of money!"

Michael's brown eyes bugged slightly. A hooded expression slipped over Gabriel's blue-eyed countenance. Gabe could tell this wasn't going well. Shifting his feet quickly, he said, "And don't be forgetting the ten dollars I tossed to that kid in the street right before I got shot. Hell, I was going to take him out for breakfast and stay over a day to see if the local preacher could get some family in town to take him in."

Michael lifted his hands. "For a man of your immense wealth, the paltry sum of ten dollars hardly offsets all the bad things you have done. Nor does the fact that you planned to give any family who would take the boy a generous monthly stipend."

Gabe felt sweat tricking from his armpits and down his ribs. If he was truly dead, how could he possibly be perspiring? Again, he shifted his feet uncomfortably. These guys wanted to help him out; he could sense that. But so far, things weren't looking good for him. He desperately tried to recall some good things he had done. "I like dogs. Does that count?"

The angel Gabriel nodded. "It certainly does. Did you ever rescue one from cruel treatment?"

Gabe had done enough gambling to know when he'd just been dealt a winning card. "You betcha. I even got into one hell of a fight with a man once for beating his dog." He quickly recounted the tale to the angels. "That's kind, ain't it?" Damn, he was so nervous that he was slipping back into using poor English. Old Mrs. Harper, an ex-schoolmarm who'd taken him in once and tried to smarten him up, the one and only person in his life aside from his mother who'd ever done him a truly good turn, was probably rolling over in her grave. "I stepped in, regardless of the risk to myself, and saved that poor dog from one hell of a working over."

Michael waved a hand, and the clouds that drifted in a heavy layer over the shack floor opened to reveal that particular scene from Gabe's past. Gabe was fascinated. It was like attending a play, only he was one of the actors. He watched himself beat the stuffing out of the dog's owner, then shove the man's head in a horse trough. The angels sighed when they saw Gabe hold the fellow's face underwater until he stopped kicking.

"The bastard isn't dead," Gabe pointed out quickly. "See? He's moving now that his head is out."

"But you nearly drowned the poor sot," the angel Gabriel sternly pointed out.

Gabe lifted his hands, palms up. "So I let my temper get the better of me for a few seconds. That doesn't mean the miserable shit didn't have it coming. He was gonna kick that dog to death. You saw him." Gabe raked a hand through his hair and then settled the Stetson back on his head. He briefly considered removing the hat out of respect, but they were being so nasty, he resisted the urge. "I have a pretty bad temper when I get riled, but surely that's forgivable under those circumstances."

"Your heart may have been in the right place," Michael conceded, "but your failure to control your temper negates that particular good deed. Have you anything else to say for yourself?"

Think, Valance, he told himself. *You're in serious trouble here, man.* "Uh, well . . . I was always real kind to my horse. After hitting town off the trail, I always took care of him first. He got washed and rubbed down before I even thought about a bath for myself. He got water and food long before I did." He frowned, realizing that he was getting a ripsnorting headache. How was that possible if he was dead? "I have to admit that Brownie never got sex during our layovers, but he was a gelding, so that kind of fun wasn't an option for him. Otherwise I would've found him a mare to visit with on occasion."

Judging by the stares and glares that greeted this remark, he could tell he was delivering the wrong address to the jury. What did these angels want from him?

"To men of your time," the angel Gabriel said, "being good to your horse is considered a necessary kindness. Where would a man be without his horse?"

"On foot," Gabe replied. "Do I get any points for being honest?" No reply from his judges. "Okay, I'll take that as a no." Gabe could almost feel the heat of hellfire inching up around his ankles again.

Michael looked at him, and the unexpected compassion in the angel's eyes punched Gabe in the gut like a mule's hind hoof. It hurt. "Okay, okay," he said. "Looking back over my life, I haven't done much you could consider, you know, saintly. I guess I'm what you fellows would call a lost soul." A lump had grown in his throat, and he struggled to speak past it. "I . . . didn't live a very good life. I wanted to. Trust me on that, but most times, when I tried for something better, I got a kick in the teeth. If that happens enough, you quit trying, you know? That's how it goes for some of us down there. If we don't have bad luck, we don't have any luck at all."

The angels conferred for a moment, then turned in tandem to regard Gabe with thoughtful eyes. The golden-haired Gabriel assumed the role of pronouncing sentence. "It is clear to us, after reviewing your life history, that you actually were among those rare individuals who truly weren't given many opportunities to redeem themselves. Abandoned after your mother's death, unacknowledged by your father, forced to live in poverty on the rough streets of Kansas City as a boy, you never had much of a chance to be anything but what you became, a worthless individual who lived his entire life without leaving a good mark on the world or improving it in any way."

Gabe opened his mouth to argue but couldn't think of one damned thing to say in his own defense, so he just closed it again, braced his shoulders, and prepared to face his punishment. Worthless? As much as it rankled to admit it, maybe they were right about that.

"In rare instances," Michael said, "we angels have the authority to offer people one more chance. Would you be interested in going back down there for a specified period of time to give life another try?"

Gabe could scarcely believe his ears. Given his recent encounter with hellfire, he figured only a fool would say no. "What would I have to do?"

Gabriel replied, "You will be given an opportunity to save a lost soul. If you succeed in your mission, if you manage to drastically alter that lost soul's life, then you will have earned salvation. It won't be easy. You may have to sacrifice a great deal, and self-sacrifice has never been one of your strong points. Are you willing?"

Willing? After standing there with his feet on fire? Of course he'd be willing. "Yes," he said firmly.

The golden-haired angel swung a hand to part the clouds again. He gestured for Gabe to peer down through the hole. "There you see Tyke Baden, a lonely, embittered old man who has lived most of his adult life in Random."

Gabe bent at the waist to have a peek and got the eerie feeling that he had fallen into the old man's sitting area. He could smell the stench of an unwashed body, rotten garbage, and newly cooked food, a blend that turned his stomach. The room was a maze of trash piles—stacks of newspapers, periodicals, and all manner of other stuff that only someone out of his mind would keep.

"Tyke was once happily married with several children," Michael said. "He lived and worked hard for the welfare of his family for many years. Then, when his children were nearly grown, disease struck his household and only Tyke survived. After grieving, he grew angry at God and everyone else in town who hadn't died from the contagion. Sadly, his only solace was found in a whiskey bottle. He is now alone, lost, wishing for just one person to care about him, but when kindly townspeople attempt to enter his home, he yells, uses foul language, and frightens them away."

"Foul language don't make my ears burn." Gabe winced. He'd done it again, allowing nerves to push him back through the years to a time when he hadn't known how to speak proper English. "If all he needs is someone to care, I could clean him up and make him feel better."

"But could you love him?" Gabriel asked. "Truly love him? That is what Tyke needs in order to find salvation, to love and be loved again."

Gabe's nostrils burned from the stench, but he figured a little elbow grease would set the house right. "How long do I get to learn to love him?"

"A month."

"A month? Isn't that a pretty tall order?" Gabe gestured downward. "It'd take me a month just to clean up that rat's nest." Then, hearing what he'd just said, he backtracked. "I'll take him. No worries. I found a dirty, stinky dog once that I learned to love real quick. He up and died on me, but it wasn't for lack of caring on my part."

"Don't choose hastily," Michael interjected. "There are many lost souls in Random. We've selected three for you to consider, and then you can reach a decision."

With a flick of his fingers, Michael changed the scene below, and Gabe saw the boy who now spent half his life huddled under the whorehouse stairwell, waiting for his mother to return. Before he thought, he said, "He'd be a tough one to save in thirty days. He's bitter, suspicious, and been done wrong so many times he has no faith in human kindness. Boys like him don't normally turn to melted butter just because somebody's nice to them."

Michael nodded. "He is a difficult one, if not impossible. Which is why we've given you three lost souls to choose from."

The angel Gabriel flung his hand to change the scene below. "Here is our final lost soul for you to consider. Nancy Sullivan, now using the surname Hoffman."

Gabe almost lost his balance when he looked down and saw the young woman who had stood at the hat shop window, watching him as he lay dying. Now she was in her bedroom, wearing only a thin chemise, bloomers, and corset as she prepared to change dresses for church. Shooting a furtive glance at the angels, Gabe inched closer for a better look. Great legs, tight little ass, breasts to make a man's mouth water. She had a very interesting freckle—or maybe a small mole—on the swell of her right breast that peeked at him over the low scoop of her chemise. Without intending to, he leaned so far over the parting in the clouds that he nearly lost his footing.

"That's the one!" he proclaimed loudly. Hell, if he had to save a lost soul, he might as well have a little fun while he was at it.

The angels frowned in disapproval. Michael spoke up. "You're free to choose whichever mission you like, of course, but looks can be deceiving. Miss Sullivan, currently known as a widow, doesn't exactly cotton to gentlemen, and of all the souls you might choose, she will probably be the most difficult to save. She distrusts men, has sworn never to let herself love one, and abhors the institution of marriage. In short, she is a lonely, un-fulfilled spinster who has denied herself the joy of marriage and bearing children because she is terrified of letting a man, any man, have authority over her. She has no true friends and ventures from her shop only for necessities and to attend church. She also has a weak sense of humor. Her only pleasures in life are her little sister and her work, the latter of which she engages in from dawn until well after midnight, seldom taking a moment for herself, not because she enjoys being exhausted, but because building her business has been a constant struggle and she is afraid to sleep."

Gabe shrugged. "I have great respect for people who work hard, and I've yet to meet a person who can't learn to laugh. Why the hell is she afraid to sleep?"

"Nan Hoffman may not give you an opportunity to teach her how to laugh. She lives in fear of discovery. And if you take her case, you will learn only from her why she has trouble sleeping."

"Discovery of what?" Gave demanded. "You say she lives in fear?"

Michael sighed. "It's a long story. Nan wrongly believes she has a murder charge hanging over her head, and she is consequently running from her past, which will make it extremely difficult for you to gain her trust. Are you still interested?"

Gabe gave Nan Hoffman's tantalizing figure another long look and flashed a grin. "I love a challenge, especially when it comes packaged like that."

The angels folded their hands and studied Gabe with somber intensity. Michael said, "This isn't a game you're engaging in, Gabe. Nan Hoffman lives in a prison of her own making, and it will be your assignment to help her escape from it. It is heaven's standard policy that lost souls be given only a month to redeem themselves. Judging by your record, you aren't exactly an expert in affairs of the heart, and making a woman like Nan Hoffman fall in love with you may be beyond your ability."

For a moment, Gabe thought he'd misunderstood the man. "Wait a minute. If I only have a month to be back on earth, why in hell would you fellows want me to make some poor woman fall in love with me? Isn't that unfair to her?"

"Because," the blond inserted, "experiencing true love, however briefly, is the only way Nan Sullivan will ever be convinced to risk falling in love again. It will be your job to help her heal in the month you're allotted, so that after your second death, Nan will be able to lead a normal life, remarry, and have children of her own. If she doesn't do that, her life will count for far less than it should, and that is a waste that our heavenly Father simply can't countenance."

Gabe threw up a hand. "Whoa, there. Did you just say *remarry*?"

Both angels raised their eyebrows. Michael took over again. "Your marrying Nan will be absolutely necessary if you hope to completely banish her fears. As it stands, she abhors the institution of marriage, convinced that once a man gains authority over her, he will turn domineering and possibly become abusive. It will be your mission to show her how wrong she is."

It was Gabe's turn to raise his eyebrows. "With only a month to gain the woman's trust, how can you possibly expect me to convince her to marry me? And after I manage that, I'll need some time to prove myself. A measly month?"

Despite Gabe's objection, which he felt was reasonable, the angels remained firm. "One month," Gabriel repeated. "It's standard policy. If you take this assignment, you'll simply have to work fast. How you go about it will be entirely up to you. By fair means or foul, all that matters is that you accomplish your mission. It will be difficult, yes, but not impossible. If you decide to take this assignment, you will be armed with enough ammunition before you return to earth to coerce Nan Hoffman into marrying you."

"Coerce? Did you say *coerce*? I've never done that to a woman in my life!" Whether his own redemption hung in the balance or not, Gabe was no longer sure that he wanted to tackle this project. He liked the ladies willing, thank you very much. "What kind of angels are you fellows, anyway? It sounds to me as if you're giving me free rein to turn that poor woman's life topsy-turvy. What if I bungle the job and leave her more afraid to trust men than she already is? What if . . . Well, the possibilities are endless, and none of them make you look too good. Do you guys pull this kind of shit very often? If so, it's little wonder so many people down there walk around asking, 'Why me, God? Why me?'"

The angel Gabriel smiled. "It isn't God who turns people's lives topsy-turvy on a regular basis. It's the influence of evil and the actions of humans who make the lives of other people miserable."

"But this time, in Nan Hoffman's case, it will be God raining misfortune on her head," Gabe pointed out.

Michael nodded. "Yes, this time it will be our heavenly Father helping to orchestrate events, but I assure you, this sort of measure is taken only in extreme cases. As for your making things worse than they already are, if that should happen, we will simply erase from Nan's memory all that occurs during your visit back to earth. Things will return to the way they are right now, with you dead and doomed to hell, and Nancy Hoffman living a pathetically sad life without any hope of ever leading a fruitful one."

"In short," Gabriel interjected, "if you fail, Nan will

recall nothing of what transpires and no damage will be done. Except, of course, to you, Gabe. For you, failure means eternal damnation."

Gabe resumed gazing down at the Hoffman woman. She seemed to be frozen in place, as if time down there had stopped. He mourned the fact that the angels had turned her motionless *after* she'd finished dressing. She had a body to make any man salivate, and Gabe had been enjoying the view. Absently, he asked, "Exactly what kind of ammunition were you referring to when you said I'd be able to coerce the woman into marrying me? I'm not pushing any woman around, no matter what you say."

Gabriel smiled slightly. "Before we get to that, you must first commit to the assignment, and to do that, you should be made aware of everything you will be expected to accomplish."

"Shoot."

"First of all, you must agree not to die intestate the second time around. You will be expected to leave all your worldly goods to Nan so she will no longer have to work so hard to make ends meet after she is widowed."

"I have no problem with that," Gabe said honestly. "My father's money has never meant all that much to me, and I don't really care who it's left to."

"Second," Gabriel went on, "you will be expected to free Nan from her past, which still haunts her and from which she is still running. Unbeknownst to her, Horace Barclay, the man she believes she killed, survived being stabbed with her knitting needle and is alive to this day."

"She went after a man with a knitting needle?" Gabe glanced down at Nan with new respect. "She doesn't look like she's got it in her."

"Normally, she doesn't," Michael said. "You of all

people should understand how it feels to be backed into a corner. Nan was trying to ward off the unwanted physical advances of Horace Barclay, a much older man to whom she'd been affianced by her father, and she threatened Barclay with the needle to hold him at bay. Unfortunately, Horace tripped on the edge of a carpet, fell on top of her, and impaled himself. Nan couldn't feel a pulse or see any sign that he was breathing, so she believed the man dead. After emptying her father's coffers, she fled with her younger sister, assumed another name, and ended up living in Random, where she's been hiding from the law ever since."

"So she still thinks they're trying to find her and put a noose around her neck?" Gabe asked.

"Precisely," Gabriel replied. "How you impart to Nan that Barclay didn't die and chose to press no charges because the incident was an embarrassment to him— well, that will be entirely up to you."

Gabe nodded. "I reckon I'll know when the moment is right—if I decide to take her on."

Michael shifted on his chair, glanced at a sheet of paper, and cleared his throat. "Third, there is your relationship with Nan to discuss. As we have already made clear, we don't care how you go about it, but you must accomplish several tasks. You must not only get Nan to marry you, but you must also gain her complete trust, make her fall in love with you, and then make physical love to her. The last is extremely important, for in Nan's mind lovemaking is yet another way in which a man exercises his control over a woman. It will, of course, have to be a pleasurable experience for her, no matter how you decide to initiate it."

He was supposed to accomplish all this in a lousy month? And had he just heard right? Once again, Gabe held up a hand. "Are you saying you don't care how I get into the lady's drawers, coercion notwithstanding, as long as I make her enjoy it? This deal is starting to smell worse than last week's fish. Am I having a weird dream or something? I mean, okay, a guy can go to hell up here for adultery, yet rape isn't against your rules?"

The angel Gabriel smiled, a gentle curve of his lips that made his face seem to glow from within. "Of course rape is against God's rules, as are all actions that cause another person pain or sadness. If we believed, even for a moment, that you would ever force a woman to submit sexually, this conversation wouldn't be taking place."

Gabe scratched behind his ear, a habit of his when he grew confused. "Pardon me for saying so, but up until now, you boys didn't seem to hold me in very high regard."

"You're basically a good man," Gabriel assured him. "You've simply never had much opportunity to prove it. That is precisely why you are being given this second chance. How you handle Nan Hoffman will be entirely up to you, just as it would have been before you died. Everyone has carte blanche in life to do whatever he pleases and in whatever fashion he chooses. This situation is no different, except that, because of time constraints, you will be armed with a good deal of knowledge about Nan, so you'll have a better chance of accomplishing your mission within a month."

Michael added, "Matters of the heart between a man and woman come with all kinds of unspoken rules. If you don't know what they are, then God and both of us have misjudged you."

Gabe decided this was no time to plead ignorance of unspoken rules. The closest he'd ever come to tugging a woman's heartstrings was when he paid a working girl double her usual rate. Recalling his brief little dance in hellfire, Gabe sighed. "I'll agree to the stipulations. Of the three lost souls you've shown me, Nan

Hoffman is the most appealing, and I think I stand a better chance of success with her than I would with the other two."

Gabe no sooner agreed than the angels began cramming his head with knowledge about Nan's past. The scene at Gabe's feet changed, showing a much younger Nan being cruelly harangued by a man named Martin Sullivan whom Gabe soon deduced was her father, which gave him cause to wonder if maybe he hadn't actually been lucky to be ignored by his own sire. As Gabe watched Nan's life flash by, he began to seethe with anger. Little wonder she shied away from men. Scene after scene unfolded, revealing bits and pieces of her past, none of them pretty. Her father constantly accused her of being stupid, ugly, clumsy. The list of faults went on and on. Gabe could only marvel that the young woman had gathered enough self-confidence to run away from home in the first place, let alone start a business of her own and manage to make a success of it.

Gabe soon realized he was no longer trying to catch glimpses of Nan's delectable figure and instead was becoming entranced by her lovely gray eyes, which seemed to darken with shadows year by year until they began to look haunted and bruised. By the time the angels concluded the viewing, his throat felt oddly tight.

Gabe turned to face the robed men. "So that fat old bastard Horace Barclay didn't die, and Nancy has been hiding all these years for nothing?"

"Do you truly feel her hiding all this time has been for naught?" Gabriel asked with a mysterious smile. "Sometimes God works in strange ways. Because of Nan's flight from home, her little sister, Laney, has been spared the ordeal of growing up in her father's household. She is consequently a happy, well-adjusted girl who might otherwise have been only a shadow of her present self. Now our heavenly Father feels it is Nan's turn to be happy. Are you ready to return to earth and see to that for Him?"

Gabe nodded his agreement. The next instant, a strange, dizzy sensation came over him, he became lost in a whirlpool of darkness, and he felt as if he were falling. Then everything went black.

Chapter Three

Gabe jerked awake to face total darkness. Had the angels double-crossed him and routed him straight to the nether regions after all? But no, hell was hot and he was drenched in icy sweat. So where had those two jokers landed him? Blindly, he groped the surfaces around him. Blankets and sheets? Afraid to move, he lay there for a moment until his vision adjusted. Clear, bright light crowded against a window shade, sending slanting beams across a room. His Stetson reposed atop a hulking dresser, and there was his towel slung over the washstand. His hotel room, he realized, and released a breath he hadn't known he was holding. It whooshed in the silent room as loudly as a frustrated bull during a mating ritual.

Damn. What a crazy dream! Bullet holes and angels and a forced marriage. That did it. He was swearing off drinking. He didn't even believe in all that pearly-gates stuff. He ran a hand over his chest to assure himself that he was all in one piece. No gunshot wound. Cautiously he sat up, stroking his jaw to check for whiskers. Normally, his fingertips rasped over the night's growth, but this morning his face felt freshly shaved. Weird. He pushed out of bed, stepped to the window, and drew aside the blind. Below lay the main thoroughfare of Random. He'd apparently slept later than usual, because he saw passersby on the boardwalks, bustling this way and that. The normalcy of the scene was reassuring, but he didn't like needing reassurance.

Forget it, Valance, he ordered silently. *Just a bad dream*. Grinning, he released the shade and shook his head. It was Christmas, and judging by the amount of sunlight bathing the window, he'd slept through quite a chunk of it. No predawn walk down Main, no slug in his chest. It had all been a figment of his imagination, undoubtedly because he'd overindulged at the saloon last night. Yahoo! He was destined to live another day. He just hoped he hadn't snoozed through the breakfast hour at the hotel restaurant. With it being a holiday, no other restaurants were likely to be serving.

After lighting the lamp on the stand beside the bed, Gabe made faster work of his morning ablutions than usual because he didn't need to shave. Then, donning his black Stetson, he went downstairs, still half smiling over the crazy dream he'd had. Tonight he'd make sure he ate a light supper and avoided the saloon.

For a dream, it had seemed incredibly real. He could call up images of the angels' faces with such clarity that he could have sworn he'd actually met the fellows. And the details. Their hairy legs and bony knees, their robes, the timbre of their voices, and the expressions in their eyes. It boggled his mind that he'd been able to conjure up something so vivid from his imagination. Angels, indeed. He was pretty sure they appeared only to the devout, and that sure as hell didn't include him.

Gabe's favorite table by a window in the hotel dining room was available. He liked it because he could keep an eye on the boardwalk through a gap in the white, frilly curtains and also see the entrance to study people coming in for a meal. A man with Gabe's reputation couldn't be too careful, and he'd learned to spot trouble with only a glance. And he never, ever sat with his back to a door. Just in case.

Agnes, the waitress, a plump, jovial redhead with merry blue eyes, hurried over to fill Gabe's coffee cup. He gave her a smile. "Merry Christmas, Agnes. I'm sorry you got stuck working when you've got a husband and kids at home who are probably lost without you."

She nearly slopped hot liquid on the white tablecloth as she gave a startled laugh. "You've got me at a disadvantage, mister. How'd you come to know my name is Agnes?"

What was this? Gabe had been patronizing the place for more than a month. He and Agnes had been on a first-name basis almost from the start. He tried to think what to say, but she forestalled him.

"One thing's for sure, stranger. You're a kidder. Christmas is a month away. Land's sake, lighten my load, Lord, please. Just thinking about fixing Thanksgiving dinner tomorrow before my shift here starts makes me feel tired. At least the boss had mercy and has me coming in for dinner preparation and serving, not breakfast and lunch."

Since her words had his tongue stuck to the roof of his mouth, Gabe was relieved when the woman barely drew a breath before she started chattering again. "I wish it was Christmas. Then I'd have all the holidays nearly behind me." She sighed and puffed at a red curl that had escaped her braid to dangle over one eye. "Working the hours I do, I'm flat dreading Christmas." She slanted her eyes toward the ceiling. "God, don't strike me dead for saying so." Then she glanced at Gabe and winked. "I'm only human. I love Christmas just as much as the next person. It's just that I have so much to do to get ready. Teddy's socks I'm knitting are only half-done, and though I've been saving as much

of my tips as I can, I still don't have enough to get my
Jenny that doll she's hankering for over at the general
store." She laughed and rolled her blue eyes. "It'll all
come right in the end. I get in a dither like this every
year."

Gabe's stomach clenched, and his hunger for a
hearty breakfast vanished. "Uh, ma'am, you said you
were going to be cooking *Thanksgiving* dinner tomorrow?"

She laughed again. "I sure did. Lost track of the
days, did you? You've been on the trail for a while, I'm
guessing. What's your name, stranger?"

"Gabe." Mind racing, his body suddenly clammy
with sweat, Gabe was relieved he wasn't so rattled that
he'd forgotten his name. "Gabriel Valance."

Agnes gave him a long study. "*The* Gabriel Valance?"

Gabe hated when people asked him that. "In the flesh,
but I'm not half as bad as my reputation paints me."

Agnes set the coffeepot on the table to pull a tablet
and pencil from her apron pocket. "I'm glad to hear it.
I have no wish to get shot if you don't like the food."
Her smile had gone faint. "What can I get for you this
morning, Mr. Valance?"

"Call me Gabe, if it's all the same to you, and I'll just
have my regular."

Agnes arched a burnished brow. "Which is? I'm no
mind reader. If I was, I'd set up shop, make heaps of
money, and quit this miserable job."

Gabe felt as if he'd just stepped from a nightmare
into another unreality. The dream . . . only now he was
coming to think maybe it hadn't been a dream after all.
Had he actually been shot last night and been in that
shack with those angels? As he thought about it in the
bright light of morning, it all seemed so crazy—too
crazy to be true. But there stood Agnes, who'd been
bringing him chicken-fried steak, spuds, eggs, and

toast for a month, and she had no recollection of having done so. One of them was plumb nuts, and he had a hunch it wasn't Agnes.

Gabe gave the woman his order. As the waitress hurried away, Gabe took in the autumn theme of the table arrangements, sprays of burnished leaves providing beds for small orange pumpkins and colorful gourds. Only yesterday—his yesterday, anyway—the centerpieces had been made with pine boughs and sprigs of holly. He could recall the evergreen scent clearly. What the hell? Unless he'd dreamed an entire month of his life, he'd gone back in time.

Just then, another waitress, a skinny little brunette named Sarah who always seemed to be battling a cold, stepped over to Simon White's table. Before the banker glanced up, he straightened his bow tie, and the gesture keyed Gabe's recall. He remembered this day—his first breakfast in this particular hotel dining room—and suddenly he knew what White was going to say before he said it. "My appetite is a little off this morning, Sarah. I'll be happy with some oatmeal mush and a glass of milk."

En route back to the kitchen, Sarah stopped to clear a table. As she turned, arms laden with dishes, Gabe nearly called out, "Don't drop them!" And the next instant, just as he knew she would, Sarah dropped everything. Cups, bowls, plates, and remaining food hit the floor and exploded at her feet, creating a mess that encompassed a full square yard.

Gabe sank back on his chair, feeling light-headed. He truly had been in that shack last night. He'd lived through this morning once before and knew every single thing that was going to happen next. Just as that unwelcome realization sank fully into his brain, Sarah, Simon White, and every other person in the room became suddenly motionless. Agnes, caught in the act of scratching her generous backside, stood still as a statue by a nearby table, her gaze sightless. The thin waitress who'd bent to pick up a shard of glass was no longer moving.

Gabe leaped up from the table, feeling panicked. What was this? This was madness, all of it. It couldn't really be happening. He was still dreaming.

And then the angel Gabriel materialized, standing in all his robed glory not three feet away. Startled, Gabe fell back a step, setting his chair off balance and nearly toppling it. "Jesus H. Christ!" he yelled. "Are you trying to scare me to death?" Distractedly he noticed that everyone but him was still frozen in place.

The golden-haired angel smiled kindly. "No, Gabe. I apologize for giving you a start. Michael and I forgot to warn you about a few things." With a wave of his hand, he indicated the people frozen in different positions around the room. "I assure you, this isn't a dream. In a moment, time will resume its pace, and everything will return to normal. In the meanwhile, no one can over-hear our conversation."

Gabe gaped at him. "Normal, did you say? You're not much good at definitions. And couldn't you have just whispered what you need to say in my ear?"

"And have you talking to someone who would be invisible to everyone else?" Gabriel shook his head, still smiling. "That wouldn't do. People would think you crazy."

Gabe wasn't prepared to argue that point, but before he got his mouth open to say so, the angel went on. "This will take only a moment. Many people, when given the same opportunity you have been given, get so wrapped up in the novelty of it all, they squander precious time. Being able to predict what everyone will do next can be vastly amusing, and it's tempting to play little games." The angel glanced over his shoulder at Sarah. "For instance, you might have cautioned that young waitress not to drop the dishes just before she did so. Or you could have scolded that matronly waitress for scratching in such an unseemly spot just before her fingertips connected with her rump. Unfortunately, such activities will rob you of opportunities to complete your mission, not to mention that they will call attention to the fact that you can somehow predict the immediate future. We don't want you to behave in any way that may make others suspicious."

Gabe struggled to collect his composure. "Okay, you've said your piece. Now you need to go."

"Not quite yet," the angel replied. "Until Christmas morning, history is going to repeat itself over and over again. The only exception to how events unfold will be you, Gabe. You have within your power the ability to alter people's behavior—what they say and even what they do—so everything that takes place around you for the next month will depend greatly upon the choices you make. Armed with so much foreknowledge, you can have a great impact on those around you. You should do everything you possibly can to improve upon your previous behavior during this coming month, but by doing so you will, in a sense, be changing history. So you must be extremely judicious."

Oh, great. Just what he needed to hear. Gabe was developing a bitch of a headache. "What exactly do you mean by that?" he demanded.

"For example," the angel began, "should you know in advance that someone is going to come to some misfortune that has nothing to do with you, was not initially caused by anything you said or did, or is completely unrelated to your mission here, you should not manipulate events to prevent it. You haven't been given this second chance on earth to play God with other people's lives. If you do that, it will be held against you in the final reckoning a month from now, no matter how successful you may be in accomplishing your mission. In short, Gabe, you may not gain entrance into heaven if you fail to abide by this rule."

Gabe started to nod his understanding, but then decided to play it safe and paraphrase what he'd understood the angel had just said. "So it's okay for me to alter my own behavior—to try to be a better person this time. But I shouldn't leap in to change things that happen outside my immediate circle unless my behavior caused it to occur in the first place."

"Precisely," the angel agreed with an inclination of his golden head.

"Well, just so we're straight, I have a couple of questions," Gabe told him. "What if, by changing my own behavior, I have an effect on someone else's life? For instance, what if I could have helped someone out the last time around and decide I want to this time? Can I do that?"

"Improving upon your own behavior in any way is fine. We just don't want you racing around town altering history for the mere satisfaction of doing so. If someone was accidentally killed the last time you were here, for instance, you should do nothing to stop it from happening again unless the death was a direct result of your failure to do something you should have done. Say you were standing beside a blind woman on a corner when you last lived through this month and should have helped her across the street. If, because you failed to do so, the blind woman stepped out in front of a wagon and was run over, you may, if you choose, help the woman this time. On the other hand, if that same woman was killed stepping into the street a block away from you last time, you should do nothing to stop her from dying this time. As harsh as it may sound, it could be her time to go, and it isn't your place to interfere with her fate."

Gabe frowned. "But now, hold on here a minute. Are you saying if I have knowledge of things that will happen—say that some kid is going to get rip-roaring drunk and gamble away his family's farm—then I should do nothing to stop him?"

"That is correct. Not unless you were instrumental in getting him drunk the first time and encouraged him to play cards. That is his destiny, one brought about by his own choices." Gabriel held up a slender finger that looked as if it had been used for nothing more strenuous than strumming a harp string made of air. "If, as a result of your own behavior last time, you led someone to misfortune, you are now allowed to correct the mistake, but you are not allowed to arbitrarily step in and prevent tragedy or misfortune. If you choose to do that, I give you dire warning that it will not bode well for you at the final reckoning. It is your mistake to make, but do be aware that it will cost you dearly."

Gabe didn't like the sound of this. Not one little bit. "There's a boy—just a kid, really—who hides under the brothel stairway, that kid you showed me last night. His mama took off with some cowpoke a while back, saying she'd return for him, but she hasn't. He's freezing half to death at night and foraging for food. Can I—"

"No!" the angel said sharply. "You are not to interfere. You never noticed that boy until just a short while before you died. Isn't that correct?"

"Yes," Gabe conceded reluctantly.

"Then you must allow the boy's life to play out the way it is supposed to. The mother's poor choice has left the child in a bad situation." Gabriel leaned slightly forward to look Gabe directly in the eye. "You are here on borrowed time, Gabe, and only by the grace of God. Though you may feel alive, you are no longer truly one of the living. Never forget that. The time you have here cannot be used to change the whole world. It is your chance to prove yourself—that you are a good, decent, caring man who deserves to be in the presence of God for eternity. It is up to the living, those who truly are still struggling through life, to bring about change for that boy under the staircase. That is their test; don't you see? They can choose to see him and help, or they can choose to ignore his plight. And in the end, they will stand before the entrance, just as you did, being called to task for the things they failed to do. Do you understand me clearly?"

Gabe did understand. "I gotta tell you, it hurts my heart not being able to help that boy. I gave him ten dollars just before I got shot, and I intended to find him a family. Doesn't that count for anything?"

"I commend you for your good intentions, Gabe, but you died before you could carry them out. Let it be someone else's responsibility now. Focus on saving Nan. That is why you're getting this second chance."

The angel vanished. Gabe blinked and said, "Don't do that, dammit! Come back here! I'm not done asking questions!"

Agnes stepped close, her ample bosom grazing Gabe's elbow. "What's that you said?"

Gabe jerked himself back to the moment—or more accurately to the past, which was replaying like kids practicing a Christmas pageant onstage, everything the same, time after time, unless he said or did something to make things happen differently. "I, um . . . I was just wanting to know why my food isn't here yet."

Agnes, ever the one wearing a smile, frowned at him. "It's only been a few seconds since you gave me your order. I'll ask the cook to hurry it up."

"No, no." Gabe took a deep breath and quickly exhaled. "You're right. No need to hurry." He gestured toward Sarah, who was in a frenzy to clean up the mess she'd made by dropping the dishes. "I'll drink my coffee. You give her a hand and don't worry about me. I'm fine."

Agnes's expression told him to make up his mind whether he was in a hurry or not, but she only shrugged. "All right, then. I'll bring your food as soon as it's ready."

Gabe repositioned his chair, which he'd knocked as crooked as a dog's hind leg, and sank onto the seat. He felt weak at the knees and hoped with all his heart that he received no more unexpected celestial visits. Smells wafting from the nearby kitchen made his stomach pitch, and he realized that his appetite had gone coon just like the orphan boy's mother. He tossed a ten-dollar gold piece on the table for Agnes, knowing it would more than cover the food he'd ordered and maybe give her enough to buy her daughter, Jenny, that doll, plus something nice for her son, Teddy.

As he turned to leave, he heard the hotel proprietor giving Sarah heck for making such a mess and breaking so many dishes. The cruel, merciless edge in the man's voice reminded Gabe of the glimpses he'd gotten last night of Nan Hoffman's life. Her father had been a nasty son of a gun, constantly ranting at her and never offering a kind word. Gabe wished he could step in and tell the restaurant owner that he'd answer for his unkind behavior someday, and that his judges would ignore any excuses he tried to offer. But Sarah and her fate were beyond Gabe's control. If he meant to complete his mission and be rewarded with salvation, he had to remember the damned rules. Especially the ones he didn't cotton to.

"Ten dollars as a gratuity?" The question boomed in

Gabe's ear, but when he whirled in a full circle, he saw no one except a few patrons staring in astonishment at him. The disembodied voice continued. "It is not part of your mission to give Agnes money to buy her children Christmas presents."

Gabe slanted a dirty look in the general direction he thought the voice came from, and snapped, "Agnes is within my circle," as he exited the restaurant and turned right into the lobby, which was fortuitously empty save for the desk clerk, who was out of earshot. "If I'd been thinking straight the last time around, I'd have tipped her more generously. She works her ass off in that place and earns precious little for her efforts."

The angel sighed. Weird. Gabe couldn't see the guy, and yet it was as if Gabriel were walking directly beside him. "All right, I see your point. You should have been more generous the last time around. But don't allow yourself to throw money at every person you see who's in trouble."

"I won't," Gabe replied. "I understand the rules. Okay? Now leave me alone. And quit following me around. You've given me only thirty days, and the first half of this one is nearly gone."

Gabe left the hotel via the lobby door, banging it shut behind him. He hoped he'd smacked the angel with it. He paused on the boardwalk and realized that he had absolutely no idea what he should do next. The crisp November air was so cold it should have glistened with bits of ice, and it knifed through his shirt like a well-honed blade, reminding him that he'd left his jacket up in his room. Why did he always forget the damned thing? For all the good a jacket did him, he might as well not own one.

Shit. He hunched his shoulders, contemplating the absolute absurdity of his situation. He'd happily have bet a hundred bucks that he could tell this story to a thousand people, and not a single soul would believe him. He still wasn't certain he believed it himself. If he'd had too much to drink last night, wasn't it possible that he'd fallen and hit his temple? People had been known to lose their memories because of severe head injury. Maybe they hallucinated, too, and saw angels that weren't really there.

"You didn't get drunk last night," the angel Gabriel murmured beside him. "You seldom get dru—"

"Shit! Will you quit doing that?" Gabe practically shouted. "If you're going to stick to me like a tick on a hound's back, can't you at least reappear? It's weird to be talking to someone I can't see! And stop reading my mind!"

"I was going to point out that you rarely get drunk. I saw your life history, remember." The angel materialized suddenly to stand on the walkway facing Gabe. He looked as real as the boards under Gabe's feet. "Of all your failings—and they were many—drowning your good sense in a bottle of spirits wasn't one of them."

"It's going to be if you don't stop scaring the hell out of me. And you can't blame me for studying this from all angles. How many people die, wake up outside a shanty, talk to angels, and get sent back to earth for a second shot at salvation?"

"I am not at liberty to give you that information. I can reveal, however, that using a shack as a meeting place was a first for both Michael and me."

"Big of you. But why? Am I the only sinner who ever died who didn't believe in the pearly gates?"

The angel chuckled. Gabe was relieved that the guy at least had some semblance of a sense of humor. "No, definitely not the only one," he admitted. "It's just that not everyone's vision of heaven—or even of hell—is the same, so we play to our audience, so to speak, creating what they believe they will see. One old lady who adored cats and had more than twenty when she died believed with all her heart that heaven would be brimming with felines, so when she passed and we greeted her, we—"

"Met her in a place with cats perched on all the clouds," Gabe finished for him.

"Yes, more or less," Gabriel replied with a smile in his voice. "And now that she has attained heaven, she is surrounded by cats."

"I'll bet you weren't supposed to tell me that," Gabe ventured.

"Probably not," the angel replied.

"So tell me something more you probably shouldn't. What happens to people who don't believe in Jesus Christ? Take Indians, for instance. A lot of them worship the sun and moon."

"The Creator considers every man, woman, and child to be His own, so He is a father with many different faces."

"I'm not following."

Gabriel smiled. "You needn't understand everything, Gabe. That is the Creator's job. Let me just say that it saddens Him to throw any of His children on the scrap pile. In other words, it isn't so much about *what* you believe but how well you live your life and how kindly you treat others. There are many people born into families or in distant places who are taught other truths. Would you condemn someone for believing what he'd been taught from birth?"

"Of course not. How would that be fair? You might not think I'm a man with much heart, but I'd never punish somebody for living his life the way he believed was right, as long as he harmed nobody else."

"Ah. Nicely put, Gabe, and I think you've just answered your own question."

"Okay, okay." Gabe frowned, trying to take it all in. Once, as a kid, he'd been cornered by a preacher who'd told him that he had to believe in Jesus in order to be saved. "So people of all faiths can go to heaven. I get that. But what about people like me, who don't really believe in much of anything?"

The angel gave Gabe a warm look. "As we said, you are a difficult case."

"And why did you choose a shack for me?"

"Well," the angel said slowly, "after considering all the places you seemed to feel most at home, we decided none was really suitable."

"Meaning saloons, brothels, and livery stables?"

"And at places you camped along the trail," Gabriel added. "In the end, it was Michael who decided on a shack. Take no offense, Gabe, but you aren't a man who seems fond of finery."

Gabe sighed, and with the release of breath, some of his tension left. "Just for the record, if I succeed at my mission here, my idea of heaven is being surrounded by great horses and faithful dogs." After considering for a second, Gabe tacked on, "And a few beautiful women wouldn't hurt."

Again, Gabriel chuckled. "Duly noted. But for the moment, you must focus on only one beautiful woman, Nan Hoffman."

Gabe nodded. "You guys can't count any too well, you know. You gave me a month, and at one point you mentioned thirty days. Or maybe that was me. Anyhow, this is the twenty-fourth of November, and if I die a second time on Christmas, that'll technically be a month and one day."

"We made an exception. Tomorrow is a holiday, so the telegraph office will be closed, and you need to contact the . . ." The angel frowned. "I forget the organization's name, but it is renowned for its detectives."

"The Pinkerton Agency?" Gabe suggested.

"Ah, yes, that's it. You must wire the Pinkerton Agency as soon as possible to get an investigation of Nan's past under way."

"Why?" Gabe asked.

"Because as soon as you feel that you no longer need to use the murder charge as leverage against Nan, you should tell her that Horace Barclay survived being impaled by her knitting needle. She will be far more likely to believe you, which will allay her fears once and for all, if you offer documented proof—in this case, a report from a Pinkerton agent."

That made sense to Gabe. "Even if I pay extra to expedite an investigation, it may take a while to get a report mailed to me."

"Which is why you should initiate the process today. It would also be wise to marry Nan today. Otherwise you'll have to wait until Monday, and time is of the essence."

The angel vanished. Gabe blinked and stifled a few choice epithets. "Wait a minute! Marry her today? I've never even met the woman! How the hell am I going to make that happen?"

Gabe heard a smile in Gabriel's voice when he replied, "You're a poker player. Create a winning hand with the cards you've been dealt."

"Well, pardon me for pointing it out, but the deck is stacked against me!"

No answer. Gabe tipped his head, listened. When he determined that the angel had left, he whispered, "Asshole. Coming and going when you damned well please. I wasn't finished talking."

Nan loved her shop. She'd started out small, making only hats, with barely enough room to exhibit her creations and have a few doodads on display for browsers to purchase. Then, two years ago, the space next door, a former shoe repair shop, had come up for sale, and she'd had just enough in the bank to buy it. She and her little sister, Laney, who was believed by the townspeople to be Nan's daughter, had suffered dearly from the drain of their funds. They'd eaten beans, occasionally flavored with a ham hock, for several months, but they'd survived the crunch, and Nan had been able to expand her business, now making not only hats, but also garments. By knocking out a wall, she had greatly increased her display footage, giving her plenty of extra space to carry sundry items that appealed to women, such as corsets and underthings, ribbons, hat pins, brooches, hair combs, and even a bit of jewelry. As a result, sales were up, Nan had a tidy sum tucked away, and she could finally say her enterprise was a success.

The clock read half past noon, the lunch hour, so she had no customers at present. Most ladies were in their kitchens right then, feeding their children, who raced home from the schoolhouse to eat, and their husbands, if their spouses were fortunate enough to have jobs that gave them a noon break. Laney, unlike most of her classmates, preferred to carry her midday meal in a pail to school so she could eat at her desk and then do homework. She was an intelligent girl, determined to do well at her studies, particularly arithmetic, so she could one day become Nan's bookkeeper and help with sales. Nan encouraged Laney in her aspirations, even though she secretly hoped her sister, who had so many talents, including a knack for playing the violin like a maestro, would set her sights far higher. Nowadays, some young ladies went to college. A few had even become doctors. In Nan's estimation, Laney was bright enough to accomplish almost anything she decided to do. Something far more exciting and challenging, Nan thought with a smile, than dusting and polishing display cases and shelves during the meal-time lull.

Not that Nan felt working in the shop was boring. Indeed, just the opposite. She seldom went anywhere unless it was to shop for food or go to church, so she enjoyed the social aspects of dealing with her customers. In fact, every time someone walked in, her spirits lifted. It gave her a chance to chat, catch up on the latest news, and sometimes even hear a bit of titillating gossip.

So her sudden dread when the bell above the shop door jangled was inexplicable. A chill washed over her. She stood too far away for a waft of icy air from outside to reach her. She knew only that the temperature in the room seemed to drop instantly by several degrees, and she sensed another change in the air as well, one of danger. The hairs on her nape prickled.

She froze in midmotion, her hand clenched on the dust cloth. Foolishness. It had been eight years since her flight from Manhattan, and two years ago, on Laney's tenth birthday, Nan had finally set aside the nagging fear that one day, when she least expected it, she would be found, arrested, and returned to New York to face charges for a crime that she'd never meant to commit. It had been a long time since she'd felt this horrible sense of doom.

The door snapped closed, followed by the sharp click of a man's boots as he walked across the waxed plank flooring. Mouth cottony, shoulders rigid with tension, Nan reminded herself that men often stopped by to purchase items for their wives. Nan's displays abounded with pretty trinkets, some inexpensive, some costly, so gentlemen of all means could afford to buy something special.

Slowly, she turned and forced a smile to her lips. "Good day," she said brightly. "How can I help you?"

The man stood with one hip braced against her jewelry case. At a glance, Nan decided Satan himself couldn't have looked more intimidating. Dressed all in black with a pair of guns riding his hips, this fellow had a dark, threatening air. Broad at the shoulder and narrow at the hip, he wore clothes that enhanced the well-toned musculature of his body, the gleaming jet of his collar-length hair, the dark-chocolate shimmer of his watchful eyes, and the burnished hue of his skin.

When he didn't answer her question, Nan nervously smoothed a hand over her pleated bodice and said, "I offer a fine line of hats, coiffure adornments, jewelry, and—" She broke off and flapped the rag. "Whatever you're looking for, I'm sure I can show you something of interest." Preferably the door.

His face, a striking combination of sharp angles and rugged planes, remained expressionless as he moved his gaze slowly from the tips of her shoes upward, as if he were taking measure of everything about her.

"I didn't come in looking for a bauble, Miss Sullivan."

Nan's heart caught. This was her worst fear come true. He *knew*. No one had addressed her by that surname in nearly a decade. She battled a wave of faintness that caused her to catch hold of the shelf just behind her. Oh, dear God, he knew. She stared stupidly at him, unable to think how she should respond. Did he want the contents of her cashbox, and if she gave it to him, would he return again and again to milk her for more funds? Forcing the starch back into her spine, she darted her gaze back to his guns, and an even worse possibility occurred to her.

"Are y-you a bounty hunter?" she asked shakily.

His firm yet full mouth tipped into a slight grin that conveyed no warmth. "In a sense, I suppose you might say that. I'm definitely here to collect a bounty, but it isn't money."

Nan felt as if someone had stirred her brains with a wire whisk. Her next words came out somewhere between a whisper and a squeak. "If you don't want money, then what is it you're after?"

"A wife," he said softly. "And you, Miss Sullivan, are my lady of choice."

Chapter Four

After a harried morning spent selecting a wedding band and wiring funds to Chicago to retain the services of a Pinkerton agent, Gabe had made a beeline to the saloon, where he'd purchased another jug of rotgut whiskey and slowly sipped two jiggers while he considered how best to handle Nan Hoffman. Creating a winning round with the cards he'd been dealt was a challenge, and in the end, he'd concluded that he couldn't corner his quarry if he approached her with his hat in hand. Gabe was a man who frightened women off the boardwalk into muddy streets to avoid getting too close to him. To herd Nan Hoffman to a preacher or justice of the peace this afternoon, he had to be ruthless and without conscience. He'd scare her into the middle of next week and marry her before she had a chance to think it through. He didn't have time for the social niceties. Not that he knew much about them anyhow.

He'd stridden into her shop with his jaw set, prepared to convince her that he was the meanest, most coldhearted bastard she'd ever met. And judging by the way she was now grinding her backbone into the shelves behind her, had turned white as flour, and dropped her dusting rag, he guessed he'd accomplished his goal. The poor woman's face was a mask of terror.

And he felt like a rotten, low-down skunk. This wasn't fair play, dammit. He knew so many of her secrets—including that her nipples were such a pretty rose pink that they showed through her chemise—that he felt horrible about using the knowledge against her. On the other hand, going to hell wasn't real high on his list of aspirations, either. This was like facing a gunman in the street, a win-or-lose contest, and Gabe stood to lose far more than Nan if he failed to convince her that her pretty little neck would soon make the acquaintance of a hangman's noose if she didn't do precisely what he said.

Lips trembling, she stared at him as if he were a coiled rattler about to strike. "Are you mad? We've never even met! What do you mean, you've chosen me to be"—she gulped and passed a shaky hand over her mercilessly tidy chignon—"your wife?"

Since explaining how he'd come to be here wasn't an option, Gabe kept his mouth shut. Nan looked different today, a mere shadow of the woman he'd seen at the window right after he'd been shot. Then, her hair had been loose and agleam with candlelight, and she'd appeared soft and feminine. He detested the severe hairstyle she sported now, which allowed not even a tiny wisp of gold to frame her lovely oval face. He also hated her blue dress, a prim garment that skimmed her corseted waist and flared with so many gathers in the skirt that her curvaceous hips and legs were invisible. The collar was so high and tight it was a wonder she could breathe.

"You're right; we haven't met," he conceded. "But I've observed you about town, and I'm a man who knows what he wants when he sees it. In short, Miss Sullivan, I want you, and it'll be extremely foolish on your part if you refuse to marry me."

Her chin came up. Gabe nearly smiled. It was a

small, delicate chin with a cute little cleft. Her cheek-bones, fragile and purely feminine, slanted back toward her ears, which were small and pink at the lobes, reminding him of the tiny seashells he'd once seen on an ocean beach during a stay in California.

In a tone that managed to quiver and drip ice at the same time, she said, "Well, foolish though it may be, I do, absolutely and unequivocally, refuse!" She straightened her narrow shoulders and stepped away from the shelves. It didn't escape Gabe's notice that she wobbled slightly on her feet. "Your suggestion is preposterous, sir. Please remove yourself from my shop. Now."

Gabe finally allowed himself to grin—a slow, humorless curve of his lips born of long practice that had made more than one man in a rage decide to think twice before he pushed his luck. "Fine, Miss Sullivan. Never let it be said that I don't know when my welcome has worn thin." He moved away from the jewelry case and touched a fingertip to the brim of his Stetson. "I'll just mosey on down to the marshal's office. I'm sure he'll be real interested to learn that the widowed milliner who's passed herself off as Nan Hoffman for eight years is actually Nancy Sullivan, a woman wanted for murdering her fiancé, Horace Barclay. The telegraph lines will be tapping quicker than a lamb shakes its tail, I'm guessing, and by dusk, you'll be on the wrong side of a jail cell's bars."

Gabe allowed his grin to broaden just slightly into a smile. "You ever been in the hoosegow, darlin'? Those cells reek of stale urine. The mattress ticking crawls with bedbugs. If nature calls, you've got to relieve yourself in a bucket that's still crusty with the leavings of the last man who used it." He held up a finger. "A word of warning about those buckets. Don't make the mistake of sitting on one. You'll sure as hell catch the crabs." At her bewildered expression, he gave a low laugh. "Crabs are a form of lice, only you get them at the wrong end. Itch like a son of a gun, and it's harder than hell to get rid of them." He sighed. "Oh, well, scratching your nether regions raw will keep you busy while you wait for the wheels of justice to turn. And they turn slowly, Nan. I don't reckon the law in New York will get all the way out here to Colorado any too fast. Might take as long as a week or two for the authorities to come fetch you—or arrange for a lawman here to transport you back to—" He broke off, pretending forgetfulness. "What's the name of that island? Ah, yes, Manhattan. Never got an urge to ride that way. I hear the eastern shores are crawling with people. I'm a man who likes some elbow room."

Gabe turned as if to leave, hating himself even as he felt victorious. Nan Sullivan wasn't a stupid woman. The success she'd made of her shop proved that. Right now, he could almost hear her mind racing as she weighed her options. And Gabe had given her none. If she let him walk out that door, he'd eat his hat and have his boots for dessert.

Nan's knees were rattling so badly that she could barely keep them locked to remain standing. She watched the stranger in black take quick strides toward the door, knowing as he covered the distance that she could not allow that overhead bell to jangle. In a very real way, it would be her death knell. And, dear God, what would become of Laney, her bright, talented, gregarious little sister? Nan knew precisely what would happen. The moment their father got word of Laney's whereabouts, he would come to fetch her, take her back to Manhattan, and marry her off at age sixteen or younger to some fat old lecher to form a shipping or industrial alliance that would make him even wealthier than he already was.

As terrified as Nan was for herself, fear for Laney

loomed foremost in her mind. Nan had tried so hard to
give her sister a better childhood than she'd had, encouraging Laney to have friends, bolstering her confidence by showering her with praise, and always urging
her on, even when the child set herself nearly impossible goals. As a result, Laney was everything that Nan
wished she were herself, if only she'd been given a
chance. She would not allow Martin Sullivan to undo
all of that.

"Wait!" Nan cried just as the man touched the doorknob. "I don't even know your name!"

He stopped, turned to face her again, and then swept
his black hat from his head in a mockery of gentlemanly politeness. "I beg your pardon, Miss Sullivan. I
should have properly introduced myself before asking
for your hand. Gabriel Valance, at your service." He
bent slightly at the waist in an offhand bow. "Gabe is
my preference."

Nan didn't think her heart could jitter any more violently, but it did when she heard his name, which was
almost legendary in Random and undoubtedly in other
towns as well. "*The* Gabriel Valance, the gunslinger?"

He settled his Stetson back on his dark head, cocking
the brim just so. "One and the same, ma'am. I don't
think I'm quite as bad a fellow as folks make me out to
be, but that's neither here nor there. Fourteen men have
tried to kill me, I didn't feel obliged to let them, and so
I got them before they could get me." A crease appeared
between his black brows. "Well, to be honest, there was
one recent exception, but though the other fellow shot
me first, my Colt also found its mark, and he fell face-
first in the street beside me, dead as a doornail, just like
all the others who went before him."

"Fourteen?"

"A good thing for me, I guess. Thirteen is a really
unlucky number."

Once again Nan felt as if she might faint. Moving unsteadily to a crate of merchandise, she sank weakly onto the splintery wooden slats. Her future plans had never included marriage, let alone marriage to a man who informed her coolly that he'd killed fourteen men. Did he carve notches on his gun belt? Her gaze slid to his hips. He lifted an eyebrow, and she realized what he must be thinking. Hastily she averted her eyes, but not before she saw his mouth quiver in quickly suppressed amusement. Her gaze darted to a beaded clutch bag on a nearby shelf. She longed to throw it in his face. Instead, she murmured faintly, "Fourteen men? Dear heaven."

"Nothing about my life has been heavenly, Miss Sullivan. My mama was a whore who got sick and died on me when I was only a little tyke. My father was a cold-hearted bastard who made a success of his first gambling establishment and then destroyed anyone who got in his way to buy another and another, until he became a man of inestimable wealth." He paused and swallowed, his Adam's apple bobbing in his sun-browned neck. "Well, maybe inestimable is a stretch, but he was a very rich man. He never acknowledged me as his son until he died. Never even saw to it that I was cared for. I grew up on the streets, scavenging for food from people's trash and stealing clothes off drying lines. When I had no shoes, I cut stolen sheets into strips and wrapped my feet in linen."

Nan stared at him, too shaken to feel sympathy, yet shocked to her core nevertheless. Her childhood had been dreadful, but the one he described was far worse.

"I was fourteen when I got tired of being kicked around," Valance continued. "And, yes, a homeless, hungry boy living hand-to-mouth does get kicked around. There are men in this world who take pleasure in hurting those who can't fight back." He rubbed beside his nose. "With a good deal of afterthought, I've got reason to believe I wasn't any too bright at that age, because stealing a sidearm off a sleeping drunk on the boardwalk was a bad mistake. Once I had a weapon, I mucked horseshit out of livery stalls to earn enough money to buy bullets, and then, every second I wasn't shoveling manure or sleeping wherever I could find shelter, I practiced shooting at targets. Once I could take the head off a matchstick without fail at fifty yards, I worked on my speed until nary a man in Kansas City could clear leather faster.

"Right about then was when my lack of good sense really began to show, because I walked into a saloon, bold as brass, with a chip on my shoulder so big it would have taken a club to knock it off. I went into the establishment to show the world that I was no longer a snot-nosed brat who couldn't fight back. I mistakenly thought that just wearing a gun would accomplish that. I never anticipated that it would take an exchange of lead to get the job done. Unfortunately for me, there was a gunslinger of some repute passing through town, and he was bellied up to the bar, washing the trail dust from his throat with a jug of whiskey. When he saw me swagger in, still a kid with peach fuzz for whiskers, acting like I could nail any man who challenged me, he took exception, told me to make fast tracks, and when I didn't, he made the mistake of going for his gun. I killed him before his Colt ever cleared the holster."

Nan closed her eyes. She had asked for an introduction, but hearing this story was more than she'd bargained for. Mr. Valance didn't seem to sense her reluctance to hear more, so he continued.

"Once a man outdraws a famous gunslinger in public—exhibiting that much speed and accuracy—he becomes, hell, I don't know, a target, I reckon you could say. Word travels fast. Before I knew it, every fellow who fancied himself a quick draw wanted to face me in the street to prove that he was faster. By the time I was eighteen, I'd killed six men, never once because I set out to, but because I had no choice. I had to defend myself or die, and I wasn't quite ready at that age to meet my maker. After six encounters, I took to the trail, trying my damnedest to stay one step ahead of the fools who were trying to find me, but over the last fifteen years, I've failed in that endeavor eight times, so, all in all, fourteen men have made the fatal mistake of challenging me."

Nan lifted her lashes. For the life of her, she couldn't think of a single word to utter.

"So," Valance said with a tip of his hat, "do you consider us to be properly introduced now, Miss Sullivan, or do I have to tell you every other ugly detail of my past to get the job done?"

Nan finally found her voice. "If this is your idea of courtship, M-Mr. Valance, I can assure you that it leaves a great deal to be desired."

He laughed, and the gruff rumble of humor came so unexpectedly that she started. "No, ma'am, it's not my idea of courtship. I'll tend to the courting part after I put a ring on your finger."

"I have *not* agreed to marry you."

"No, but if you refuse, I can promise that you won't like the consequences, and neither will your sister."

Nan clenched her fists over the gathers of her skirt. "I never meant to kill Horace Barclay. He was . . . Well, he meant to take liberties he had no right to take prior to marriage. I got away from him long enough to grab a knitting needle from my yarn basket to warn him off. He just laughed and lunged at me, tripped, and fell forward, taking me down under his vast weight. I never meant to stab him."

Valance leaned his back against the door and crossed

his booted feet. "I've no doubt you're telling the truth. As dumb as I've been a few times in my life, I've smartened up over the years. I'd never marry a woman I thought might stab me when I turned my back on her."

"Then why?" Nan cried, her voice turning shrill. "If you believe I'm innocent, why are you doing this to me? You can't possibly bear me any affection. You know only enough about me to send me to the gallows, and if I end up there, my little sister will suffer even more than I will, and for far longer. Why? You walk into my shop from out of nowhere, a man I've never seen in my life, and demand that I marry you. I don't understand. What can you possibly hope to gain? You don't seem interested in money."

"I've got plenty of money of my own without tapping a woman who works from dawn until late at night to make a success of her business." His coffee-dark gaze locked with hers. "So, you're right: I'm not interested in your bank account. Maybe I'd just like a chance to spend time with a beautiful, refined woman. Or a chance, maybe, to hang my hat on the same hook for a spell and see how it feels to have a normal life. I've countless reasons, Miss Sullivan, but time's a-wasting, and I'm finished talking. You can get your cloak and go with me to the preacher—or a justice of the peace, if you prefer—and become my wife. Or you can tell me to go to hell, and I'll walk down to the marshal's office. Your choice."

"Choice?" Nan's voice shot up an octave. Catching herself, she continued in a calmer tone. "What do you mean, *choice*? And even if I agree to this madness, how can I be certain you won't soon tire of the situation and turn me in anyway?"

"You don't for certain yet." He shrugged one thick shoulder. "On down the road, you'll come to know me better and realize I'd never make a bargain like this with you and then renege later. But for now, all you've got is my word. If you marry me, the truth of your real identity will be a secret I'll carry with me to the grave."

Nan realized her blurred image of him was caused by tears, and that infuriated her. She never allowed herself to cry in front of anyone. She'd learned under her father's harsh tutelage that weeping only encouraged a merciless person to be crueler.

And there was not the slightest doubt in her mind that Gabriel Valance was merciless, perhaps even more so than her sire. He was the kind of man who would rule a woman with an iron fist, and crush her with the brute force of a blow if she dared to defy him.

Even so, Nan had no options. She didn't want to hang for a crime she hadn't intentionally committed, and she would endure anything, even marriage to a self-confessed killer, to protect Laney.

She pushed shakily to her feet. "Please excuse me while I go upstairs to my living quarters and fetch my wrap."

He inclined his head. Then he moved quickly forward as the door opened behind him and bumped his back. Geneva White, the banker's wife, walked in, smiling brightly. Atop her brown coiffure, she sported a gaudy, overdecorated hat that Nan had made, per Geneva's specifications, cringing as she'd added the requested stuffed canary to a crowning and unattractively flamboyant abundance of flowers and feathers. According to Geneva, such hats were all the rage back east, and it was the silly woman's primary aspiration to set the fashion standards in Random, keeping its female population apace with the latest fads. Over her rose walking dress, she wore a lush cape of burgundy wool and suede gloves of exactly the same hue.

Her blue eyes twinkled with eager excitement. "I've finally succumbed to temptation, Nan, and Simon has relented. I want to commission you to design that gown for me."

Nan glanced at Valance. He gave a slight shake of his head. Nan tried to smile at her customer, but her face felt as if it were painted with dried egg white.

"I'm terribly sorry, Geneva, but I'm closing for the day. A matter of some urgency has come up."

"Oh, dear, is Laney all right?" Geneva asked.

"Laney is fine." Nan groped for an explanation and settled for, "It's a private matter."

Geneva finally noticed the man who loomed to her right like a dark specter. She paled, flashed a horrified look at Nan, and made a fast retreat to the door. "Later, then. Perhaps I shall return on Monday after the holiday weekend."

"Perfect," Nan managed to reply with some semblance of a normal tone. "I'll look forward to coming up with a fabulous design."

Geneva gave Valance a last, wary glance and exited the shop with a loud jingle and bang of the closing door.

Valance gazed through the windows at the fleeing woman. "Was that a bird on her head?"

"Yes." Nan's stomach rolled, and for a moment she feared she might gag and purge her stomach on her gleaming plank floors.

"Not a real one, I hope."

Bile burned in Nan's throat. "The fake ones don't look that real." She remembered how she'd hated handling the stuffed creature—ever conscious of how tiny, fragile, and defenseless it must have been in life. She'd read, afterward, that people painted the insides of shoe boxes with varnish, stuffed the live canaries inside, closed the lid, and killed them with the fumes. A quick and painless death that left the birds unmarked, the article had claimed. But Nan didn't believe it was painless.

Her world had become a varnish-coated box, the lid was closing, and she could attest to the fact that struggling for breath was agonizing.

A biting chill sliced through Nan's green wool cape, making her already cold body feel like a chunk of ice. She couldn't imagine how Gabriel Valance could bear being outside without a coat, but if he suffered from the near-freezing temperature, he gave no sign of it. He stopped just outside her shop to arch a raven brow at her.

"Which do you prefer," he asked, "a justice of the peace or a preacher?"

Nan definitely didn't want to marry this man in a spiritual ceremony. If they kept it as merely a legal union, recognized only by the state, she could at least tell herself that the vows she was about to make wouldn't be binding in heaven. "The justice of the peace suits me fine."

He nodded, and for a man who had to be new in town, he turned right, needing no direction. With surprisingly good manners, he stepped to the outside of the boardwalk and cupped her elbow in his hand, keeping her sheltered between him and the storefronts as they walked. Nan tried not to think about how large his hand felt—or how even the relaxed press of his fingers emanated strength through her wool wrap. If he chose, he could probably crush her bones with the sheer force of his grip.

This isn't happening, she thought a little wildly. *It can't be. I swore never to marry, and it was a promise I meant to keep.* And yet here she was, striding along beside him as if nothing out of the ordinary were about to occur. Madness. How would she explain this to Laney? Even worse, how would she survive the coming night? Gabriel Valance wasn't one to prevaricate; he'd been brutally honest about his reasons for doing this. He'd seen her and decided that he wanted her. Though Nan had never lain with a man, she was no twitter-brained young girl who had no idea what occurred in a marriage bed, and in her opinion, the whole process would be not only disgusting, but also possibly painful. She seriously doubted that Gabriel Valence knew the meaning of the word *gentle*.

"How did you find out about me?" she asked, her voice twanging with panic.

His grasp on her arm tightened as he guided her around a loose plank. "Well, now, there's a story, and one you wouldn't believe if I told you. So let's just say a little bird whispered in my ear."

Nan's panic mounted. "If you were told about me, then someone else must know as well."

"Two individuals—no, make that three—know every detail about your past, but they're in no position to talk."

"You can't be sure of that!" she responded shrilly.

He laughed, and with surprise she realized his amusement was genuine. "Oh, ma'am, I think I can. They're no longer of this world."

"You killed them?"

Just then, a drunk burst through the bat-wing doors of the saloon out onto the boardwalk. Valance caught Nan back, drew her to a stop, and gave her a perturbed frown. "Why the hell would you think that?"

"You said they're no longer of this world; that means dead."

"Well, they're not dead," he shot back. "Not the way you're thinking, anyhow." Using his free hand, he fidgeted with his hat. "It's hard to explain, and I'm not going to stand here trying until I talk myself blue. You just have to take my word for it; they won't be yapping to anybody."

Nan gaped up at his tanned face, wishing his coffee-dark eyes were easier to read. The drunk finally staggered from the boardwalk into the street, heedless of the fact that he forced a farmer to bring his wagon team to a rearing stop, and apparently deaf to the insults shouted after him as he wove across the thoroughfare toward the general store.

Valance guided Nan back into a walk. Only a few doorways ahead was the office of the justice of the peace, a man named Walter Hamm, who also served the community as an attorney at law, occasionally sat on the judicial bench, and sold eggs from his wife's chickens on the side, undercutting Burke Redmond's prices at the general store by a penny a dozen. Ellen Hamm's eggs were superb, with yolks that were nearly orange, and whites that held their shape in a hot skillet, testimony to the good care and feed her hens received. Nan often came up the street to buy eggs from Walter. Today the walk seemed much longer, yet at the same time all too brief.

When they reached the door, Nan jerked to a halt well away from the threshold. She felt Valance's grip lighten on her elbow.

"If you want to bolt, I won't try to stop you," he said. "If you can't go in there and do this willingly, I won't—"

"Willingly?" she challenged, her voice reed thin with anger. "You've given me no choice. It's go in or be hanged by the neck until dead."

"With that *or* you just contradicted yourself. You do have a choice." He angled a meaningful look across the street at the marshal's office. When he looked back at her, a muscle along his jaw ticked, and his eyes seemed as black as a moonless night. "Make up your mind, Miss Sullivan. Marriage or the gallows? I think I'm the better bargain."

Nan couldn't argue the point, so she covered the remaining distance to the entrance. She couldn't make herself believe, really believe, that she was going to marry a man she had never clapped eyes on until an hour ago, if, indeed, it had even been that long. But do it she would. No matter how badly he treated her, she would somehow protect Laney, and in the end, being his wife would be better than dying. She'd escaped from an intolerable situation before and started a whole new life. If she had to, she would withdraw what money she had in the bank and do it again.

Chapter Five

For Nan, the experience inside Walter Hamm's office passed in a nightmarish blur. Gabriel Valance's voice rumbled distantly in her ears, and her own responses sounded tinny and unreal. Vague impressions assaulted her brain of witnesses to the nuptials being called in off the street, and then casting her horrified looks when they realized the identity of her groom. She repressed a shudder as her new husband slipped a gold band onto her left finger. He whispered that he'd gotten the ring earlier at the jewelry shop. It disturbed her that he'd been so confident she would marry him prior to meeting her, and it bothered her even more that the circlet of gold fit perfectly. She was unable to suppress the shudder that shook her body when he lightly kissed her on the lips to conclude the ceremony. Then she was unable to steady her hand as she put her name to paper. She stared blankly at the register, wondering for a fleeting instant if the huge ink blot she'd made would render her signature worthless. If so, it would be the only bit of luck she'd had today.

Walter, who'd worn a concerned expression on his bony face during the entire ordeal, tried to catch her gaze with a question in his own. Nan managed to avoid looking him in the eye, leaving him with no alternative but to sigh and say that he would go directly across the

street to the Office of Public Records, Random's version
of a courthouse, to record the marriage and instruct the
clerk to send copies of the documents to Denver.

Gabe wasn't in the least rattled during the ceremony.
He was well accustomed to the wary expressions of
distaste on people's faces when they first saw him, had
fully expected Nan to be a quivering mass of trepidation, and was able to repeat his vows without a single
qualm. He could swear to love, honor, and protect his
wife until death did they part. He had to play the role
of husband for only a month, after all. And then he'd
be among the dearly—or not so dearly—departed. He
had absolutely nothing to lose and eternal salvation to
gain.

His calm lasted until he guided his bride onto the
boardwalk and turned her toward her shop, which was
now locked, with a closed sign hanging at an angle on
the door window. *What the hell am I supposed to do now?*
He felt so uneasy that he even hoped the chatterbox
angel who liked scaring the crap out of him would materialize and give him some advice. But the ever-elo-
quent Gabriel had chosen this moment to remain silent.
Gabe had absolutely *no* experience with women who
didn't earn their livings on their backs. How could he
put Nan at ease? What should he say to her now? How
was he supposed to act?

He knew only that she was as jumpy as a bug on a
fiery-hot rock, and every time he shifted his grip on her
elbow, he felt her body snap taut with what he guessed
was fear. Did she think he might shove her between
two buildings and force himself on her in broad daylight? And if she was this nervous out in the open, with
people and wagons passing by, she'd be in a fine state
once they were alone in her shop.

Gabe mentally groped for comforting sentences. *I
have no intention of forcing you to have physical relations*

with me. No, that wouldn't work. If he said that, she'd immediately think that was precisely what was on his mind and that he meant to bed her posthaste. *I'm not going to hurt you.* Scratch that off the list. Then she'd have reason to believe that he did indeed mean to have sex with her immediately and was only promising to go about his business gently. *Don't worry. Everything will be just fine.* That was the worst yet.

Shit. Gabriel, where are you? I need advice! Gabe nearly parted company with his boots when the angel's deep voice finally vibrated in his ear. *I have no experience with ladies, Gabe. I'm an angel, remember, not a man.* Gabe circled that reply in his mind and silently shot back, *But you must have been a man at some point. Right? You had to die to become an angel. Did you cock up your toes right after you were born or something?* The angel's response made Gabe miss a step, which earned him a startled glance from Nan. *Clearly you're a stranger to scripture, my friend. I was never born. God created me as an angel, and I've never been anything else.* That made absolutely *no* sense to Gabe. How could somebody become an angel if he'd never lived on earth to be tested and prove that he was holy?

"You've *never* had sex?" Gabe blurted aloud.

Nan jerked as if he'd jabbed her with one of those long hat pins he'd seen in her shop. "I most certainly have *not*, sir," she snapped back, "and hereafter, I would greatly appreciate any attempt on your part to speak in politer terms!"

Gabe couldn't admit that he had been addressing someone else. He could just imagine her reaction if he told her he was conversing with an invisible angel who had not only arranged their marriage but had also told Gabe her ring size. And, *damn*, did that mean proper ladies like Nan didn't refer to the activities behind closed doors as having sex? If not, what the hell did they call it? Intercourse? Physical intimacy? Before he could stop to think it through, he blurted, "Well, if not sex, what the hell do you call it then?"

The words no sooner passed his lips than Gabriel, his inconstant adviser, yelped, "Don't ask her *that*!"

Nan stopped dead in her tracks at Gabe's inquiry, causing him to jerk so hard on her arm that she staggered. He barely managed to catch her from falling. Then, with her body pressed so firmly against his, he could have sworn he felt the tips of her nipples burning their way through all the layers of her clothing and his as well. She peered up at him, looking nonplussed.

"What do we—um—call it?" she echoed. Flicking the tip of her tongue over her lower lip, which made his manhood snap to attention, she added, "I . . . well, I honestly don't know. It is not a topic ladies discuss."

I told you, the angel Gabriel said. Gabe was so dumbfounded by Nan's response that he barely heard his golden-haired adviser. "Ladies *never* discuss it?" he asked incredulously.

Nan's fair brows snapped together. "Never," she affirmed. Then, taut as a fiddle string and still pressed full-length against him, she added, "My mother, who might have discussed the subject with me, died before I was of an appropriate age, and the ladies who frequent my shop . . . Well, our conversations never stray to topics of such a personal nature."

Gabe tried to let that sink into his overtaxed brain. "Well, when people *do* discuss topics of such a personal nature, they refer to the act as—"

She clamped her fingertips over his mouth, sending a jolt slamming through him. "Please, *must* we talk about this? Having to engage in the act will be burden enough."

Gabe searched the depths of her beautiful gray eyes, and the fear he saw there gave him pause. "Well, we're going to have to call it something, because sooner or later, husbands and wives do discuss it."

Her lashes, thick, luxurious, and several shades darker than her golden hair, dipped low. Then a muscle jerked in her delicately hollowed cheek. "Very well," she said stonily. "If and when we must discuss it, we shall refer to it as engaging in the act." He suspected she'd have used the same tone to refer to a particularly loathsome type of vermin. Besides, the formality of that phrase was above and beyond ridiculous. Still, he was on untraveled paths with this woman, and it wasn't his aim to upset her any more than he already had.

"All right," he consented. "I can do that."

He hoped some of the tension might ease from her small frame, but she remained rigid. He belatedly realized that he'd grasped both her shoulders and was holding her fast against him. He released his grip instantly, which resulted in her losing her balance, which prompted him to grab her by one arm again.

"Are you all right? Don't fall. I don't want you getting hurt."

"Let go of me. I won't fall," she assured him. With a glance both up and down the boardwalk, she visibly cringed and added in a fierce whisper, "We are making a *spectacle* of ourselves. People are *staring*."

Gabe started to turn to see who was staring, but she stopped him with, "Don't *look!*" Her eyes filled with supplication. "That will only make everything worse!"

How returning someone's stare could make anything worse totally escaped Gabe, but he honored her edict.

"We must get off the street. *Please.* The moment news of our marriage gets out, tongues will be wagging nonstop. I don't want to add fuel to the fire by standing here on the boardwalk like two well-rooted stumps."

Gabe felt a little like a stump. Making his feet move

required concentration. He guided his rigid bride to the door of her shop, watched her struggle with wildly shaking hands to insert the skeleton key into the hole, and, in frustrated silence, bit down so hard on his back molars that he started to get a toothache.

"Here, honey, let me." He snatched the key from her grasp, a feat that took unerringly good aim, because the thing was bouncing about erratically in her hand. He hit the hole on the first try, gave a sharp twist, and pushed the door open. Stepping back, he gestured her forward. "Ladies first."

He couldn't say that she actually leaped across the threshold, but she did enter with frenzied haste. As Gabe stepped inside behind her, she whirled to slam the door closed with such force that the walls vibrated, creating a muted noise to underscore the cacophony of the jangling bell. Then, trembling like an aspen leaf in a brisk wind, she leaned against the portal, her forehead resting on the doorframe.

Feeling helpless, Gabe hooked his thumbs over his gun belt and watched her try to regain her composure. When he'd accepted this mission, he'd never for an instant imagined that pushing this woman into marriage would upset her so much. He'd had mostly his own concerns in mind, and been so glad to be offered a second chance that he'd thought of little else.

"I should have chosen Tyke," he muttered.

She turned to stare at him, her face so drained of color that it worried him. "Pardon me?"

"Nothing. Just talking to myself."

She straightened, unfastened the frog of her cloak, and then reached up as if to flip over the sign.

"Uh, I wouldn't if I were you," he said, making her freeze midmotion. "Do you really want to deal with customers right now? Chances are, the news of our marriage is traveling through town like a wildfire licking at August prairie grass. Anyone who comes in probably won't be looking to buy anything. They'll be wanting information, and even if you refuse to give them any, they'll still race out to tell anyone who'll listen every word you said, everything I didn't say, and that you look like you're about to faint."

"Do I?" She touched trembling fingers to her cheek. "Look as if I'm about to faint, I mean."

"If you turn any paler, I'm going to stand close enough to catch you before you hit the floor."

Apparently she preferred that he keep his distance. She rubbed her cheeks vigorously with the heels of her hands. With a quivering intake of breath, she swept off her cloak, hung it on a hook by the door, and stood like a soldier at attention when she turned to face him again. "I have *never* fainted," she informed him, "and I have no intention of starting now." She peered down at her bodice watch to check the hour. Gabe hadn't noticed the dainty little timepiece until she touched it. When his gaze settled on her chest, where he'd been trying really hard not to look, he noticed nothing but the thrust of her breasts against the blue cloth of her dress. "Laney will be back from school in an hour and twenty minutes," she announced.

Gabe realized she was letting him know that he had a limited time if he wished to "engage in the act." He nearly smiled, stifled the urge, and managed to keep his expression suitably solemn. "I was hoping she'd be here sooner. I'm looking forward to meeting her."

His response clearly wasn't what she expected. "Sooner?" she echoed in a thin voice. "I thought that you'd—"

Gabe finally allowed the grin twitching at the corners of his mouth to curve his lips. He looked deeply into his bride's worried eyes, took a moment to think before he spoke, and then said, "I know what you thought, Nan. But you misjudged me. As I said earlier, now it's time for the courting part to begin. 'Engaging in the act' isn't on my agenda for tonight, or for tomorrow night, or for *any* night unless you are a willing participant."

"I will *never* be a willing participant."

Gabe was a man who enjoyed laughing. Even as a kid who'd had little to be happy about, he'd always felt better with a smile on his lips. So he allowed himself to chuckle now. "Never is a very long time, but I'll still stand behind my word. If the moment never comes when you can *willingly* engage in the act, I won't press you. It's not my way."

Her worried expression turned to one of pure and undiluted bewilderment. "Why on earth did you insist on marrying me then?"

He ventured a grin. "Because you're beautiful, and I enjoy looking at you. And also because any single man with eyes who didn't want to marry you would be a damned fool." He glanced toward the rear door that led upstairs to her living quarters. "I'm thirty-three years old, and except for a year of my life when an elderly ex-schoolmarm took me in to clean me up and teach me to read, I've never enjoyed a home-cooked meal, never slept in a real bedroom, or spent an evening doing whatever it is families do after supper." He winked at her. "If your prediction of never turns out to be true, then I'll still count myself lucky to have the opportunity to be in your home and spend time with you and your sister."

"Daughter," she corrected. "You mustn't refer to Laney as my sister. No one but you knows the truth."

"Daughter, then," he said with a shrug.

Well-done, the angel Gabriel murmured in Gabe's ear. Gabe barely managed to stifle a response to his heavenly mentor. *Damn.* If Nan heard him talking to himself again, she'd feel certain he was crazy, and he wouldn't blame her. The last thing he needed was for her opinion of him to sink even lower.

Time to back off, he silently conveyed to Gabriel. *From this point forward, you have to leave me alone and let me handle this my way.*

The angel laughed softly, causing a waft of air to tickle Gabe's ear. *The instant I leave you to your own devices, you'll be calling upon me for advice.*

Gabe couldn't deny the possibility. He'd only ever dealt with eager, willing females, and he knew he was totally out of his depth with Nan. Even so, the angel needed to scat. *I can't say I deserve my privacy,* Gabe replied in his mind, *but Nan has never deliberately harmed anyone, and she does deserve hers. What happens between us from this moment forward needs to be between her and me and nobody else, not even an angel. You can't hover invisibly in the air, watching us and listening to every word we say. It wouldn't be right or fair to her.*

Gabe heard the angel sigh. *All right, my friend, I'll leave you to proceed without my inestimable wisdom to help you along. Before I leave, however, I'd like to give you a few last words of advice. When you have no idea what to do or say next, take a moment to listen to your heart.*

Gabe wasn't sure his heart did much talking.

"Would you like to see my shop and the upstairs?"

Nan's question jerked him back to the moment. Her nervousness and the anxiety in her expression told him she'd issued the invitation with great reluctance. "I'd love to see everything."

She gave him a quick tour of the downstairs. He found her curtained-off workroom far more interesting than the storage closet and display areas, because it reflected more of her character. The right and left walls sported shelves and cubbyholes that held yardage, trims, and other sewing sundries, all tidily arranged. A new-looking Singer sewing machine held court at the back of the room, its gleaming walnut stand draped with what appeared to be a woman's dress in progress. A roomy square table took center stage. Scissors, a neatly wound measuring tape, a sketch tablet, and a wine-red pincushion adorned its smooth surface.

She rested her slender fingers on the black scissor handles, making Gabe wonder if she planned to stab him. With a quick search of her expression, he chased away the thought. Nan didn't have it in her to deliberately harm anyone, not even a man who had forced her into matrimony.

"This is where I work," she said shakily. "I also consult with my customers in here."

"That is a beautiful sewing machine. It must have cost a small fortune."

Pink slashed her pale cheeks. "A necessary purchase. I've doubled my sales since buying it."

She brushed by him to exit the room and turned toward the door that led to the upstairs living area. Gabe stopped her short. "Shouldn't we lock up? Even with the closed sign showing, curiosity seekers are liable to walk right in."

Nan glanced down at the key he still held in one hand. "Laney will be home soon, and her only way in is through the shop." She held out a slender hand for the key. After taking it from Gabe, exercising care as she did to avoid a touch of their fingertips, she slipped the instrument into her skirt pocket. "As for the gossipmongers, as sharp as their tongues can be, most of them are honest to a fault. I doubt any of my customers would steal."

Gabe didn't share her faith in the goodness of most people, but then, when he thought about it, he decided that his opinion of others might be more than a little biased. He'd spent much of his life seeing the dark side of human nature, and as a kid, he'd suffered cruelties that not even Nan, emotionally injured by her father though she had been, could probably imagine. Maybe his perspective had come to him through a narrow lens, focused on the gutter scum, while Nan had seen the world through a multifaceted prism, allowing her to glimpse more brightness and hope.

Remaining two steps behind her, Gabe followed her up a steep, narrow staircase, the kind he called a neck breaker. One misstep could cause a person to take a very nasty fall, and if that occurred on one of the top risers, a somersault to death could easily result.

"You need some nice, sturdy handrails," he observed.

"I know," she admitted as she paused to push open the door to the apartment. "Hiring a carpenter is expensive, though. I recently enlarged the shop and our quarters after buying the place next door. The renovations, simple though they were, cost me dearly. I also paid a lot extra to put in a kitchen water pump and some drainpipes. Handrails in this stairwell must wait until next year."

Gabe made a mental note to visit the lumberyard and the hardware section at the general store. He didn't want Nan or Laney to take a tumble.

After passing through the doorway to enter the room beyond, Nan stood in its center with her hands clasped at her waist, the fingers of her right hand twisting the wedding band around and around as if the circle of gold seared her flesh. She waited for him to join her. He noticed that her pointy little knuckles were white, a telltale sign that she still expected him to jump her at any second. Recalling the scenes of her life that he'd been shown by the angels, most particularly the obscenely fat Horace Barclay's sexual assault upon her person, he felt a little sick to his stomach. Nobody who'd seen all that could blame this woman for fearing men.

Most nauseating of all to Gabe was the inescapable fact that Martin Sullivan had been in his upstairs study during the attack upon his daughter, well aware of what was occurring down in the sitting room, because he and Barclay had discussed the situation and agreed it needed to happen. Nan's premature deflowering would have ensured that she offered no last-minute objections on the day of the fast-approaching nuptials. Grinning like a cat lapping cream, Sullivan had reclined on a velvet chair in front of the fire, enjoying an expensive cigar while wreathing his head with aromatic smoke. So far as he was concerned, nothing could be allowed to prevent the wedding. Nan's feelings about it were inconsequential. The union of the Sullivan and Barclay families would create a formidable financial alliance that would greatly benefit both men. Nan would settle down quickly enough once Barclay got her pregnant. She'd forget about her silly, girlish revulsion at marrying a much older man and focus on raising a family, just as countless other women of her station had done for centuries. Martin wasn't about to let his daughter's foolish notions about becoming a spinster get in the way. What a bunch of poppycock. Females had been created for one reason, and one reason only: to provide men with progeny.

Fortunately, at least to Gabe's way of thinking, Sullivan hadn't counted on Nan's knitting needle coming into play, and he'd seriously underestimated his elder daughter's intelligence, courage, and ingenuity. While Martin Sullivan had sipped fine brandy and lit a second cigar, Nan, in shock and quivering with terror, had been emptying his study safe, stuffing possessions into pillowcases, and spiriting her little sister from the huge house through the servants' quarters.

Gabe wasn't sure how Nan had found her way to Random. The angels hadn't shown him that part of her life. He had glimpsed scenes of her early years here in a much smaller shop, and had seen the meager existence she'd led in order to get her ledgers in the black. He also knew that she'd done without many necessities in order to give Laney everything she'd felt a little girl should have.

In short, though Gabe knew he had only a short time to enjoy it, he was proud to be Nan's husband. She was, in his estimation, one hell of a lady. A little too prim for his taste, perhaps, and she definitely needed to learn how to laugh. But over the next month, he'd work on that.

During the renovations, Nan had enlarged the kitchen, turning the previously tiny nook into a spacious room reminiscent of the few farmhouse kitchens around Random that she'd seen. There was a wide window above the new sink, which was actually plumbed, and the counter space was ample, providing plenty of room for rolling out dough and cooling baked goods. She'd even gotten a long table, large enough to seat six, because it felt homier, as if a real family lived here.

Gabriel Valance made the area seem smallish and cramped. Nan wasn't sure how that could be. Though he was a tall and well-muscled man, he wasn't *that* big. Yet he seemed to dominate the room, towering over her and robbing her lungs of breath.

"This is nice," he said, drawing his gaze from the frilly lace curtains above the sink to scan the adornments she'd hung on the yellow walls and set on the waxed wood counters. He smiled slightly. "Your decorating talent extends to more than just hats, I see."

Nan felt an odd warmth spread up her spine. She loved what she'd done with the kitchen, and of course

Laney had given it high marks, but no one else, except the workmen, had seen the finished product. Having a stranger praise the room's appearance felt . . . nice.

She nearly smiled, but squelched the urge. Gabriel Valance wasn't just any stranger. He was her husband, and he might give her compliments merely to butter her up. Everything she'd heard about this man and from him made it clear that he took what he wanted. And she wasn't at all sure she believed his avowals that he had no intention of consummating the marriage unless she was willing. "Flattery will get you nowhere, Mr. Valance."

He chuckled. The deep timbre of his laughter was a pleasant sound, but Nan knew from hard experience that the kindliest, most pleasant of men could turn into heartless monsters in the blink of an eye. She'd seen her father charm his houseguests, then whisper a scathing remark to her mother that had shattered what little self-esteem Helena Sullivan still possessed. By the time Nan was thirteen, her mother had been slowly killing herself for years by trying, over and over again, to give her husband a son. Between miscarriages, Helena would barely give her body time to heal before she tried to get pregnant again, and her successes at that had always ended with hemorrhaging, loss of the baby, and Martin raging at her for failing yet again.

Nan's memories of her mother's last miscarriage, which had occurred right before Helena became pregnant with Laney, would haunt her for the rest of her life. Nan had just finished with her lessons for the day and had run upstairs to dress for their formal dinner, a daily ritual her father insisted on each evening, as befitted a man of his social status.

Nan had rounded a corner in the long hallway to find her mother lying on the marble floor in a spreading pool of blood just outside the master suite. Martin

Sullivan had stood over his wife, white-faced with anger, his hands knotted into fists.

"You stupid, skinny little cow!" he'd yelled. "The midwife says it was a boy. A *son*, Helena, *finally* a son. I swear to God, you can do *nothing* right."

"I stayed in bed just as the doctor advised," Helena cried, her voice weak from blood loss and exhaustion. "It wasn't my fault, Martin. It just happened."

"That's your song, and you sing it so well!" Martin toed his wife's hip, not putting enough force behind the kick to actually do her physical harm, but jostling her body nevertheless. "Get out of my sight, you useless bitch."

Nan could still remember how she'd stared down in horror at the spreading pool of her mother's blood. Yet Helena had struggled to gain her feet, sobbing and begging for her husband's forgiveness even as she slipped and fell again. Nine months later, Helena had gone into early labor and died giving birth to Laney, another female for Martin Sullivan to despise.

Jerking her thoughts back to the present, Nan gave Gabriel Valance a long, deliberate study. His eyes twinkled in the afternoon light that shone through the window. Try though she might, she could find no glint of cruelty in their dark depths. Even so, she knew only a ruthless man could kill as many times as he had and still feel lighthearted enough to laugh.

With a deliberately cool edge to her voice, Nan said, "I did the kitchen to please myself. Your opinion really doesn't matter to me."

He shrugged, still smiling. "Fair enough." Glancing toward the archway, he asked, "And where does that lead?"

"The sitting room." Nan moved toward the opening, determined to give him a tour and be done with it. "Expanding into the shop next door provided us with a lot more space upstairs as well. This used to be a tiny sitting area and bedroom, which Laney and I shared, and that was the entirety of our quarters. During the remodel, I focused mainly on our living area, so down that short hallway we now have two bedrooms, a water closet, and another room where I work at night. Laney often has nightmares, so I don't go back downstairs to my shop after she's asleep."

She saw him give the horsehair settee a measuring glance and followed his gaze. He was far too tall to stretch out on it, she realized, and knew he was thinking the same thing.

"What does she have nightmares about?"

Worrying about the coming night's sleeping arrangements, Nan took a moment to assimilate the question. "Why do you ask?"

"Just curious. With you to mother her and a home as fine as this, I'd think she would be a happy, carefree girl." He stepped over to the fireplace, glanced at the burgundy parlor chairs at each hearth corner, and then flicked a look at the empty leather sling that she used to bring up wood from the backyard pile each evening. Fingering the gray mortar between two red bricks, he asked, "Does this put out enough heat to keep you cozy on a cold winter night?"

"I keep the fire going in the cookstove most evenings as well. We stay warm enough."

"It must be an ongoing chore to carry enough loads of wood up that staircase to keep two fires going."

"Laney helps. Between the two of us, we manage fine."

He turned from examining the brick to face her again. Her nervous gaze became fixed on the breadth of his shoulders. A suffocating sensation filled her throat. "In other words," he said with a touch of amusement, "you have absolutely no need of a man in the house."

Nan supposed she had been a trifle transparent in their exchanges thus far, but if her honesty made him feel unwelcome, that was his burden to bear. She had not entered into this marriage willingly, and she would not pretend she had.

"Absolutely no need of a man at all, Mr. Valance. If it angers you that I refuse to say otherwise, I suppose you can shoot me." She flicked a glance at his guns. "That is your expertise, correct? Shooting people?"

"I've never shot anyone who didn't try to shoot me first," he replied. Then he arched a black eyebrow, calling to her mind the shape of a raven's wing. "And from this moment on, my name is Gabe. If you prefer, you can call me Gabriel. But I don't think it's fitting for you to address me formally any longer."

Nan couldn't argue the point. Laney would be home soon, and somehow Nan had to protect the child from the harsh realities of this impossible situation. Laney was a spirited girl and could easily become feisty if she thought Nan might be in peril.

"How am I going to explain this mess to my sister?" Nan asked him.

His firm lips tipped into a crooked grin. "Well, now, I'm thinking you should tell her the truth: that I came into your shop, asked you to marry me, and you simply couldn't bring yourself to say no."

"Laney will never believe that. She's heard me say too many times that I have no use for men and that I abhor the institution of marriage."

"You'd better make it convincing then. Otherwise I'll have two wet hens pecking at me, and my patience may wear thin."

"And if your patience wears thin?" Nan forced herself to look him directly in the eye. "I truly didn't mean to harm Horace Barclay. His death was an accident. But I will tell you right now, if you ever harm Laney, by word or by action, I'll kill you without blinking an eye."

He nodded. "If I hurt your sister, by word or by action, I'll help you slit my own throat."

That wasn't the response Nan had expected. Mentally teetering, she wasn't prepared when he added, "Now that we've got that covered, we should spend what remains of our time alone discussing our sleeping arrangements."

Nan gulped. "You may sleep on the settee or the floor."

A muscle began to tic in his jaw. "Not on your life. We're man and wife. We'll share a bed."

"But you said you had no intention—"

"And I meant it," he inserted, cutting off her protests. "But that's where I draw the line. If you insist, I'll sleep in my trousers, but that's all the compromise I'm willing to make on that front."

Nan realized that her arms had gone stiff at her sides and that her hands were knotted into painful fists, her nails digging into her palms. "Do you truly think I'm so naive that I believe you won't force yourself on me? Until this marriage is consummated, I can have it annulled at any time. You don't strike me as being a stupid man. You've surely considered that and plan to make this union legally binding as soon as you possibly can."

He turned toward the sitting room window, which looked out over the main street of town. "I'm content to leave things as they stand." He drew his watch from his pocket and perused its face. "Hamm's office should still be open. You're free to head out of here and file for an annulment before he closes up shop, if you like. The same goes for tomorrow, and the day after that."

Nan felt suddenly cold and hugged her waist. "The instant I filed for an annulment, you'd pay a visit to the marshal's office and have me arrested! I'm not that stupid, Mr. Valance."

"Gabe—or Gabriel," he corrected. Then he slipped the watch back into his pocket and flashed her a grin over his shoulder. "I'd say we're off to a good start, darlin'. We clearly understand each other. That's more than a lot of couples can say after twenty long years of marriage."

Nan couldn't recall ever having hated anyone quite so much. She parted her lips to fling a nasty retort at him, but just then she heard the shop bell ring, and an instant later Laney's light footsteps sounded on the stairs.

"Well?" he said, challenging her with his gaze. "I see no point in burdening that child with this, so either slap a smile on your face or make tracks for Hamm's office."

Nan forced her arms from around her waist, sent him a look that she hoped sliced through him like a knife, and then turned just as the apartment door flew open. When Laney bounded into the kitchen, Nan was beaming a smile that made her face feel as if it might crack.

Chapter Six

Gabe had taken a chair at the far end of the kitchen table as Laney Hoffman entered the apartment and closed the door. He hoped he wouldn't seem as intimidating if he was seated. Wearing a dark green dress, intricately pleated at the bodice and trimmed with pearl-like beads at the throat and cuffs, along with black patent-leather slippers with arch straps sporting shiny bows, the girl was window-display perfect from the top of her head to the tips of her toes. She greatly resembled Nan, with the same ivory skin, delicate features, lovely gray eyes, and golden hair. At twelve she was still coltishly thin, with only the merest hint of budding breasts, but Gabe knew she'd be a beauty soon who'd turn men's heads just as her sister did now.

Gabe sensed, however, that the striking resemblance ran only skin deep. There was a spark in Laney's eyes that Nan's lacked, and as the girl listened to Nan's disjointed, high-pitched, nervous explanation of how her sudden marriage to Gabe had come about that morning, Laney gave him a glare hot enough to melt sand and make glass. Laney wasn't buying a word of her sister's jerky explanations, and Gabe didn't blame the kid. Nan was the most abysmally unconvincing liar he'd ever encountered. *Interesting.* He filed a mental note to remember that his wife fluttered her hands, got a squeak in her larynx, and couldn't look a person in the eye when she spouted falsehoods.

After concluding her spiel, Nan gestured for Laney to sit down, and then started bustling around the sunny yellow kitchen, putting on a pot of coffee, warming a pan of milk for hot cocoa, and arranging cookies she'd baked last night on a serving tray. Aside from Nan's twittered comments, directed over her shoulder as she worked, the silence was so marked that Gabe noted for the first time that the sitting room wall clock had an unusually loud tick. Laney, perched stiffly on a chair at the opposite end of the table, kept her gaze fixed on him, and to say her expression was filled with hostility would have been an understatement. He'd seen friendlier looks slanted down the barrel of a pistol.

Soon Nan was ready to serve the after-school beverages and treats. Because the recipients of her offerings sat so far apart, she arranged cookies on two dessert plates and then poured Gabe a cup of coffee and Laney some cocoa. Gabe eyed the dainty teacup she'd set before him, hoping his forefinger wouldn't get stuck in the tiny handle.

"There we go!" Nan said brightly. "As you two enjoy the afternoon snack, perhaps you can become better acquainted while I go down to the shop to lock up and count down my till."

That suited Gabe just fine. Judging by the fire in Laney's eyes, he figured she had a peck of words backed up in her throat and that they would rain upon his head like bits of ice in a hailstorm the instant Nan left the room.

After the door closed, Laney sat stock-still, listening to Nan's receding footsteps on the stairs. The instant the sounds indicated that Nan was down in the shop, well out of earshot, Laney leaned over her cookie plate, her dimpled chin, so very like Nan's, jutting at him like that of a prizefighter asking for a solid punch. "That was a stupid pack of lies, every word of it!" she cried. "She doesn't want any man mucking up her life, never has and never will, and if she ever changed her mind and decided to get married, it wouldn't be to someone like *you.*" Gabe nearly winced as that barb struck home, but before he could get his mouth open to defend himself, Laney rushed on. "Do either of you really think I'm dumb enough to believe this?"

He definitely didn't think the girl lacked intelligence. Just by searching her gaze, Gabe could see that she was sharper than a new tack. "Your sister didn't lie," he offered. "It sounds incredible, Laney, but that's what happened. Every word Nan said is the absolute truth. I did come into the shop this morning. I did offer for her hand. And just as she told you, she couldn't say no."

Laney's eyes widened until they looked as big as half-dollars. She couldn't have looked more horrified— or more frightened—if he'd suddenly turned into a scorpion. "My *sister*?"

Oh, shit. He never should have referred to Nan as the child's sister. Everyone in Random believed that Laney was Nan's daughter. "Well . . ." he began.

"You *know*! Don't say otherwise! And somehow you coerced her into marrying you because of it! You know everything!" She was practically screaming. And everybody in town was going to know if he didn't manage to get her to calm down and shut up.

"Yeah, okay, I know everything. You're right, absolutely right. But if you don't quit yelling, Nan will be flying up here in a panic. Give me a second here, okay?"

Laney subsided, but he had a feeling it was only temporary. Her use of the word *coerce* didn't surprise him. Most kids would have fallen back on something simpler and more commonly used, but he suspected that Laney had an impressive vocabulary for a twelve-year-old and could spell every word correctly. Gabe had studied hard on his own after old widow Harper died, and over the years, he'd developed a handshake relationship with proper English. He could read almost anything, and use bigger words than he'd ever once imagined, but his spelling was still on the downside of passable. Laney Hoffman made him feel like a sow's ear sitting across from a silk purse.

A stare-down ensued, and Gabe used the seconds that passed to weigh the situation. He'd never been much good at lying, not because it was a religious issue for him, but more because he considered himself to be an honorable sort, and telling falsehoods, in his estimation, was unethical. If a man wasn't as good as his word, he wasn't worth the powder it'd take to blow him to hell.

But his reluctance to lie to Laney went deeper than that. Gabe knew a straight shooter when he met one, and this girl was exactly that: a person who said what was on her mind, minced no words, and let the chips fall where they might. She deserved better than lies from him. Even worse, Gabe doubted he could get creative enough with a story to make her believe it anyway.

"You're right," he finally admitted again. "I know everything about your sister's past, and I used that knowledge to force her to marry me. I told her that if she refused, I'd go to the marshal, reveal her true identity, and have her arrested."

If he'd expected Laney to be scared at the idea of exposure, he'd figured wrong. Bright spots of angry color sprang to her cheeks. "*Why?* Are you hoping to lie around here, being good for nothing, while she supports you with her income from the shop?"

Gabe almost smiled. "I don't need your sister to support me, cupcake. I have so much money stashed away in a Kansas City bank that I could live in high style until I'm an old man without ever turning my hand to an honest day's work."

Her brows, which, like Nan's, were several shades darker than her golden hair, snapped together in a scowl. "Oh, sure you do. If that was true you'd have no need to force some woman to marry you. If you have that much money, you could find a wife on your own. So what do you want with Nan, anyhow? A man like you usually consorts with saloon girls, not proper ladies like my mama. And don't call me cupcake!"

Gabe lifted the coffee cup to his lips to hide a grin. She had spunk, no doubt about it. "A man like me?" He took a slow swallow. "All that glitters is not gold, little lady, and the same goes for anything that appears to be all dark."

After he spoke, he saw a shift of emotion in Laney's eyes, but it quickly vanished, to be replaced by anger again. "Are you saying I shouldn't judge you, Mr. Valance? You're a gunslinger. I heard about your being in town at school today. A boy who went home for lunch got it straight from his father that you ate breakfast in the hotel dining room this morning."

"Yes, I'm a gunslinger," Gabe conceded. "And one of some repute, I might add. That doesn't mean I like being what I am or that I ever wanted this kind of life for myself." Gabe gave her a brief overview of his history, much as he had for Nan that morning. "Sometimes our lives can change direction at the turn of a leaf or the shift of a breeze," he finished. "We don't see it coming, but one incident can change everything."

"Like what happened to Nan when she accidentally killed that fat old man?"

Gabe was heartened by the softening of Laney's expression. "Exactly like that, only for each person, the pivotal moment is caused by different things."

"How'd you learn to use a word like *pivotal* if you never went to school?" she asked.

Gabe allowed himself to smile slightly. "An old widow who'd once been a schoolmarm took me under her wing for about a year and did her best to smarten me up."

"You didn't learn words like that in a year."

"No, but living with her for that short time opened up the world of books for me, and after she died, I hungered to learn more, so I studied on my own."

"So you're self-taught."

"More or less."

Laney took a bite of cookie and pocketed the morsel in her cheek. Her gaze locked with his, offering him no quarter. "I don't believe what you said about marrying my sister to get a taste of how it feels to live like other folks. I'm sort of starting to like you, Mr. Valance. But like you say, things can change fast, and I can start hating you again real quick if you try to blow smoke in my eyes."

Gabe had to laugh at that, and with some surprise, he realized that he was starting to like her, too. "If I told you the real truth, Laney, you'd never believe it."

"Try me," she challenged.

Gabe was tempted—oh, how badly he was tempted. But it was a crazy, incredible story that he still couldn't quite believe himself. He finished his coffee in two big gulps, intending to end the conversation by going down to help Nan in the shop. But as he set the dainty little cup back on the saucer and pushed to his feet, he remembered the last bit of advice that the angel Gabriel had given him. *Listen to your heart.*

At the time, Gabe hadn't been able to recall a single time when his heart had spoken to him, but it was definitely speaking to him now. He sank back in the chair, studied Laney soberly for a long moment, and finally decided that having the little imp in his corner sure as hell couldn't hurt, and might very well help him to accomplish his goals. "If you want to hear the truth—the *real* truth—it's a long story, and it's one Nan must never hear. If I tell it to you, will you give me your word that you will repeat nothing I say to her?"

Laney didn't hesitate. "No. You've herded my sister into a marriage she doesn't want, and for all I know, you're up to a heap of no good. My first loyalty is to her, not to you."

Gabe admired her for her honesty. Yep, she was a straight shooter if ever he'd met one. "What if, by telling you the story, I convince you that I mean Nan no harm? That I am, in fact, here to do exactly the opposite and try to help her?"

Laney swallowed the bite of cookie. Her gray eyes darkened with shadows. "Nan doesn't need help."

Gabe shook his head. "Ah, Laney, don't lie to yourself after being so brutally honest with me. Look me in the eye and tell me, without blinking, that Nan is completely happy with her life, that there's nothing more that she yearns for, nothing else that she once dreamed of but has now given up on ever having. Can you do that?"

Laney searched the depths of her untouched hot cocoa, her shimmery lashes feathering over her cheeks. "Well . . . she did tell me once that there was a time when she was still young and stupid that she believed she'd find her one true love." Looking up again, the girl shrugged. "She doesn't believe in all that nonsense anymore."

"Do you think it's all nonsense?" Gabe asked softly.

He listened to the clock tick while she struggled for an answer. "I don't know. No, I guess I don't think it's nonsense." She shrugged her narrow shoulders. "I love Nan with my whole heart, and if I can love *her* that

way, it only makes sense to me that I could love someone else just as much, maybe someday even a man."

Gabe was relieved to hear that. Being raised by a
woman who disliked men and feared the institution of
marriage could have affected Laney's view of the
world, its male population in particular.

"And babies," Gabe ventured. "Don't you think
Nan's ever wished she could have her very own baby? I
know how much she loves you, and I'm not trying to
take anything away from that, but having your own
child—well, I think that's something most women want,
even if they never say so."

Laney narrowed her eyes. "Are you saying you're
here to help Nan fall in love with somebody and have
babies of her own before she gets too old?"

Gabe stood and carried his cup and saucer to the
sink. "If you want to hear my story, cupcake, it isn't
going to happen here." Ignoring her mean look at his
use of the nickname again, he went on. "Nan will be
coming back up any minute, and it's very important
that she never hears a word of this." As Gabe rinsed his
cup, he sent up a silent prayer that confiding in Laney
wasn't a huge mistake. *Listen to your heart,* Gabriel had
told him. Well, Gabe sorely feared that his heart might
be so rusty from disuse that it was talking nonsense.
"Where's your cloak?" he asked the child.

"Hanging on the hook downstairs by the door."

Gabe turned from the counter. "Good. You can grab
it as you go out with me to help get wood."

Gabe went to collect the leather firewood sling that
he'd seen lying by the sitting room hearth. Laney
grabbed the sling near the woodstove. When they met
again in the kitchen, she lifted her fair brows at him in
question. "You don't act like you're any too happy
about telling me this tale."

Gabe saw no reason to deny the truth. "I'm afraid it

may be a huge mistake, and if it is, I'm going to pay dearly."

Laney considered that for a second and then nodded. "I won't repeat to Nan any of what you tell me if you can convince me you're actually here to help her."

Not good enough, he realized. This tale was too farfetched to gamble on the understanding of someone so young, however well-intentioned. "Look," he said. "Let me put this another way. Will you promise to keep quiet about what I tell you, even if you don't believe it, if I can convince you that I mean your sister no harm?"

She didn't answer right away. Instead, she studied him like she might a curious bug in a display case. He had a feeling she was looking clear into the depths of his mind and heart. After what seemed a minor eternity, she nodded slowly. "Okay. Deal."

Gabe figured that was about as much as he could hope for and led the way downstairs, braced with every step to catch Laney from falling if she tripped. If he did nothing else useful around here, he'd get some sturdy handrails installed.

Nan had nearly finished emptying the merchandise crate that she'd collapsed upon that morning. She stopped arranging items on a shelf to turn and give them a surprised look.

"We're going out to bring in some wood," Gabe told her. "You're out upstairs, and it's liable to get real cold tonight."

He saw Nan's shoulders stiffen. "Laney and I can do that. We always have."

"I know, but now that I'm here I may as well make myself useful."

She shrugged, as if it made her no never mind, but Gabe knew it bothered her to accept any kind of help from him. "While you're about that, I'll get supper started then." She glanced at her sister. "Be sure to wear your cloak, Laney. I don't want you catching a chill." When Gabe reached the door, she added, "If you're bent on bringing in wood, Gabriel, I'll need a load down here in the shop come morning as well."

He glanced over his shoulder at the woodstove, which occupied the left rear corner of the room. "No problem. I'll make sure you have plenty to last you the day."

After they filled the wood slings, Gabe braced a boot on a half-empty layer of the long woodpile and slipped his pack of Marquis of Lorne cigarettes from his shirt pocket. Laney hugged her cloak close, watching as he tapped out a smoke, struck a match on the outer thigh seam of his jeans, and lighted up.

"You'll be getting phossy jaw if you aren't careful," Laney warned him as he drew on the Marquis to get it burning well. "That phosphorous is dangerous. It puts off fumes, you know, and people get sick from them."

Gabe grinned. "How do you light your lanterns at night, with your finger?"

"Mama always lights them, and she's very careful not to breathe the fumes."

Gabe shrugged. "I mostly only smoke outside, and even then only occasionally. I doubt I inhale enough phosphorous fumes to bother me."

Laney looked unconvinced, but she apparently put the concern behind her to ask, "You going to tell me that tale, or are you just going to stand there, puffing the whole time?"

Gabe exhaled a waft of smoke, glad for the calming effect. "I'm working my way up to it. I'm just not sure where to start."

"At the beginning," Laney told him.

A fine suggestion, but what was the beginning? Gabe couldn't quite determine when it had all started—

as far back as his childhood, maybe?—so he settled on beginning when he found the boy under the stairway on Christmas morning, being careful not to mention that it had been the stairway leading up to the prostitute quarters. He didn't figure Laney needed to know about such places until she grew older.

When he got to the part where Pete Raintree shot him in the chest, Laney's eyes went as round as pennies. "Praise God he didn't kill you!" she cried. Her gaze sharpened, and he saw her eyes narrow. She was adding two plus two and getting seven. "You don't look shot to me. Even after almost a year to heal, you'd still show some sign of having been that seriously injured."

Gabe tossed away his cigarette and ground it out under his heel. "That's where this story gets real strange, cupcake, because Pete Raintree did kill me. He came out of the shadows, yelling that Pete Raintree had shot Gabriel Valance, still unaware that I'd gotten him dead in the chest. When he reached me where I lay in the street, he looked down at the blood, all bewildered, and then he fell dead just a few feet away from me."

"But you didn't die—not really—because you're still here, almost a year later."

Gabe chose not to correct her chronology. That could come later. Instead he told her about seeing Nan standing at the window. "She stood there, with evergreen boughs framing her person, almost like a picture frame, and the light of the candle shone in her hair, making it radiant, almost like a halo. I knew I was dying—I felt cold, really cold, and it was getting hard to breathe. Nan was so damned beautiful I thought maybe I'd already died and was seeing an angel."

"Nan is pretty," Laney agreed, "especially with her hair down."

"Yep, pretty as an angel. I stared at her as long as I

could, trying my best to hang on, but black spots started blocking my vision, and pretty soon everything went black, like when all the lantern wicks are turned down at once, and a room goes so dark you can't see. Only difference was, I wasn't thinking anymore, or even feeling anything. That was it. I just died. It happened really fast."

"And then Doc Peterson came and saved you. Right?"

"Nope. I woke up standing in front of a rickety old shack. It was eerie, I can tell you that, but I didn't get any too scared until I looked down."

Laney leaned closer. "What did you see that frightened you?"

"I was standing on nothing but a cloud—walking on air, I guess you could say."

Laney rolled her eyes. "That's the craziest thing I ever heard. Nobody can walk on air."

"You can if you're dead," Gabe replied. Then he glanced back over his shoulder at the narrow opening between the two buildings, which provided passage to the shop's backyard. "We'd better take in a load of wood before I continue. Otherwise Nan's going to get worried and come searching for us. If we go in, she'll get busy in the kitchen cooking, and maybe she won't keep track of time."

"You can't stop the story there!" Laney cried. He had a strong feeling that was just what she thought his tale was—a story he'd invented. But a good one.

Gabe laughed. "It's what they call a cliff-hanger, keeping your audience in suspense."

"It isn't fair to use a cliff-hanger right this minute. Tell me just a little bit more before we take the wood in."

"Nope," Gabe said. "Top off your sling, sweetheart. Otherwise Nan will soon be tracking us down to find out what's taking so long."

With a huff, Laney began collecting split lengths of wood and stacking them on what she'd already deposited on the unfurled sling. "It's a stupid story, anyway," she grumped. "And I don't care what happens next."

"Fine, then. If you don't want to hear it, I won't bother myself with finishing."

The searing glare the child arced toward him set Gabe to laughing again.

Thirty minutes later, when they returned to the backyard woodpile, Gabe resumed telling his story. He left out the identities of the other two lost souls in Random whom he might have chosen to save and focused on his decision to pick Nan. "Those angels, they're clever fellows," he told Laney. "They parted the clouds so I could look down and see Nan during certain moments of her life. Your father, Martin Sullivan—do you remember him at all? You were pretty little when Nan got you out of his house and ran away with you."

Dark shadows shifted in the girl's eyes. "No, I don't remember him," she said without a trace of doubt in her voice. Then she met Gabe's gaze and added, "But sometimes I think maybe—" She broke off and shook her head.

"Sometimes you think what?" Gabe pressed.

She shrugged and gazed off at the backyard of a house facing the next street over. "I have bad dreams," she said, her voice pitched so low it was almost a whisper. "Really awful dreams, and sometimes I think the man in them who's being so mean to Nan might be my father."

Gabe sighed. "As much as I hate to say it, Laney, I think you're probably right. Your father . . . well, he was *very* mean to Nan, and if you saw some of that going on when you were really little, it may come back to you in nightmares, even though you can't remember any of it when you're awake."

She gave him a questioning look. "I'm not sure I believe this story, Mr. Valance. Talking to archangels and looking through holes in the clouds to see Nan doing things years ago?" She wrinkled her nose. "It smells to me of imagination and trickery."

"Then how do I know the things I know?" Gabe challenged.

"You could have discovered Nan's identity, done some digging, and learned things about her past. It was in the newspapers in New York that she murdered Horace Barclay, I'm sure. Nobody needs a couple of angels to tell him that."

Gabe knew he was losing his audience. He could see it in Laney's eyes. *Ah, well*, he thought grimly, *I knew making her believe me would be difficult—and risky.* "Okay, fine," he told the child. "I know it all sounds pretty farfetched."

"Finish anyway," Laney replied. "It really is a good story."

Gabe cocked his head. "You are going to be some man's undoing one day, Laney Hoffman, sweet as sugar on the one hand and as difficult as a mathematical equation on the other."

She dimpled a cheek. "If refusing to suffer nonsense gladly makes me difficult, I'll happily accept the judgment."

Gabe almost told her to go pick wildflowers—which, during a Colorado winter, were nonexistent. But then he decided that finishing the tale might sway her in his direction.

"Well, you're definitely difficult, and now that I've got that said, let me entertain you with this little bit of information. Nan didn't mean to murder Horace Barclay. When he tried to force himself on her, she got away from him long enough to grab a knitting needle. She meant only to hold him off by threatening him, but he just laughed and lunged at her. Big and fat like he was, he was too clumsy by half, and he tripped on the rug, fell on top of Nan, and skewered himself. She never meant to stab him."

Laney nibbled the inside of her lower lip. "Nan could have told you that this morning when you were threatening to turn her in. Your knowing that she didn't mean to hurt him means nothing."

She had him there, Gabe decided, because Nan had, in fact, tried to convince him of her innocence that morning. *Careful, Gabe.* He had only three aces left in his hand: the knowledge that Horace Barclay wasn't dead; that the fat old bugger had been too embarrassed about the incident to report his injury to the authorities; and that Nan had no murder charge hanging over her head. Over his lifetime, Gabe had made some pretty stupid mistakes, but he'd learned from experience and wasn't about to make another. If he gave Laney even one of those tidbits of information, she'd go running to Nan with the news. If that happened, Gabe would no longer have any leverage in this situation, and Nan would make fast tracks to Hamm's office first thing in the morning to file for that annulment.

No way was Gabe going to let that happen. Laney would believe what she chose to believe, and if the two of them remained at loggerheads because of it, he'd simply tough it out for the next month. After all he'd gone through as a kid, living for thirty days with two sharp-tongued females taking shots at him every chance they got . . . Well, Gabe had survived far worse.

"There has to be more to your story," Laney observed. "You claim you're here to save Nan. There's no way you can clear her name, not unless you've left out something important."

Gabe smiled grimly. Laney Hoffman had a mind like a steel trap, and he wasn't about to stick his foot on the spring release. "You're right. There's more to the story, but I'm no longer in the mood to finish. You don't believe me anyway, so why waste my breath?" When all she did was shrug, Gabe hit her with another question. "Do I strike you as being a stupid man?"

"No, you seem smart enough to me."

"Then why, if I was going to make up a story, would I choose to make one up that nobody in his right mind would ever believe? Hell, no. If I were lying, I'd come up with something a lot better, believe me."

"I don't understand why you chose to tell me in the first place."

"To get you on my side, of course. If I can get you to come around, you might help ease my way with Nan."

Laney huffed. She had a way of rolling her eyes that Gabe might have found adorable under other circumstances. "I'll only ever be on Nan's side, never on yours."

"It's one and the same. Whether you believe me or not, I'm here to help the woman."

Once again hugging her cloak against the cold, Laney peered at him through the deepening twilight. "You know what I think, Mr. Valance?"

"No, but I've got a feeling you're going to tell me anyway."

"I think maybe you did get shot, and maybe you did almost die, and maybe sometime during your recovery, you grew delirious and *dreamed* about meeting those angels."

Gabe bent to throw some more wood into both slings. "Well, thank you for that much. At least you aren't out and out calling me a liar."

Laney watched him work, tapping the toe of her patent-leather slipper on the sparse winter yellow grass. "No, I think it's more likely that you're simply very confused, Mr. Valance, and that worries me, because if you're *that* confused, hearing angels talking to you and all, you may believe you're here to help my sister, but instead you might somehow do her harm."

Gabe straightened with a sling of wood in both hands. "Rest assured, I'll try my darnedest to keep my confused self under control."

Laney shook her head. "No, I'm sorry. That's not good enough. I want you out of our house."

"What you want and what you'll get may be two different things." Gabe started for the narrow alleyway, then paused midstride to swing back around. "And fair warning, little miss. If you say or do anything to interfere between me and Nan—if you tell a single soul a word of the story I just told you—I'll follow through on my threat to visit the marshal. If your sister winds up in jail, it'll be on your head, and you'll have to live with the knowledge that you're the one who sent her there."

Laney paled, and her face took on that closed-in expression again. "Now you're showing your true colors, Mr. Valance. If you cared about my sister, you'd never consider turning her in. I don't know what you really want, but I don't trust you an inch, and as long as you're around, I'll be watching you close. Nan could hang for murdering Horace Barclay."

Hating himself, he said, "Yep. She could. So before you get on your high horse, you'd best remember that."

Despite the fine food on the table—pan-fried salt pork, mashed potatoes and gravy, and corn Nan had preserved at the end of summer—supper was a dismal affair. Gabe sat at one end of the table, Nan at the other, with Laney in the chair to Nan's immediate right. No one spoke. They just ate. The silence was so loud it almost hurt Gabe's ears. He discovered during the meal that his jaw popped when he chewed—just a soft click that he normally didn't notice in public dining areas, where people actually engaged in conversation.

Apparently Nan had given up on pretending she was happy about their marriage, or the prospect of sleeping with him that night had her in such a dither, she'd forgotten about putting on a good face for Laney. She sat so straight that Gabe could have ruled paper with her spine, and she picked at her food, taking a tiny bite of one serving and chewing while she pushed another around on her plate. Laney kept sending Gabe long, unnerving stares. At one point, he thought she might be trying to convey something to him, but then he decided she was just glaring. The girl was way too big for her britches—well, in her case, bloomers—and needed a sterner disciplinarian than Nan apparently was to take her down to size. Gabe had no inclination to volunteer for the job, and even if he had, he doubted he could accomplish much in only thirty days.

The countdown started tomorrow morning right before dawn, he realized gloomily, and he was starting to have serious reservations about this business of trying to save a lost soul. It was a lot harder than the angels thought, if not downright impossible. Nan Sullivan—no, *Hoffman*—didn't want to be saved. In fact, if she hadn't had a murder charge hanging over her head and was stronger of arm, he'd be kicked out of here in two seconds flat.

After the meal, Nan told Laney to sit at the back side of the table to study or complete her assignments while Nan tidied up. Gabe had little experience in a kitchen. Out on the trail, he'd washed his eating tins plenty of times, but he hadn't stood at a sink since the widow Harper died. Nevertheless, he was willing—no, *determined*—to help clean away the mess, partly because it wasn't his way to sit while someone else worked, but mainly because he knew Nan needed to learn that it wasn't an indication of weakness to accept a man's assistance. When it came to doing for herself, she was downright stubborn.

Under less sober circumstances, Gabe would have laughed at Nan's efforts to keep her distance from him as they put the leftovers away. If his shirtsleeve so much as grazed her arm, she jerked back, and in the relatively small space, they brushed against each other often as they emptied serving bowls, scraped plates, and moved the meat from the platter onto a smaller dish. The icebox was crowded. Nan had to shift containers around to make more room, and with the cooling chest so low to the floor, it was a task that required her to bend over. Even concealed by an overabundance of gathers and the bustle of her skirt, her nicely rounded posterior drew his gaze like metal to a magnet. *Damn.* When Gabe imagined how enticing she'd look in a nightgown with her hair down, he felt a film of sweat on his brow and started to think that sleeping on the settee might be easier all around.

Once the kitchen was clean, Nan began adding wood to the cookstove's burning chamber, so Gabe, hoping to lighten her load, went to build a fire in the sitting room for her. He was kneeling in front of the hearth, blowing softly on the ignited kindling to encourage a flame, when Laney startled him half out of his wits by tapping him on the shoulder. He went for his gun, caught himself in the nick of time, and in the process nearly lost his balance and pitched headfirst onto the wood grate.

"Jesus H. Christ. Give a man some warning, why don't you?"

"Shhh!" Laney angled a finger over his lips. "Mama mustn't know I'm talking to you. She thinks I went to use the water closet."

Gabe regained his balance, turned still in a crouch to

peer up at her, and asked, "Well, what's such a secret? Or is there a general rule around here against talking like normal people?"

"I believe you," she whispered. "About dying and talking to angels. I believe it happened, all of it."

That caught Gabe by surprise, and not trusting Laney to be above trickery, he said, "Really? That's a quick change of heart. Now the tables are turned, because I'm not sure I believe you."

"You have to!" she whispered in urgent appeal. "He talked to me! Right before supper when I went to my room to change out of my school dress. I couldn't see him, but I heard him, clear as a bell."

Gabe sent a cautious glance toward the kitchen. "You heard *who*?"

"Gabriel. At least, that's who he said he was, Gabriel the messenger." Laney leaned over at the waist, getting almost nose-to-nose with Gabe. "If you've ever read scripture—"

"I haven't."

"Well, it makes complete sense if you have. Gabriel is referred to as the messenger. I remember reading that in the Old Testament, I think, but maybe in the New as well. Wasn't he the one who appeared to people to foretell the births of Jesus and John the Baptist, or something like that?"

"Don't ask me. I've done a lot of reading, but I steered clear of the Good Book. I've met too many people who seem half-crazed because they read passages from scripture every day. Too much of a good thing, I reckon, because they act like practically everything is a sin. No playing poker, no drinking, no— Well, never you mind. If I started thinking that way, I'd never have any fun."

Laney grasped his shoulder. "He came to me; I'm *telling* you. When I first heard his voice, it scared me half-witless! He told me it all really happened, that it wasn't a dream and you aren't confused. He said I shouldn't breathe a word of what you told me to Nan, and he said I should help you instead of trying to hinder you."

The fire had finally caught without Gabe's help, so he pushed to his feet. "Like I said before, this is a mighty fast turnaround, Laney, and after the things you said out back, I'm not too sure I can trust you. You haven't said one thing that you couldn't be making up."

"He was afraid you might not believe me," Laney whispered, "so he told me to remind you of the last thing he said to you before you made him go away."

"And what was that?" Gabe asked, wondering how Laney knew he'd asked Gabriel to back off. He caught movement from the corner of his eye and realized Nan was walking toward the sitting room. "Make it quick. Here comes your sister."

"Listen to your heart!" Laney wheeled away toward the short hallway. "That's what he told me to tell you."

As the child vanished around the corner, Gabe stared into the feeble lick of the flames, mesmerized by the spurts of blue as tiny beads of pitch ignited. *Listen to your heart.* There was absolutely no way Laney could know about that—unless the angel Gabriel actually *had* visited her.

A smile moved slowly over Gabe's mouth. That golden-haired son of a gun truly had been created by God and never been a man. Otherwise, he would have known better than to drop in on a young girl when she was pulling off one dress to don another. *Poor Laney.* Little wonder the angel had scared her half out of her wits. Gabe knew the feeling. It was eerie to have someone speak in your ear when you least expected it and couldn't see him.

He felt rather than saw Nan come to stand in the archway.

"What were you and Laney talking about?" she asked, a ring of suspicion edging her voice.

"Nothing much. Just about some passages in scripture about an angel named Gabriel. Laney seems to think he is referred to in the Good Book somewhere as the messenger. Do you know if that's accurate?"

Gabe turned to face his nervous bride, feeling more confident than he had all evening. Maybe this business of saving a lost soul wouldn't be so hard, after all. Not with a very determined archangel guarding his back.

"*You* are familiar with scripture?" Nan moved over to a table at the end of the settee, where a decorative lantern sat. As Laney had told him, Nan averted her face slightly to one side after striking the match and held her breath as she put flame to wick. After waving her wrist to put out the match, she added, "You don't strike me as the kind of man who's spent much time reading the Bible."

Gabe moved slowly toward her. She stiffened, clearly apprehensive. When all he did was relieve her of the match and walk back to the hearth to toss it on the fire, he heard her sigh with relief.

"You've got me pegged," he admitted. "I don't poke my nose in a Bible often. But that doesn't mean I don't believe in God."

"Really?" She slipped her slender arms around her equally slender waist. "Does that mean you're a churchgoing man, Mr. Valance?"

"Gabriel is my name. I'll settle for being called Gabe. As for church attendance, I guess you might say I haven't gone often, but I'll gladly do so if that will make you happy."

"What would make me happy, Mr. Valance, is if you'd disappear from my life."

Chapter Seven

After Laney had gone to bed, casting a significant look over her shoulder as she departed, Nan informed Gabe that it was her habit to work late into the evening, either on special orders or on her own designs, which she displayed for sale downstairs. The glimpses he'd been given of her life bore out her statement, and because theirs was no ordinary wedding night, he saw no reason to upset her usual routine. He wasn't entirely certain he didn't feel slightly relieved.

"Okay," he said agreeably. "Anything I can help with?"

She flung a startled look at him and firmed her lips, giving him a tantalizing peek at a dimple in her right cheek. He wondered how it would look if she smiled. "You, help with tedious work? Not with those gigantic hands. I swear, they're the size of dessert plates."

Gabe flashed her a grin. "You're addressing a man so fast with a gun that some folks swear they can't see me draw. I'm pretty nimble-fingered, and I'll be happy to lend you some assistance."

"I appreciate the offer, but I shan't be taking you up on it."

As she made her way along the hall to her small workroom, Gabe strode directly behind her, noting as he did that shortening his steps was totally unnecessary, because she was in such a hurry to get away from him. When he followed her through the doorway, she swung around, effectively bringing him to a halt, and planted her hands on her hips. Whatever idiot had said that gray eyes were seas of tranquillity had never seen the sparks of lightning shooting from Nan's. Now he understood where Laney got her spunk. Nan hid it well, but beneath that facade of rigid control, she had a temper. You had only to get her riled in order to glimpse it. And he was more than glimpsing it.

"I said I don't *want* your help," she bit out.

Gabe glanced at the small table behind her. "I see two chairs. Laney must help sometimes."

"Laney doesn't have paws instead of hands."

Gabe took a half step forward. Given the choice of having him collide with her or retreating, Nan took a step backward. He circled her and sat down gingerly on a chair that looked designed for a medium-size lady, not a six-foot man. He'd chosen the less cluttered side of the table, and he smiled at her with a nonchalance that he was far from feeling. "Give me something simple to do, then."

She huffed in exasperation. "You'll interfere with my concentration. This is my *livelihood*, sir. Without my income, Laney and I will be in the streets."

"No, you won't. You've got a husband to support you now."

Her expression said that her faith in that statement was about as strong as her faith in Santa Claus, and a good deal less benign. "So far as I can tell, Mr. Valance, you are not gainfully employed."

Gabe arched a brow at her. He was on firmer ground now. "I told you that my father was wealthy and that he finally recognized me as his son when he died. I don't need to be gainfully employed to support you. I'll just walk over to the bank, the clerk will wire Kansas

City, and as soon as my account balances are verified, I'll have an advance on the soon-to-be transferred funds in my pocket."

"So you don't bother with toil?" Her voice rang with censure.

Gabe allowed himself a smile. "Make up your mind, lady. First I'm in trouble because I'm not 'gainfully employed,' as you put it. Then you get upset when you find out that I have enough money to support you. As for toil, I bother with it when I'm of a mind, which happens often enough to keep my back strong. It's not in my nature to sit around twiddling my thumbs. So put me to work. Before you know it, you'll forget I'm even here."

Her eyes narrowed. She sat down across from him, but there was about as much repose in her posture as if she'd sat down on a giant pinecone. Gabe suspected he was about to be assigned the most boring task imaginable. He didn't care. He could entertain himself with the view. With a woman as lovely as Nan, no single man this side of the grave would ever get tired of looking. A lot of married ones wouldn't, either.

"If you insist on being here, then you may as well be useful." She pushed a wooden box toward him. "Sort beads."

Gabe peered over the side of the large, rectangular container. It was filled with a loose assortment of tiny rainbow-colored beads, among which were nestled rows of small, sturdy glass cups without handles that already held beads sorted by size and shape. Hmm. He knew Nan expected him to fumble the job. What she didn't know was that he relished doing intricate work with his fingers to keep his knuckles well oiled. He removed the cups from the box and lined them up like soldiers at muster. Then, after grabbing a handful of beads, he started dropping them, one by one, into containers holding matching pieces. Some were barely bigger than the tip of a pencil's lead, others were large, and there were varying sizes in between.

"There aren't enough cups," he observed as he returned a partial handful of driblets to the box.

"I have only so many sorting cups. Just search for beads to match what's already in the ones there."

Now Gabe saw her aim: to make him go blind from eyestrain. He went to work, knowing she believed that he'd find it difficult, if not impossible, to grasp some of the more minute spheres. That wasn't going to happen.

They worked in frigid silence for several minutes. Occasionally Gabe paused to watch her fuss over a hat she was decorating. Her frown told him that she found something not quite right about the arrangement of flowers on one side of the crown, which she'd temporarily attached to the felt with straight pins.

"What's the problem?" he asked when she sighed and jerked the arrangement off a third time.

"It's missing something, and with you in here, I'm so distracted I can't figure out what."

"You could always plop a poor, dead bird in the middle of it."

She glanced up, visibly struggling not to smile. "Isn't that hat the most *awful* mess you've ever seen?"

"Everything on it is pretty," he observed. "It's only that there's so much pretty that it's . . . well, gaudy, I guess is the word."

"Or tasteless," she said. "Geneva is one of those people who fails to understand that sometimes less is more."

"Do you hate working under her direction?"

"I hate working under anyone's direction." She glanced up from a rose she was pinning back on the hat, her expression conveying that she'd spoken before she thought. "What I mean is—"

"You don't have to explain. You're an artist, and when you work, you're trying to create a vision in your mind. It must be frustrating when you have to follow someone else's dictates and design something that you think looks terrible."

"An artist?" She didn't roll those gray eyes toward the ceiling, but he had a strong hunch she wanted to. "Hardly that. I make hats, pretty little hats, yes, but they aren't works of art."

Gabe dropped a fake seed pearl into a cup. "Spoken like a true artist, ever humble. I looked at your stuff today—not only the hats, which are great, but at some of the dresses, too. You're very talented. That deep brown hat, the one with the brownish white blossoms on it?"

"Silk dogwood blossoms."

"Ah, I thought they looked familiar. I've come across a lot of dogwood in bloom along the trail over the years. Anyway, your choice of colors and eye for contrast—well, that is one nice hat. Some lady is drooling over it, and when she's saved enough money, she'll be in to buy it, unless someone else beats her to it. You can bet your bloomers on it."

Color surged to her cheeks. Gabe wasn't sure if she was blushing with pleasure at the compliment or embarrassment at his tactless language.

"That was *polite* for me," he hurriedly explained. "My *gentlemanly* way of saying you can bet your ass on it." As soon as the words were out, he realized he'd just made things worse. "I mean—uh, sorry, ma'am. Nan."

A shimmery look entered her eyes, making them sparkle like morning sunlight on fresh-fallen snow. He saw a cheek muscle twitch. Was she appalled beyond measure or trying not to laugh? "You, Mr. Valance, have an earthy way with words."

"Gabe," he corrected. "And you've got a grand way

with hats." He went back to sorting. "As for my words, I'm trying to watch what I say. It's just . . . well, this isn't the world I'm used to. Being with a lady like you . . . it's new to me. I may slip sometimes and say things that shock you."

She shifted the rose, angling it one way, then another. "Just don't say shocking things around Laney, please. I've tried very hard to give her a proper upbringing, and I will not be pleased if you fill her head with language a young lady shouldn't hear, let alone say."

"I'll try my best." He glanced up. "The thing is, I may say some things that I think are fine, and you'll disapprove. Maybe you can keep track of my slips and tell me later."

Her fingers stilled on the flower, and her gaze sought his. "Are you asking me to critique your speech?"

"Critique? Now, there's a word."

"It means—"

"I know what it means. I'm just not used to hearing it spoken. And, yes, that's what I'm asking, I reckon."

She still studied him. "You won't grow angry if I correct you?"

It was Gabe's turn to pause in his work. The sudden cessation of beads plopping into containers created a taut silence between them as she waited for his reply. He sensed that there was a heap of anxiety behind her question. "Not if you're halfway nice about it. Why do you ask?"

"Because most men don't like it when a woman finds fault with—"

"I'm not most men. I'm Gabriel Valance." He winked at her. "We men aren't like your beads, Nan. Don't try to sort us into cups by size and color. All of us have imperfections, but no two of us are the same."

He noticed she took time to glance pointedly at the

cup of matched beads he was holding before she answered. *Point taken, lady. You don't believe me.* "Yes, well, not growing perturbed if I criticize you may be easier said than done. My father grew furious if my mother or I even hinted that—"

Irritation stabbed Gabe low in his middle. "I'm *nothing* like your father, and I'd venture a bet that ninety percent of the men in Random aren't, either."

"You know nothing about my father!" she cried.

"I know that he was at home and allowed your fiancé to assault you in your own sitting room."

The bright flags of color on her cheeks turned ashen, and Gabe realized, a second too late, that there was no way in hell he could have come by that information— unless he'd been talking to angels.

"How did—" The words snagged in her throat. She swallowed and tried again. "How can you possibly know if my father was home when it happened?"

Thinking fast, he said, "Because in the highfalutin society you come from, no proper young lady would entertain a gentleman if she were at home without a chaperone. Talk about a scandal. If word got out of such goings-on, a girl's reputation would be destroyed."

The crease between her brows deepened. "How do you know my chaperone wasn't an older female relative?"

"An older female relative would have been stuck to your side like a tick to a hound's back, and *she* would have skewered that bastard Barclay with the knitting needle." Recalling the attack he'd witnessed through the parted clouds, Gabe felt anger roiling in the pit of his stomach. And then, before he could stifle himself, words he knew he shouldn't say began shooting from his mouth. "Nope, your father was in the house. He deliberately left you alone with Barclay, knowing full well what would occur in his absence." Gabe leaned forward, his gaze locked with hers. "He heard your cries for help. But he didn't intervene, did he?"

At that, all the color, even the hints of gray, drained from Nan's face. She shook her head. "Only a horrible excuse for a father would do something so reprehensible."

"You said it. You had a horrible excuse for a father." Gabe dropped a blue bead into a cup. As glass struck glass, the resultant report seemed as loud as a rifle shot. "Don't pretend with me, Nan. You were aware then, just as you are now, that your father knew what Barclay was going to do, and he was okay with it. Otherwise, Barclay wouldn't have *dared*. Men have died for doing far less. *That's* why you hate men, why you distrust all of us and never wanted to be married—because the one male in this world who should have loved and protected you was a sorry, good-for-nothing, rotten son of a bitch."

Nan released an anguished cry and, without pushing back her chair, lunged to her feet, catching the table's edge with her hip. The bead box tipped and slid toward Gabe, along with all the sorting cups, and fast though he was with his hands, he could stop only the large container from falling, not the cups or the hundreds of beads that cascaded over the box edge to bounce and roll to all corners of the room. One got him straight in the eye. Right then, the stinging sensation was the least of his worries.

Nan whirled to leave the room. Her high-heeled boots found a carpet of tiny orbs, and her feet started shooting out from under her. For an instant she fought for balance, wheeling her arms like someone who'd stepped onto wet ice. Then down she went.

When Gabe leaped up to make sure she hadn't hurt herself, his own boots found no purchase. His right leg shot sideways, his left skidded forward, and the next thing he knew, he fell on top of her, barely managing to catch the brunt of his weight with his hands to avoid squashing her. He ended up sprawled across her legs with his head nearly level with hers.

"You okay?" he demanded. She'd gone down hard, and she was made so delicately that he feared the impact might have broken one of her bones. His hands smarted like hell from catching himself with his palms and connecting with beads instead of planks. Needle-like pain shot to his shoulders. "Nan? Are you hurt? Talk to me."

Her eyes met his, but he had the feeling she wasn't seeing him at all. She looked right through him and then cupped her hands over her face. A dry, shrill cry tore up her throat, a prelude to body-wrenching sobs. Against her palms, she keened, "Oh, God, oh, God, oh, *God*. He kn-*knew*! How c-could he d-do that to m-me? To his own d-*daughter*!"

Gabe realized that she was in pain, all right, but it wasn't merely physical. He levered himself off her and sat beside her, one bent leg pressed from hip to knee against her side. *Damn.* He wished now that he'd left it alone. But, oh, no. Instead of keeping his mouth shut, he'd gotten his back up over the "most men" comment, and defended himself and his gender without thinking. One thing had led to another, and . . . *Well, shit.* Now she was crying, curling up into a tight ball, and judging by how hard the sobs seemed to come, he had a bad feeling she didn't often weep.

No surprise. In that way, he suspected he and Nan were cut from the same cloth. It was okay to reveal anger, but never any untidy emotions, no feelings that ran deep. Now he'd stripped her feelings bare, taking her back in time to an incident that had destroyed her life and haunted her to this day. Her loss of control was his fault, and he couldn't blame her a bit for crying. But if he didn't get the volume toned down, and soon, they'd have Laney in here to investigate, and things might go from bad to horrible.

"I'm sorry," he rasped. "I had no right to say those things. No business even bringing it up. I'm so sorry." He put a tentative hand on her slender shoulder.

"You never mind about being sorry!" she practically screamed at him. "It's *true!*" As he shot an alarmed glance at the hall, Nan jerked her hands from her face and white-knuckled them over the bodice of her dress. Tears poured down her cheeks, and distended veins pulsed at her temples. The tremors that ran through her slender body vibrated into his thigh and seemed to radiate up from there, sending shudders along his spine. She choked back another sob and burst out, "My father w-went to his upstairs s-study and left me there, *knowing* wh-what Barclay meant to d-do. He *w-wanted* it to h-happen so I'd feel trapped and st-stop objecting to th-the marriage!" Her voice went squeaky. She squeezed her eyes closed, tears cascading toward each of her ears. Somewhere in the middle of all this he heard a door bang open down the hall, but he had more immediate concerns. The sobs that Nan tried to stifle tore from her chest with such force he worried that she might injure her insides. "My *f-father*, my own *father*."

"What happened?" Laney cried from the doorway. "Did she fall? Is she hurt?"

Given the fact that Gabe was sitting beside the girl's prostrate sister, he was amazed she didn't fly at him with her claws bared, no questions asked. He knew this looked bad.

"No, she isn't hurt," he said, his voice grating in his ears like a rock on sandpaper. "The beads spilled, and her feet went out from under her, but she's okay."

Upon hearing Laney's voice, Nan had gone abruptly

quiet, and Gabe had a nasty suspicion she was holding her breath to accomplish the feat.

"Why's she crying then?" Laney's tone was laced with suspicion, and her expression made it clear that she wanted the truth, not a wagonload of bullshit.

Gabe looked up, and after holding the girl's gaze for a second, he said, "Something I said reminded her of something her father did. She's upset, is all. I'll handle it. Trust me and just go back to bed."

Instead of rushing to her sister's side, as Gabe half expected, Laney remained in the doorway. She searched Gabe's eyes for an interminably long moment, and then said softly, "Listen to your heart." With a last worried look at Nan, she wheeled away down the hall.

This was no time to let his throat close up at Laney's expression of faith in him. He felt like an idiot for losing control of his tongue and mucking everything up this way. Now that Nan felt sure her sister had left, she was sobbing again, and Gabe suspected that it would be a while before she stopped. He felt like an organ monkey that had just pulled the cork from a shaken-up bottle of root beer.

One thing was for sure: He couldn't leave Nan lying there on all those beads. They jabbed into the flesh like pebbles. With a sweep of his arm, he cleared a section of flooring, rose on one knee, and gathered her against his chest to stand. She didn't resist. Instead, she hugged his neck and buried her face against his shoulder. He knew better than to take it as a personal compliment. She was barely aware of him at the moment.

Gabe carried his wife to her bedchamber. He'd never dealt with a sobbing woman, but he guessed some things just came naturally. He kicked the door closed, sat on the front edge of the mattress, and cradled her on his lap.

"It's over," he whispered. "I never should have

brought it up. It happened a long time ago, honey. Eight years. It's over."

Only, Gabe knew it wasn't over for Nan. It was a horrible event in her past that she'd never been able to forget or forgive, a terrible truth that she'd probably kept buried deep, never taking it out in the light to face it. He understood how that went. He had some dark truths of his own that he tried not to think about. He mostly pretended they never happened, unless the memory sneaked in to haunt him in a dream.

The angels had told him that Nan dreaded sleep and worked long into the night to avoid it, but they hadn't told him why. Now he wondered if she worked to the point of exhaustion because sleeping left her vulnerable to nightmares. Maybe, like Laney, the horrible memories she kept buried resurfaced when she tried to rest and brought her awake with a scream on her lips. The thought made Gabe's heart hurt. Though a woman grown, in many ways Nan had never moved beyond her terrible childhood. Again, he could understand; he had awakened countless times from bad dreams with his body drenched in cold sweat.

Her sobs finally turned soft and irregular, and then she quieted. Gabe knew the instant she came back to *him* instead of lingering in the past, because she stiffened in his embrace. She didn't seem sure what to do with her hands. Touching him again clearly wasn't appealing.

"Oh, my." When she pushed against his chest with a pointy elbow, he relaxed his hold and allowed her to put some distance between their bodies. She wiped her cheeks, sniffed, and sprang from his lap. "I do a-apologize, Mr. Valance. I don't know wh-what came over me."

The lantern in the room hadn't yet been lit, but moonlight poured through the parted window curtains to illuminate her face and figure. Her eyes glimmered like drenched quicksilver, huge in her small face and filled with shifting shadows.

"Don't apologize," he told her, his voice still gravelly. He wished . . . Hell, he didn't know what he wished. He only knew that upsetting her this way had been unforgivable, even worse than putting a bullet in a man's chest. At least they'd asked for it. Nan had been an innocent victim. "I've got this feeling," he said softly, "that it was high time for you to let some of that out."

As if her legs were about to buckle, she sank down beside him, shook her head, and straightened her shoulders. There was something unbearably touching to him about the way she held herself, as if she were ready to defy the whole world, alone.

"It isn't like me—to c-cry, I mean. I never, *ever* cry."

Gabe decided he must be unconsciously doing what Laney and the angels had recommended, because his heart was sure hearing that sentence. *I never, ever cry*, she'd said. The last two words should have been, "In public." He believed Nan never allowed herself to weep in front of anyone, even Laney, but he didn't buy that she was a total stranger to tears. The pain in her voice, the agony conveyed by her sobs—that kind of hurting ran clear to the bone. He suspected that she'd soaked her pillow with silent tears on many a lonely night.

"All of us need a good cry at some point." It was all he could think to say, but at least it was neutral. He'd stuck his foot in his mouth enough for one night.

"You don't—" A residual sob zigzagged up her throat and cut her short. She passed a hand over her eyes again, trembling so badly that her skirt hem fluttered. "You don't s-strike me as a man who'd ever cry—over anything."

Gabe searched for words. "Uh, well, not often. But it's happened. And just so you know, sometimes I'm crying on the inside. You know, where no one can see."

She hugged her trim waist and hunched her shoulders. "About what? What do you cry inside about, Gabriel Valance?"

He wasn't sure if she was asking the question because she really cared to hear the answer, or if she was talking to forestall a void of silence. He decided whichever it was, he'd give her a straight answer, no matter how uncomfortable it made him. He owed her that.

"A lot of things. Mistakes I've made. Stuff that happened to me when I was too young and small to defend myself. Sometimes even for the men I've killed, even though it was my only choice if I wanted to stay alive myself."

It felt funny saying that. He'd sure never done it before, but it felt as if a huge weight had rolled off him along with the words. "Is there anybody on this earth who never weeps inside?" he asked.

She stared at him in what seemed like stony silence for several seconds. Her voice quavered as she replied in a thin voice, "My father. I don't think he's ever cried or even felt the urge. He definitely felt no regret when my mother died."

Gabe had observed enough to hate the man. "Some people . . . I don't know—it's like they're born with something missing inside them. I think your father is like that, a man who doesn't have it in him to love anyone but himself."

She unlocked her arms from around her waist just long enough to push a stray lock of golden hair from her eyes. "He definitely never loved my mother, or me—and when Laney was born, he despised her, too, because he'd wanted a son. Even when she was tiny, he'd tell her that she was the worst disappointment of his life. She wasn't old enough to understand his words, but she got the message."

Gabe could see her drooping with exhaustion and decided the rest of this conversation needed to wait for tomorrow. A man couldn't kill every snake in a field with one swing of a hoe. Right now, she needed rest more than any comfort he might give her. After she was tucked in, he'd listen if she still felt inclined to talk. But he doubted that would be the case. Once she regained her composure, he'd probably have to pry the words out of her with an iron lever.

He pushed up from the bed, which made her jerk. "I'm just going to light the lantern, Nan. Then, while you're dressing for bed, I'll see to turning off the others and banking both fires."

"I don't think I can sleep."

Gabe almost offered to stretch out on the sitting room floor with his bedroll. After bringing in the wood earlier, he'd gone up the street to the hotel to collect his personal belongings, which were now stowed in one corner of the room. But before he could form the words, he decided against saying them. How they began this marriage would set the rhythm for the next thirty days, and he would never be able to breach Nan's defenses in so short a time if he allowed her to sleep apart from him.

"You need to try," he said instead. "You look dead on your feet."

By the light of the moon, Gabe turned up the lantern wick, struck a match he found on the bedside table, which was covered with a dainty crocheted runner as creamy white as his wife's skin, and then ignited the thick, kerosene-soaked cotton. A yellow glow burst brightly. With practiced ease, Gabe replaced the globe and turned back the key to adjust the flare.

He could feel the tension radiating from Nan. "I

meant what I said earlier today," he assured her. "I won't be going back on my word. You needn't feel uneasy."

If nothing else, that got her mind off her father. *"Uneasy?* I've never slept in the same room with a man, let alone in the same bed, and you're a stranger."

"I'm sorry if this is unsettling for you." It was all he could give her, and he knew it was precious little. She needed more from him. He searched for something, anything to ease her mind. "I'll bring you one of the kitchen knives, if that'll make you feel better. If I make a wrong move, you can stab me."

She laughed, the sound shaky and laced with bitterness. "As if you couldn't take it away from me in the blink of an eye?"

Gabe couldn't and wouldn't deny the truth of that. She was a woman of diminutive stature, no match for a man—any man. He felt as if he'd been set adrift in a boat without a paddle. He could only hope those two angels knew what they were doing, because Gabe sure as hell didn't. And he'd already made enough mistakes for one day.

He stepped over to the door. Her voice made him pause before turning the knob. "Do you promise to keep your trousers on?"

Gabe was glad he had his back to her, because the question made him smile, although not with mirth. He felt sad for her—sad and a little angry, both at once. She was a sweet, loving person. He'd seen that firsthand during the glimpses he'd gotten of her life. She'd done nothing to deserve all the trials and mistreatment she had endured.

"I swear it."

Nan was shaking so badly that she could barely unfasten her bodice buttons. Once she'd worked her way down to just below her waist, she shrugged off her dress, hung it in the armoire, and then stripped to quickly don her white nightgown. Even though it was heavy cotton, designed for winter nights, she felt naked in it. Gabriel Valance had a way about him that could have made her feel bare even if she were rolled up in a carpet and covered head to toe.

He knew things about her that no normal human being could possibly know. It was eerie, almost as if he'd been around all her life and present to witness the most awful parts of it. Was he a clairvoyant? Nan shook her head and then reached up to pull the pins from her hair. She didn't believe that any human being could see into the past or future. She was simply rattled, still battling tears, and grasping for anything to explain how the man knew so much about her.

His voice rang in her mind. *I know that he was at home and allowed your fiancé to assault you in your own sitting room.* He'd said it with such conviction, not as a stranger fishing for information might have, but like a man certain of his facts. Only three adults had been at the Sullivan residence that night: her father, Horace Barclay, and Nan herself. All the servants had been given an unexpected night off, an unprecedented gesture everyone had misinterpreted as the generosity of Martin Sullivan. Normally, he'd treated the help with even less kindness than he did his daughters, complaining if employees asked for a brief leave of absence and docking their pay for any hours missed. Not that night, though. Nan could still remember the chill that had run down her spine when her father had told all the household staff that they weren't needed for the rest of the evening and assured them that they'd be paid for the unexpected time off.

Nan had suspected what was coming then—if only briefly. She had assured herself that not even her father

would do something so vile. Though she'd been protesting the marriage, she hadn't yet been openly defiant.
She'd given her father no reason to sic Barclay on her.

Remembering the particulars of that evening once
again brought tears to Nan's eyes and a quiver to her
knees. She went to sit on the edge of her bed, trying
frantically to drive the images from her mind. But it
was no use. Gabriel Valance had opened the thick black
curtain in her mind, allowing the memories to escape.
It was as if she were trapped in one of her nightmares,
only she was wide-awake.

Her father had poured Barclay a snifter of brandy.
Then, rubbing his hands together, Martin Sullivan had
said, "I think I'll retire to my study for a bit and give
you two a chance to grow better acquainted."

"But, Papa!" Nan had protested. "That isn't proper.
Until the marriage, I should be chaperoned at all times
when I'm in Mr. Barclay's company."

"Oh, poppycock," Martin had said with a smile—
the cold, well-practiced, calculating smile that always
put her on guard. "No one is in the house to carry tales,
and the fact that you still refuse to address your fiancé
by his given name proves my point: that the two of you
need to become better acquainted."

Nan quickly learned what *better acquainted* meant in
the language of men. Barclay had wasted no time on
pleasantries before pouncing. When Nan realized his
intent, she'd screamed for her father's help, but of
course Martin hadn't come, even though Nan knew he
had heard her cries.

How could Gabriel Valance possibly know about
that? It was, for Nan, such a dark, terrible truth that
during her waking hours she refused to let herself
think about it, let alone speak of it to anyone, not even
Laney. And of the other two people in the house that
night, one was dead, leaving only Martin Sullivan to

have blabbed the story, and he was far too protective of his sterling reputation ever to admit that he'd committed a deed so foul.

Nan tossed her hairpins onto the table and thoughtfully ran her fingers through her loosened tresses. No matter how she circled it, she could think of no way Gabriel could have ascertained that particular bit of information about her past, so she was left with only two probable explanations: that he was either clairvoyant or a very good guesser. Either way, he'd destroyed her composure by throwing the truth in her face. She'd been caught completely off guard. It shamed her to recall weeping in front of him. Even more humiliating, she had allowed him to hold her on his lap, rocking slightly as if to comfort a child. It made her feel like a fool—and she greatly feared that Valance might now have the impression that she was weak.

The weak became victims. If an animal rolled onto its back during a fight, its opponent ripped open its belly. It was no different with human beings. The strong ruled the world, and the namby-pambies got kicked in the teeth.

Nan thought she heard a hall floorboard squeak. Fearful that her unwanted bedmate would return at any moment, she hurriedly threw back the covers, slipped between the sheets, and then huddled as close to the edge of the bed as possible, blankets and spread clutched under her chin. Was Valance a man of his word? Did he truly have no intention of touching her? His voice rang in her mind. *I swear*. He'd sounded sincere, but Nan had learned long ago that promises uttered by men meant nothing.

When he tapped on the door to enter, she could barely manage to say, "Come in."

As he stepped into the room, the lantern light threw his shadow across the wall behind him, making him seem even larger than he actually was. She wanted to squeeze her eyes closed and not look at him, but her lids seemed to be frozen open. He strode over to turn off the lamp. The device hissed and sputtered, still giving off an amber radiance for several seconds before the wick finally went out. She could see nothing until her eyes adjusted, and even then, all she could make out was his silhouette as he circled the foot of the bed. Lying there with her back to him, she tried to guess where he was in the room and what he was up to. Being unable to watch him made her skin crawl, but if she turned over, she might catch him undressing.

His boots made soft thumps as he toed them off. Then she heard cloth rustle. She imagined him doffing his shirt. A floorboard creaked once more under his weight. She sensed rather than heard him approach at the opposite side of the bed.

"If it's all right with you, I'll hang my gun belt over the headboard on my side. I—um—can't sleep without my Colts near at hand."

Nan understood that in a way she never before could have. Right then, though she'd never owned or even touched a firearm, she wished she had a gun in the drawer of her bedside table. If so, she'd grab it and hide it under her pillow for protection. His professed intentions were merely words, as insubstantial as dandelion fluff. The only thing a smart woman counted on from a man was that he'd take advantage of her every chance he got.

Oh, God. She remembered the brutal dig of Barclay's fingers into her flesh, how he'd panted and torn at her bodice, trying to bare her breasts. And he'd succeeded. To this day, recalling the touch of his pudgy, moist hand on her skin made bile surge up the back of her throat. She couldn't bear to endure that again. Everything within her recoiled at the thought.

The blankets shifted, letting in a draft of cool air to lick at her back. Then the mattress sank under him, and she felt the warmth of his body radiating under the canopied sheet to curl around her. Judging by the sounds he made and all the jiggling, he was settling onto his back. Frightened, she rolled over to face him, taking care not to close any of the scant distance between them. Faint moonlight bathed his face and glistened on his hair, making the strands that fell loosely over his high forehead look bluish black. He'd folded his arms beneath his head, and to her dismay, his upper body wasn't covered. Most men wore one-piece knitted underwear that covered them from throat to ankle. At least, she'd always surmised that they did.

Until now, Nan had only been able to imagine the bulging muscles in Gabriel's shoulders, chest, and arms. Without the black shirt to cover him, she realized that her imagination had done him a grave injustice. His was a body that had been tempered by hard work to a steely strength. That frightened and fascinated her, both at once.

"You okay?" he whispered.

Nan wasn't sure if she'd ever be really okay again. In a voice that rang flat even to her, she replied, "I'm fine."

He stifled a yawn. "Been a long day, and tomorrow's Thanksgiving. Do you and Laney have any special plans?"

The question had Nan's thoughts circling. *Thanksgiving.* How was she supposed to focus on the holiday at a moment like this? She'd forgotten all about it. Finally, she collected her composure enough to say, "Just a quiet meal here."

"No invites to join other families in their homes for dinner?"

"I don't often go calling."

"Why is that?" he asked.

Nan considered for a long moment before answering. "Given my past, which must remain a secret, I've avoided forming friendships. If I get too relaxed around anyone, I may slip up and say something I shouldn't."

He sighed, sounding weary beyond measure. "And Laney? What keeps her from slipping up?"

Relaxing slightly because he'd thus far made no move to grab her, Nan considered the question. "For Laney, it's different. She remembers nothing from before. In her mind, life began here in Random. The shop and our living quarters are her world. From the very first, I taught her to call me Mama, even when we were alone. This is her only reality."

"But it isn't your only reality."

"You know very well that it isn't. Until Laney's tenth birthday, nearly a full six years after we came here, I lived in fear that someone might learn of my whereabouts. Some days while working in the shop, I jumped at my own shadow. When the doorbell jangled, my heart would leap into my throat. I constantly felt as if I were treading on thin ice, waiting for it to crack and swallow me whole."

He sighed again. "That's no way to live."

"I had no choice, and then today, after two years of feeling confident I'd never be found, you walked into my shop."

"I'll never go back on my word and turn you in," he said, his voice going coarse again.

"If you grow bored with this situation—"

"Then I'll scat. I mean you no harm, Nan. Try to believe that."

Nan thought to herself that the word *harm* had many definitions. Even if Gabriel Valance never revealed her true identity to the marshal, he'd single-handedly managed to turn her whole life topsy-turvy.

He shifted to get more comfortable, and her heart jerked. He must have felt her stiffen, for he said, "I'm not going to force myself on you, honey. You can take that promise to the bank."

With that, he let his eyes fall closed. A moment later he emitted a soft rumble, and she realized he'd fallen asleep. She felt a crazy indignation, which baffled her no end. She should be glad he'd drifted off. What was wrong with her? She stared at his sharply chiseled profile until her eyes burned with exhaustion, and still she couldn't lower her lashes. A miserable night awaited her. She felt certain, absolutely certain, that she'd still be wide-awake when dawn broke and sunlight first bathed the window.

Chapter Eight

Something coarse and fluttery tickled Nan's nose, and a lovely blend of scents—a faint muskiness, a hint of cologne, and traces of piney bath soap—teased her sleep-numbed senses and beckoned her from the dark dregs of dreamless oblivion. *How odd*, she thought drowsily. The layered blankets on her bed kept her cozy even on the coldest of winter nights, but as she drifted slowly toward wakefulness, she became aware of radiant heat enveloping her, almost as if she'd curled up against an oversize bed warmer. She struggled to open her eyes, squinted a moment until her pupils adjusted to the morning light, and then stared in bewilderment at a bare male chest only inches from her face. It was sparsely furred with black hair and was the delightful color of café au lait, her favorite kind of coffee.

Nan blinked. Memories came storming back, most of them alarming and the rest unacceptable. This man was her *husband*. As if dashed in the face with cold water, she came instantly alert and smothered a moan of abject dismay. Her nose was buried in Gabriel Valance's armpit. It was his hair tickling her nostrils.

Nan stopped breathing, acutely conscious that Gabriel still lay on his back with his folded arms pillowing his head. It was not *he* who had moved toward *her*. She had closed the distance between their bodies in her sleep. And, oh, sweet *Lord*, she'd curled her left arm over his bare waist. Even worse, she'd propped a bent knee on his denim-sheathed thigh. She was snuggled full-length against him with certain very *private* parts of her body in unnervingly close contact with his.

Fully awake now, Nan tried to think what to do. If she moved quickly away, she'd startle him from slumber, and she absolutely did not want that. He'd kept his promise and not touched her. He would undoubtedly find it highly humorous if he opened his eyes to find her lying nearly on top of him.

Very carefully Nan drew her arm back, then focused intently on ever so slowly moving her knee off his leg. She nearly parted company with the mattress when his voice rumbled near her ear.

"I'm already awake. I was afraid to move for fear of startling you."

"Consternation!" Nan rolled quickly away from him. "I'm sorry. I don't know how that happened."

"You were asleep. I reckon you got a little cold and just moved close to get warm."

Close didn't say it by half. Now Nan understood why some people claimed they'd nearly died of embarrassment at certain moments of their lives. She wanted to cover her head with her pillow and never have to look him in the eye again. Instead, she swung her legs over the edge of the bed. When the bare pads of her feet touched the floor, she felt no chill, but shivered as if she did.

"I didn't mean to—um—crowd you," she managed to say. *What must he think?* Undoubtedly that she was a wanton hiding behind a facade of propriety. "The last I remember, I was on my own side of the bed."

"You weren't crowding me. It was nice, actually. You have a very cute little snore." The smile she heard in his voice made her wince.

"Snore?" Nan cast him an incredulous glance over her shoulder. "Ladies do not snore."

He chuckled and sat up to rake his fingers through his hair. "It's a very *ladylike* snore." His dark eyes, twinkling with laugher, met hers. "Soft, sort of whispery." After studying her for a moment, he seemed to sense her dismay. With a shrug, he added, "Maybe you're right, and I really shouldn't call it a snore. The sound is definitely nothing like what some men make when they sleep. Over the years, I've heard some real wall shakers."

Nan had moved past the snoring issue to a new concern: How could she get up and move about in front of him without being decently clad? She cast a glance at the armoire, where her wrapper hung inside on a door hook, and wished she'd had the forethought last night to drape it across the foot of the bed. Even though her gown was made of heavy cotton, it would provide her with precious little cover if she got between him and the sunlight that slanted over the half curtains at the window. She couldn't bear the thought of him seeing her naked, even if only in silhouette.

"Is something wrong?" Gabriel asked. She felt the mattress jiggle as he swung off the bed. "You're staring at the armoire as if it holds a bucket of gold nuggets."

Nan turned slightly to look at him. "My wrapper's in there. I forgot to get it last night."

"Wrapper?" he echoed, his tone implying bewilderment. He rubbed one well-muscled shoulder as if to get the cricks out and stifled a yawn. Nan noted how the furring of hair across his chest narrowed into a diminishing dark line that descended to the waistband of his black jeans and then disappeared. A blush seared her cheeks when he caught her looking. He studied her, his brow pleating in a thoughtful scowl. Then, startling her, he snapped his fingers. "Ah, yes, your *wrapper*. Of course! Every proper lady wears a wrapper." He drew open the armoire doors and fisted his hand over the deep pink robe. "This it?"

"Yes." The garment looked effete in his big hand. When he stepped toward her, proffering it, Nan took it and said, "Thank you. It's—um . . . The air has quite a nip in it this morning." Curling the fingers of one hand over the cuff of her sleeve to anchor it at her wrist, she thrust her arm into the wrapper. "I'll be warmer now."

His firm mouth quirked at one corner. She half expected him to call her on the lie. She wasn't really cold, after all. Instead, he went to collect his shirt, which he'd tossed over the back of a chair. As he shoved his arms through the sleeves and began fastening the buttons, he said, "I'll go add wood to the fires. I don't want you or Laney taking a chill."

He sat behind her at the opposite side of the bed to pull on his boots. Then, circling around to face her, he tucked in his shirttails, apparently oblivious to the fact that a gentleman would never do such a thing. Nan sighed inwardly. She'd been so focused on all the physical aspects of this union that she hadn't stopped to think how difficult it might be to teach this man some proper manners.

He started for the door, then stopped dead. "My guns. I can't believe I almost forgot them."

He retraced his steps to collect his weapons. Why he felt he needed to wear them this morning, she didn't know. But she refrained from asking, mostly because she wasn't sure she wanted to hear his answer.

Once armed, with the plain leather holsters anchored snugly to his muscular thighs, he left the room, softly closing the door behind him. The starch drained from Nan's spine, and her shoulders slumped. Though she knew she'd slept deeply, she didn't feel rested and dreaded the day ahead.

The door popped back open and Gabriel poked his

raven head in through the crack. "Happy Thanksgiving," he said with a grin that flashed strong, even white teeth.

It was a charming smile, Nan thought. A little *too* charming for her taste. It hinted of long practice. And she wasn't about to be fooled by it. "Happy Thanksgiving," she replied stiffly.

"I'm excited about it," he told her. "It'll be my first."

She didn't understand. "Your first . . . ? Your first what?"

"My first real Thanksgiving."

Long after the door closed again, Nan sat on the bed, staring blankly at nothing. *My first real Thanksgiving.* Surely he'd been joking.

But something told her he hadn't been.

After performing her morning ablutions behind a locked door in the water closet, Nan emerged into the hallway properly attired for the day. She'd chosen a rust-colored gown trimmed with brown—autumn colors appropriate for the holiday. After checking on Laney, who was still fast asleep, Nan crossed the sitting room and entered the kitchen, expecting to find Gabriel sitting at the table, waiting for her to make coffee and breakfast, expecting, as most men did, to be waited on as if he were a king. Instead the coffeepot was already set to boil atop the woodstove and her new husband was nowhere to be seen. She'd put away her nightclothes, so she knew he wasn't in the bedroom.

"Mr. Valance?" she called. "Gabriel?"

"Back here!"

Nan followed the deep ring of his voice down the short hallway and stopped in the open doorway of her workroom. On his knees, her husband was scooping up handfuls of beads and returning them to the wooden box on the floor beside him. The sight was so astonishing that for a moment she was speechless.

"That's my mess to clean up," she told him when she found her voice. "There's no need for you to do it. I'll make fast work of it after breakfast with my broom and dustpan."

He shook his head. "If you sweep them up, dirt from the floor will get in the box and all over the other beads."

Nan couldn't argue the point. She tried to keep a tidy home, but it was impossible to sweep even well-waxed floorboards perfectly clean. She wanted to thank him for being so thoughtful and willing to help, but a lifetime of bitterness toward men held her tongue. She would not be taken in by his pleasant demeanor. Nor would she lower her guard. Sooner or later, he would show his true colors. All of them eventually did.

Nan would be ready when that happened. Colorado had been a state now for more than four years, but women still weren't allowed the right to vote, and Nan had little faith that the male populace was in any hurry to rectify that. Until women here were granted suffrage, they would remain lesser citizens without a voice, and in the interim, the men controlled everything. Nan had seen few overt demonstrations of dominance in Random, but the public demeanor of men in no way reflected what actually occurred in their homes behind closed doors.

She wasn't sure what Colorado's laws were in regards to a woman's financial wealth after she married. In some states, the new husband automatically took possession of all his bride's assets. In others, a wife could retain possession and control. Nan only knew that she wasn't going to take any chances. She'd worked too hard and scrimped too long to save what little she had, and there was no way she would allow Gabriel Valance to take a single dime of it.

On Monday morning right after the bank opened, she'd slip across the street and empty her savings account before Gabriel thought to visit the bank himself.

A floor plank in her downstairs workroom had started to work loose. With the claws of a hammer, she could easily pry it up, slip her money into the crawl space, and then nail the board back into place. It would be a perfect hiding spot. When Gabriel Valance grew weary of acting nice and started trying to rule her every word and action, she would be ready to act. She was certainly no stranger to packing everything she could carry in pillowcases and vanishing.

At her silence, Gabriel glanced up. "If my doing this upsets you, Nan, I can stop. I only wanted to get it cleaned up before someone else took a tumble."

"No, no." Nan forced a smile that stretched her stiff cheek muscles. It wasn't only men who could hide behind a charming facade. She would pretend to accept this marriage. For the duration of the holiday weekend, she would be sweetness itself. After Monday came and went, and she had her money safely tucked away, she'd figure out an escape plan that she could execute in short order. Then she'd simply bide her time. If all went well, she'd be pleasantly surprised and more than willing to admit, if only to herself, that she'd misjudged this man. If all didn't go well, she would spirit Laney away from this town and never look back. It would be difficult, and both she and Laney would feel sad, but in the end they would both be better off without a man ruling their lives. "I appreciate the help, actually," she continued. "After throwing together a quick breakfast, I have to make bread and put it aside to rise while I make pies. It'll be a very busy morning and early afternoon for me."

"Pies?" He sat back on a boot heel and grinned from ear to ear. "You're a pie maker?"

Weren't all women? He made it sound as if making pies were the equivalent of roping the moon or plucking stars from the sky. Nan could almost see him salivating, and this time her smile wasn't forced. "Ah, so you like pies, do you?"

"Like 'em? I *love* 'em. Even the bad ones at restaurants taste good to me."

Nan folded her arms. "What's your favorite?"

"No favorite. Apple, peach, rhubarb, any kind of berry."

"How about pumpkin?"

"You've got a pumpkin? Where? I'll gut it if you'll make some pies with it."

Nan grinned. She couldn't help herself. "It's a deal. I bought a pumpkin on Tuesday from Burke Redmond at the general store. It's in the cabinet under the sink. Last Thanksgiving I cut myself trying to stab a knife through a pumpkin shell. I've no wish to repeat the experience."

He tossed some beads into the box. "Not too handy with knives, I take it."

Nan tapped the toe of her boot, a nervous habit she'd never been able to break. "My talent runs more to knitting needles."

"I'll bear that in mind." He chuckled and bent to his task again. "Don't overdo on breakfast. If pies are on the menu, I don't want to waste much room on everyday fare."

"I was thinking of oatmeal porridge and toast. That'll be quick and filling."

"Sounds grand to me."

Twenty minutes later, Nan was about to put breakfast on the table when Laney emerged from her bedroom. Still in her nightgown with her hair loose and astir from her pillow, the girl tottered across the sitting room into the kitchen, stifling a yawn with her hand.

"Good morning, dear heart," Nan said. "I hope you're hungry. Breakfast is almost ready."

Laney rubbed her eyes with both fists. "What are we having?"

Nan glanced at the child's attire. Wearing only a nightgown had been okay before, but now that there was a man in the house, the child needed to change her habits. "Oatmeal porridge and cinnamon toast. While I'm setting the table, run get your wrapper on, sweetie. Now that we have a gentleman in the house, it's important that we not parade around half-dressed."

Gabriel appeared behind Laney in the sitting room archway. He'd apparently overheard Nan's edict, for he swept a measuring look over the girl's gown, arched a winged brow, and then met Nan's gaze with a question in his own. Nan knew precisely what he was thinking: namely that the child was already decently covered. To Nan, that was beside the point. It was her job to teach Laney how to comport herself as a lady, and ladies did *not* keep company with men while en dishabille.

Laney retraced her footsteps to her room to don her robe. Nan set bowls of porridge and plates of toast on the table. Then she went to a drawer for spoons. She deliberately avoided Gabriel's gaze, because it was not her intent to debate with him her parenting decisions. The man had no idea how to raise a girl to become a proper young woman, so his opinions were not only impertinent but also unwelcome.

To his credit, he voiced no objections, and by the time Nan joined him and Laney at the table to break their fast, some of the tension had eased from her spine. Laney tucked into her meal without speaking. She tended to be less talkative upon waking than she normally was. As a result, Nan often leafed through fashion periodicals during the first meal of the day. Studying fashion plates was something she rarely found time to do, so she jumped at any opportunity.

Unfortunately, with Gabriel at the table, she felt obligated to rigidly observe the rules of proper etiquette.

She yearned briefly for one of the fashion issues she kept tucked away in a kitchen cupboard, but Gabriel's low moan of pleasure when he took a bite of cinnamon toast soon distracted her. He actually closed his eyes to savor the taste. Then, lifting his lashes, he grinned at her and said, "This is *delicious*. I've never tasted the like."

Nan noted that he at least swallowed his food before speaking. Otherwise, his manners were deplorable. He had one elbow propped by his bowl. He didn't bother to put down his spoon before taking a sip of coffee, choosing to use both hands, as if dining were a race to the finish line. The linen napkin she'd put at his place remained folded on the tablecloth and, she surmised, would never make it to his lap. She decided to be grateful for small blessings: He had not yet slurped or used his spoon as if it were a shovel, so he wasn't completely beyond salvation.

"You've never had cinnamon toast?"

"No. How the hell do you make it?"

Nan shot him a meaningful look. He appeared to be puzzled for a second, but then he glanced at the quiet Laney and said, "Pardon my language."

Nan bit back a smile, feeling heartened. *Definitely trainable*, she decided, but giving the man even a glimmer of polish would take unflagging determination on her part. "Cinnamon toast is easy to make." She quickly told him how. "It's difficult for me to imagine never having tasted it. It became a favorite breakfast treat for me when I was a small child."

He took another bite, once again humming appreciatively at the taste. "I wonder if they serve this in restaurants. I don't recall ever seeing it on the menu."

As a young woman, Nan had gone with her father to restaurants for supper, but she'd eaten out in the morning only while traveling out west, and then during a brief layover at the Random Hotel while Laney recovered from pneumonia. Though Laney's illness had frightened Nan at the time, she now felt it had been fortuitous because she had discovered the hat shop during their stay. "My experience with breakfast menus is limited, I'm afraid. In the future, perhaps you should suggest to a café or restaurant entrepreneur that cinnamon toast be added to the morning selections."

His ebon brows snapped together. "A restaurant *what*?"

Laney giggled. Battling a smile herself, Nan sent the girl an admonishing glance. "*Entrepreneur* is a word of French origin, meaning business owner or proprietor."

"Ah. Thank God it's French. I've worked hard to build my vocabulary, but I've stuck to only English. For a second there, I thought I'd missed a big word. They're my main focus—learning how to say them, what they mean, and how to use them. The widow Harper stressed to me during the year I stayed with her that being well-spoken is important."

Nan felt it unnecessary to say that *entrepreneur* was commonly used by English-speaking people. Given what little she knew about Gabriel's appalling childhood and lack of formal education, she found it admirable that he'd studied so hard on his own to learn his letters and build his language skills.

"The next time you make this, will you show me how?" he asked.

Nan quite liked cinnamon toast herself and wouldn't mind having it two days in a row. "Tomorrow morning then," she agreed. "It's truly very simple."

"It doesn't taste simple to me," he said, his voice ringing with sincerity.

Nan refused to believe he would remain so easy to please at mealtimes. She'd once seen her father bludgeon her mother in the face with a full platter of hot meat because it had not been prepared to his taste. Though the fault had lain with the kitchen staff, Helena had still taken the brunt of her husband's temper.

Unaccustomed to company in the kitchen, Nan was rattled by Gabriel's intent observation of every move she made as she prepared yeast bread, mixed up a batch of corn bread to go in the stuffing, and then began pie dough. He was full of questions, asking why she did this and why she did that. A careful measurer when she cooked, Nan grew so distracted while adding ingredients to a bowl that she feared she might have put in twice the amount of baking powder.

Hoping for a brief respite, Nan set him to the task of cutting into the pumpkin. Behind her, she heard him ask Laney, "Did you have a jack-o'-lantern for Halloween?"

"We did! Mama helped me carve it. She saves our candle stubs all year long so we can have ours lit in the shop window until right before we go to bed and still have some fat stubs left over for our Christmas tree." Laney was a great fan of holidays. "Ours was the best jack-o'-lantern in all of Random."

"Do you often use candles?" he inquired.

"Fairly often. When we're doing nothing that requires a lot of light, candles are cheaper to burn than kerosene."

"Less expensive," Nan corrected over her shoulder. She could almost see Laney rolling her eyes. "You won't run low on breath using that term, little miss, and it is far more ladylike."

"Burning candles is *less expensive*," Laney complied, her tone implying that the trials she endured under Nan's tutelage were nearly unbearable.

"I figured Nan for being big on decorations during the holidays," Gabriel mused. "The Christmas boughs that framed the shop window were beautiful."

Nan turned to give him a curious study. "When were you here at Christmas?" she asked. "I thought this was your first visit to Random."

Darting worried looks at their pumpkin carver, Laney avoided Nan's gaze, which struck Nan as being rather odd. Gabriel, however, didn't miss a beat. "Yes, I've been here before."

Nan was about to ask when, but he forestalled by saying, "Are we having turkey? I know some folks around here raise domesticated ones. Not that I care. I only ask because you mentioned making stuffing."

Since coming to Random, Nan had served turkey at Thanksgiving only once. Though it had been a small bird, she and Laney had been unable to consume but a portion of it, and the remainder had gone to waste. "With only the two of us, I serve roasted chicken as a substitute. It's quite good, the stuffing is just as marvelous, and we aren't left with meat going bad. Hope you don't mind."

"Mind?" His white teeth flashed in a teasing grin. Not for the first time, Nan noticed how the creases in his lean cheeks deepened when his mouth curved. "I'll bet your roast chicken today puts all the turkeys cooked in Random to shame."

"If you're implying that I'm the best cook in town, you're in for a big disappointment," she replied. "Luckily, it's hard to go wrong with one of Ellen Hamm's hens. I don't know what she feeds her chickens, but their eggs are superior, and so is their meat."

Gabriel had scooped out the pumpkin seeds onto an open newspaper, and one bit had fallen to the floor. Nan stooped to pick it up.

"I'm sure it will be delicious," he assured her. "Hell, I'd be happy if you served shit on a stick. You're just that good a cook."

Chapter Nine

By nightfall, Nan had grown so weary of Gabriel's lavish and nonstop compliments on the Thanksgiving Day meal she'd prepared that she was feeling a bit waspish as he stoked both fires while she prepared for bed. Granted, he'd done full justice to the meal, actually helping himself to thirds of everything, but no man could be as nice and easy to please as he pretended to be. *Drat him.* Was this what it felt like to play chess with a master? *No*, she decided. *It's a vicious game of cat and mouse, and I am the unfortunate mouse.*

Nan was too miffed to be worried overmuch tonight about being raped in her own bed as she jerked off her clothing. *This pumpkin pie could take a blue ribbon at any state fair in the country.* She couldn't get over that one. Nan considered herself a fairly accomplished baker, but she'd never produced anything from her kitchen that deserved such accolades. Gabriel Valance was a master, all right—a master at spouting poppycock. He didn't miss a trick at figuring out what a person would want to hear.

She wasn't buying any of it. The man was doing his deliberate best to charm her. Playing along with him, and formulating an escape plan if needed, was her only option while she waited for the ax to fall. What irritated her most was that she'd enjoyed hearing the compliments. She wasn't sure if that made her madder at Gabriel or at herself.

As for the ax . . . well, she knew it *would* fall. It always did with men. Right when she least expected it, he'd turn vicious, lacerating her with words—or fists. Every time she looked at his broad, work-hardened hands, her stomach knotted. Martin Sullivan had been possessed of a wicked backhand, which he hadn't hesitated to use on Nan when, in his view, she spoke out of turn. She had vivid memories of mind-numbing pain radiating through her jaw after he smacked her. Sometimes in very cold weather, her jaw still ached. Gabriel topped her father by several inches, and outweighed him, too. If he ever dealt her such a blow, she'd be picking herself up off the floor nursing a shattered cheekbone. Better not to irritate the man.

Nan donned her nightgown and then jerked so hard on her hairpins that several strands came away with them. Tears stung her eyes. Laney was totally bamboozled by Gabriel. Nan didn't like that one bit, either. In the space of a single day, the girl had burst out laughing more times than she had over the last six months. It bruised Nan's feelings. She wasn't sure why. There was no harm in laughter. It was just such a marked change, with Laney giggling so much more than she usually did. Was Nan so somber and unsmiling that she smothered Laney's natural high spirits?

Nan sank wearily onto the edge of the bed. She'd tried so hard to be a good mother, doing for Laney all that she'd yearned for herself as a child—doling out lots of hugs, giving plenty of praise, using endearments, buying presents the child coveted, and spending fun time with her each evening, sometimes playing cards or board games, other times just talking. And Laney had seemed happy.

Now she seemed *happier*. Nan tried to tamp down

the resentment that welled within her. She had been born with a tendency to open her mouth when she shouldn't. Years of living under her father's stern rule had taught her a certain reticence, but she still had a temper that could flare quickly and make her forget to control her tongue. If she allowed herself to feel angry with Gabriel, if she stupidly grew lippy with him . . . Well, the possible consequences didn't bear thinking about.

She heard a board creak in the hallway, a prelude to his imminent invasion of her cherished privacy. She leaped up and dashed to the armoire to fetch her wrapper, tossed it on the foot of the mattress, and then dived under the covers, drawing them firmly beneath her chin just as he tapped at the door.

"Come in," she called.

He stepped into the room rubbing his middle and smiling. "I am so full I feel like I'm going to pop. Never should've had that fourth piece of pie, I guess. It was too delicious to resist, though." Standing just inside the closed door, he began unbuttoning his shirt. "The one and only time I ever got homemade pumpkin pie before today was the Thanksgiving I lived with old widow Harper. She was feeble and had bad eyesight, so it wasn't a very good meal. The whole time I stuffed my face, I had my eye on the pie she'd set out by the stove. I could barely *wait* for a piece."

Nan tried to imagine him as a hungry little boy brought in off the streets by a sickly but well-intentioned old woman. "Was it good?" she couldn't resist asking.

He laughed and shrugged out of the shirt, his well-muscled shoulders rippling in the lantern light as he moved. Nan was reminded of a beautiful sculpture of dark teak, rubbed to a high sheen. *Beautiful?* The thought no sooner settled in her mind than she shoved both it, and her gaze, away. Men could be handsome, she supposed, but never comely or beautiful. What in tarnation was she thinking?

"It was *horrible*. She added salt instead of sugar."

Startled from her discomfiture, Nan said, *"What?"*

"You heard me, salt. I took a huge first bite, chewed once, and then tried not to gag or spit it out." Seemingly comfortable in a half-naked state, he strode around the foot of the bed. "She was a sweet old gal, stern and unsmiling most of the time, but God rest her, she never laid an angry hand on me. Aside from the fairly brief time I had with my mother, I have no memory of kindnesses from anybody except that frail, shaky old lady." He sighed. "She no longer cared for sweets at that age, so she never tasted the pie. She'd worked so hard to make it, and I didn't want to hurt her feelings, so I pretended to eat the whole thing. Mostly I spit it in my napkin and became an expert at rinsing out the linen after supper, but sometimes she wouldn't look away so I could do that, and I had to swallow it."

Nan's eyes burned. Only a boy with a very gentle heart would have done that to save an old lady's feelings. How, she wondered, had that boy matured into a man who coerced a woman into marriage simply because he liked her looks?

"I'm sorry your childhood was so awful." Despite her resentment and distrust of him, Nan sincerely meant that. No youngster should have to endure what he had. "It's so sad."

"Hey, I lived through it," he said as he hung his guns on the bedstead. "If it doesn't kill you, it makes you stronger."

Nan wasn't sure the trials she'd survived had strengthened her. She often felt like a puppy trying to paddle in a swift current and barely managing to keep its nose above water.

Gabe sat behind her to kick off his boots. "Can you

turn off the lantern tonight? I'm so full I'd have to roll over there to do it."

Not wishing to be treated to another display of amazing masculine musculature, Nan complied, pushing up on an elbow, quickly dousing the light, and then huddling under the covers until the residual amber glow faded away to leave them in blackness.

Gabe hated that he made Nan so nervous. When she shifted to face him, he knew it wasn't to snuggle down and get more comfortable, but to watch every move he made so she'd be ready if he decided to grab her. What she planned to do about it, he couldn't imagine. She wasn't much bigger than a minute.

As he'd done last night, he stretched out on his back, using his folded arms as a pillow. It was a comfortable enough position for him; he used his saddle as a pillow out on the trail and often slept this way. Not that he wouldn't have enjoyed lying on his side or stretching out a little, but that would make Nan even more uneasy. She needed her rest, and if he meant to let her get any, he had to play like a corpse laid out in a coffin: ankles together, legs straight, arms folded. His only exception to that pose was to have his hands behind his head instead of resting on his chest.

Once he got settled, he whispered, "Good night." After she responded, he closed his eyes, waited a couple of seconds, and then emitted a snore that he hoped sounded real. She'd fallen for it last night, thank God. Only after she'd heard him snore had she been able to relax.

He forced out another sputter, trying not to overdo it, and waited, feeling the mattress shift under her slight weight as she snuggled down and sighed. The sound was laced with relief. He bit back a smile, wondering how long he'd have to do this before she finally started to trust him.

It didn't surprise him when he soon heard a change in the rhythm of her breathing. She'd worked her little fanny off all day, and had to be exhausted. So exhausted, in fact, that she hadn't insisted on sewing in her workroom long into the night. Soon there came that soft little snuffle of hers. He smiled into the moon-silvered darkness. *Ladies do not snore.*

Gabe was still grinning slightly as he drifted off to join her in slumber.

Gabe wasn't sure how long he'd been asleep when a choked cry jerked him back to consciousness. It took him a second to recall where he was and, more important, with whom. His heart caught when he realized Nan was jerking and muttering nonsensically in her sleep. In the shaft of moonlight that bathed the bed, she thrashed with her fists, tossed her head from side to side on the pillow, and then strained as if to escape a great weight on top of her.

Gabe's sleepy bewilderment was swiftly replaced by understanding. *A nightmare.* And he knew exactly what it was about. *Barclay, the fat bastard pig.* Nan was either pinned under her attacker's limp, massive body, or she was enduring a cruel pawing of her breasts. The memory of it that flashed through Gabe's head made him angry enough to kill. If he'd had another year to live, instead of only a measly month, he would have hit the trail for Manhattan to have ten meaningful minutes alone with Horace Barclay. Hell, while he was at it, he'd give Martin Sullivan a good ass kicking, too.

Wanting to wake Nan and bring the torture to a swift end, Gabe grasped her shoulder. "Nan. Hey, honey. Wake up. It's only a—"

A small, bony fist caught him in the mouth, and the next thing he knew, his wife was grunting, scratching, and slugging. He ducked his head, trying to protect his eyes. "Nan! Stop it. It's a dream, only a dream!"

With a low wail, she nailed him on the ear with the heel of her hand, which sent a peal of loud ringing through his temples. Then she brought up a knee and almost got him in the groin. He snaked out an arm to catch her around the waist, rose up on his other elbow, and pinned her flat on her back in a two-count move.

"It's me, Gabe," he told her. "Wake up, Nan. It's only a dream."

With him holding both her wrists in one hand, she could no longer swing at him. So instead she panted— whiny, jerky pants brought on by panic—and bucked with her hips. The futility of her efforts drove home to Gabe just how helpless she'd been to defend herself against Barclay. Gabe knew the instant she escaped the clutches of the dream and came awake. She dragged in a deep breath and went absolutely still.

"A dream," he said again. "Only a bad dream. You know who I am now?"

"Gabriel?" she whispered. "Oh, mercy."

Her nightgown was damp with sweat. He felt the tips of her breasts harden and thrust against his bare chest. A certain part of his body reacted, but Gabe didn't allow his mind to follow its lead. He was too concerned about Nan right then to entertain such thoughts.

She stared up at him, her large eyes shimmery with tears. "I'm sorry. Oh, dear, I'm so sorry."

Confident now that she'd come fully awake and wouldn't swing at him again, Gabe released her hands and levered his weight off her. As he drew slightly away, she reached out with wildly shaky fingers to touch his mouth. "You're bleeding."

He tasted with his tongue. "Well, shit, you busted my lip." Gabe shifted onto his back and got his head comfortably cradled on his pillow. "That's quite a right hook you've got going there, darlin'."

He had hoped to make her laugh. Instead she said, "It wasn't you. I never meant to hit you."

Gabe wiped his mouth. "I know that. And no harm done. It's not the first time I've been served a knuckle sandwich. At least you didn't loosen my front teeth." He angled her a glance. "That must have been some nasty dream you were having."

She drew the covers over her shoulders and huddled on her side, facing him. He wanted her to tell him about it, but she remained silent for so long that he was about to give up on that when she said, "I have bad nights sometimes, one nightmare after another. That's one reason I always work so late, because I dread going to bed. I never know when the dreams will come, and the one I just had is the worst of all."

"Barclay?"

She pushed at her tousled hair and nodded. No words to describe the dream slipped from her lips, though. That worried him.

Her delicate features were defined by moonlight and shadow, enabling him to see the soft arch of her brows, the dainty bridge of her small nose, and the fullness of her soft mouth. A very kissable mouth.

Whoa, son. The last thing she needs is for you to get as horny as a two-pronged goat. All the same, he wanted her. She was so beautiful, how could he not? During his adult years, he'd bedded a lot of women, prostitutes one and all. Maybe gals like that started out in their profession looking fresh and sweet, but if so, Gabe had never run across one. It was a hard, punishing life that they led. Most of them grew old and worn before their time. By contrast, Nan was like a fine bit of lace fresh from the bolt.

"I'm not going to be able to go back to sleep," she confessed. "I think I'll go to my workroom for a while. I can finish trimming Mrs. Hamilton's dress with lace. Sewing helps calm my nerves." She sat up. "I truly am sorry about your lip."

Gabe hated to think of Nan working well into the night while he lay in bed sleeping. "You've already had a long day. Won't you at least try to get some rest?"

"I . . . can't." Perched on the edge of the bed, she craned her neck to look back at him. "Once this starts, it goes on all night, one dream after another."

Gabe understood all too well. It had taken him years to outgrow his nightmares, and even now, they still woke him occasionally. "You can't go the rest of your life avoiding sleep. It'll take you to an early grave."

"I tried sleeping drops once. That was even worse. The dose the doctor prescribed was so strong, I'd go to sleep, still dream, but couldn't wake up."

"Did you try a lesser dose?"

She nodded. "And I was still good for nothing the next day, so rummy I could barely take care of Laney, let alone run my shop."

"Probably laudanum," Gabe ventured. "And you're lucky it didn't agree with you. People get addicted."

"I hated the way it made me feel."

Gabe sighed, recalling how relieved he'd felt when he'd told her why he sometimes cried inside where no one could see. It had been as if a huge weight had eased from his chest and shoulders, flowing out of him with the words. He wished Nan would talk to him about the incident with Barclay. She'd never been able to tell any-one about the assault, he felt certain. She'd fled from Manhattan and never uttered a word about it to anyone for fear she'd be turned in and hanged for murder. The only exceptions had occurred yesterday morning when he'd invaded her life, and then again last night when he'd stupidly brought up her father's incomprehensible treatment of her.

That outburst from Nan had been about Martin Sullivan, though, not about Barclay. Gabe studied her pale face and hated himself a little—no, a lot—for what he was about to do. But if there was anything he'd come to learn about Nan, it was that she held her cards way too close to her chest. She would never speak of Barclay's attack on her person unless Gabe got her so riled that she forgot to guard her tongue. And, dammit, she *needed* to talk about it.

"Explain something to me," he said. "Not much really happened with Barclay. Right? The fat slob was so clumsy that before he could do you any real harm, he tripped, fell, and skewered himself. So why does something so . . ." He deliberately let his voice trail away as if searching for words. "Why does something that inconsequential still bother you so much all these years later—so much that you can't sleep at night? I mean, well, it was mostly just an unpleasant tussle. The man never actually raped you or anything."

As he knew she would, Nan shot up from the bed, turned to face him with her hands knotted at her sides, and cried, "*Inconsequential?*" She laughed bitterly. "Spoken like a man. No *harm*?"

"What did he do that was so terrible?" Gabe jabbed.

She threw up her hands. "I was *completely* naive about things like that!" she cried in an outraged voice. "After living with my father all my life, do you think I eagerly accepted the attentions of men? No! I wanted no part of the courtship business, and even when my father forced me to entertain potential husbands in the sitting room, I let each of them know, straightaway, that I abhorred the institution of marriage. Prior to Barclay's attack on me, I'd never even been kissed!"

That tidbit of information shocked Gabe—and made

his heart hurt for her. "Never? Not even innocent pecks on your lips?"

"Innocent?" She shuddered. "I knew what those men wanted, what *all* of you want, when it comes right down to it. I wasn't born blind and deaf, after all."

"I'm not following."

She pierced him with a stiletto glare. "Do you think I never heard my mother's cries of anguish when my father demanded his conjugal rights? Do you believe me to be so stupid that I didn't know—or at least imagine, in my girlish mind—what he was doing to her? Or that I was oblivious to the beatings he meted out when she refused him for fear the next miscarriage might kill her?"

Gabe saw that his wife was shaking now, with anger or horror.

She pointed a quivering finger at him. "Don't you *dare* speak to me of what is inconsequential and what isn't! My mother died giving birth to Laney. She *died* because my father insisted that she get pregnant again and again and again to give him a son. And God help her if she didn't pretend to be glad when her courses stopped. A *son*, mind you; that's all he wanted from her. Daughters were lesser beings." She spread a slender hand over her waist. "*I* was a lesser being, a bit of brainless fluff and completely without worth to him."

Though Gabe was glad he had her talking, he hated the way he'd gone about it—and he hated even more that he needed to steer her off the topic of her father and back to Horace Barclay. "I know your father was a bastard, but he's not the person haunting your dreams."

"It's all tied together!" She bent slightly forward at the waist. "Barclay and my father were in cahoots! They *planned* what would happen to me that night. It was all about *control*. I wasn't happily falling in with my father's wishes. I was protesting the union with

Barclay, not openly defying my father yet, but coming close. In truth, even open defiance wouldn't have saved me. My father could have forced me into the marriage." She flung out a hand, but she was so upset she didn't see him duck. "And, oh, my, what if I had turned the wedding into a public spectacle? What if, at the very last moment, I refused to say, 'I do'? My father prized his social connections. No one in his circles knew the *real* Martin Sullivan. In most wealthy families of Manhattan, it was common practice to arrange advantageous marriages for sons and daughters, but it rarely happened that a young lady protested at the altar. What would his friends have thought if they witnessed him forcing his daughter into marriage with a disgustingly fat man nearly three times her age?" She grabbed for breath. "It's all one *thing*, not separate instances. What did you say to me last night? Oh, yes, you told me not to sort men into cups as if they were beads of the same color and size. Well, don't *you* sort the incidents of my past into cups, either! It's all related—my father, the marital arrangements, Barclay's attack on me. You're trying to make light of what happened to me that night? Damn you to *hell*!"

Gabe was very close to going there, without her wishing it on him. And he was not unaware that goading her like this might doom him to that fate. She wasn't likely to forgive him for this anytime soon, and he had only twenty-nine days left to make her fall in love with him. *No matter.* He'd been given a second chance down here to save Nan, not himself. Granted, a side benefit, if he was successful, would be salvation for himself, but he couldn't allow that concern to cloud his thinking to the point that he tossed away chances to make Nan's life less conflicted. If talking about Barclay's attack could possibly set her free of the memory, he'd be a heartless, conscienceless skunk if he didn't push her to do it. Even though she had one hell of a right hook.

"If what happened with Barclay was all that bad, explain it to me. From where I'm standing, it sounds fairly trivial." He silently congratulated himself on the use of *that* word. It would push her right over the edge.

"Trivial? Why, you . . . you—" She broke off, but he had a feeling it wasn't because she couldn't find the right words. Rather, it was because the words she was finding weren't ones that a lady would ever dream of using. "Being thrown to the dogs by your own father? He gave all the staff the evening off, which he'd never done before, to set me up! And then he left me in the sitting room to be raped!"

"But you weren't raped. Barclay roughed you up a bit, and I'm sure the knitting-needle business must have shaken you up. Killing someone . . . Well, let's just say I understand how you must have felt when you realized the fat bastard was dead, but all in all, he barely touched you before he cocked up his toes."

"Barely touched me? Ha! When I tried to avoid his slobbery kisses, he made a fist in my hair and held me still." Her throat worked as if she might gag at the memory. "He didn't care if he ripped my hair out. His lips were as fat as the rest of him, hot and slimy with saliva. And then—" She gulped. "Then he shoved his tongue so far into my mouth, I swear he swabbed my tonsils. It was disgusting. I couldn't breathe. I couldn't move. I thought I was going to throw up. It wasn't so much his strength that overpowered me, but his breadth and weight. I couldn't have set him off his feet if I'd dived at him in a full run, hitting him with everything I had."

Gabe made a mental note to teach her a few tricks about how to take a man down. With proper training, she'd never be so defenseless again. The bigger the bastards were, the harder they fell. "If he was that fat and ungainly, why the hell didn't you run? He never could have caught you."

Indignant rage sparked in her eyes. "You think I wanted it to happen? I tried to run. Perhaps, with luck, I could have gotten around him, but I'll never know, because I couldn't move." Her eyes went bright with tears again. "I froze. He set down the snifter of brandy my father had poured for him and smiled at me—an awful, leering, victorious grin. I knew then what he meant to do—what my father had given him permission to do. I *knew*, but for some reason, I couldn't make my feet move. Even as he lumbered toward me, I just stood there, helpless to save myself."

"Ah, honey." Gabe winced. He was playing the evil inquisitor in this scene, and he couldn't afford to slip out of character, no matter how sharply her words struck chords within him. Nevertheless, he understood how it felt to be frozen with fear. As a boy, he'd been so terrified a few times that it had felt as if bags of bricks were tied to his feet. Clearing his throat, he forced himself back into his role. "So you just stood there and did absolutely nothing to fend him off?"

As if her legs threatened to fold, she sank onto the edge of the bed, one hip angled so she still faced him. Tightly hugging her waist, she rasped, "I wanted to run. I *tried*. I don't know why I just stood there." Her voice lifted a notch. "But it wasn't because I *invited* what came! And before I could collect my senses and get my feet to move, he was upon me. After forcing his disgusting tongue halfway down my throat, he ripped my dress open, baring me clear to the waist."

Gabe settled back to listen. It was coming now, spewing out of her as if a small volcano inside her were erupting.

"He wasn't out to merely *deflower* me," she said in a cold, flat voice. "Oh, no, he was establishing his dominance over me, determined to train me up the way he wanted me to go, much as it says in the Bible, only his way was *evil*. I would be cowed. I would perform my wifely duties without complaint. If he wanted to beat me, I would accept it as my due. *That* was his aim, to put me in my proper place." She dragged in a shaky breath and slowly exhaled. "I struggled, but he only laughed at my attempts to escape. He didn't merely *touch* m-my feminine protrusions; he laid claim, digging in hard with his fingers to cause pain. Months later, I still had purple marks on my skin, left there by his fingernails cutting into my flesh.

"I don't remember how I broke his hold. Maybe horror lent me strength. I only know that I somehow wiggled free, and because he stood between me and the door, my only choice was to find a weapon to hold him off. I ran for my yarn basket, snatched up a needle, and whirled to threaten him away with it." She paused to swallow. "He only laughed. He wasn't afraid of me and my pathetic weapon. As he came toward me, he said he would teach me a lesson I'd never forget, and I saw in his eyes—they were little and beady in his flabby face, as cold and unfeeling as a lizard's—that he intended to punish me in private, personal ways that I would never forget or risk inviting again."

Gabe's heart twisted.

"Then, just when I thought he'd grab me again, he tripped. It happened so *fast*. I would have tossed away the needle, I swear. I never meant to kill him!" Her chest began to rise and fall rapidly, and by the cadence, Gabe knew she was no longer with him in the bedroom, but in the past, with Barclay nearly upon her. "He was so close when he tripped that he came down on top of me. I fell backward under his weight. When we hit the floor, my breath was knocked out of me. I couldn't breathe. Every time I tried, it was as if cotton batting had been shoved down my throat. I panicked, felt like I was suffocating. I couldn't see. Black spots bounced before my eyes.

"When I could finally drag in breaths again and my senses began to clear, I realized that the mountain of flesh on top of me was deathly still. It was then I f-felt the blood—sticky wetness all over my bared skin. I *knew* then. I knew. He was *dead*. Killed by my knitting needle. Who would believe that I hadn't meant to stab him? Or that he had sexually assaulted me? He was Horace Barclay, a man of sterling character and reputation, a deacon at our church who kissed babies and sang baritone. He was big and jolly. Everyone who knew him loved him. My side of the story would never be believed."

She turned a haunted gaze on Gabe. "The rest comes to me in nightmarish bits and snatches. Trying to roll his immense weight off. Praying for a miracle as I felt to see if his heart was beating—if he still breathed. And then the hysteria that came over me when I knew for certain he was dead. I remember huddling on the floor with my arms crossed over my nakedness, saying, 'No, no, no. Don't let him be dead. No, no, no.' But God wasn't hearing my prayer." She closed her eyes and tipped her head back, treating him to an unimpeded view of her arched neck, which put him in mind of a swan's. "I finally collected myself and had the presence of mind to know I had to run. Run and never look back. Only I couldn't leave Laney. She presented nothing but complications for me, but I couldn't abandon her. I knew my father would treat her just as badly as he had me. I had no choice but to make off with her."

She'd gotten all of it out now. Gabe felt almost as exhausted and drained as she probably did. "Of course you couldn't leave Laney. Your father would have had her on the auction block at thirteen, hoping to marry her off and form an empowering alliance with her husband's family."

"Yes, and then *she* would have been a victim. Perhaps her attacker wouldn't have been Barclay, but sure as rain in March, it would have been someone. Growing up under my father's rule, Laney would have come to hate men, just as I did, and she would have resisted any arranged marriage. My father does not countenance rebellion, not even a hint of it."

Gabe had accomplished what he'd set out to do. She'd finally talked about the attack. Judging by the slump of her shoulders, she felt empty now, no longer buried under a mountain of unspoken horror. He'd aimed, fired, and hit the bull's-eye. So, now what? If she hadn't hated him before, she sure as hell did now. *I'm no good at this, Gabriel*, he thought, hoping the message would wing its way straight to the archangel. He needed some advice, and he needed it fast. Unfortunately, Gabe had told his namesake to scat, and apparently his request had been granted.

"Well," Gabe ventured, "hate me though you might, at least now maybe you'll no longer dread sleep."

She jerked her head around to stare at him. "Pardon me?"

Gabe settled back with his folded arms under his head again. "You heard me. You've kept that bottled up and tightly corked for too many years. Talking about shit like that helps us turn loose of it and move on."

Silence. It stretched between them, as taut as an archer's bowstring. Then, in a shrill, squeaky voice, she asked, "Are you implying that you manipulated me into talking about it?"

"There's a word I don't use often, *manipulated*."

"Answer the question!" she cried.

Gabe released a breath and slowly inhaled. "Do you honestly believe any man with a heart could believe what you endured at Barclay's hands was *inconsequential*? Or trivial? Using that word was a stroke of genius. It pushed you right over the cliff."

She leaped to her feet. "You, a man with a *heart*? Damn you!"

Gabe winced. She'd probably cursed more in the last half hour than she had in her whole life. "I knew you'd hate me for it, but it needed doing. Now it's time for you to come back to bed and get some sleep."

"I shan't sleep a wink! Not on a bad-dream night. I told you that."

"Care to make a wager on that?"

"Make your bet!" she flung back. "I'll match you!"

"A hundred dollars."

"You're on!"

Gabe knew she couldn't afford to lose a hundred dollars, so her willingness to put it on the table told him far more than she could know. For one, she was beside herself with anger—at *him*. And second, she believed, without a single doubt, that she wouldn't sleep tonight.

"Good." He patted the mattress. "Fair wagering obligates you to at least *try* to sleep. Get in bed."

She huffed, did a turn in place that lifted her long hair to swirl around her, and then jerked the covers back. "Very well. But I swear to God, if you so much as *breathe* on me, Gabriel Valance, I'll shoot you dead with one of your own guns."

"Fair enough. I believe you. I probably have pumpkin breath anyway."

She finally crawled into bed. Gabe didn't look her way. He just closed his eyes and listened to her rain what he suspected were curses upon his head, but she muttered them into her pillow so he couldn't make them out. *Ah, well.* He'd been cursed before; it was nothing new to him.

Once again, he pretended to fall asleep. Then he waited. He had to give Nan credit: She managed to stay wide-awake for at least thirty minutes. But in the end, he heard that cute little snuffle—not a snore. God forbid that he call it that!—that told him she'd given up the ghost.

He grinned into the moon-washed shadows. He was a hundred bucks richer, and she would slumber like a baby in its mother's arms for the rest of the night. If she had another nightmare, he'd eat the socks he'd been wearing for two days straight.

All in all, not bad for one day's work.

Chapter Ten

A warm glow of brightness disrupted the night. Nan squeezed her eyes shut. The irritating glare didn't go away. She frowned and pulled the covers over her head. Then, slowly, as she inched toward awareness, she realized that a light in the middle of the night was usually a sign of distress. Had Laney come in with a candle, ill or needing her? She jerked upright and opened her eyes.

The harsh glare was no candle. It was sunlight, *full* sunlight, indicating a late morning hour. Her mind rejected what her eyes were telling her. It couldn't be morning. Nan blinked. Squinted at her bedroom window. *My stars!* It had to be after nine. She twisted to peer at the windup alarm clock on her bedside table, which she rarely used to rouse herself but kept wound to be sure of the time. *Sixteen after ten?* No! It couldn't be. She'd forgotten to wind it, and it had stopped last night. That was the only explanation.

Rattled and incredulous, Nan sprang from bed, noting as she did that Gabriel wasn't in it. She hurried over to the armoire, shifting hangers back and forth on the rod to find the russet gown she'd worn yesterday. Her bodice watch would give her the correct time. It couldn't possibly be sixteen after ten in the morning.

Seventeen after ten. Two timepieces couldn't be

wrong. She'd slept half the day away. What would Gabriel say? Worse, what would he *think*?

Snatching her wrapper, she shoved her arms through the sleeves in case Gabriel made an unannounced entry, then gathered her clothing and crept from the bedroom, up the mercifully empty hall, and into the water closet. After locking the door, she gazed with yearning at the metal bathtub—one of the plumbing luxuries she'd allowed herself when she redid the upstairs— which emptied through a hose into a pipe under the floor that ran across her apartment and connected with the drainage outlet under her kitchen sink. Other shop owners along Main Street had thought her mad when she'd asked Elbert Rasper to plumb her kitchen sink and tub. Indoor plumbing was, as yet, far from the norm in Random and possibly even in Denver. But Nan had ignored the gainsayers, paying Elbert a small fortune to do the work and then run a hollow drainage log from the building to a buried gravel pit at the back edge of the shop's backyard.

Now she wished she could sneak to the kitchen in her nightclothes to pump some water and put it on to boil for a wonderful hot bath. *Not.* When she faced Gabriel Valance—gambler, drinker, blackmailer of women, and gunfighter—she wanted to be fully dressed and perfectly coiffed. She'd given him every reason to feel smug, sleeping all night without dreaming and snoozing until nearly noon. Manipulating her into speaking of Barclay's attack on her had been cruel of him. She'd never spoken of it to anyone, and doing so last night had *nothing* to do with her deep, dreamless sleep. She'd been exhausted; that was all.

Oh, *lands*, she owed him a hundred dollars! A small fortune. What on earth had she been thinking when she made that wager? Nan filled the washbowl, hastily completed her morning ablutions, and got dressed. After putting away her gown and wrapper, she headed for the kitchen, nervously fiddling with her hairpins. Her husband and Laney were undoubtedly awake, hungry, and awaiting breakfast.

Still incredulous that she'd slept so deeply and for so long, Nan stepped briskly through the sitting room archway, saying, "Good heavens, why didn't someone wake me? You both must be starv—"

She broke off to gape in startled amazement at Gabriel, who stood at the stove wearing a makeshift apron, a white kitchen towel tucked over the front of his gun belt. Laney hovered at his elbow, giggling.

"Good morning." He left off stirring something in a pot to flash her a smile. "You're just in time for the breakfast of the century: pumpkin pie oatmeal and cinnamon toast."

Laney, her cheeks as red as September apples, turned a sparkling gaze on Nan. "It was Gabe's idea. We had leftover pie filling, and oh, Mama, you should taste! It's ever so good!"

Nan, who'd frozen in motion, collected herself and took another step toward them. The sight of a man, any man, turning a hand in the kitchen was so foreign to her that she feared she was gawking at him like an idiot. All she could manage was, "Laney, I see no tasting spoon."

A flush crept up Gabriel's dark neck. He darted a glance at Laney, quirked an eyebrow, and sent the girl dashing over to the flatware drawer to get a utensil. This told Nan that they'd both been sampling with the stirring spoon. Nan did the same thing herself sometimes, but only on the sly when Laney wasn't watching.

"Pumpkin oatmeal. Hmm." Actually, it sounded delicious, and Nan couldn't help but wonder why she hadn't thought of it herself. "I'm amazed you know how to cook, Gabriel."

"I don't, really, at least not much. My experience runs only to an open fire. I can serve you up a tasty pot of beans, and my skillet corn bread isn't too bad. I'm also a quick learner if someone takes the time to teach me." He grinned and sniffed the pot's contents. "That was a hint."

He looked clean-shaven, his burnished jaw shiny in the light that came through the window over the sink. His black shirt, though slightly wrinkled, appeared crisp and clean. The memory of his bare chest, shoulders, and arms chose that moment to invade her mind, and she felt heat creeping up her throat.

"When our holiday food is all gone, perhaps you can treat us to one of your suppers." Nan fetched an apron and tied the strings in a bow at the small of her back. She stepped over to a cupboard to collect dishes for the table. "It was thoughtful of you both to postpone breakfast until I woke up. You must be starving."

"Actually, this'll be our second breakfast. We had pie when we first got up." His deep voice curled around Nan like warm smoke. "We controlled ourselves and left you a piece."

Nan's stomach felt as knotted as a skein of kitten-tumbled yarn. She pretended to be intent on setting the table. "Well, since you apparently aren't going to mention it, Gabriel, I suppose I will. It appears that I owe you a hundred dollars. Gloat all you like." *Please don't.* "It shan't bother me."

Laney gasped. "A hundred dollars? For what?"

Nan glanced up just then, and Gabriel winked at her. "That was a silly bet. I don't expect you to pay up."

"It wasn't a silly bet to me." Nan placed fresh napkins beside each bowl. "And I am a woman who honors her debts."

"Okay, fine," he volleyed back. "You can put it in the family pot. Now that we're man and wife, what's yours is mine, and what's mine is yours. We can make bets any old time we want, and nobody ever really loses."

Ha. As of Monday, all the money in Nan's pot would be under the floorboard in her downstairs workroom. No way was he getting his hands on her precious hoard. It was all the security she and Laney had.

"I can't believe Mama made a bet. She doesn't believe in wagering!" Laney glanced back and forth at both adults. "What did you bet on?"

Gabriel grinned at the girl. "Whether or not you could stop talking for thirty seconds."

Laney giggled and rolled her eyes. "No, sir. You're fibbing. What did you *really* bet on?"

"That, young miss, is none of your business," Gabriel replied. "Right, Nan?"

A rush of relief filled Nan. She truly didn't wish to have her nightmares become a topic of breakfast conversation. There were things that Laney shouldn't know—things that Nan had relentlessly endeavored to keep secret from her. As a result, Laney, while aware of the stark facts about what had occurred eight years ago in Manhattan, remained unaware of any lurid details. Little girls should remain innocent.

"Right," she said, confirming Gabriel's statement with an emphasis that made him turn to stare at her. "Now that I'm married, Laney, there will be some things Gabriel and I discuss only between ourselves."

"How is that fair? I don't like secrets!"

"Too bad," Gabriel inserted. Then he distracted the girl by slapping a hot pad into her hand. "You can dish up the oatmeal while I get the toast out of the oven."

Moments later, Nan was seated at the opposite end of the table from her husband, with Laney at her right. The blessing had been said, and now the child was laughing because Gabriel had tasted the porridge, closed his eyes, and was moaning as if his bowl were filled with ambrosia. Nan braced herself and took a taste. She nearly moaned, too. The stuff was almost as good as the pies had been. As for the cinnamon toast, she felt that the slices had been slathered with too much butter, but when she bit into her piece, she couldn't quarrel with the results. *Delicious.*

Suddenly Nan felt unusually hungry. Normally she ate smallish portions and never had second servings of anything, but she quickly dispensed with her porridge, helped herself to a second piece of toast, because there were still three left on the platter, and then poured herself a glass of milk from the chilled pitcher. As she took a sip, she found her gaze locked with her husband's over the rim of her tumbler. An odd shiver ran up her spine and radiated out over her shoulders, making her skin prickle. The sensation wasn't unpleasant, but it did take her by surprise. *Good heavens.* Was this how it felt to be attracted to a man? No wonder some women acted like morons, simpering and blushing and fanning their cheeks.

Nan would *never* allow herself to behave in such an unseemly way. It mattered little that Gabriel Valance was devilishly handsome when he grinned at her. She would *not* melt under the twinkling warmth in his coffee brown eyes. She averted her gaze and carefully set down her milk. A burning sensation crept over her cheeks. She filled her mouth with toast, chewed industriously, and nearly choked when she tried to swallow.

"I think that getting a good night's rest agreed with you," he commented. "Your color is better. Don't you agree, Laney?"

Nan endured a long study from her much younger sister. Finally the child replied, "I do agree. Her cheeks are nearly as pink as my Sunday dress."

Over the remainder of the holiday weekend, Nan tried her best to stick with her regular routine, which included any hand-stitching needed on garments in progress, and cleaning tasks too time-consuming to manage when the shop was open. Gabriel Valance insisted on helping, and when he decided to sweep, Nan watched in startled amazement as he put all his strength into each pass with the straw bristles, sending more dirt airborne than into the pile on the floor. She confiscated the broom at the first opportunity and suggested that her new husband dust the sitting room, her thought being that he couldn't do much damage with feathers attached to the end of a handle. Wrong. He knocked over knickknacks, toppled a display of books, and used the tool so vigorously that bits of down soon decorated the upholstery. Despite his ineptitude, he took criticism from Laney with good grace, attempted to lighten his touch, and later collected all the feathers. Nan was incredulous that a man would turn his hand to household tasks, let alone take instruction from a twelve-year-old.

Gabriel continued to play the role of charming husband—ever patient, warmly accepting, and brimming with compliments. He was good at it. . . . She had to give him credit, but it constantly remained at the forefront of Nan's mind that he was only putting on an act. And that act wore on Nan's nerves so badly that she felt like an overwound clock with inner springs about to snap.

By Sunday, feeling extraordinarily well rested and having experienced four reasonably tolerable nights in bed with her husband, Nan was finding it increasingly difficult to hold fast to her determination to resist Gabriel's allure. Was he real, this man with his crooked grin and playful sense of humor? Her lovely apartment, once so quiet, now rang with laughter. And her life, once so predictable, had become a moment-by-moment surprise.

Hoping for some time alone to sort out her chaotic thoughts and emotions, Nan went downstairs to work in her shop that afternoon. To her dismay, Gabriel and Laney soon joined her, and what might have been a peaceful and productive few hours for Nan became a stint of alternating amusement and frustration. While she dusted shelves and cataloged her new inventory, man and child engaged in a ludicrous game of dress-up. Laney started it by plopping a hat on her head and pretending to be a fastidious and difficult-to-satisfy customer. Gabriel followed the child's lead, and the next thing Nan knew, her dark, intimidating gunslinger wore one of her more colorful headpieces, a mauve felt cap adorned with pink and green feathers and silk carnations nestled among sprigs of angel's breath. He draped a knitted green shawl over his broad shoulders and hooked the handle of a beaded black handbag over his wrist.

If anyone on the street saw this performance, it would be all over town faster than a tumbleweed in a hurricane. Hurriedly Nan drew the curtains across the windows, muttering something about the light hurting her eyes.

Neither Gabriel nor Laney paid her much attention. Flapping one hand and placing his other on a cocked hip, Gabriel tried to speak in a high-pitched voice, but his natural baritone thrummed deeply in between squeaks. "I have my heart set on a hat with a dead bird perched on top, Mrs. Valance. I'm told you are a milliner of inestimable repute who happily works under the direction of her clients to create *stunning* originals."

It was the first time Nan had been addressed as Mrs. Valance. It gave her a jolt, but she couldn't very well protest. Like it or not, it was her name. She might have resented the reminder, but Gabriel looked so silly she couldn't help but smile. Playing along, she said, "I've a broad inventory of stuffed critters in storage. What kind of bird are you yearning for?" She slanted him a wicked look. "Perhaps a hummingbird? Or a canary?"

"Not a hummingbird or a canary!" Laney cried. "They're too little and sweet to suit him." Her gray eyes danced with mischief. "Do you have a big, black, *ugly* crow?"

"No, but I do have a vulture," Nan said.

That set Laney to giggling so hard that she bent her knees and hugged her sides. Gabriel growled and, still in costume, snatched the girl off her feet and slung her over his shoulder. "A big, black, *ugly* crow? I'd much rather be a vulture and have you for supper."

Laney squealed. "Help me, Mama! Help!"

Glancing at the window curtains to make sure no one outside could peek through a crack between the panels, Nan only smiled and shook her head, convinced that the child was in no imminent danger—unless, of course, Gabriel dropped her on her head. "Do take care," she cautioned.

He grinned and set Laney back on her feet.

"A badger," Laney suggested, straightening her skirt. "He should have a stuffed one on his head. They're nearly as fearsome as he is."

Nan was no longer certain Gabriel was as fearsome as his reputation painted him. The thought came into her mind from out of nowhere, and she didn't welcome it. But once the sentiment took root, she found it difficult to dislodge. She knew her own reputation in town was that of a woman who did quality work and paid her bills on time, but was standoffish and made no friends. She'd even heard it said that she felt she was too good for the rest of the town. It wasn't true, but people held fiercely to their own perceptions. Was Gabriel's reputation as inaccurate as her own?

Before Nan could pursue that thought, a knock came

at the door. Laney's expression turned horrified. With a squeak, she stripped off her acting garb, grabbed Gabriel's as he shed it, and then raced to hide the evidence of their foolishness in the storage closet. As Nan went to answer the summons, Laney was pretending to tidy shelves, and Gabriel was standing with one hip braced against the jewelry case, his dark eyes dancing with laughter.

Prudence James and Loretta Michaels, two of the worst gossips in town, stood on the threshold. As they hurriedly explained that they were in desperate need of red and green trim for a Christmas table runner they'd decided to make over the weekend, they craned their necks to peer past Nan into the shop.

"I hope you don't mind the intrusion," Prudence said. "We thought we had everything we needed, discovered that we didn't, and want to finish our project today."

Nan knew very well that they'd come to snoop, but she allowed them entry. "My till is counted down for the weekend. Anything you buy will have to be put on your bills."

"Oh, no worries," Loretta said with a flap of her hand as she swept past Nan with a rustle of her skirts. "We'll settle with you tomorrow." She jerked to a stop when she saw Gabriel and placed a splayed hand over her heart. "And who might you be? It's not often I see a gentleman in Nan's shop."

Nan quickly made introductions. Gabriel grasped the fingertips of each woman's proffered hand, and then engaged in polite small talk until Nan intervened by reminding the two busybodies that they'd come to buy trim. Gabriel took advantage of the distraction to go upstairs, leaving Nan to deal with her customers' nosy questions. She kept her responses vague and was relieved when the two women finally left.

"They didn't need trim!" Laney exclaimed. "All they wanted was to see Gabe up close. If he hadn't been down here, they would have tried to wangle an invitation from you to go upstairs for tea."

Nan couldn't argue the point. "Gabriel handled it well, giving them no fuel for gossip."

Laney snorted. "Those ladies lie, Mama. They don't need a reason to say awful things about people."

"True," Nan agreed. "But looking on the bright side, if their story is intriguing enough, I may sell a lot of Christmas trim."

Laney laughed. "Better yet, we could sell tickets! A nickel for a peek at the infamous gunslinger Gabriel Valance. We could get rich!"

The following morning, Nan dressed for the day, prepared breakfast, got Laney off to school, and then told Gabriel she had to walk over to the bank for one-dollar bills and coins to set up her cashbox for the week. Her new husband seemed to think nothing of it, and instead of offering to escort Nan to the bank, as she expected he might, he said he wanted to take a turn around town, get a breath of fresh air, and try to find a newspaper.

Nan was breathless and jumpy when she entered the bank. Simon White, as plump as his wife, Geneva, was thin, sat behind his desk off to the right. He had been attempting to grow a mustache over the last few weeks, and this morning, in the golden light coming through the barred, painted window, Nan saw that he'd tried to shape the bedraggled thing with pomade. It looked as if two fat gray mice were perched on his upper lip, noses touching in the center and their tails extended stiffly behind them.

"Mrs. Hoffman—er, Valance!" He struggled to his feet and came around his desk to greet her.

"Mr. White." Nan offered her gloved hand, and the

banker executed a half bow as he lightly grasped her fingers. "Lovely to see you," she said, wondering as she spoke how Geneva could bear to kiss him with that bush sprouting beneath his nose. Nan would have much preferred kissing Gabriel, who kept his face clean-shaven. *And where did that thought come from?* "I trust Geneva is doing well after the rigors of the holiday."

"Fit as a fiddle, and jabbering nonstop about the gown you're going to design for her." He arched a silver brow. "How may I assist you this fine morning?"

Nan smiled and gestured at the teller window, where Hank Mortimer, a pencil-thin man whose only outstanding features were a hawk nose that turned red when he smiled, and ears that stood out as if they were being blown from behind by a strong wind, stood ready to help her. "Nothing but a routine withdrawal," she replied. "I'm sure Mr. Mortimer can handle it."

Simon held on to her fingers. "I understand that congratulations are in order."

For an instant, Nan couldn't think what he meant. "Oh! On my marriage, you mean. Yes, indeed, and thank you."

Tipping his head slightly back, Simon studied her with unabashed curiosity. "When, may I ask, did you come to meet Gabriel Valance? So far as I know, he arrived in town only last week. I never would have guessed you to be possessed of an impetuous nature."

Nan kept her smile firmly in place. "I'm not, Mr. White. This isn't Mr. Valance's first visit to Random. He came once before at Christmas."

Simon frowned. "Hmm. I don't recall anyone ever mentioning that. A man of his ilk usually causes quite a stir when—" He released her hand to cover his mouth as he coughed. "Er—ah . . . ahem. My apologies. I seem to be catching a nasty cold."

Nan took advantage of the break in conversation to

say, "I really must hurry, Mr. White. I've left my shop unattended." She turned toward the teller window. "Please give Geneva my regards."

Ten minutes later, Nan ducked between two wagons to gain the opposite boardwalk. In one hand, she carried a satchel filled with all her life savings, except for one dollar, which she'd had to leave in the account to keep it open. Once inside her shop, she leaned against the wall to catch her breath, annoyed with herself for feeling apprehensive and slightly guilty. This was *her* money, earned honestly by the sweat of her brow. She had every right to withdraw it from the bank. If she chose to paper her sitting room walls with it, that would be no one's business but hers.

Leaving the Closed sign up so passersby would know she wasn't yet open for business, Nan hurried into her downstairs workroom, sorely wishing that she'd installed a door instead of merely hanging a curtain to separate this area from the front of the store. If Gabriel returned, only the drape of green cotton would conceal her activities from him.

Dropping the satchel on her project table, Nan swept off her cloak and tossed it over a chair. Then, grabbing the hammer she'd ferreted from the closet toolbox earlier, she went to work. *Easy as making pumpkin pie oatmeal*, she thought, as the plank gave way with one pull of the claws. The satchel was a bit fat for the opening, but she managed to stuff it through. After replacing the board, she stuck the heads of three nails in her mouth and poised a fourth one on the wood, gingerly holding it as straight as possible while she took aim with the hammer. She swung and grinned with triumph when she hit her target. Men liked to pretend that this sort of thing was difficult, but Nan wasn't finding it so. She pounded industriously, feeling certain that anyone with half a brain could take up carpentry.

Then she somehow missed the nail and hit her thumb. *Ouch!* She nearly broke her teeth biting down on the metal pegs in her mouth as pain shot up her arm. It hurt so much that for a few moments she actually saw black dots. A shriek was beyond her. Dropping the hammer, she grabbed the wrist of her injured hand and released a smothered humming sound as she rocked back and forth, squeezing her eyes shut against the agony.

"When you hit your thumb with a hammer, you're supposed to throw the hammer, kick something, and then turn the air blue with curses," a deep, silky, and all too familiar voice said from behind her.

Gabriel. Nan scrunched her eyelids together even more tightly, afraid to look at her injured digit for fear she would see bleeding pulp and shattered bone. She still didn't think she could manage to speak, and what could she say, anyway?

She felt her husband grasp her forearm. "Let me see what you've done to yourself." Her strength no match for his, Nan surrendered her hand to him. "Well, shit," he muttered. "If you needed something nailed, why the hell didn't you ask me to do it?"

"Is it bad?" Nan cracked open one eye, which she focused on the floor. Anywhere but the thumb. "I think I've broken it. Did I shatter the nail?" How could she do fine sewing with a hand out of commission?

"It isn't *that* bad," he assured her. "God made our thumbs to take a lot of punishment. It's going to be sore for a few days, though."

The pain had gone from mind-numbing to merely throbbing, and Nan opened both eyes. Her digit was red and slightly swollen, but it looked intact and wasn't bleeding. "Well, that's not fair," she blurted. "Anything that hurts so much should at least *look* injured so a person can get some sympathy."

Gabriel chuckled and lifted her hand. She watched in stunned amazement as he drew her thumb into his mouth. It felt as if warm, wet silk had gloved her flesh. She jerked her hand, but he held tight. As he sucked, she felt the pulsating pain give way to a dull ache. She also felt a hot, drizzly sensation low in her belly that made her want to gather her skirts, leap to her feet, and run for her life. This wasn't supposed to happen.

When he finally stopped his ministrations, he smiled and said, "Next time, after you kick something and curse, pop the injured part in your mouth. Works every time."

Shaken by the unwanted arousal coursing through her, Nan managed to say, "Apparently you've hit your own thumb a number of times."

"A few. Once you get your swing perfected, you don't miss as often." Weight balanced on the heel of one boot, he shifted to glance over her shoulder. "A loose board, huh? I'll fix that for you lickety-split." He reached for the hammer. Nan's good hand shot out and grabbed it first.

"I can do it!"

He closed his fingers over hers and came away with the tool. "Judging by the way that nail's bent almost double, I don't think so."

Oh, no. Heart in her throat, Nan watched as he located the nails she'd spit out, found another on the tabletop, and then knelt on one knee, hammer in hand, to pry the board loose again. Muscle rippled in his shoulders and across his back as he put his strength into the job. She knew he was bound to see the satchel when the board popped free, and for the life of her, she couldn't think what she should say.

"Well, now, what have we here?" he asked when the inevitable occurred. He reached through the crack and lifted the bag out. With a quick twist of his fingers, he opened the catch and stared at the money. Nan's face went hot when he directed a questioning look at her. "Do you really think this is necessary?"

"It's mine," she cried. The words came unbidden. "I won't let you claim it. I won't. I worked hard to earn every cent. Do you think I'm stupid enough to leave it in the bank so you can take it away from me?"

Never in her life had she seen anyone's expression change so fast. His face so grim that it frightened her, he closed the satchel, returned it to its hiding place, and nailed the plank down with hard, precise swings that filled the shop with deafening reports. She wondered if he was wishing he was hammering her instead of the nails. When finished, he straightened, tossed the hammer on her desk, and thrust her cloak at her. Nan flinched every time he moved. His anger was so intense that she could almost feel its heat.

"Come with me," he said.

It was an order. Nan, who'd been liberated from masculine rule for eight years, protested. "I'm not going anywhere. I've a child to support and a business to run."

His dark eyes had gone as black and flat as smut in a stovepipe. "Oh, yes, you are, Nan," he said with soft menace. "Either you put on your cloak and come with me willingly, right now, or I'm going to throw you over my shoulder and carry you. Given your love of propriety, I don't think you want that to happen. Everyone on both boardwalks will see you riding my shoulder with your fanny pointed skyward. And if you think I won't do it—try me."

Five minutes later, Nan was sitting beside her husband in front of Walter Hamm's desk. In stunned silence and not quite trusting her ears, she attended the conversation between the two men. Gabriel instructed the attorney to draw up an affidavit stating that he, Ga-

briel Valance, Nan's lawfully wedded husband, relin-
quished all rights to his wife's assets. The title to her
shop would remain solely in her name, and her husband would have no access to her bank accounts. After
two copies were signed and notarized, Gabriel took
one, folded it neatly, and slipped it into his shirt pocket.
The other copy would be filed as a public record.

Nan shrank in her chair, feeling . . . Oh, she couldn't
find words for how she felt. Numb, definitely. A little
like the time she'd fallen off a horse, hit her head, and
felt disconnected after regaining consciousness. And
also ashamed. She'd badly misjudged Gabriel, and her
actions had hurt him. She'd made him bleed way deep
inside where no one could see—in that secret place
where he cried over events in his past that could never
be changed or erased. She wasn't sure how she knew,
but she knew. Certainly his face didn't give it away.
Those strong features looked carved out of granite.

When the business about her assets was completed,
Nan stood, thinking that they would leave, but Gabriel
indicated by gesture that she should sit back down. To
Hamm he said, "Now I'd like you to draw up my will,
and make Nan my sole beneficiary. It should be simple
enough. I liquidated all of my father's assets after he
died, so there's no real property involved, only some
money in my Kansas City bank account." He paused.
"Well, that's not exactly right. I do have a horse down
at the livery." He glanced at Nan. "When I die, will you
take care of him for me? Maybe rent some pasture at
the edge of town, have a shelter built, and see to it that
he's fed and watered every day? His name's Brownie,
and he's been a loyal friend to me. I don't want him
sold."

Nan stared at her husband. She'd ridden often in
New York, but she hadn't been near an equine since,
except for when she and Laney had traveled cross

country, partly by stagecoach. "You're not going to die, Gabriel. And you've made your point. There's no need to draw up a will."

"Everyone dies," he replied. "Will you take care of my horse or not?"

"Of course. I just think—"

"How you *think* is what got us here," he snapped, cutting her off. To Hamm, who was staring at them both in bemused amazement, he continued. "That takes care of it, then. When I cock up my toes, Nan gets everything, including my horse. If anything happens to her, it goes next to Laney. I don't give a damn about my personal effects."

Hamm shifted papers on his desk and cleared his throat. "I can certainly draw up a will for you, Mr. Valance, but in order to make it ironclad, I should include all the pertinent financial information, the name of your bank, the names or numbers of your accounts, and—"

"There's only one account." Gabe gave the attorney the name of the bank and his account number. "It's also under my name, Gabriel Valance."

Hamm hunched over his desk, jotting down the information. "And your middle name?"

"I don't have one. My mother just named me Gabriel. Maybe she didn't know about middle names. I don't think she came from educated folk."

Nan's heart squeezed.

"And, roughly estimating, of course, how much would you say is in the account?" the attorney asked.

Gabe frowned thoughtfully. "It's been a while since I looked at the balance, but the best as I can recollect, about one point five, give or take a few thousand."

Hamm's pen jerked to a stop. He lifted his head to stare at Gabriel. "I'm sorry. You mean one point five thousand, surely. Fifteen hundred?"

Gabriel's mouth tipped into a humorless grin. "I don't know where you learned your numbers, Hamm, but where I learned mine, you can't give or take a few thousand from fifteen hundred dollars. My father left me all his money, plus gambling and whorehouses in four different states. After I sold all the damned businesses, I had a little over one point five million in the bank. I don't live high on the hog and haven't spent much of it, so I'm guessing what's left is still on the plus side of one point five."

Walter Hamm emitted a sound that reminded Nan of a cat trying to cough up a hairball. He wasn't the only one who was stunned. Nan nearly fell off her chair.

After concluding business at Hamm's office, Gabriel, without speaking a word, ushered Nan across the street to Simon White's banking establishment, where he arranged to transfer ten thousand dollars into Nan's bank account. During the transaction, Gabriel never looked Nan's way. Feet numb, thoughts circling, she stood at his side, her gaze pinned to the muscle that ticked in his lean cheek as he signed the necessary paperwork. *Ten thousand.* Nan's father was wealthy, and she'd grown up in palatial surroundings, but never in her life had she had access to so much money. And to top it off, Gabriel had signed away his right to touch a single cent of it.

If his purpose had been to make her feel like a worm, he'd certainly succeeded by the time they exited the bank and started across the dirt thoroughfare to her shop. When they reached the boardwalk, Nan groped in her cloak pocket for the key. Gabriel didn't follow her over to the door. When she turned to glance back at him, she felt sure the memory of him standing there on the boardwalk, feet spread, hands resting at his hips, would be forever branded in her mind. Black Stetson, black hair, black clothing, and black boots. He still looked like Satan himself, only Nan now knew he wasn't. The anger had gone from his face. It was completely expressionless. She thought she preferred the anger. Behind those fathomless dark eyes, she suspected, swirled a world of hurt. And she was responsible.

There was a lump in the middle of her chest that ached like a sore tooth. She owed him an apology. She knew that. But so many feelings were tangled within her that she couldn't sort one from another to form a coherent thought, let alone a sentence. Besides, a busy boardwalk wasn't the place to conduct that sort of conversation.

"About that bet we made," he said slowly and succinctly. "When I come back, you need to pay up. I want a hundred dollars out of that satchel."

"What?" Nan wasn't sure she'd heard him right. "You nailed the plank back down at all four corners."

His eyes burned into hers. "In between waiting on customers, I guess you'll be plenty busy, then, won't you? I want my hundred dollars, no ifs, ands, or buts."

"You just transferred ten thousand dollars into my bank account. Why can't you wait and let me withdraw a hundred?"

"That's *my* money." He jabbed a thumb at his chest. "I want a hundred of *yours*."

Nan searched his dark face, but she found no trace of emotion there. What difference did it make where the hundred dollars came from? He'd just given her far more than that.

"Gabriel, you're making no sense."

He spun on a boot heel to walk away. Over his shoulder, he said, "Why do I have to make sense, Nan? You sure as hell don't."

Chapter Eleven

Nan spent an hour working the floorboard loose. Gabriel had not only nailed the silly thing down, but apparently glued it into place as well. Sweat trickled down her spine and dripped from her nose before she finished. Then she pulled, tugged, and finally braced her feet on the floor to pull the stupid satchel up through the opening. When the bag finally popped free, Nan was unprepared for the sudden give and lost her balance, staggering backward into shelving. *Ouch.* It was her second injury of the day. Now in addition to a tender thumb, she had an aching shoulder blade. And both injuries were her own fault for doubting Gabriel Valence.

No sooner had Nan regained her balance than she heard Geneva out front, calling, "Na-an? Na-an, dear, where are you?"

Usually Geneva's habit of giving her name two syllables amused Nan, but today it irked her. She didn't feel like dealing with a demanding customer right then, but she set the satchel on her project table and pushed aside the curtain anyway. "Well, hello, Geneva. How *lovely* to see you." *Please, God, don't let her insist on another stuffed canary.* "I spoke with Mr. White early this morning, and he mentioned that you've been talking nonstop about your new gown. I can't wait to hear your ideas."

Geneva, who considered herself to be up-to-date on all the latest Parisian fashions, having as a cherished possession a six-year-old copy of a French ladies magazine, swept off her luxurious wool cape, an eye-popping blue one today, and hung it on a hook by the door. "I do, Nan. And I am eager to share them." She fluttered her fingertips over her puffed sleeves, which were hopelessly passé, and then swatted her bustle, which ballooned behind her, giving the viewer a general impression of a ship approaching at full sail. Though Nan had tried at least a dozen times to tell the woman that subtler bustles were now in style, Geneva had turned a deaf ear. Laney called it selective deafness. Pressing her palms together as if she were at prayer, Geneva cried, "I have the most beautiful gown pictured in my mind! It is going to be *astounding!*"

It would be astounding, all right, Nan thought grimly. Just then Prudence and Loretta swanned into the shop to pay for their trim, and before Nan could collect their money, three other ladies walked in. Nan felt like a curiosity on display in a traveling circus. Sometimes she had browsers in her establishment, but seldom five women at once. Perhaps Laney had it right, and Nan should sell tickets. Problem: Her husband, the main attraction, had vanished.

Four hours later, after finally clearing her shop of customers, Nan had a brutal headache, felt sick to her stomach, and yearned to lie down before she had to start supper. Geneva's gown would be memorable, but not in the way the fool woman intended. Silver and red sequins on a black day gown? Nan shuddered at the very thought.

After closing the shop, she went upstairs and settled for dabbing lavender water at her temples. Glancing at her bodice watch, she determined that Gabriel had been gone now for more than five hours. She gazed solemnly at her bed. Even though she'd tidied the covers and drawn up the coverlet that morning, she could almost see him lying there, naked from the waist up, his muscular arms folded behind his head. He'd slept beside her for five nights running, and he'd yet to touch her in any improper way. Not that she was complaining.

She sank onto the edge of the bed and rested her forehead on the heels of her hands. Oh, how she wished he would return before Laney came in from school. Nan needed to apologize to him, and she preferred to do it in private. *Ten thousand dollars.* The man was wealthy beyond most people's measure, yet all he owned was a horse, a saddle, a bedroll, and clothing. From the moment he had appeared in her shop last Wednesday, Nan had believed he was after *her* worldly possessions. Or her person. Yet he'd laid claim to neither one, had made her the sole beneficiary in his will, and now . . . well, now she no longer knew what to think. She still wasn't *entirely* certain he wasn't after her person, but she'd had irrefutable proof that he wasn't after her money.

His appearance in her life made no sense to her. Absolutely *none.* Unless, of course . . . Oh, no, not that. It couldn't be.

Deep in her heart, Nan had always believed that her heavenly Father looked after her. Thinking back over her life, she couldn't count the times, using all her fingers and toes, when divine intervention had either saved her from a dastardly fate, sent precisely the right person to help her, or led her directly where she needed to go. But Gabriel Valance? He was completely *wrong* for her, as well as for Laney, more of a catastrophic visitation than a blessing.

All the same, Nan couldn't deny how many times she'd failed to recognize a blessing in disguise until months or even years later. Barclay's attack on her, for instance. At the time, Nan had felt that it was the most *terrible* thing that could possibly have happened to her, but in retrospect, she knew the assault and Barclay's consequential death had been the catalysts that had given her the courage to grab Laney and run. A horrific occurrence, yes, and it haunted her to this day. But Nan knew, beyond a doubt, that if not for the events of that night, she would have been forced to wed Horace Barclay and would now be his desperately unhappy, browbeaten, physically abused broodmare. And Laney, raised by Martin Sullivan, would now be nearing a marriageable age and possibly even be already betrothed to a man she detested. Nan couldn't help but feel that they'd both escaped a dire future and landed in a far better place.

As for landing where they had, here in Random? Nan's decision to stay in this town had not come about because she'd wanted to live in a tiny community off the beaten track, but because Laney had sickened with pneumonia during their journey west. Nan had rented a room at the Random Hotel and sent for the doctor, nursed Laney back to wellness, and then decided to remain for a few more days to let the child regain her strength. It had been turning spring at the time, and as happened in Colorado, the cold, stormy weather suddenly gave way to a delightfully warm day, enabling Nan to take her sister outside for a little walk. During that outing, Nan had spied the For Sale sign on a milliner's shop. For an amazingly low price, the considerable inventory would go with the building, and the place had been in ready-to-open condition.

According to the notice posted on the shop window, the elderly Mrs. Barker, who owned the shop, had taken sick and never recovered enough to resume her entrepreneurial duties. She'd decided to sell and had moved to the edge of town to live with her daughter. Nevertheless, she loved her store and came in weekly to dust and polish, keeping everything in excellent shape. Nan remembered how her heart had leaped with excitement when she'd peered through the windows. Then she'd pooh-poohed the idea, laughing at herself for being so ludicrous. She couldn't become a milliner. She didn't know the first thing about making hats.

The thought had no sooner settled in her mind than a crackly voice behind her said, "Ah, interested, are you?" And Nan turned to see a bent lady with snow-white hair who just happened to be Mrs. Barker, the shop owner. She had taken an instant liking to Nan, encouraged her to buy the business, and then had come every single day to teach Nan her trade. Eight years later, Nan couldn't say she'd gotten rich being a milliner-cum-seamstress, but she had managed to build a good life for herself and her sister. Random and this shop had become their salvation, something Nan never would have predicted when she first clapped eyes on this dusty little town.

And now there was Gabriel Valance, who'd blackmailed Nan into marrying him. Only, for what reason? He didn't want her money, and if he wanted her body, he was taking his own sweet time in availing himself of her favors. So, why, why, *why*? If he'd suddenly decided he wanted to get married and any woman would do, then why pick her? Was Gabriel himself even clear on his reasons for being here?

Nan knew only that he'd somehow worked his way past all the barriers she had erected around her heart, and he was making her feel things she'd been determined all her life *never* to feel. Though her instincts told her not to trust him, she was coming to consider now that her instincts weren't instincts at all, but learned reactions, taught to her by her father. Was it possible that Gabriel was right, and not all men were like Martin Sullivan? Taking that one step further, was it possible that Gabriel was everything he seemed to be: a wonderful, caring man whose exterior had been tempered to steel by a horrible childhood and an even sadder adulthood? *My first real Thanksgiving.*

Tears burned at the backs of Nan's eyes. She sighed and sat erect, so confused and upset that she could barely sort her thoughts. *Gabriel.* He was like a storm in her life, turning everything topsy-turvy. Nan had always liked order—in her home and in her shop—and there was nothing wrong with that, really, but being around Gabriel was starting to make her realize that she'd become so focused on being responsible that she'd forgotten how to laugh and enjoy life. Or, even more troubling, Nan wondered if she'd ever learned how to do either in the first place. She'd been raised in a singularly somber and unpleasant home.

Was it any wonder Laney seemed so much happier now that Gabriel brightened their lives? Her sister had laughed more in the past few days than she'd done in the last few years.

Nan wasn't ready to concede, even to herself, that Gabriel's invasion of her world might have been divine intervention. Divine intervention and blackmail didn't mix, at least not in her view. But she was coming to believe that he intended no harm to either her or Laney. So why did it matter *why* he was here? For once in her life, could she not simply go with the flow and see where the current led?

Nan collected the stuffed satchel from the foot of her bed and put it in a drawer. She had a lot of sorting out to do, and not the kind one did with one's hands.

Despite the chill breeze, Gabe's brow beaded with sweat, and his shirt, damp from toil, filmed his skin like wet flour glue. He'd lost track of how many times he'd swung Nan's ax. He knew only that he'd split a mountain of logs and now had a huge pile of wood to stack. As he attacked each piece, he thought, "Dammit, Gabriel, where are you?" But his heavenly namesake refused to answer him.

Gabe needed to talk to the angel and get a few things straightened out, first and foremost that this plan wasn't working. He wasn't *saving* Nan. Instead he was upsetting her constantly. To add frosting to the cake, he'd gotten angry with her this morning and acted like a total ass over something that he never should have held against her. She'd known him for less than a week, for God's sake. Who could blame her for drawing all her money out of the bank and trying to hide it from him? She'd been watching out for herself and her sister. There was no crime in that. Gabe had been guarding his own back since childhood. So why had it pissed him off that she'd tried to do the same?

Bottom line, he was wasting his time down here, still miles from the goal the archangels had set for him. Even worse, today when he'd been walking off his ire, he'd seen that boy again huddling under the whorehouse staircase, cold, hungry, and alone. The kid's mother would never come back, and the good people of Random were turning a blind eye to the child's plight. It gnawed at Gabe deep in his gut. He'd met the boy prior to dying, and he'd meant to help him. So why would it be held against him in the final accounting if he helped now?

It made no sense to Gabe. And after being around Nan for five days, he was sick to death of rules that made no sense. The angel Gabriel needed to come down here and take a good hard look at the realities. It wasn't only humans who were suffering. Gabe's meandering walk had taken him out behind Lizzy's Café, where he had come across a half-grown pup huddled in a lean-to on a piece of wet blanket. The poor thing obviously stayed there hoping to get scraps of food, but apparently Lizzy, the owner of the place, didn't have a generous soul. The animal was nothing but yellow fur and bones, and it had gone against everything in Gabe's nature to turn his back and walk away.

But he'd done it, because helping the dog was against the damned *rules* he'd been told he had to follow. Gabe understood that he couldn't be turned loose down here with advance knowledge of future events and the ability to alter history. If a person was supposed to die, it wasn't up to Gabe to stop it from happening. But how about being free to practice common decency? It wouldn't alter the course of world events if he saved a dog from starvation.

"Gabriel?"

In the middle of a swing, Gabe gave such a start at the sound of Nan's voice that he nearly nailed his boot instead of the log. *"Dammit!* Don't call me that. Okay? My namesake is a fellow I don't much like at the moment." He tossed the ax aside and turned to face her. "I prefer plain old Gabe. It may not be fancy enough to suit you, but it sure as hell suits me just fine."

The words no sooner erupted from Gabe than he winced. He'd spent half the afternoon wondering how to tell this woman he was sorry for his contemptible behavior that morning, and now he was biting her head off.

The wind picked up just then, whipping her dark green skirt to twist it around her legs. Her hair, always so perfectly arranged, tore loose in places from the pins and fluttered around her head like curlicues of spun gold. But as beautiful as she looked to his hungry eyes, it was the expression in hers that caught and held his attention.

I never cry, she'd told him once. And Gabe believed it. Nan was a woman who guarded her feelings and revealed them to no one. At least, that was how she'd been before meeting him. Now her eyes were swimming with tears, *again*, and it was all his fault.

"I'm so sorry," she said shakily. A gust caught her words and flung them away, but he caught the faint ring of each one. "I don't know what else to say, only that I'm very, *very* sorry."

Well, hell. This was a new one. Here he'd been trying to figure out a way to apologize to her, and she'd beaten him to the draw. That didn't happen often. He already felt bad enough about the whole stupid mess.

"Don't," Gabe pushed out. "It's me who should be saying I'm sorry. You did nothing this morning that any sane woman in the same situation wouldn't have done, and I acted like a total ass."

She brushed at her cheeks with her free hand. In the other, he finally noticed that she held the satchel. He almost groaned. She'd actually pried up that damned board, and he'd been so mad when he pounded in the nails, he knew he'd driven them deep. Loosening them had to have been an arduous task for a slightly built woman.

She stepped toward him, extending the bag. "I want you to have this, every dime of it. And with it, I extend my abject apologies. I misjudged you from the start, and I've—" She broke off and swallowed. "Though I've tried to make you feel welcome in many ways, I've withheld my trust. I'd like to rectify that."

Only Nan could turn a heartfelt apology into a formal speech. But Gabe knew it truly was heartfelt. He saw that in every taut line of her body and also in her eyes. She laid the bag at his feet and walked over to the chopping block to sit down. That surprised him. He doubted she often sat on anything but a straight-backed chair, and he'd sure never seen her spine come into contact with one. He suspected she was afraid a slump in her posture might snap her vertebrae.

"Would you mind joining me for a moment?" she asked, patting the blade-scarred surface of the stump next to her hip. "I have a few things I'd like to say."

Gabe was so exhausted from cutting wood that the thought of sitting for a few minutes held some appeal. He took a seat beside her, careful not to crowd her. Fortunately it was a huge block, the lower end of a monstrous ponderosa pine that had met up with a saw years ago, judging by the grayed hue of its grain.

"Shoot," he said.

She smiled slightly. Then she released a shaky breath and leaned her head back to look up at the darkening winter sky. After an endlessly long moment, she finally said, "Do you know what I realized about myself this afternoon?" She licked her bottom lip and turned that quicksilver gaze on him. "I never learned how to laugh." The dimple in her cheek flashed, not with a genuine smile, but more a sad twist of her lips. "There was no real laughter in my childhood home. Once the guests left, there was none at all, in fact. My mother— her name was Helena—was a beautiful woman, born into a wealthy family, and thinking back, I can't recall seeing her smile. Not *real* smiles, anyway, only the polite kind, which are for show and not heartfelt. I wonder now if she wasn't raised in much the same fashion that I was, with a father who expected daughters to be decorative ornaments of barter, not living, breathing people."

Gabe felt something shift in his chest. He couldn't say it hurt, but it didn't feel particularly good, either.

"You love to laugh," she observed softly. "I don't know who taught you how, but whoever it was gave you a priceless gift."

Gabe followed her lead and stared up at the sky for a long while. "My mother," he finally revealed. "It was my mother who taught me how to laugh."

"Will you tell me about her? She must have been wonderful."

Startled by the request, Gabe gave her a curious study. "Nan, my mother was a—" He couldn't push the word *whore* past his lips. Not now, with his memories of Mary Susan Miller resurfacing in a painful yet sweet rush. "She was . . ."

"An unfortunate?" Nan offered.

"Yes, an unfortunate, and no, I won't tell you about her." Gabe's memories of his mother were precious and intensely personal. He'd never shared them with anyone, and he didn't intend to start now. "Sorry."

"But I shared so much with you about my father—and other things. How is that fair?"

"You *needed* to share those memories."

"Well, as defensive as you are, perhaps you need to share yours, too!"

"You don't see me not sleeping for fear of bad dreams. Since I got you to talk, you've slept like a baby."

She lifted her hands, conveying bewilderment. "I didn't ask to hear bad things, only about what she was like and how she taught you to laugh."

"Everything about her was *bad*, Nan. At least, you'd think so. I'm not about to tell you about my mother so you can look down your *ladylike* nose at her. I loved her with all my heart, and I still love my memories of her."

"You think I would do that? Look down on her, I mean?"

Gabe gave a bitter laugh. "Yes. How could you not? For you, the whole world turns around propriety. A lady does this, and a lady does that. Well, cupcake, my mama was no *lady*, not by your standards anyway."

"But by yours she was?"

"Damn straight, the finest lady who ever walked."

Nan puffed air into her cheeks and went back to sky watching. After a second, she softly said, "So you think it impossible for me to comprehend how life can back one into a corner and make one do unthinkable things. Me, Nan Sullivan, who murdered a man."

That was another thing Gabe meant to discuss with the angels if he ever got another audience. It wasn't right that Nan still scourged herself for killing a man who was actually alive and well. Being responsible for another person's death . . . Well, Gabe knew from first-hand experience how heavy a burden that was.

"All right," he heard himself say. "I'll tell you a little about my mother, but God as my witness, if you criticize her, by word, action, or a noise in your throat, I'll leave you to sit here on your stump throne and never tell you anything else."

To his surprise, she replied, "You shan't hear a word of criticism from me or see any sign of it. I promise."

Gabe had been so bent on not talking about his mother that he had to collect his thoughts and invite the memories back again. "I don't know what she found to laugh about. She had a horrible life from start to finish. Well, maybe not *horrible*. A better word might be *difficult*, at least when she was young and still at home. The horrible parts didn't come until later." Memories unfurled inside Gabe's mind, nearly too sweet and precious for words. "Like your mother, she was pretty. Beautiful, in fact, with merry blue eyes and long, curly brown hair that shone like she gave it a good polish every morning."

"She probably gave it a hundred strokes with a brush every night before she went to bed. I used to do that before you came."

"You're right. She did brush her hair at night." Gabe recalled that now. "That was how I first learned to count, while she brushed her hair." He settled a questioning regard on Nan. "Why'd you stop brushing yours when I came?"

She shrugged. "It's a bedtime ritual, and it seemed improper to do it in front of you."

Gabe chuckled. He couldn't help himself. "Brushing your hair?" He shook his head. "We've got a whole different idea of proper, apparently."

"Enough about me," she said. "I want to hear about your mother."

Gabe settled his elbows on his knees, more comfortable talking when he leaned forward slightly. That way, if Nan stuck her nose in the air, maybe he wouldn't notice. "She came from poor folks, the oldest of fourteen kids. Only nine of them survived infancy, so by the time she turned fifteen, she'd loved and lost three baby sisters and two brothers. Her father was a farmer with a hurt back. After having so many babies and laboring to raise the ones who lived, her mama grew old before her time."

"I'm sure the grief aged her as well," Nan observed solemnly. "Imagine the pain of losing five babies."

"Yeah, well, they couldn't afford to send for the doctor, so home remedies were all they had. Given the conditions, it's probably amazing that nine of the fourteen kids survived. Babies sicken more often than not when they're born into poverty. Food was scarce. My grandmother probably never got enough nourishment when she was carrying them."

"Oh, Gabriel, not enough food? How awful. It makes me feel terrible for whining about my own childhood. At least there was always plenty to eat."

Hearing the sincere ring in Nan's voice, Gabe started to relax. Maybe he'd misjudged her, and she truly wouldn't grow condescending. "At fifteen, my mother felt it was up to her to save her family, so she packed a knapsack and walked barefoot all the way to Kansas City to get a job so she could send money home to keep food on the table."

"Oh, my stars. I doubt I'd have that kind of courage even now."

"It was courageous, all right. Sadly, being brave of heart isn't always enough. She quickly learned that there were no jobs worth having for a girl her age, with the exception of one: selling her body to men. So that's what she did." Gabe waited, but he heard no muffled snort to indicate a negative reaction. "And somewhere along the trail, she met my father, a fancy gambling man with a lot of money and no heart. She went to work in one of his establishments, and he took a temporary liking to her, insisting that she service only him."

Gabe paused, trying to recall where he'd come by all this information. He knew his mother had told him some of it—about her family and how she'd ended up in Kansas City. But he couldn't picture her telling a little boy the rest of it. He guessed he'd ferreted out most of the story as a grown man, after he'd found his father and confronted him. What a shocker that had been. Gabe had learned during the meeting that he was the spitting image of his sire, and even now, the resemblance didn't sit well with him. Luther Valance had been a conscienceless, greedy, and viciously cruel man who'd used other people like ladder rungs to reach the top. Gabe had no doubt that he had illegitimate half brothers and sisters scattered helter-skelter across four states, but Luther had chosen to acknowledge only his firstborn when he died.

"Anyway, she got pregnant with me, and when my father found out that he'd put a bun in her oven, he tossed her out on the street. I was born in a seedy Kansas City brothel. I don't know what she did with a baby while she worked. Maybe the other whores helped her out by taking turns looking after me." Gabe shrugged. "When I was old enough, I hid out under the brothel staircase until the men stopped tapping on my mother's door. Then I got to go up to her room." He smiled at the memory. "She could make a feast out of one cookie and a cup of tea. She'd pretend to nibble while I ate most everything. We didn't have plenty, like you, so when we got something, she always made sure I got the lion's share. We'd sit cross-legged on her bed. It was the only furniture in the room besides a dresser. But it was home to me—the only one I ever really had. We had good times there, really good times. She'd tell me stories. I remember the ring of her laughter and how she was always ruffling my hair. Somehow, no matter how rotten her work that night may have been, she always found something to laugh about."

"And you thought I might feel moral indignation? A woman who could laugh in the face of desperation and heartbreak, and give love and laughter to her little boy despite horrific circumstances, deserves honor and respect, not condemnation. Despite her circumstances, she tried to be a good mother."

Gabe felt relieved to hear her say that. "Better than that. She *was* a good mother. The best she could be, anyway. Believe it or not, I was a fairly happy kid." He shrugged. "I know the way we lived must sound horrible to you, but it was all I knew, and she made what little we had seem special. Not to say there weren't some awful moments." He remembered the night he'd tried to defend his mother against an abusive client and been tossed down a steep stairway for his trouble, but he hesitated mentioning something like that to Nan. "Mostly my memories, vague as they've become over the years, are good ones. Then Mama got sick. I was five, maybe six. When there is no adult around to remind a kid, he loses track of how old he is until he's mature enough to do some digging to learn his birth date. I don't know what took my mother, but she up and died on me, and from that point forward, I grew up on the streets." Gabe sighed. "I guess you're right, though. She gave me a great gift by teaching me to laugh. In this nasty old world, if we don't laugh, what can we do but cry?"

Nan's gaze clung to his. "Will you share it with me?"

"Share what with you?"

Her throat convulsed in a hard swallow before she replied, "The gift your mother left you—the ability to laugh at silly things."

Gabe's heart caught at the yearning in her expression. "Honey, laughing is the simplest thing in the world. You just let go and do it."

She shook her head. "No, first you have to see the humor in something." The corner of her mouth quivered, and in her attempt to suppress that, she flashed the dimple at him again. "I'm blind to those things, so bent on everything being done properly and having order in my life that I'm stifling Laney's ability to be carefree. Save her from that, Gabriel. Save *me* from that. If she grows up to be a killjoy like me, I'll never forgive myself."

It was Gabe's turn to swallow hard. "You're not a killjoy, Nan. You're just a little too serious about stuff." *Way too serious, mostly.* But not for anything would Gabe have hurt her feelings by saying so. "Relax a little bit, and laughing will just come naturally."

"I need help." She turned up her palms where they rested on her lap and stared at them. "I've heard we all have a life line and a love line. Do you suppose I was born with a serious line?"

"Nobody's born with a serious line," he refuted. "You're going to be fine. You're already a great mother.

Let up on yourself. It's hard to improve on damned near perfect."

"That's the problem, don't you see, my penchant for perfection." She bent her head, fell quiet for a moment, and then stood. "Your answer is no, isn't it?"

"It's not that, Nan. I just don't like to make promises I'm not sure I can keep. I'll try. How's that sound?"

She nodded. "That's all that can be asked of anyone." She gestured toward the building. "Supper is in the warmer. I hope you'll leave off chopping wood and come upstairs before everything ruins."

Gabe watched her walk away: shoulders straight, head high, each step precisely measured. At the narrow alleyway, she stopped and turned her golden head to say, "Don't forget the satchel of money. It may not seem like much to you, but I worked hard for every cent."

After she vanished into the shadowy chasm, Gabe sat and stared at the dusky gray sky. He could almost hear the angel Gabriel whispering, *You see? You are not down there wasting your time.*

With a frustrated sigh, Gabe softly said, "You crazy sons of bitches. Is that why you sent me here, to teach the poor woman how to *laugh*?" No answer. Not that he expected one.

He swore, swung off the stump to grab the satchel, and followed Nan. If he meant to help her develop a sense of humor before his time here ended, he'd best get started.

Gabriel. That very night, he taught Nan a lesson she would never be likely to forget. After supper, she'd gone to her bedchamber to synchronize the alarm clock and her bodice watch, which had been off by one minute's difference the other morning. Gabriel found her muttering under her breath in frustration.

"What is it?" he asked, coming to stand over her

where she sat on the edge of the bed. He leaned slightly in and sideways to see the faces of both timepieces. "Is one broken?"

"Not broken, really. They simply aren't keeping the same time. One insists on being a minute ahead of the other, or perhaps it's the other way around. It makes me crazy when clocks don't show the same time. Never being late is important, you know."

"And you think one measly minute matters that much?"

Nan glanced up at him. "Of course it matters. One minute, ten minutes—it's *very* important to know the right time of day." She fiddled with her bodice watch. "It's a simple matter of getting the second hands synchronized, I think. Only, when I'm setting one, the other one is ticking ahead."

Gabe reached down and caught her wrists, startling her so that she jerked and then gaped at him.

"Stop it," he said. "Remember what you asked me earlier, to teach you how to laugh? The first thing you have to learn is that a little thing like two clocks being a minute apart doesn't matter. It just *doesn't*."

"Perhaps not to you, but it does to me."

"And there in a nutshell is your whole problem." He released her hands and sat beside her on the bed. "Go ahead. Keep messing with both timepieces until your nerves are frazzled."

Nan twisted the stem of her bodice watch. "Thank you. I will. Both Laney and I must live by the clock. Not all of us are so fortunate as to be millionaires."

He started to laugh, tipping back his head and releasing deep guffaws. Nan had no doubt that he was making fun of her, and she began to feel more than a little cross.

"What, precisely, is so funny?"

He waved a hand before his face and shook his head,

apparently so overcome with mirth that he couldn't speak. Nan waited until it passed. He finally sighed and rubbed his side as if it ached.

"It's just . . ." He smiled that crooked, wonderful smile that she was beginning to anticipate. "Fair question, okay? How do you know which timepiece is correct?"

"Well, I—" Nan broke off to stare down at both clocks, and a strange suffocating sensation crawled up her throat. "I, um . . . I don't, actually."

"So you're going to spend half your evening struggling to set both clocks to the *incorrect* time?"

A shaky squeak erupted from Nan, and the next thing she knew, she was helplessly giggling. What had seemed so important to her only seconds before now suddenly struck her as being absolutely *trivial*.

Gabriel joined in, and they laughed until they were so weak they flopped onto their backs on the bed, both of them holding their stomachs. Nan decided she would never try to synchronize her clocks again. If they gained a minute or lost one, she no longer cared.

Because a minute in time was only just that, a silly minute.

Gabriel. Time spun forward for Nan like a winding path gilded with gold. He filled her and Laney's world with so many precious gifts, laughter being only one of them. Morning or night, and anywhere in between, Nan never knew what might happen next. One evening, Laney got out her violin, which she'd become very accomplished at playing, and the first thing Nan knew, Gabriel had swept her up from her chair into a waltz around the kitchen. Nan had danced with many men back in Manhattan, but never had she been held so close, her body braced against ironlike muscle, her feet barely touching the ground. In his arms, she felt as if she were floating. Laney, delighted, moved from one melody to another, allowing Nan to enjoy the feeling for several minutes. She was breathless when the waltzing finally ended, and her heart caught when she realized that Gabriel still held her close, his cheek pressed against the top of her head.

"Ah, Nan," he whispered for her ears only. "You're killing me, you know."

Startled, she reared back to stare up at his face. "How? *What?* Did I tromp your toes?"

He started to laugh, that deep, warm, vibrant rumble of humor that she was quickly coming to adore. His dark eyes sparkled with mischief as he winked at her. "You are *priceless.*"

Nan held that comment close to her heart. *Priceless.* She wasn't certain what had prompted him to say it, but it meant the world to her.

Most evenings while Nan labored over tedious sewing tasks she couldn't do on her machine, Gabriel spent his time with Laney, either helping her with homework or playing games. Nan tried to put her foot down when he decided to teach the girl how to play poker, but Gabriel forestalled her.

"Every female should know how to play poker," he insisted. "Even *you.*" He grabbed Nan's sewing and set it aside on another chair. "It isn't just a game; it's a wagering game. And by learning how to be good at it, you learn how to read men. *That* ability could save your bacon someday." He looked at Laney. "Especially yours, young miss. You're going to be a beauty just like your mama, and the time is fast coming when young men are going to be sniffing after your skirts."

"*Gabriel!*" Nan admonished. Laney giggled and rolled her eyes at him, obviously enjoying the idea.

"That's not inappropriate," he informed Nan. "It's just a saying, and trust me, it's also a fact of life. Men sniff after a woman's skirts. You may know that, Nan, but Laney doesn't, and trying to shield her from the facts of life is no kindness. You want her to get her bloomers charmed off by some lying, no-good scoundrel?"

"Gabriel!" Her voice shot upward again in reproof.

"Don't 'Gabriel' me," he shot back. "Ninety-nine percent of the men outside this building are scoundrels."

"I thought you said most of them were—"

"Forget what I said that night. I was speaking about the *character* of most men then, and the fact is, when it comes to skirt sniffing, the character of most males leaks out through the bottoms of their boots. That doesn't mean all of them are terrible people, only that . . . well, their brains can play second fiddle to their urges, that's all. Laney should learn how to tell if a young man is honest and decent, or if he's lying through his teeth to charm her, and playing poker is a grand teacher."

"That's absurd," Nan protested.

Gabriel shuffled the cards with an expert flourish. "You think so? Listen up, darlin'. There are two things in this world that fire a man up enough to make him forget his principles: skirt sniffing and laying his money on a table." He slapped the deck down, asked Nan to make the cut, and then began dividing the red beans at his elbow into three separate piles. After pushing one mound toward Laney, he shoved one at Nan. Then he dealt each of them and himself five cards, hands moving at dizzying speed.

"The first game I'm going to teach you is five-card stud."

He quickly explained the rules, most of which Nan promptly forgot. Her knowledge of poker ran to sayings she'd heard about it—someone holding the trump card or all of the aces. She didn't know how those things figured into an actual game.

"It's pretty simple, all in all." After they'd studied their hands, he said, "Ante up." At their bewildered looks, he said, "That means put out some money, in this case however many beans you want to risk. You're betting on the odds that you've either got a better hand than everyone else, or you've got good base cards that you may be able to win with if you draw the right cards to go with them. It's called anteing up at most gambling houses."

Nan put out one bean. Gabriel sent her a glance rife with amusement. "We've got a cautious better at the table, Laney. You can match her, or you can raise her." He leaned forward, giving the child an imploring look. "*Please* raise her. It's only *beans*. Put at least five out there, or this is going to be plumb boring."

Laney grinned, shoving out six beans. "I put out five more than you, Mama."

"Just say, 'Raise you by five,'" Gabriel corrected. And then to Nan, he said, "That means you have to put out five more beans to stay in the game. Later, I'll tell you about folding, but that's pretty much unheard-of when players first look at their hands, the rare exception being when some poor fellow sees his wife peeking over the bat-wing doors, shooting daggers at him with her eyes."

"No lady would *ever* approach the bat-wing doors of a saloon or gambling establishment," Nan told him.

"She will if her husband is gambling with money she needs to buy food for her children."

"You see, Laney?" Nan sent the child a meaningful look. "It's an evil game that drives men to deprive their children of necessities."

"The game itself isn't evil," Gabriel countered. "It's the evil things some men will do in order to play—and the even eviler things they'll do to win." He examined his cards and rearranged them. Nan followed his example.

"Are two jacks good?" she asked.

Gabriel huffed out a breath that stirred the gleaming black hair on his forehead. "You shouldn't tell us what you've got, Nan."

"But we're just learning. Fine, fine." Nan wrinkled her nose.

Gabriel chuckled. "Two jacks aren't bad for the first deal. Throw the other cards down now and tell me to hit you with three, because I need to deal the draw."

"Hit me with three." Nan picked up her draw and studied her hand. She now had three jacks. She decided that if two were good, three had to be better. "Do I bet again now?"

"Yep," Gabriel replied with a grin. "Look at you, playing like a sharp already."

Nan pushed out three beans, and the raising process began again. When it came Gabriel's turn, he pushed out twenty beans. "*Twenty?*" Nan cried. "You must have something really good."

Both she and Laney matched his bet. "Now comes the face reading," he told Laney. "Do I have a pat hand, or am I bluffing?"

"You raised us as if you had something wonderful!" Laney accused.

Gabriel grinned. "Exactly. But *do* I have something wonderful? If I can make you both believe I've got a winning hand, you may fold and let me have the whole pot." He settled back on his chair to rearrange his cards. "I've been told I give myself away when I bluff, so watch my face. See if I'm playing straight or trying to clean you out of beans."

Nan saw nothing different; it was the same devilishly handsome countenance that she feared was becoming branded on her heart. Laney stared so hard at Gabe's face that she nearly squinted. "Your eyebrow!" she shouted. "It twitches!"

"Very good," Gabriel said with a laugh. "Before you know it, you'll be able to read a man so easily, it'll be second nature. Always remember, there are mainly two things that will make a fellow play dirty: a strong attraction to a young lady, or money. And *never* trust a man who won't look you dead in the eye."

As the game continued, Nan found herself laughing so hard that tears ran from her eyes. Both Laney and Gabriel said that a spot on the tip of her nose turned bright pink when she bluffed. After that, Nan tried holding her cards high to hide her face, but her opponents called her on it.

"There are all kinds of warning signs to watch for when a man's lying or bluffing," Gabriel told them. "Some fellows tug on their ears or rub beside their noses. I've seen lots of temple scratchers in my day as well. You have to be careful with nervous gestures, though, because sometimes a straight shooter will do things like that if he's really tense." He looked directly at Laney. "Like, say some young fellow decides he loves you so much that he can't live without you and asks you to marry him. If he truly loves you, he may be so nervous waiting for your answer that he'll rub his nose plumb off."

Toward the evening's end, Nan decided that playing the evil game of poker was actually stimulating and fun. Laney brought the hilarity to an end with a question for Gabriel. "So how do I know for sure if a young man is lying when he says he loves me?"

Gabriel laid down his cards and rested his arms on the table to give Laney a solemn look. "I care very deeply for you, Laney. I mean that from the bottom of my heart. I care so much that I'd take a bullet to protect you." He let his words hang in the air for a long moment. Then he asked the girl, "Am I lying or telling you the truth, straight from my heart?"

Laney stared hard at his face. "Your eyebrow isn't twitching."

"Nope," Gabriel said with a crooked smile. "What else?"

"You aren't shifty eyed."

"Nope." His larynx bobbed as he swallowed. "The most important thing, cupcake, is to listen to your own heart. When you look into my eyes, do you believe me?"

Laney's gaze went misty. "I do," she whispered. "I think you truly mean it."

Gabriel reached across the table and chucked the child under the chin. "You're right; I do. So keep your sweet little self out of harm's way so I don't get shot trying to keep you safe." He began gathering the cards. "We'll play again tomorrow night. But now I'm afraid it's bedtime. You've got school in the morning, and Nan has to open the shop."

Laney planted a good-night kiss on Nan's cheek. Then she glanced hesitantly at Gabriel before suddenly circling Nan's chair to throw her thin arms around his neck. "I love you, too, Gabe. I really do."

Nan saw Gabriel squeeze his eyes closed as he hugged the girl against him. "I know you do, honey. But thanks for telling me so."

A few minutes later, when Gabriel joined Nan in bed, she rolled onto her side to face him. In the darkness, he was limned by soft moonlight coming through the window. Nan's throat felt tight. He truly did love her little sister in an avuncular way, deeply enough to lay down his life to protect her. Nan had seen the truth of that in his eyes when he'd said the words.

It was a wonderful thing to know that Laney now

had a strong male protector. Nan wouldn't have changed that for the world. All the same, she felt sad. She wasn't certain why, but there was no denying the ache at the base of her throat. Perhaps, she decided, it was merely that she felt set aside. Laney had never loved anyone else but Nan.

Yes, that was it. Nan clung to the explanation like a drowning woman might a log. But even as she did, a little voice in the back of her mind taunted her. *You want him to say those words to you! That's the truth of it. It's not sadness that you feel; you're green with jealousy. And of your own little sister, no less. What kind of person are you?*

Nan flipped onto her back to glare at a ceiling she couldn't even see. She felt Gabriel stir beside her. "You okay over there?" he asked.

"I'm fine," Nan said, almost too quickly. She'd never been a good liar. Thank goodness he couldn't see her nose.

The truthful answer would have been that she wasn't okay and wasn't sure she'd ever be truly okay again. She'd gone and let herself make one of the stupidest mistakes of her life: She was falling head over heels in love with Gabriel Valance.

Chapter Twelve

Ever aware that his days were numbered and his fate might be less than pleasant if he didn't accomplish all the tasks assigned to him, Gabe had, from the start, been keeping a mental checklist. He'd been told to hire a Pinkerton agent. *Done.* He'd been told to make Nan the sole beneficiary of his will. *Done.* He'd been told to make her trust him. *Almost there.* By never touching her intimately in bed without an invitation—which, damn it to hell, he hadn't yet received—he'd succeeded in convincing her that she needn't anticipate a physical attack every time the lamp went out. His second great move had been forcing her to be present while he had Hamm draw up his will. Immediately afterward, Gabe had regretted doing that, but in retrospect, he knew that visit to the attorney's office had erased all fear in Nan's mind that Gabe was after her money. Also, by signing documents that protected her assets and then transferring ten thousand dollars into her bank account, he'd given her financial independence *and* the ability to flee if she chose. Those three actions had gone a long way toward convincing Nan that not all men wanted or needed to be in complete control of a woman. Though Gabe couldn't yet say Nan trusted him completely, he believed she was coming close.

Two things remained on his to-do list: making Nan

fall in love with him and then seducing her. Even in the shack, when Gabe had first heard those conditions, he'd had some serious reservations. What kind of man deliberately wooed a woman, tricked her into loving him, and made use of her body when he knew from the start that he couldn't stay with her? And how was it right to *pretend* he loved a woman with the sole aim of getting between her legs? The angels had strongly disapproved of Gabe's former practice of paying women to satisfy his male urges, but to Gabe's way of thinking, that had been an honest exchange, money in return for service. And he'd always been generous, leaving more than was asked. It had been his way of paying tribute to his mother.

Not that he wasn't coming to care for Nan. The more relaxed she became around him, the more she tugged on his heartstrings. The fact that she didn't know she was doing it made it all the more poignant. There was no artifice about her. She was real. If he'd known he could spend a lifetime with her—loving her, protecting her, and providing for her—he would have gladly let go and moved beyond mere affection to a deep and abiding devotion. What man in his right mind wouldn't? But the remainder of Gabe's life was numbered in days, not years.

The big question that troubled him was, just how far was he willing to go in order to save his own ass? He'd done plenty in his life that didn't make him proud, but deliberately setting somebody else up for a world of hurt wasn't one of them. He yearned to tell Nan that her knitting needle hadn't killed Barclay, to hell with waiting for the damned Pinkerton report. But if he did that, he would lose the only leverage he had to make her remain in the marriage. He liked to think that she'd come to care enough for him that she wouldn't kick him out, but what if she hadn't? The moment he told her she had no murder charge hanging over her head, she might get an annulment and send him packing. He couldn't take that chance.

Where were the boundaries? Or were there any? Gabe found himself wavering back and forth on that question. So for a few days, he cogitated on it. One minute, he told himself that making love to Nan would be for her own good. Enjoying sex—and Gabe was pretty damned sure he could make her enjoy it—would show her that the physical intimacies between a man and a woman could be not only beautiful but also fabulously pleasurable. Where was the harm in that? After he died again and she got over feeling sad, she'd see men in a whole new light and would no longer cringe at the thought of marriage. That would be good not only for Nan but also for Laney. Gabe sure didn't want that cute little girl to reach womanhood with a deeply ingrained disgust for the opposite sex.

Oh, how easy it was for Gabe to justify his reasoning and embrace the thought of seducing Nan. She was beautiful. At night, lying beside her in bed, he sometimes wanted her so badly that he ached. He knew she was ready for some gentle persuasion, and physically, he was *more* than ready. And, he assured himself, it would be for a good cause.

Only, would it really be in Nan's best interest? Just when Gabe got himself convinced that the answer was an unequivocal yes, a bothersome little voice whispered inside his head that pushing Nan to be physically intimate was *wrong*. In all his life, Gabe had never worried much about being a gentleman. All those highfalutin manners and social mores were for other fellows, not him. So it was unsettling to discover that he had countless scruples that were now suddenly rearing their ugly heads to torment him with indecision. Right now, it was also a damn nuisance. His conscience may have been late in making an appearance, but it sure was making up for lost time.

He began to feel that his brain was a seesaw, up with positive thoughts one second, and down with negative ones the next. In the end, Gabe decided to concede to his scruples, the bothersome little buggers. *Let it be Nan's choice*, he decided. If she made a romantic over-ture, he'd make love to her so fast that her head would swim. But if she didn't—well, he'd have to live with the consequences, he guessed. When he tried to imag-ine eternity, he felt overwhelmed—and, okay, a little afraid. A *lot* afraid, if he was honest with himself. But waiting Nan out was the only decision he could live with.

So instead of trying to woo Nan, Gabe found himself fashioning sturdy rails for the dangerously steep stair-case that led upstairs, rebuilding some of her down-stairs shelving, which had gone a little rickety with age, and then fixing her shop flooring, the planks of which had worked loose in spots to create trip hazards. On Christmas morning, when he had to take that inevita-ble predawn walk from the saloon toward her shop, he would take his last breaths knowing that he'd made some improvements, and maybe, if the angels didn't wipe Nan's memory clean because he'd failed in his mission, she would think of him with a smile after he was gone.

In the meanwhile, Gabe could congratulate himself on accomplishing a few things that the angels hadn't specified. He had Nan laughing now. Granted, she was still the most prissy-mannered woman he'd ever run across, but she was developing a sense of humor about that and was even starting to alter her thinking about some things. Laney was now allowed to be in the up-stairs living area in her long flannel nightgown, sans wrapper. The girl was covered from head to toe, after all, and Nan had finally accepted that unless Laney needed extra layers to keep warm, it was silly to make her wear them. Nan had also stopped sitting rigidly straight during meals, and sometimes she even let go enough to rest an elbow on the table while she ate. Her appetite had improved by leaps and bounds, and Gabe was more than pleased to note that she no longer avoided sleep by working long into the night. The dreams that had interrupted her rest for so many years seemed to have stopped. She'd also become a participant in the evening games, and slowly but surely, her poker-playing skills had improved. Gabe was pleased when she learned to read his expressions well enough to know when he truly held a winning hand and when he was bluffing. As silly as it sounded spoken aloud, life was one big poker game, at least in Gabe's estimation, and a woman who knew when to hold 'em and when to fold 'em wasn't as likely to be bamboozled by shysters.

Gabe even started accompanying his ladies to church on Sunday morning. It made him uneasy, having to hang his guns on a wall hook at the front door, but he did it, not because he was filled with a sudden rush of good feelings or even liked being inside the church, but because his presence there seemed to make Nan and Laney happy.

Gabe tried to find religion in that place; he truly did. Hell, he knew better than anyone that something more waited on the other side of this life. So why was it so difficult to sing the songs and rejoice in the Lord? Gabe worried on it and decided in the end that though he believed in the basic principles of Christianity and that Christ had died for everyone's sins, he didn't agree with the way these people were working their way toward salvation. Believing wasn't some exclusive club, dammit, shutting out others who didn't think exactly the same way. There were people out there who'd never stepped foot inside a building crowned by a steeple and cross, and though they had faith in other things, or possibly a divinity of another name, that didn't mean they'd be banned from heaven.

What, exactly, *was* heaven, anyway? The way Gabe saw it, heaven existed mainly in people's hearts, not really as a place with streets paved in gold, but a peaceful state of being in the presence of divine goodness, attained by believing in something and living your life on earth by those tenets. Was a Cheyenne Indian less likely to find that because he worshiped Mother Earth, the four directions, the sun, and the moon? The people in this building seemed convinced that *they* had it right, and everyone else had it wrong.

Gabe didn't buy that. He'd run into a lot of Indians out on the trail who'd shared their food with him because he had none and had left him with his scalp because he meant them no harm. They had been good men, and back in their villages, they'd had wives and children whom they loved just as much as any white man did his.

Judging by what Gabe had thus far heard, Jesus had been all about love, and that had been at the core of every word he said. *Do unto others as you'd have them do unto you.* Well, Gabe knew for a fact that none of these men and women in their Sunday best was living by that edict. Not a single one of them had helped that boy under the staircase, and though most of them ate fairly often at Lizzy's, not a scrap of the food left on their plates had ever found its way to that poor dog in the lean-to.

Jesus would have given his whole supper to the boy, and then he would have pitched a holy fit inside the café, berating everyone there for ignoring the plight of a helpless critter outside.

That was it for Gabe in a nutshell: He couldn't believe that it was the holy songs people sang or the devout prayers they could recite by memory that earned them a ticket to their idea of heaven. It was one's actions toward others, human or animal, that saved one's soul. *I'm here every week*, these people seemed to be saying. *I'm holier than others who don't come.* Yet some of the men snored through the preacher's long sermons, and a lot of the women seemed more concerned with how they looked than with why they were there.

All his life, Gabe had felt set apart from religious people, never quite understanding what they found so special about the inside of a building, and more than once as a kid, he'd envied other children who regularly attended church with their parents. Now he no longer felt left out or even slightly jealous. If he wanted to feel close to his Creator, he'd go outside, away from all this sanctimony, and appreciate creation—the power of a high wind, the miraculous formation of an icicle, the incredible blue of a summer sky, or the beauty of a dog that never lost faith and continued to wait for a handout that none of these people was ever likely to offer him.

Nan seemed to sense that Gabe didn't like going to church, but when she asked him about it, he skirted the question. It wasn't right to make light of another person's beliefs or to criticize the rituals she held dear. Nan was sincere in her worship. She hung on every word the preacher uttered and said every prayer with reverence. Her face fairly glowed as she sang the hymns. For Nan, going to church meant everything, and Gabe respected that. It truly was *Nan's* way, and Gabe had no doubt that God looked into her heart and saw that.

It just wasn't for Gabe.

He did like the Lord's Prayer, which he'd never before heard in its entirety. He sorely wished he could memorize the words without studying on them, because, in his opinion, Jesus had laid out a set of rules in that prayer for every decent human being to follow, regardless of what name they gave their god.

When Gabe had completed all the needed repairs in the shop, he tried to make himself scarce during the day so Nan could do business. Most of the ladies had overcome their fear of him after seeing him in the shop a few times, but it didn't escape him that there were some purchasing needs that they would never mention to Nan when a man was present. Mrs. Tandy, a stout matron with black hair, entered the shop one afternoon, glanced from the corset case to Gabe, and then turned as red as a ripe tomato. She left without buying anything. Mrs. Hamm, who walked a lot like her chickens, bobbing her head with every step, whispered behind a cupped hand of her more personal needs and then went into the work area, where Nan could show her merchandise behind the curtain. Patience Cole, a hunched and frail widow woman with bad hearing, stopped in every day to browse and visit, and announced each time she left that men had no business in a ladies' apparel shop. Each day, a number of ladies came into the shop, but few of them bought anything. Gabe couldn't help but wonder if he was causing a drop in sales.

Staying upstairs too long made Gabe feel caged. Of a morning, he'd go across the street to get a newspaper or periodical, which entertained him for a couple of hours while he finished off the morning pot of coffee. Then he cleaned the apartment, a task he considered to be obligatory, since he lived in the place and helped create the messes.

By noon, though, he ran out of things to do. He spent the lunch hour with Nan, sharing a meal with her that he usually prepared, mostly sandwiches, since he wasn't an accomplished cook, and then helping her in the shop with little chores she couldn't do while waiting on customers.

When one o'clock rolled around, Gabe developed the habit of hitting the boardwalks to get some fresh air and exercise. He always went to the livery first to visit Brownie. Giving the horse a good rubdown and some treats took only a few minutes, but Gabe stretched his time there into an hour by exercising the gelding in the corral out back. Once he'd left the stable, Gabe walked the streets of Random. He strolled up one and down another; then he retraced his steps, not caring if anyone noticed that he passed the same buildings again and again. If they thought he was casing a joint, so be it.

Going inside any of the businesses was out unless he actually wanted to buy something, a task he tried to do early in the morning, far earlier than he'd been out and about the first time he'd lived through this month. Otherwise he ran the risk of stumbling into reenactments. Knowing exactly what would happen next and what people were going to say before they said it . . . well, it gave him the fidgets. He didn't find it entertaining, as the angel Gabriel had feared he might. Instead he was filled with an urgent need to escape.

So Gabe walked—something he had rarely done the last time. No more bellying up to a poker table in the saloon of an afternoon, where he might be tempted to fleece another player simply because he knew what cards would be dealt and to whom. No more lingering in the hotel restaurant, hearing the same conversations take place again. Out on the boardwalks, Gabe occasionally encountered someone that he'd bumped into before, but mostly he experienced no repeat performances.

During his outings, Gabe always stepped behind Lizzy's Café at least once to check on the starving dog.

Not dead yet. Gabe wasn't sure why he went, because it made him feel bad when he walked away. He was drawn there, nevertheless. He didn't allow himself to scratch the poor critter behind its ears. He said no kind words. Going there was pointless, and the animal's begging eyes always made him feel guilty. But he went anyway.

And then there was the boy, who huddled under the staircase when he wasn't skulking around town in search of nourishment. *That* really broke Gabe's heart. He yearned to toss the kid money. Barring that, why couldn't he at least give him some food? But he'd been given his instructions, and if he meant to get this right, he couldn't disregard them.

One afternoon while walking, Gabe was passing Doc Peterson's for the third time when the sight of a little girl and her mother stepping into the office waiting room stopped him dead in his tracks. Next week, on Tuesday the twenty-first, four days prior to Christmas, that young mother was going to take her little girl back into the doctor's waiting room, where the child, who had a weak heart, would be exposed to a very nasty chest ailment that would take her life on Christmas Eve.

Gabe's knees went suddenly weak, and he had to lean against the damn building to stay erect. His entire body broke out into a cold sweat. He knew that precious child was going to die, and he had it within his power to stop it from happening. Except that he could do nothing, absolutely *nothing*. Last week, Gabe had been able to reason his way past a deaf and frail old lady stepping off the boardwalk and dying under the wheels of a wagon. *Not my place to intervene.* Okay, yes, he could accept that. Everyone had to die at some point, and that old lady's time had come. But the child? She was only about three, barely out of diapers. Maybe the weak heart would take her later in childhood anyway, but what if it didn't? What if, by stepping in, Gabe could give her a chance to live a happy and fruitful life well into old age?

Walking back toward Nan's shop, Gabe felt physically sick. *It's not my place to mess with stuff like that. I'm not supposed to alter events while I'm here.* But the words pinged inside his head like shotgun pellets rattling around in a tin can.

By the time he reached home—or what he'd come to think of as home, anyhow—Nan had flipped her door sign over to read CLOSED. Gabe was relieved that he'd be able to cross the store and escape upstairs without having to exchange pleasantries with Geneva White or some other female customer. He stepped inside and pushed the door shut behind him, feeling as exhausted as if he'd just outrun a pack of flesh-devouring hounds.

"Gabriel?" Interrupted from tidying her cashbox counter, Nan fixed a worried gaze on him. "Are you all right?"

"Fine, I'm fine," Gabe told her, but he couldn't say it with any conviction.

Nan circled out from behind the partition and moved toward him. "Oh, dear, are you coming down sick? Geneva says there's a nasty illness going around. Simon caught it and took to his bed for nearly a week. He's all right now, but Geneva says he grew so congested that she had to send for Doc. Now, apparently, it's sweeping through town like wildfire."

Pushing up on her tiptoes, she reached to check Gabe's forehead for fever. He caught her slender wrist before her fingers connected. He didn't want her to feel how clammy his skin was. "I'm fine, Nan, only a little tired for some reason."

"Tired? You look gray. Get yourself upstairs. I'll hurry along as quickly as I can, and I'll dose you with some of Mr. Redmond's tonic. He swears by the stuff, so I always keep a bottle on hand."

"I don't need any tonic," Gabe protested. "Maybe just a fresh cup of hot coffee to perk me up. I got chilled during my walk."

She frowned up at him. "Well, silly you. That's to be expected when you haven't the good sense to wear a coat."

"I can't wear a coat when I'm walking fast for exercise. I get too hot."

She gave that derisive little snort that he'd come to expect whenever she disagreed with him. "You didn't get too hot today. Upstairs with you. I'll build up both fires, and you'll be toasty in no time."

As Gabe climbed the stairs to the apartment, he wasn't sure if he'd ever feel warm again.

While Nan fussed over him, Gabe's mind circled the dilemma he found himself facing. If he did anything to alter the course of events that was destined to occur, he would be in trouble up to his eyebrows. But what if he found a way to change some things—only a few—without actually turning a hand to do anything himself? Once the idea took hold in his mind, it wouldn't leave.

That evening, over another of Nan's wonderful suppers—beef gravy and mashed potatoes with hot rolls slathered with butter, preserved corn, and green beans as sides—Gabe said casually, "I sure do see some sad things during my walks."

Both Laney and Nan said, "You do?"

Careful, Gabe. Even though neither angel had made his presence known for quite some time, Gabe figured they had celestial spies keeping a close eye on him. "Oh, yeah. So sad that it makes me question the goodness of humanity sometimes. How can people turn a blind eye to obvious suffering? I just don't understand it."

Nan let go of her fork, making a loud clink against her plate. Her eyes filled with concern. She so seldom left her shop to mingle with others that she honestly didn't know what was happening in the town she now called home. And Laney wasn't allowed to go near the saloon, and had no reason to venture behind Lizzy's Café on her way to and from school.

"Suffering?" Nan echoed. "What suffering?"

Gabe shook his head. "Never mind. Let's enjoy our meal. I don't want to upset you or Laney." If he could herd them around to *pressing* him for the information he wished to impart, maybe the angels would give him a pass. "Some things are just meant to be, I suppose."

"What things?" Nan glanced at Laney. "Is it too awful for young ears?"

Gabe forced a smile that he knew *looked* forced, because he honestly didn't have a real smile in him tonight. "Oh, no, nothing like that."

He resumed eating, counting off the seconds. Through his lowered lashes, he saw Nan retrieve her fork, but she put nothing in her mouth.

"Well, now that you've said something, you can't leave it at that," she complained. "What on earth is happening in our town that people are ignoring? Do tell, or my imagination shall bedevil me all night."

"Mine, too!" Laney cried. "I shan't turn a blind eye if *I* see suffering."

Gabe prayed not. Now that he had his ladies waiting with bated breath for him to enlighten them, he couldn't decide whom he wanted them to help first, the boy or the dog. Being human, the boy took priority; there wasn't a question in Gabe's mind about that. On the other hand, he wasn't any too sure the dog could last much longer without food.

"I've seen two things that really disturb me," he finally said. "And I'm unable to do anything in both cases." He made a show of peppering his meat, deliberately taking his time. "There's a half-grown pup under a lean-to out behind Lizzy's. Aside from the fact that all he's got for a bed is a tattered hunk of wet blanket, he's slowly starving to death. I think he smells the food inside the café and hopes to get handouts, but apparently Lizzy and her customers who pass through the backyard aren't possessed of generous hearts."

"He's *starving*?" Laney's eyes bugged. "Truly?"

Gabe nodded. "He'd be a good-size dog if he had any meat on his bones. Longish yellow fur. It's all matted right now, and his ribs poke out like Conestoga wagon hoops. He's on his last legs, I'm afraid."

Laney directed a yearning glance at Nan, to which Nan responded with, "No, little miss, you absolutely *cannot* bring the poor thing home. We've no place here for a dog. No fenced area out back. Animals must have access to the outdoors to tend to . . . Well, *that* goes without saying." Nan sighed. "You're at school all day, except on weekends, and I'm busy in the shop. There's no one to take him out for walks."

"Gabe could do it, Mama! He walks all afternoon." Laney sent Gabe a pleading look. "Right, Gabe?"

Aware that he'd be gone soon, Gabe couldn't bring himself to saddle Nan with a dog she honestly couldn't care for. Thinking quickly, he said, "I'm not so sure that would work. The poor fellow is scared to death of me." That was one of the biggest lies Gabe had ever told. Dogs always took right up with him, and he had no doubt that the starving mutt behind Lizzy's would as well if Gabe offered so much as a kindly word of encouragement. "That's why I haven't taken him any food. He's so scared of me, I doubt he'd touch it."

Nan frowned. "Can't you just"—forgetting her table

manners, she swung her fork and tossed a bit of gravy onto the front of Laney's pink dress—"*throw* the poor thing some food? We have plenty of stuff left over, so much that the icebox won't hold all of it, and it's always going bad on me. We could feed two dogs and a small child on a daily basis with what I throw out."

Laney mopped at her dress. Nan was so upset about the dog that she hadn't even noticed what she'd done. In that moment, Gabe realized how easily he could completely lose his heart to this woman. If she had a mean bone in her body, he'd never yet seen it.

"He won't let me get that close." Another lie, but Gabe, who normally avoided speaking untruths, had decided he wasn't counting. "Even if I put all my muscle into it, the offering would wind up in the middle of Lizzy's rear dooryard. Some customer would step in the muck, and then there'd be hell to pay for the dog. Lizzy would immediately put two and two together. She might even ask somebody to shoot it for her."

"You *are* rather fearsome, Gabe." Laney tossed her soiled napkin down beside her plate. "If I were a starving dog, I'd be a mite scared of you, too. But I bet—"

"Young ladies do *not* bet," Nan interrupted.

"Oh, for heaven's sake, Nan." Gabe gave her a loaded look. "We bet all the time when we play poker. The sky won't rain rocks upon the child's head for saying such an innocent word."

Nan made a fist over her heart, swept her eyes closed for a moment, and then said, "You are correct. I'm sorry for getting off topic. Old habits die hard." She offered Laney an apologetic smile. "You may continue, dear heart. I'm sorry for interrupting you."

Laney, still wide-eyed, revised her approach. "I will venture a *guess* that the dog won't be afraid of me, and I could take food right into the lean-to without upsetting him at all."

Nan nodded. "I think your *guess* is probably correct. Gabriel does have a—" She broke off and sent Gabe another penitent look. "Well, let me just say that you scared the sand out of me the first time we met."

"It's his black attire and those frightful guns that he wears," Laney observed. "If he'd dress like a normal person, he wouldn't look quite so intimidating. He'd just look interesting."

"*Laney!*" Nan admonished. "It is extremely careless of Gabriel's feelings to criticize his choice of clothing. He doesn't dress abnormally."

"He doesn't dress like all the other men in town," the child protested.

Gabe shot up a hand. "Ladies, ladies." To Nan, he said, "My feelings are not in the least hurt by Laney's observation. I dress for effect and deliberately try to look mean. I'm a fast draw, remember. Looking mean discourages upstarts who want to take me on. Usually," he added, remembering Pete Raintree. Then, to Laney, he said, "I'm glad to hear that I look intimidating. That's my aim. So can we return to discussing a solution for the poor dog?"

"I can get close enough to feed him," Laney pronounced. "I'm certain I can. I'm only a girl. Nobody, not even a possibly mistreated dog, is afraid of a girl."

She struck fear into Gabe's heart every time he looked at her, only not in the way she meant. Pretty soon boys would be lining up at Nan's door to see Laney. Gabe wouldn't be around to oversee the situation or step in to teach the unruly young pups proper calling manners.

"It's settled then." Nan studied her uneaten meal with a forlorn expression. "I've lost my appetite, thinking about the poor thing. He can have what's left of my supper."

"Mine, too," Laney seconded.

Gabe's usual hunger for Nan's cooking had vanished that afternoon when he'd seen the little girl. "Mine goes into the pot, for sure. I won't die sometime during the night if I don't get something to eat. The poor mutt might." Before his ladies could leap into action, Gabe forestalled them with, "But the dog is only part of the problem."

Nan, caught in midmotion as she rose from her chair, sank back onto her seat. "Oh, no! Is there another homeless animal that's starving?"

"Not an animal," Gabe replied. "It's a cold, hungry boy, about Laney's age, maybe a little older. He huddles under the—" Catching himself just in time, Gabe refrained from using the word *brothel* in front of Laney. "Just this side of the saloon, there's a staircase open to the street. He hides in the far left corner, where the shadows help to conceal him. His mother took off with some cowpoke, promising to return. I have no idea what happened to her, but I don't believe she'll come back." Gabe held up a staying finger. "I know you, Nan. You'll want to gather him up and bring him home. But this boy has led a hard life. What he really needs is to be taken in by a family—a family with at least a couple of other children *and* an experienced father to ride herd on him. This boy may be given to violent acts. He may be a thief. His language may be even rougher than mine."

"Well, we *can't* just leave him under that staircase!" Nan cried. "And if he's hungry, why on earth haven't you been taking him food, Gabriel? We've plenty to share."

Once again, Gabe had no choice but to lie. "The boy is afraid of me, too, just like the dog. If I went under that staircase, he'd probably drench his drawers." The kid had been extremely wary of Gabe, but not quite *that* wary. "And you can't just throw food at a child as if he's an animal. That would be horrible."

"I can hide my cashbox so we can bring him here until—"

"No," Gabe said softly.

He sincerely did have concerns about the kid's character, and he could not, in good conscience, put Nan or Laney at risk. As long as Gabe was present, he could deal with the boy, but the clock kept moving forward. If Nan took the child in until more permanent arrangements could be made, Gabe might die before it happened, leaving Nan and Laney alone with a possible miscreant. There was also the inescapable fact that someone up there had to be watching, and Gabe would pay dearly if he encouraged Nan to be the one who took the kid in.

"I think what you should do is see to the boy's immediate needs—food to fill his belly and blankets to keep him warm. Then, Nan, when you can steal time away from the shop, perhaps you can whisper in the preacher's ear, making him aware of the child's plight. The preacher knows all the good families in town, and he is the perfect person to place the boy in a proper home."

Nan expression went bewildered. "Why haven't you whispered in the preacher's ear yourself? You've met him twice now on Sunday."

"Did you notice the way he looks at me?" Gabe challenged. In truth, the minister had been friendly enough and seemed to practice what he preached, accepting even a gunslinger into his church. "He's wary of me, too. I'm definitely not the best person to speak with him." Gabe could only hope that Michael and Gabriel were presently preoccupied with other concerns, possibly an old lady whose idea of heaven meant that it had to be brimming with cats. Otherwise, he was going to get caught. "You understand, I hope?"

"I didn't notice him looking oddly at you, Gabriel, and I know for a fact that he's a very caring man, but if you say he feels nervous of you, I can only take your word for it."

Gabe settled back in his chair, hugely relieved. Both the boy and dog would be saved, yet Gabe would be able to look the angels dead in the eye and honestly say he hadn't lifted a finger to help either one. He'd done some exaggerating—and tossed in a couple of whoppers—but he figured he could get away with that.

The little girl with a weak heart still presented a huge problem, and Gabe had no ideas up his sleeve yet as to how he might prevent her death without actually doing anything himself. But he'd think on it.

Nan pushed up from her chair. "We've work to do, little miss. We can clean our garbage pail and toss some food into it for the dog, but feeding the boy will take a bit more preparation." Moving toward the sink, Nan glanced from the window glass toward Gabe. "It's dark out. Isn't that staircase right beside the saloon and in front of . . . uh—" She broke off and lifted her brows at him. "I'm not sure it's safe for two females to go there at this time of night unescorted."

Gabe didn't want Laney or Nan going near the place alone even in broad daylight. They could encounter a drunk at almost any time of day. Most women in town crossed the street and walked on the other boardwalk while passing the brothel and drinking establishment. Maybe that was part of the reason the kid had received no help, because no one had seen him. *Yeah, right.* The boy left his hidey-hole to forage for food, and unless people were blind, they had seen him. The reason the good ladies of this town ignored the kid was because he was the child of a whore, and going near him might soil their fancy skirts. Or force them to face the unpleasant fact that an "unfortunate" had a booming business going upstairs. Were their husbands contributors to her income?

"I suggest that all three of us go," Gabe said. "At the staircase, Nan, Laney and I will stand well back so I don't scare the boy, but I'll still be close enough to step in if anyone bothers you. As for the dog, you and I can hold back while Laney goes inside the lean-to with food. Again, I'll be there if needed, but not close enough to alarm the poor mutt."

Nan nodded. "That sounds like a champion plan to me."

"If I were a hungry boy under a staircase, I'd want sandwiches," Laney announced. "They're easy to eat. No plate or flatware to bother with."

"Good idea, sweetness. Sandwiches it shall be. How many do you think he can eat, Gabriel?"

Gabe bit back a smile, wondering why it had taken him so long to come up with this idea. "Three should do it. If they're wrapped in paper or a towel, he can eat all he likes and save the rest for later. In the morning, I'm sure he'd welcome a couple of bacon-and-egg sandwiches, especially if you could get them to him warm."

"He'll need something to drink," Laney observed.

"Milk," Nan inserted. "We've a quart bottle with a cork that I can fill with a funnel." She glanced over her shoulder at Gabe. "While we prepare the food, can you get some quilts? You'll find them on the high right shelf of my workroom at the end of the hall. There's a worn one I've been thinking about tossing. We can use that one as a bed for the dog. The boy should have nicer ones. If they get stained, so be it. I can always make new ones if and when my stacks run low."

Twenty minutes later, Gabe walked with his ladies, who were bundled up against the cold, to watch while the boy received food and bedding. *I'm not lifting a hand*, he assured himself, hoping one of the angels was listening. Then he quickly scratched that wish. He'd be better off if Gabriel and Michael were perching cats on clouds and their spies were watching someone else. He wasn't physically doing anything himself, but he'd sure connived to set things in motion.

Standing back with Laney, Gabe couldn't clearly see how the boy reacted to Nan, but when she emerged from under the stairwell and reached him, he saw that she was smiling tremulously and had tears in her eyes. For the second time in the space of an evening, Gabe realized how easily he could fall head over boot heels in love with her.

"He's got plenty of quilts now to keep him warm and comfortable," she said brightly. "And he's gobbling sandwiches so fast I'm afraid he'll make himself sick."

"Was he scared of you?" Laney asked, saving Gabe the trouble.

"After exhibiting an initial bit of fright, he quickly got over it," Nan answered. "I think the food distracted him from worrying overmuch about the delivery person's possible intent."

Gabe felt as if the weight of the world had been lifted from his chest. "He'll be starving again come morning," he observed.

"No, he won't. This delivery lady has every intention of taking him a huge, hot-from-the-stove breakfast. And I will carve out time tomorrow to pay a call on our minister to let him know there's a boy who needs placement in a good home."

"You can sweeten the deal by telling the preacher that the generous family will receive a tidy amount of money each month to offset the cost of feeding and clothing an extra child."

Nan smiled up at him. "Are you truly willing to do that for him, on a monthly basis without fail?"

"Sure."

Fortunately Gabe knew that Nan would see to it after he died. She would then have a bank account balance nearly as big as her kind and gentle heart.

He felt at peace as he escorted the two females to Lizzy's. He handed Laney the quilt he'd been carrying under one arm. Nan, apparently chilled, leaned against Gabe's side as they watched the girl scurry across the café's back dooryard to the lean-to. Even through the darkness, Gabe saw the painfully thin yellow dog struggle to his feet, beside himself with happiness to have a visitor. Laney set aside the bucket and went down on her knees to hug the animal's neck. *Not good.* Gabe had a bad feeling it might be love at first lick. Soon the dog was devouring the offerings. Laney stayed there until the food was gone to collect the pail.

"I think I need a new trash bucket," Nan observed. "That one is going to be in constant use."

Gabe was happy to agree that she was probably right.

During the short walk home, he congratulated himself on outwitting the angels. He'd followed their rules, almost. Surely *almost* would be counted as good enough, even up there.

Gabe was too happy to worry about it overmuch tonight. He took it as a very good sign that he hadn't heard the angel Gabriel's admonishing voice boom in his ear.

Now Gabe had only to dream up some way to prevent that little girl from going to the doctor next week. That was going to be a tough one, he knew.

But, dammit, he had to think of something.

Chapter Thirteen

After that night of helping the boy and dog, Gabe yearned to do more, so very much more. He kept reminding himself that he could not keep intervening, that he needed to stay focused on his immediate circle, but, damn, it was hard. There were so many things he could have prevented from happening with the fore-knowledge he had—the death of a dog that ran between two quarreling drunks and got shot, the nasty fall of a toddler on the boardwalk that resulted in badly scraped knees, and the financial ruin of a young man at the poker tables who bet all he owned on a supposedly unbeatable poker hand. The list of things Gabe could stop from happening was endless inside his mind.

He tried to concentrate on his singular reason for being here: saving Nan. She was why he had been given this second chance. He couldn't forget that even for an instant. No one else mattered.

In the beginning, Gabe had been so grateful to be given another chance, but as Christmas approached, he was filled with heartache. Ah, yes . . . he had succeeded in accomplishing nearly all of his assignments. Today he had finally received the Pinkerton report in the mail, which documented that Horace Barclay had survived being impaled by Nan's knitting needle. When the moment was right, Gabe would hand Nan the paperwork.

She would no longer have to live in dread of the murder charge that she now believed hung over her head. She'd still have to be cautious about how much she revealed about her past if she forged friendships, of course. To protect Laney, she would have to remain in hiding until the child reached her majority. Martin Sullivan was the girl's legal guardian, and if the man got wind of Nan's whereabouts, he'd waste no time in coming to Random to collect his younger daughter.

Gabe worried about what would become of his ladies after he died the second time, but one concern he didn't have was that Nan would be careless and reveal her location. She'd managed to keep her head down for eight years, and she would continue to do that. With all the money Gabe was leaving her, she and Laney could remain in Random, a tiny town lost in the wilds of Colorado, and live in high cotton for the rest of their lives.

Gabe tried—*really* tried—to be satisfied with the good he had accomplished. The dog was putting on weight, and the boy, though not yet placed in a caring home, was warm and had a full belly. But thoughts of the little girl with the weak heart haunted him. He attempted to keep a smile on his face, but apparently he was no loss to the stage, because Nan picked up on his gloomy mood.

One evening as they worked together to prepare supper, she suddenly reached out and clasped Gabe's wrist, stopping him from opening a cupboard door. "Gabriel, what's troubling you?" she asked softly.

Gabe avoided meeting her silvery gaze. Sometime over the last couple of weeks, he'd started to feel as if Nan could see clear to his soul, and he figured his soul was probably a pretty dark place right now. Using his greater strength, he broke Nan's grip by grabbing the cupboard knob. "What makes you think something's troubling me?" He took a serving bowl from the shelf.

"I've got nothing on my mind but the hunger in my belly. Pretty soon it'll be growling so loud, you'll think a wild beast is hiding behind me."

Nan left off trying to make him look at her, but when she spoke from behind him as he tried to walk away, her words jerked his feet to a stop as surely as if they were invisible strings knotted around his ankles. "You don't laugh anymore."

Gabe kept his back to her and briefly closed his eyes. Laughter, his gift to her, and now he'd become the killjoy. "I'm sorry." He moved over to the stove to empty a hot pan of peas into the bowl, wishing Laney would emerge from her room to interrupt this exchange. She'd come home from school feeling tired and was taking a before-supper nap. "I didn't realize I haven't been laughing. It's nothing to do with you, honey. I guess we all have a gloomy side, and now you're glimpsing mine, I reckon."

"Are you—" She broke off and made fists in her pretty white apron, which she'd embroidered with roses and curlicues of green. "From the start, I feared that you'd grow bored with all this domesticity. Is that the problem, that you're yearning to be out on the trail again?"

Gabe almost groaned. He'd hated his former life, camping along streams or laying over in strange towns, never daring to linger for long and always waiting for a slug to nail him in the back. This brief time in Nan's world . . . Well, these had been his best days ever. He'd gotten to experience life in a real home. He'd even been able to pretend sometimes that Nan was his wife and Laney his very own child, giving him an addictive taste of family. If he'd had his druthers, he would have stayed here in Random forever. Maybe build a real house at the edge of town with enough land around it to keep horses and a few farm animals, plus grow some crops. Hell, maybe he'd even raise chickens. While Nan made hats, he could try his damnedest to produce hens that laid better eggs than Ellen Hamm's.

"I'm not hankering for the trail, Nan. You don't have to worry that you'll wake up tomorrow morning and find me gone." He laughed at the thought, the sound wistful. "As if you'd care if I suddenly disappeared. If you could, I think you'd sweep me out the shop door with all the street dust your customers track in."

"No, I wouldn't. I've come to think very highly of you, Gabriel. You're . . . my friend."

Gabe searched her gaze and knew, finally, that she wouldn't send him packing if he told her Horace Barclay was alive and well. He wished for more than mere friendship with her, but he had to settle for whatever she offered him. "Nan, there's something really important that I've been wanting to tell you."

"What?"

"About Horace Barclay and that mur—"

"Mama?" Laney called hoarsely as she stumbled sleepily from her room toward the kitchen. "I don't feel well."

Distracted, Nan met the child in the archway, felt her forehead, and said, "Oh, lands, you're burning up!" She sent Gabe a frightened look. "I mean it; she's on fire. We need to tonic her up and try to get this fever down."

Frustrated by the interruption, Gabe stepped over to place a hand on the girl's forehead. Nan was right: Laney had a very high fever. Just then, the girl coughed, and Gabe heard a slight rattle in her chest. Nan went as white as her apron.

"She's had pneumonia once before." She directed an imploring look at Gabe. "Do you think—"

"I don't hold much with tonic," Gabe inserted. "Peddlers mix it in their wagons half the time, using measures of rotgut whiskey, honey, and God only knows what else. For all we know, they could spit tobacco juice in for good measure. Then they swear it'll cure near anything. The truth is, people feel a little better right after taking it because they're a bit drunk."

Nan teetered on the edge of panic. Gabe saw it in her face. "Get her back to bed, honey. When she's settled, fill the washbasin with cool water, strip off her clothes, and bathe her with wet cloths. She'll get the shudders and beg you to stop, but don't. And when she tries to hug the covers, don't let her."

Gabe stepped over to the wall hook where he'd taken to hanging his Stetson. As he settled the hat on his head, Nan, holding a slumped Laney to her side, cried, "Don't leave us, Gabriel! I'm not strong enough to bathe her if she goes out of her head with the fever and fights me."

Instilling into his voice a calmness he didn't quite feel, Gabe said, "I'm only stepping out briefly to fetch Doc Peterson. I'll be back in two shakes. Then I'll help, if I'm needed."

Laney leaned more heavily against Nan. "My heart hurts, Mama, like a knife is poking into me. I can't barely breathe."

When the child used incorrect English, Gabe knew how very sick she truly was. *Pneumonia, sure as hell.*

Gabe collected the physician in short order. Doc Peterson, the same man whose gaze Gabe had met in the saloon mirrors on that Christmas morning right before he'd been shot, took a listen to Laney's chest and pronounced, "It could turn on us and become pneumonia, but for now, I don't think she's there yet. Just very congested."

"I nearly lost her to pneumonia the last time," Nan said softly, her voice twanging with hysteria. "What if she has a tendency toward it?"

Doc patted Nan's arm and got up from the bed. "She's older now, Mrs. Valance, a healthy young lady with a strong constitution. This stuff is nasty, and I can't promise it won't turn into pneumonia, but let's not start draping black over the windows just yet." His prominent Adam's apple bobbed as he spoke. Gabe noticed that his thin gray hair spiked straight up atop his bony head, a sure sign that he'd been raking his fingers through it, possibly with hopelessness. His gray suit, the same one he'd worn last time, looked as if he'd been sleeping in it for days. He opened his black bag and started fishing around in the cluttered depths. "I've seen some patients tonight who may not be so lucky, but I'm not too worried about this little gal. Do like your husband told you. Keep the fever at bay with cool baths." He set a brown bottle on the small table. "This tonic will help her to rest. Dose her with two tablespoonsful every four hours."

"It wasn't mixed by a peddler, I hope," Nan said shakily.

Doc chuckled. "No, ma'am, I don't deal in snake-oil cures. I order this tonic in from Frisco. There's some laudanum in it, what we doctors call tincture of opium. Strong stuff, so don't overdose her. It's mainly to help her sleep while her body fights this off."

Gabe knew Laney wasn't going to die. For one, he hadn't heard rumors of her death the last time he'd lived through this month. He'd also seen Nan at a bough-draped shop window on Christmas morning. She never would have decorated for the holiday if her little sister had just passed on.

He escorted the exhausted physician downstairs to see him out. As they crossed the shadowy shop, Gabe said, "This illness—it's sweeping clear through town, isn't it?" The last time Gabe had lived through this month, he'd heard people in the hotel restaurant speaking of the awful contagion that others were catching right and left. It was the same affliction that would kill the little girl with the weak heart on Christmas Eve. "It started with Simon White about three weeks back."

Doc nodded. "Simon went to Denver on business. I don't know if he caught it in the city or while he was traveling, but it took him down." Lifting an eyebrow, the physician smiled wearily as they moved through the shadowy shop. "Call me crazy if you like, but I've been practicing medicine for a long time, and though I've got no proof, I believe contagious illness is passed from person to person, possibly by touch or through the air when stricken people cough."

Gabe had done some reading but didn't count himself an expert. "So you don't hold with the miasma theory?"

"I don't discount it, but I don't ignore what I've seen with my own eyes, either. Close contact—hell, just being in the same room a sick person recently left—can make you sick, too." The doctor shrugged. "I've seen it happen. It's happened to *me*. I've started washing my hands before and after I treat a patient, and my wife, who assists me, frequently sterilizes all the surfaces in my treatment room. I don't get ill nearly as much now, and neither does she. I highly recommend that you and your wife wash your hands often while you're caring for Laney."

Gabe was a firm believer that experience was a great teacher, so he thought the physician could be right. And deep in his heart, Gabe was convinced that the little girl destined to die on Christmas Eve could be saved if he could prevent her from entering that office where so many sick people would be waiting for treatment. "You won't hear any argument from me, Doc. If illness travels in a cloud of bad air from one community to another, why do I never get sick out on the trail?

I remember once—the name of the place escapes me now—when a stage full of ailing people pulled in and stayed over until everyone was well enough to travel again. The sickness spread all over town."

Doc nodded. "I've seen similar incidents. A sick cowpoke rides in to have a drink, and before I know it, my waiting room is brimming with people who have the same illness. Before Simon realized he was getting sick, he made contact with a lot of people. He's a shaker of hands and a cheek busser, as much a politician as he is a banker. Now a good third of the population has taken ill. I caution people to stay home if they can and to wash their hands often if they are around others, but very few listen."

"That's too bad." Gabe's thoughts drifted to the little girl again. "Whatever this is, it's really nasty."

"Yes. It's hitting the little ones and the elderly the hardest. I lost Mrs. Barker tonight. She was the old lady who originally opened this shop. I didn't mention it in front of your wife for fear of upsetting her even more." At the door, Peterson stopped to look up at Gabe. "I did all I could. It was her time to go, I guess." He shifted his bag to his left palm and mimed shaking hands with Gabe. "No point in touching. I've been handling the sick all day, most recently that girl upstairs. Don't know for sure if it helps, but I try not to pass any contamination around. It's been a pleasure meeting you. I can finally size you up on something besides rumor."

"Rumor?" Gabe echoed.

Peterson chuckled. "That the gunslinger in town isn't really such a bad fellow once you get to know him. I don't put much stock in gossip normally, but I'm pleased to learn that it rings with truth this time. That fine lady upstairs deserves to have a good man."

Gabe locked up after the doctor, then leaned his forehead against the cool glass above the Closed sign.

Her time to go. He felt as if he'd chewed up a razor and swallowed the chunks, wooden handle and all. Knifelike pains pricked his innards. That sweet little girl would go into Doc's waiting room next Tuesday, and she'd be afflicted with the same illness that Laney fought off right now. And Gabe wasn't supposed to do anything.

After helping Nan nurse Laney—holding the girl still while Nan bathed her, hauling in boiling-hot pots of water to set them under a sheet canopy to create steam, and grasping the girl's thrashing head between his hands while Nan dosed her with the tonic—Gabe prepared food for the boy and dog. Laney was sleeping now, albeit fitfully. Nan was resting in the rocker that Gabe had moved from the sitting room into the bedchamber.

In short, there was no one but Gabe to play food deliverer tonight. He formed a sack with one of Nan's kitchen towels to hold the boy's sandwiches and milk bottle, filled the pail with scraps for the dog, and retraced his steps downstairs. Outside Nan's shop, he stood motionless for a moment, wondering how in the hell he could do this and get away with it. He could only hope that angels had lousy night vision. And what were the chances of that?

Gabe stopped several yards from the whorehouse staircase and softly called, "There's food and milk in a satchel out here on this boardwalk. I wonder who in the world left it here."

Before the boy could slip out from his hiding place to fetch the food, Gabe had turned heel and was walking away, swinging the pail of dog scraps at his side with every other step. No personal contact, no forbidden act of intervention. *Nope.* He was just dropping off nourishment, helter-skelter, and if a hungry boy and dog ran out to eat, it wasn't any of his doing.

Gabe whistled the tune to "Yankee Doodle" as he approached Lizzy's Café, which was now closed down for the night. Circling the side of the building and stopping just short of the backyard, he set down the pail and slightly changed the cadence of his whistle, two sharp tweets that most dogs recognized as a "come here" signal. Never missing stride, Gabe loped toward the opposite side of the street, gained the boardwalk, and leaned against the barber's pole to strike a match and have himself a leisurely smoke. *Every man needs to escape sometimes*, he told himself, *and enjoy a cigarette.* There was no crime in that. If some stray dog devoured the contents of a bucket he'd left unattended, it wasn't his fault.

Though the moon had ducked behind the clouds, the mongrel, golden fur brushed to a fare-thee-well by Laney yesterday, was easy to spot as it came out from behind the café to wolf down the pail's contents. Gabe gazed off up the street, casually blowing smoke rings. *Do I see a dog? Hell, no, I don't see a dog. It's dark as smut out here.*

When the dog slipped away to its lean-to, Gabe stamped out his smoke and crossed the street to collect the bucket.

Striding off the distance, he returned to the shop in record time. He was slightly breathless after stepping inside and leaned against the closed door to recover. His skin itched as if he'd raced through a mile-long patch of poison ivy. His scalp had gone clammy beneath his hat. Deep down, he knew that his celestial watchdogs saw almost everything, and they'd probably seen him as well.

"Play me out a little rope, Gabriel," he whispered, then paused to listen. *Nothing.* "For a bothersome angel who scared the shit out of me on purpose a couple of times, you sure know how to keep quiet when it suits you."

It was all Gabe could think of to plead his case. If he got punished for what he'd done, he guessed he had it coming. At least he'd be able to sleep tonight, knowing the boy and dog had been fed.

Well before daylight, Gabe once again delivered food, using the cloak of darkness to conceal his activities. By dawn, Laney's fever had broken, and about ten the next morning, she hacked up what looked like a quarter cup of green glue. Gabe rinsed out towels while Nan held the child's head. By noon the crackling sound in the girl's chest had lessened to a slight wheeze when she breathed, prompting Gabe to announce, "We've seen the worst of it now."

Nan, pale from lack of sleep and worry, smiled wearily. "I hope you're right."

"Of course I'm right."

By six that evening, Laney was clamoring for something to eat. No, she didn't want *broth*. She was hungry and wanted real food. Nan conceded by making her finger-size slices of toasted bread, which Laney dunked in the *dratted* beef bouillon. Gabe wished he could laugh at the youngster's shrewish behavior as she started to rally. But his chest felt as if he'd swallowed one of his boots and gotten it caught crosswise in his windpipe. Not all little girls in Random had Laney's sturdy constitution, and Gabe knew for sure that one of them was going to cock up her toes unless he did something.

Even as he stole through the night again later to take food to the boy and dog, Gabe couldn't shake the dark gloom that had settled over him. He could only be thankful that Nan sought their bed early, so tuckered out from caring for Laney that she couldn't stay awake once the danger had passed.

When Gabe joined her, sleep eluded him. He tried counting sheep. When that didn't work, he came so close to reaching for Nan that he had to ball his hands into fists and clench his teeth to resist the urge. Oh, how he wanted her. He imagined how sweet she'd feel in his arms, how the silky, gentle warmth of her bare skin would mold against his. How damned good it would be to bury himself deep inside her moistness and forget everything for a while.

He was still imagining the glory of it when he finally fell asleep.

By the weekend, Laney was well on her way to recovery. In the interim, Gabe tried several times to broach the subject of the Pinkerton report with Nan, but when she wasn't racing about to care for Laney, she was nodding off in the rocker. On Saturday night, he sat at the end of a sleeping Laney's bed, rested his arms on his knees, and leaned slightly forward to catch Nan's gaze. Head bent, she intently studied a dress bodice to which she was affixing seed pearls.

"Honey, there's something I need to tell you," he said softly so as not to awaken the girl.

Nan lowered her sewing to her lap and smiled at him. "You don't look very happy about it."

"I'm delighted about it," Gabe assured her. "It's only that I feel bad about not telling you sooner." He swallowed, whether to clear his throat or gain time before speaking again, he wasn't sure. "Horace Barclay didn't die, Nan."

She stared at him with parted lips. *"What?"*

Gabe repeated himself.

"How can you possibly know that?"

"I hired a Pinkerton agent to investigate. Barclay is

not only alive and well, but he never even filed a report about the incident, probably because the whole situation embarrassed him and he feared that the truth might come out—namely that he assaulted you, not the other way around. How could he have explained being stabbed with a knitting needle?"

The chair creaked as she shifted her weight to lean forward slightly. "Are you certain he's alive? Manhattan is very far away, and the agent may be mistaken."

Now Gabe understood why he'd been told by the angel to get a detailed report. Until Nan saw it, her fears could never be completely allayed. He set her sewing on the foot of the bed and drew her up from the rocker. "Come downstairs with me."

Nan glanced at Laney. Gabe tugged on her hand. "She's fine. After a good night's rest, she'll be fit as a fiddle tomorrow."

Gabe had hidden the report on a top shelf in Nan's downstairs work area. When he withdrew the missive, she took it and sat at the table, staring at the writing on the envelope. "Pinkerton," she said softly. "It's a company of incomparable reputation. I didn't know they were based in Chicago."

"They run investigations all over the country." Gabe took a seat across from her. "Don't study the address all night. Look at the report."

Slender fingers trembling slightly, she lifted the envelope flap and drew out the document. Gabe settled back on his chair, watching her expressions as she read. She glanced up. "It's the correct Horace Barclay. I recognize the street they say he lives on, and the age is about right."

"Of course it's the right man, honey. Pinkerton doesn't hire imbeciles, and his men are very well trained."

Nan finished reading and closed her eyes. "Oh, my."

Her lashes fluttered up. "All this time, with me worrying myself sick about being arrested and also feeling guilty for killing him, he's been carrying on as if nothing ever happened. It says here that he remarried barely six months after I stabbed him."

"He stabbed himself," Gabe reminded her. "And God help the young woman he selected to take your place as his second wife. She's probably miserable."

"No 'probably' to it. He's an awful man." She searched Gabe's gaze. "You said you wished you'd told me sooner. When did you initiate this investigation?"

Gabe wished he could ignore that question. "The day of our marriage."

"Whatever prompted you? I never implied that Barclay might be alive—just the opposite, in fact. What made you suspect he survived?"

"Intuition." Gabe wasn't sure where that had come from, but he was glad the word had popped into his mind. "A huge man like Barclay is thickly layered with blubber, and a knitting needle isn't *that* long. To kill him, it had to have pierced a vital organ, and unless you took aim, which you said you didn't, there was a chance the needle hit nothing vital."

"But . . ." She studied him in bewilderment. "How did you know he was fat? I said he was huge, but I don't remember telling you that he's fat."

Oops. Gabe had never been good at telling half-truths. "You must have mentioned it." He shrugged and tugged on his earlobe. "What does it matter? I wanted to know for certain, one way or the other, so I wired Chicago, transferred funds to cover the costs, and then waited for the report. It came in the mail last week, just before Laney got sick. I tried to tell you about it that night in the kitchen, but I got interrupted when she woke up with a fever, and we haven't had any chance to talk privately until now."

Nan passed a hand over her eyes. "I can't believe it. He's alive. All this time I've been so afraid, and now I learn there was no reason to hide." She smiled. "Gabriel, have you any idea what this means? I'm not a fugitive!"

He could almost see the weight of guilt lifting from her shoulders. That alone made him glad that the angels had sent him here. Even so, he had to say, "No, you aren't a fugitive, but Laney's whereabouts still can't be revealed."

Nan's smile dimmed. "True. If our father learns where she is, he'll come for her immediately." She sighed and settled her gaze on the document again. "I'll have to remain in hiding until she comes of age. Even so, knowing I didn't kill Barclay . . . Well, words cannot describe how I feel! It's terrible to believe you've ended a man's life." Her eyes went sparkly. "Thank you so much, Gabriel, not only for believing me when I said he fell on the needle, but also for hiring an agent to investigate. I might have gone to my grave believing that I'd killed him."

She sprang up from the chair and spun in a circle, her skirts billowing around her legs. Lifting her arms, she cried, "I feel *free*, like a bird just released from its cage."

Gabe understood exactly what she meant and shared her feeling of release. Allowing Nan to go on believing that she'd killed Barclay had bothered him deeply. Now, if he could only think of a way to save that little girl, he'd die a happy man.

By Sunday afternoon, Laney was pestering Nan unmercifully to be allowed to visit the dog. Nan, fearful that the cold air would give the girl a setback, kept saying no.

"I'll wear two capes and my heavy wool gloves!"

Laney argued. "I'm fine now, Mama. You already said I can return to school tomorrow and sleep over at Melody's after the Christmas sing-along tomorrow night! What difference can one day make?"

Nan felt that giving Laney permission to attend the party tomorrow, plus stay the night so soon after being sick, was already a huge concession on her part, and she quickly grew cross with the girl for asking repeatedly to visit the dog. She was about to get stern and tell the child that she would countenance no more arguing when Gabriel intervened.

"How's about if she wears a muffler and keeps her face covered?" he suggested. "You're mostly worried about her breathing the cold air. A thick muffler would take care of that. She does have one, doesn't she?"

"Yes!" Laney cried. "Mama knitted me an extra heavy one. After the snows come, I wear it every day to school and back!"

Stirring the contents of a pot on the stove, Nan let go of the spoon and threw up her hands. "Oh, all right!" she cried. "But mind that you keep that muffler over your face every single second, and—"

Laney was already racing for her room. "I will!" she promised over her shoulder.

Nan gave Gabriel, who sat hunched over a periodical she felt certain he hadn't been reading, an admonishing frown. "You've been as quiet as a Methodist at a Baptist revival all day, and you choose now to get chatty?"

Normally he would have smiled and winked at her, but this afternoon, his expression remained somber. Nan, still feeling joyous over the Pinkerton report, felt irked because he didn't seem to share her elation. He sat back on the chair, rocking it onto its two rear legs. "I'm sorry, but it's clear to me that she's fine as a frog's hair. If she wears the muffler, she'll be safe."

Laney raced back out of her room, wrapping the length of knitted yarn around her neck without missing a step. She grabbed the food pail, hit the door, slammed from the apartment, and, judging by the sound of her footfalls, descended the stairs at a dangerous speed, banging the bucket against the wall all the way down.

"I hope you're right," Nan said.

"She doesn't die," he replied. "So stop coddling her."

Nan turned slightly from the stove, bewildered by the way he'd worded that pronouncement. She *doesn't* die. It was as if he were referring to a character in a story he was telling her about. "What does that mean, 'She doesn't die'?"

He shoved so quickly to his feet that the chair teetered before it landed on all four legs with a loud *thunk*. "I just misspoke. What's the matter with you today? You're picking at every little thing." He wheeled toward the archway. "Let the child be a child. She'll grow up way too fast as it is."

"And where are you off to?" Nan asked, her voice laced with irritation because his criticism had hurt her feelings.

"I'm taking a short nap. Maybe you'll be in a happier mood when I come back out."

The way Nan saw it, she wasn't the one in need of a mood change. Normally Gabriel laughed, cracked jokes, and made light of things. He also usually helped her fix dinner, but he hadn't the last few nights. Nan had laid that off on the fact that he'd been stuck with the duty of delivering food to the boy and dog morning and night, but deep down, she knew she was only making excuses. Something was troubling Gabriel, and he was in grim spirits because of it. Now that he'd shown her the Pinkerton report, that couldn't be what ate at him.

Concerned, Nan set the pot on the warming shelf so the contents wouldn't scorch, and followed her husband to the bedroom. Whatever was wrong, she sensed it was serious. It wasn't in Gabriel's nature to get in a black mood over anything trivial.

She found him sitting on his side of the bed, his elbows braced on his knees, his head in his hands. The dejected slump of his strong, broad shoulders made her heart pang. She closed the door softly behind her and then went to sit beside him.

She chose to say nothing for a moment, giving him the opportunity to shoo her away if he didn't want her there. When no rejection occurred, she said, "Something is troubling you, Gabriel, and has been for days. Won't you please tell me about it? A problem shared is often a problem solved."

"The problem isn't one I can solve, Nan, or you either."

Studying the side of his dark face, every line of which had been etched upon her heart, Nan saw him grimace, as if he wished he might call back the words. Then he straightened and released a long breath.

"It's just that a lot of people have gotten sick, and more people are bound to come down ill over the next week." He slanted her a quick glance but failed to meet her gaze. She was reminded of how often he'd said during games of poker that a woman should never believe a man who wouldn't look her dead in the eye. "We were so lucky with Laney. She's strong, and getting sick was barely a hitch in her get-along. But not everyone has been or will be that fortunate."

Nan had learned of Mrs. Barker's death, and despite the fabulous news Gabriel had given her last night about Barclay being alive, she'd spent the morning engaged in a battle with tears. She'd loved that old lady, and accepting her death hadn't been easy. Now Nan kept Mrs. Barker and the family in her prayers, hoping that her dear friend was in a better place and that her loved ones would recover quickly from their grief.

"And that's what is troubling you?" she asked, strongly suspecting that Gabriel was circling the truth. "Contagions strike towns all the time, sometimes taking lives, sometimes not. We can only hope we don't get sick ourselves and pray for our friends and neighbors. There's little else to be done. Getting in a dark mood surely won't help."

"What if you could do more?" He swung around to look at her, and the intensity in his dark eyes made her nape prickle. "If you knew how to save someone else from dying, but in the doing, you knew you'd catch this ailment and die yourself, would you risk your own life to save that person?"

Nan took a moment to mull that over. "Gabriel, why torture yourself this way? If not even Doc Peterson, with all his knowledge and tonics, can save those with weak constitutions, you and I surely can't. It's a purely hypothetical question you've asked me."

"Well, hypothesize, then! If you had the cure for this and could save someone, but you knew—if you were absolutely convinced—that going into the person's home would end up killing you, would you go anyway?"

His expression was so tortured that Nan yearned to cup her hand to his lean cheek, or pull him into her arms as she often did Laney. But tension rolled off him in waves, and she knew any sympathetic overture from her would be unwelcome.

"If I had a cure I'd go in a heartbeat, and then, after leaving the house, I'd have a dose myself."

He stared at her for an endlessly long moment. "Sweet Christ, the way your mind works could drive a man mad. What if you had only enough cure for that one person, Nan, and if you went to administer it, you knew you were going to die? Is that defined enough for your linear-thinking brain?" The moment he finished speaking, he closed his eyes and held up his hand. "I'm sorry. I shouldn't have said that." His lashes fluttered back up. "I admire your mind, and your thinking patterns don't really irk me. It's just that I need you to answer the question, and you're dancing around it."

Nan could tell that he truly did need her to answer him. She simply couldn't understand why. There was no cure for this illness, and even the town doctor was at his wit's end. That said, she thought carefully, trying to imagine herself in the situation Gabriel had just described.

"To protect myself from the miasma, I suppose that I would cover my face with a cloth soaked in camphor and go to save the person's life."

"Even if you knew the camphor wouldn't work and you'd die?"

Nan lifted her shoulders high and held them rigid. "It's a very difficult question, isn't it?"

"You're telling me."

Nan gave herself a little body shake. "I don't know why you're torturing yourself with what-ifs that can never possibly happen, but hypothetically, it is a commonly held belief that all decent, God-fearing human beings would, under certain circumstances, sacrifice their own lives to save another's."

He sighed, tipped his head back, and closed his eyes. Nan stared at the muscular column of his arched throat, fascinated by the bob of his large Adam's apple as he swallowed. "I was afraid you'd say that."

Nan stifled an urge to laugh, wondering even as she did how they had come to switch roles. She was supposed to be the serious one who worried about silly things. She rested a comforting hand on his arm, her fingertips immediately feeling the heat of his skin through his shirtsleeve. "I did say 'hypothetically.' It would take an incredible amount of courage to die in order to save someone else, Gabriel. While we all like to believe that we possess that kind of courage, the reality is that most of us do not."

He lowered his chin to search her face. "People commit heroic acts all the time."

Nan allowed herself to smile again—only slightly, so he wouldn't think she was laughing at him. "Yes, but do they have an opportunity to consider the consequences first?"

His mouth tipped into a mere shadow of the wide, slightly crooked grin that she'd come to enjoy so much. "In other words, you hold with the belief that most of us have a yellow streak and wouldn't sacrifice our own lives to save someone else if we had so much as a second to think about it first."

Nan nodded. "It's sad, isn't it? But I think the only man who possessed that kind of courage died on a cross nearly two thousand years ago. The rest of us are sorry excuses compared to him."

He blinked and raked his fingers through his black hair, which had been longish when she met him and was now in desperate need of a trim. "Thank you," he told her. "I really needed to hear that." He winked at her. "Sometimes I get to thinking I'm the only coward in a whole world of heroes."

"You, Gabriel Valance, are no coward," Nan informed him, inserting a stern tone of absolute certainty into her voice. "You've faced death fourteen times without even getting the shakes. If someone aimed a gun at me, I'd be so scared I'd fall to my knees on the spot, begging for my life." Remembering that supper was only half-finished, she stood. "As for a whole world of heroes?" She finally found the courage to cup her palm lightly over his hard jaw. "I've yet to meet one—unless, of course, I count you."

"Me?"

Nan drew her arm back. Her fingers tingled from touching him, and little zings darted up her arm. "You've had many men try to kill you, and you remain ever ready to defend yourself against the next one who tries."

"Defending myself is a natural human instinct."

"True, but a lot of men would live in constant fear. You don't. Instead you live in the moment and find things to laugh about. At least, you did until sometime last week."

He rotated his shoulders as if to work out the kinks. "You're right. I've been downright gloomy, haven't I? I'm sorry. I'll try to brighten up."

"Please do. I sorely miss your laughter." Nan went to the door, then paused with her hand on the knob to look back at him. "This whole conversation—it was hypothetical, was it not?"

He'd gotten up to follow her, and as he closed the distance, she admired the loose, masculine swing of his stride. "Purely hypothetical."

"So you're not thinking about dying in order to save someone else?"

He tweaked the tip of her nose. "No, honey, I'm not thinking about dying to save someone else."

Nan was relieved to note that he looked her dead in the eye as he said it.

The evening that followed was, in Nan's opinion, glorious. Gabriel jumped in to help finish making supper. He gave her lavish compliments on the food. Laughter rang out in her sunny yellow kitchen again. After cleaning up the cooking mess and washing the dishes, the two of them packed sandwiches for the boy. Laney, having already enjoyed one outing, was busy at the table, hurrying to complete her makeup work, which had been sent home to her by the teacher via a classmate.

"Don't dawdle," Gabe cautioned the girl. "If you're not finished when we get back, we'll play poker without you."

"No, sir! I'm nearly done."

A few seconds later, Nan took a deep breath of the crisp night air. "I can't believe you've been plopping that boy's food down on the boardwalk!"

"He's afraid of me, I told you. He didn't suddenly get over it simply because I was the only person who could bring him his meals."

While Gabriel paused some distance from the staircase, Nan went ahead without him. In the shadowy darkness beneath the steep plank steps, she could barely see the boy, but a picture of him had been imprinted in her mind, because she'd seen him of a morning. Aside from wearing rags, being filthy, and needing someone to shear off his long brown hair, he was a handsome child with beautiful blue eyes and nice features. So far, Nan hadn't been able to get him to talk much. He mostly said thank you and then grunted when she ventured questions. She'd yet to learn his name.

"It's Mrs. Valance with your supper," she said as she approached him.

"No need to say that every time. Who else do you think brings me food?"

The answer to that question was a torment to Nan's heart. How could people she knew and counted as decent pretend not to see this child? If she lived to be a hundred, she would never understand it. Most of her customers were good, generous women, yet not a single one had brought the boy as much as a slice of bread. Perhaps, Nan decided, it was more a case of the child's location than a lack of caring. Nan was unafraid to slip under the brothel staircase because she had Gabriel standing guard. Her female acquaintances might not have such gallant husbands.

"Well, here it is, then." Nan bent forward to plop the makeshift sack on his lap. "We had pan-fried pork tonight, and your sandwiches are still warm. I hope you enjoy them. And, of course, I brought you milk."

"Thanks," he said with an unappreciative grunt. "Where the hell have you been? The last few nights only that gunslinger has come. I don't like him one bit. I bet he'd just as soon shoot my ass off as look at me."

Nan guessed him to be about Laney's age, possibly a bit older. His language shocked her, but not quite so much as it might have before she'd met Gabriel, who had a colorful vocabulary himself at times. "In truth, it was that gunslinger who told me about you and encouraged me to bring you food. He is deeply concerned about you."

Even in the darkness, Nan saw the boy's head snap up. "Why does he care? I'm nobody to him."

Nan sighed inwardly. Preacher Hayes was going to have a hard go when it came to convincing this young sir to accept help. "Just like you, my husband was once a boy who lived under staircases and went hungry. No one ever brought him food. I guess he thinks someone should have, and he has no wish to see history repeat itself. It was despicable then, and if it happens now, it will still be despicable."

"You talk a lot," he informed her, "and use big words. Are you highfalutin or somethin'?"

Nan bit back a smile. In some strange way she couldn't define, this boy reminded her of Gabriel. "Let us just say that I was raised in a totally different environment than you. I don't intend to sound highfalutin. I make hats and dresses for a living. I have a daughter about your age."

"I've seen her."

This was the most the boy had ever said to her, and Nan hugged the realization close, hoping it meant he was starting to think of her as a friend.

"Too fancy for me," he said around a mouthful of food that slurred his words. "All them ruffles and such, with bows on her pigtails. She's a fussy little snot, I bet." He stopped chewing to peer through the darkness at Nan. "Like mother, like daughter."

Nan bristled but managed to guard her tongue. Instead of responding in kind, she said, "That fussy little snot could clean you out in a poker game, young sir. Don't judge a girl by her ruffles and bows lest others judge you just as quickly."

"I've already been judged, lady. My mama is a whore." He gave a bitter laugh. "I bet you don't even know what that means."

Nan's heart broke for him. Little wonder he reminded her of Gabriel. She could only hope he grew up to be as fine a man. "Yes, I do know what it means, and I think you have the makings to pull yourself up by your bootstraps and put all of this behind you if you get half a chance."

"I don't got any boots. Hell, lady, I don't even have shoes. I outgrew them until my toes poked out the ends and they squeezed my feet so hard they ached."

Nan couldn't see what covered his feet now, but she wondered if he'd stolen a sheet from someone's drying line and cut it into strips to create makeshift footwear like Gabriel once had. Now that she came to think of it, a sheet had gone missing from her own line a couple of weeks back. She'd believed some dog had dragged it off, but now she suspected the thief had been an angry, two-legged boy. If so, he was more than welcome.

"What size shoe do you wear?" she asked.

"How should I know? My mama bought me my last

pair from a peddler two years back. She never said what size, and even if she had, that'd be wrong now."

Nan felt saddened as she left the boy to his supper. When she reached Gabriel, she said, "He has no footwear. I think he may have stolen my good sheet off the line a couple of weeks ago. It went mysteriously missing."

"Smart boy." Gabriel grasped her arm. The touch of his hand radiated warmth through her cloak and set her skin to tingling again. "I know a lady with ten thousand dollars in the bank. Maybe she should get the kid some boots."

"I shall."

Nan couldn't resist the urge that overcame her to lean against him. It felt lovely and right when he released her elbow to curl a strong arm around her shoulders. Her reaction should have shocked her, but somehow, nothing about Gabriel or her feelings toward him could surprise her anymore. Now that she knew Barclay wasn't dead, the only thing she still had to hide was Laney's whereabouts. She knew in her heart that Gabriel would never put the girl's happiness at risk. Nan could get her marriage to this man annulled, if she wished. But an annulment was the last thing she wanted now. She'd fallen in love with him, and she didn't know what to do about it. So she rested more heavily into the circle of his embrace and enjoyed the undulating bump of his hip against her side as they walked.

"I have no idea what size shoe the boy wears," she found the presence of mind to say.

"Just guess and buy him three pairs. Redmond will take back the ones that don't fit."

"Champion idea!"

Nan regretted their arrival at the shop door. Gabriel drew away to open it and ushered her inside.

Later, as they played poker with Laney, Nan couldn't concentrate on the game. Instead she studied his handsome, dark face, the graceful way his big hands moved as he shuffled and dealt cards, and how muscle played under his black shirt whenever he moved. Later, after they went to bed, Nan lay curled on her side, facing him. As always, he pillowed his head on his folded arms, closed his eyes, and drifted off to sleep before she could blink.

She yearned to reach out and touch his bare chest. Her fingertips ached to explore the mat of curly black hair and test the texture of his skin. An ache formed low in her belly, and she felt hot and wet between her legs. The lady in her wanted to pretend she had no idea what caused that, but Nan had long since left behind the innocence of girlhood, and the woman in her demanded honesty, at least with herself. She wanted—no, needed—him to hold her, to make love to her. She wasn't sure what that kind of intimacy entailed, but she trusted Gabriel, and the niggling fears at the edges of her mind weren't enough to dampen her desire.

The problem was, she had no idea how to tell him that.

Nan believed that Gabriel's dark mood had passed after their talk the night before, but on Monday, she noticed that his facial expressions were once again tense and grim. Before the morning was out, he'd left and then returned with a Christmas tree, which he had selected from Burke Redmond's boardwalk display. While Nan dealt with the occasional customer, Gabriel left and soon came back with a board from the building supply store at the south end of Main, which he quickly fashioned into a sturdy tree stand. He worked like a dervish, and she got the disturbing impression that he was trying to avoid thinking by keeping busy.

When he suddenly turned to her and asked, "If you could wish for anything you wanted for Christmas this year—I mean absolutely anything, no matter how outlandish—what would it be?"

Hoping to make him laugh, Nan quipped, "Roses, a huge bouquet."

When he didn't even smile, Nan laughed for him. "I'm funning with you, Gabriel. It's the dead of December. There isn't a rose in bloom within a thousand miles."

He finally relented and grinned, but she could tell his heart wasn't in it. "Not true. Haven't you ever heard of hothouses?"

"I grew up in Manhattan. Yes, I've even *seen* a few. But no such thing exists here in Random. People who grow vegetables in this climate have starts on their windowsills until sometime in June! And even then we can get a killing frost."

He rubbed the nape of his neck and went back to scowling. "Do you believe in Santa Claus?"

Nan sighed. "No, of course not. I don't think I ever did. In my childhood home, Saint Nick never got soot on his suit from our chimney, and our tree was only for show. I had packages under it every year, but only because guests over the holiday season would have thought it strange if I didn't. My father didn't believe in filling a child's head with nonsense about magical beings."

"Have you filled Laney's head with nonsense?"

Nan brushed dust away from a hat perched on a rack that she'd been neglecting of late. "I have. Santa always brings her something special."

Gabe studied her so intently that Nan stilled her fingers on a silk flower. "Will you promise me something?" he asked.

His tone made her heart catch. It was as if he were

telling her good-bye. "Anything," she said, throwing caution to the wind.

"On Christmas morning, no matter what happens, go out to the woodpile to see what Santa left for you."

The backs of Nan's eyes burned. "So you mean to surprise me with something, do you?" An ache crawled up from her chest to crowd her throat. "You're not planning to leave, I hope. I mean . . . you're so solemn. And you seem so sad. If you mean to go, Gabriel, please don't do so without at least bidding me farewell. I won't make it difficult for you. I promise. I'll only . . . wish you Godspeed."

He met and held her gaze. "I won't ever leave Random, Nan. You can count on that. Just don't forget to check that woodpile. It'd be a shame for a Santa gift to get covered with snow."

"Ah, so you predict we'll have a white Christmas?" Nan was shaking inside.

"I'll even go so far as to guarantee one."

Nan had to break eye contact. She hugged her waist and turned to survey the tree. "It's beautiful, Gabriel. You have a good eye for shape. It's a shame we can't decorate it tonight, but it should wait until tomorrow, when Laney will be home to help. It's her favorite part of Christmas."

"Well, then, we'll wait and have a decorating party!" he said, his voice jovial and yet oddly hollow. "I've never trimmed a tree. I'll probably muck it up good, and Laney will be fixing everything I do."

Gabriel vanished for the rest of the afternoon and returned just as Nan was about to conclude business for the day. With a somber nod of greeting to her, he went directly upstairs without a word. Nan might have followed him but for Laney's sudden arrival home from school. In a whirlwind of excitement about the party at

Melody's that evening, the girl packed her things for an overnight stay and left again so quickly that Nan could barely get a word in. As Laney raced from the shop with a stuffed satchel in one hand, Nan was in the process of telling her not to forget her toothbrush.

Her voice trailed away when the door slammed. Stepping over to turn the sign and close for the day, Nan watched her sister skip across the dirt thoroughfare with Melody, her blue skirt bouncing beneath the hem of her cape, her beribboned pigtails swirling like golden ropes around her shoulders. *Fussy little snot.* Nan smiled sadly at the memory. The boy saw in Laney all that he wished for himself—and would never have by accident of birth. Nan hoped that Preacher Hayes found a family for the child soon. He deserved to have a home and people who cared about him. She would pray that he'd be settled somewhere before Christmas.

Until last night, Nan had been thinking about going against Gabriel's advice and taking the kid in herself. She could turn her upstairs workroom into a bedroom for him. She no longer used it anymore, anyway. And in her opinion, Gabriel was the perfect candidate to take that bitter boy in hand. No matter how experienced some other man in town might be at fathering, he would never comprehend what that poor child had endured. Gabriel could, because he'd experienced it himself.

But, though Nan hated to admit it, Gabriel was right: The boy would be a handful, and she had to think of the effect his rebellious behavior would have on Laney. Not a good situation. Gabriel at least tried to mind his manners and curb his tongue.

Sighing, Nan went upstairs to start supper. Though Laney would eat at Melody's tonight, Nan still had two hungry fellows and a dog to feed. She expected to find Gabriel in the kitchen, either making fresh coffee or drinking the cold dregs from that morning. The man did love his coffee.

Nan frowned when her husband wasn't where she expected him to be. She stood just inside the closed door, listening for movement in the apartment and telling herself he might be in the water closet, but she heard nothing, not even the slight creak of a floor plank. Oh, no. She sincerely hoped he wasn't in the bedchamber, lost in morose thoughts again. She'd heard from a customer that the contagion had taken another life this morning—that of an elderly man at the east side of town. Nan had never made the gentleman's acquaintance, so though the news of his passing saddened her, she wasn't affected in a personal way. Gabriel, however, seemed to take every death to heart—as if he might somehow have stopped it from happening.

That was totally irrational, in Nan's opinion, and it disturbed her that Gabriel's usual practical nature had abandoned him. No one could save people from a contagion like this. It swept through a town, hitting here and there like a twister touching down, no rhyme or reason to it. Nan could only pray that no one else died and that she and her loved ones would be spared.

Her fear was realized when she quietly entered the bedroom. Gabriel sat on the far side of the bed, once again hunched over with his head in his hands, as if the weight of all the world's sorrows bore down on his shoulders. Nan couldn't understand why he was reacting this way to something he couldn't prevent. Perhaps it was because his mother had taken suddenly sick and died as a result. Gabriel might have horrible recollections of another contagion, and this one was dredging up all the old memories.

As she had last night, she went to sit beside him. When she glanced over, she saw that his whole body was taut with tension. The cuffs of his shirtsleeves, folded back from his wide wrists, were tight over the knotted muscles in his forearms. She rested a hand lightly on his shoulder.

He jerked and shifted away. "Don't. I'm not myself right now. Stay away from me."

"Gabriel, I don't under—"

"You don't need to understand," he nearly shouted. "What you need to do is listen to me and stay the hell away from me."

Nan froze with her hand inches from touching his shoulder again. A threat laced his tone, and she realized with a start that he was warning her that he might hurt her, which was stuff and nonsense. Nan wasn't sure when she'd come to trust Gabriel so completely; she only knew that she had.

"I'm not afraid of you, Gabriel. You'd never harm a hair on my head."

"Oh, yeah? Well, cozy up, honey, because right now I'm in sore need of something to drown my sorrows in—either whiskey or a woman, I don't really care which, and you're closer than the damned saloon."

Nan heard his words, but she still felt no fear. She didn't know what tormented him, but if he needed comfort, she was more than willing to give it. She laid her hand on his shoulder and pressed in with her fingertips. "Whatever is wrong, let me help you. Please?"

He turned so suddenly to clutch Nan in his arms that her breath hitched in her chest. The next thing she knew, his hot, hungry mouth slanted over hers. For an instant, she recoiled. His embrace vised around her like a crushing band of steel. He traced her teeth with his tongue. She couldn't get any air. This wasn't her Gabriel. Her Gabriel was gentle, never taking what wasn't offered, never even asking.

But he was asking now. Rigid, her breasts flattened against the hard planes of his chest, she made fists over his shirt, fully intending to struggle. Between one heartbeat and the next, though, she forgot why. That hot, melting sensation she'd experienced last night invaded her center again, making that secret place between her legs throb with every pulse beat and go wet. She could have sworn lightning threads were ribboning from the sky to lick at her skin. Gabriel released her only to catch her head between his hands.

"Oh, Jesus," he muttered as he pillaged her mouth, tasting and suckling as a starving man might sweet nectar. Between thrusts with his tongue, he said hoarsely, "Don't . . . say . . . no. Please . . . don't . . . say . . . no."

Nan couldn't have spoken if she tried, and she didn't wish to try. Gabriel. Oh, how she'd come to love him—and yearn for him, for this. She wouldn't have refused him for all the tea in China.

Chapter Fourteen

Nan was like a fire in Gabe's blood, and his helplessness to save the life of a little girl fanned the flames. He wanted to tear off Nan's clothing, shed his own, and lose himself in her, not only once, but again and again, letting himself become so dizzy with desire and passion that he wouldn't be able to think.

But, oh, God, she was so incredibly sweet, a precious package that should be carefully unwrapped so as not to damage the ribbons and pretty paper. Though need slammed through him in urgent waves, more intense than he'd felt with any other woman, he tried to gentle his kisses and his touch, nibbling hungrily but persuasively at her lips to teach her the primal dance of tongues that would fan the embers of her ardor, so long banked and buried. He stretched out with her on the coverlet, canopying her slender body with his own, his weight resting on one arm and hip. Feathering light kisses along the curve of her cheek, he found the sensitive hollow under her shell-like ear and traced teasing circles there with his tongue. He had imagined doing this so many times that it seemed as if he'd done it before, only nothing he'd conjured in his mind could compare to the reality. Lavender and silken skin. Tendrils of golden hair that wisped against his jaw like bits of goose down, so soft, so fine, so absolutely feminine.

When she moaned and arched her body against him, he nearly lost control.

But this was *Nan*, not some woman he'd hired to satisfy his physical needs. Nan, whose laughter had been a prize hard won, whose trust was a priceless gift, and whose innocence humbled him. She caught his face between her slender hands and angled her head to settle her mouth over his, flicking shyly at his lips with the tip of her tongue. Need knotted in his groin, the ache spreading upward. His manhood throbbed and pushed against the fly of his jeans.

In between kisses, she whispered, "I love you, Gabriel. I love you so very *much*." She sighed into his mouth, her breath honey sweet. "I shall thank God every day for the rest of my life for bringing you to me."

"I love you, too," he whispered back, his voice thick with desire. "Oh, God, sweetheart, I love you, too."

As Gabe uttered the words, they slithered through his mind like venomous snakes, sinking their fangs into his conscience and releasing their poison. He froze above her, his breath coming in tortured, ragged gasps. He loved her. This wasn't mere fondness that he felt. He'd fallen completely and irrevocably in love with this gentle, wonderful woman, and now he was about to betray her trust by taking the gift of her body when a monstrous lie and a web of deceit hung between them.

He jerked away from her, filled with self-loathing. She *wouldn't* thank God every day for the rest of her life. On Friday at dawn, he was going to die and leave her, and there was nothing, absolutely *nothing* within his power to change that. He could hold her and cherish her and protect her for only three more days.

Gabe sprang from the bed, caught his balance, and stared at her, his aching lungs grabbing for breaths that couldn't breach the clench of his throat. Nan stirred and blinked up at him in bewilderment.

"Gabriel?" She stretched a hand toward him. "What is it? Come back to me. Whatever I did, I—I'll not d-do it again."

"It's not you," he rasped, thrusting his hands into his hair and making hard fists, glad of the pain, because he hoped it would clear his head. His throat felt as if it were being vised by a hangman's noose. "I . . . can't . . . do . . . this," he squeezed out. And then, as if driven by a demon within him, he threw back his head and screamed the words. "I can't do this, damn you!" He heard Nan's frightened gasp and saw her recoil as words boiled past his lips. "I *won't* do this! It's a bargain with the devil I've made! Do you hear me! I'm done with it!"

A jolt shot through Nan's body as Gabriel left the room and slammed the door behind him. The portal hit its frame with such force the walls vibrated. She heard his feet pounding down the stairs. Breathing fast, her body still thrumming with yearning, she sat up slowly, so astounded—no, *stunned*—that her brain felt frozen. Then the reality of the situation slowly sank in. She'd just offered herself to the man she loved, and he'd turned her down flat.

Nan didn't cry. The pain that lacerated her chest ran so deep it made her bones ache. *Gabriel.* She hugged her arms around her waist and slowly started to rock, so tortured with myriad emotions—pain, bewilderment, and a sick sense of rejection—that she wanted to scream, but she had no voice. The silence of the room, broken only by the incessant ticking of the alarm clock, pounded against her ears. Her eyes remained dry, burning in their sockets like smoldering coals. Love, she realized, wasn't always a priceless gift; sometimes it was a person's worst agony.

Gabe went to the livery, threw a saddle on Brownie, and sent the horse down the silent street at breakneck speed to get out of Random. He didn't know where he meant to go, just that he needed to escape. The hard blowing of the gelding finally forced Gabe to slow the pace to a walk, and then, his head so muddled he couldn't reason past the tangle of his thoughts, only lifelong habit made him continue at that speed to cool down his mount.

When Brownie's lathered neck finally dried, Gabe drew the horse to a stop and swung down from the saddle. He left the gelding's reins to dangle, not really caring if the horse spooked and ran. Not that Brownie would ever hare off and leave. Over the last ten years, the equine had been Gabe's only true friend, ever faithful, never faltering.

This far from town, beyond even the farms that skirted the community, Gabe knew he could scream at the top of his lungs and be heard by only the horse and wild critters. And that was precisely what he did—scream. The immeasurable anger that churned within him was impossible to contain, and the worst part of all was that Gabe didn't know for sure with whom he was most furious, the angels or himself.

"I'm finished!" He yelled the words with such rage that the tendons along his throat stung. "The deal is off!" When he heard no response, he doubled his fist and punched at the darkening sky. "I was a fool to agree to your terms in the first place! I'm not *saving* Nan! I'm destroying her! Breaking her heart! Ruining her life!" Heaving for breath, Gabe stood with his feet spread and his head hanging back to glare at the sky. Brownie cocked his ears at his master. Gabe ignored the horse's mildly astonished expression. "Gabriel! Do you hear me?" he roared. "Dammit, *answer* me! To *hell* with my mission! I quit! I don't *care*! Just do like you said you would if I mucked this up and erase her memory! *Now!* She's hurting! Do you understand that?" He stared wildly around to see if the angel was going to materialize but saw only a startled-looking prairie dog peering cautiously at him, his head and forepaws poked out of his hole. Somehow that made him even madder. He'd never liked being ignored, even by an angel.

"You listen to me, dammit, Gabriel! I let her fall in love with a *lie*! I set her up to break her heart! She believed it could be *forever*, that if she let herself care, I'd always be there for her! But that's not the way of it. I don't have a lifetime to give her, only three miserable days!"

Silence answered him. The prairie dog vanished. The gloaming began to deepen, and Gabe started to panic. Where the hell was Gabriel? Why wasn't he at least answering? Gabe didn't care if all the fury of heaven rained down on him; he was reneging on the deal, finished, done.

Exhaustion finally drove him toward a boulder, where he sat and hung his head. He'd yelled himself out. Darkness settled over the rolling, grassy landscape, making Gabe feel like a tiny speck in its vastness. His throat felt raw. The bite of the wind cut through his shirt, chilling him to the bone. Soon not even a star winked to brighten the darkness. Brownie came to nuzzle at his shoulder, his warm breath somehow making Gabe feel less alone. He hugged the horse's silky neck, pressing his cheek against the animal's solid reality. The gelding chuffed, gave Gabe a gentle bump, and moved away.

"I don't understand," Gabe whispered. "Why'd you send me here? *Why?* A second chance, you told me." He searched the endless expanse of sky. "I was supposed to get it all right this time. Only, the truth of it is, by following your damned rules, all I did was make the same mistakes all over again. Guard my own back, save my own ass; those were always my mottoes. And that hasn't changed. It's still all about saving myself."

Gabe listened to the low moan of the night wind, the swishing whispers of countless blades of grass, the faint grinding sound of Brownie's jaws as he snatched a few mouthfuls of prairie grass. The horse's teeth clanked slightly against the bit as he chewed. And then a truly *horrible* thought struck Gabe: What if he had imagined it all? What if he'd never taken that predawn walk up Main and been shot dead? What if Pete Raintree didn't even exist? That first morning, Gabe had toyed with the idea that he might have had too many whiskeys the prior night and somehow injured his head. Only the angel Gabriel's rebuttal on the boardwalk in front of the hotel had driven that suspicion from Gabe's mind.

But what if the angel hadn't been *real*? What if everything Gabe believed he'd experienced had never happened? Was his mind playing tricks on him?

No, no. That couldn't be right, Gabe assured himself. He couldn't have conjured up all those details about Nan's past without help. He'd known too much, things no one could possibly learn, not even if he hired the best agents available and had them investigate Nan for years. Gabe recalled the scenes he'd witnessed through the parting of the clouds, and he knew, way deep inside, that he couldn't have dreamed all those details. In person, he'd never yet seen Nan half-dressed, but he was willing to bet she had a dark little freckle or mole on the swell of her right breast.

He slowly released a weary breath. Clearly neither angel planned to communicate with him. Why, he couldn't imagine. He'd just scotched the bargain, and now, unless they reined him in, he would, in a sense, be like a runaway horse, unpredictable and without direction. Maybe he'd automatically damned himself through both his actions and his screaming that the deal was off. He'd certainly yelled loud enough for his words to echo for miles.

So be it. Gabe pushed up from the rock, stood gazing at the sky for several seconds to give his celestial mentors a final chance to speak, and then strode to his horse. *Fine*, he thought as he swung back into the saddle. *Leave me to muddle through on my own. If that's your plan, then I'm doing this my way from here on out. And I'm starting with Nan. Even if she doesn't believe me and thinks I'm crazy, I'm telling her the truth, every last bit of it.*

As Gabe rode toward Random, at a much slower pace this time, he wondered if Nan would even know him now. The angels had promised that they'd erase her memory if he messed up. And he'd sure as hell messed up. She was *not* supposed to be hurt. The thought that Nan might not recognize him stabbed Gabe's heart. But, hey, it wasn't as if he could offer her anything. Three lousy days. In a way, he'd be relieved— at least for her—if she remembered nothing about him.

Now he had to figure out how to approach her so that if she knew him, he wouldn't ram his boot into his mouth any farther than he already had, but not scare the crap out of her if her memory had been erased. *Great choices here, Gabriel.* Gabe hoped the angels were having themselves a good laugh.

When Nan grew upset, she worked. It was her way of escaping—losing herself in a project, finding calm in the mindless rhythm of simply doing, and blocking out whatever pained her. From long habit, she had done that this evening, seeking refuge in her project room downstairs. She had three hats in progress, and the dratted gown for Geneva. She couldn't face that hideous gown tonight, so she gravitated toward a particularly challenging hat, which begged for something—a different angle with the arrangement, a focal point of color, or perhaps a complete new start.

Normally, growing immersed in her work lulled Nan into a numb state, compartmentalizing her mind so that her emotions were tucked neatly away in a corner. Not tonight. Her husband's eyes, the memory of those burning kisses, the feel of his arms crushing her close, refused to be dislodged by bits of millinery. She stabbed her fingertip with a pin and bled on a flower. The appearance of the hat frustrated her so much that she ended up tearing everything off it. And then, after fussing with it for well over two more hours, she finally gave up.

What she needed was a good long cry, but the tears wouldn't come. She recalled hearing or reading that some heartbreak ran too deep for tears. And the pain she felt over Gabriel ran very deep. She'd sworn never to love a man, and fool that she was, she'd gone and done it anyway. If she lived to be a very old woman, she would never forget the humiliation she'd felt when he sprang away from her. *Just deserts.* Any woman who lost her heart to a man was asking for grief. Now she had to pick up the pieces, glue them back together, and move forward. If she couldn't do it for herself, she had to do it for Laney.

With a start, she remembered that the boy and dog hadn't yet been fed. Dark and late though it now was, she couldn't leave them to go hungry all night. Glad to have something, anything, to distract her from thoughts of Gabriel, she rushed upstairs, rifled through the icebox, and found enough leftover food to fill both of their bellies. *Champion.* This way, she wouldn't have to cook when the mere thought of eating made her stomach clench. She prepared sandwiches for the boy, filled a bottle with milk, and tossed what remained into the pail.

When she stepped from her shop, a rush of uneasiness came over her. A lady should never walk about town unescorted after dark. It could be dangerous, especially near the saloon. *Stuff and nonsense.* She would make fast work of delivering a meal to the boy and be gone in a blink. If some drunk did start down the brothel stairway, she'd be out of sight before he ever gained the walkway. As for going out behind Lizzy's, Nan thought that would be safe enough. No miscreant was likely to be sharing the lean-to with a dog.

Hurrying through the night, Nan swiftly executed her acts of kindness and made her way back to the shop. She half expected to find Gabriel there when she stepped inside. He'd left his personal effects and would have to return at some point to fetch them. He was a decisive individual, and it would be just like him to waste no time in coming. Somehow, though, she knew the moment she stepped into the building that her husband wasn't there. Gabriel had a way of filling the very air with his presence, and Nan's senses always picked up on that.

She sighed, relieved that she didn't have to face him right then. When he did show up, she intended to be the very picture of serenity. Never would she reveal to him how deep his rejection had pierced. Never would she let him see that he'd broken her heart.

After returning to the livery, Gabe spent nearly an hour grooming Brownie, not because the horse actually required that amount of attention, but because Gabe needed time to think before he faced Nan. If the angels had kept their promise and she didn't remember him, he at least had to learn where she'd tucked the Pinkerton Agency report. She'd probably think he was a lunatic if he began searching her shop, but he absolutely had to find the document and then place it where Nan would be sure to come across it later. The Pinkerton investigation had set her free from her past. No dead fiancé, no murder charge. The angels could erase every other memory of Gabe from Nan's mind, but Gabe wouldn't allow that information to be taken from her.

Apart from that, Gabe would accept what came. With no recollection of him, she would revert back to the Nan he'd first met, a fussy spinster who fretted over her clocks, rigidly adhered to the rules of propriety, and rarely laughed. Even if she happened upon the roses he'd ordered from Denver and planned to leave atop a fence post behind the woodpile right before he walked up Main on Christmas morning, she wouldn't recall their conversation about Santa and wouldn't know the flowers were from him.

On the other hand, if she *did* remember him, Gabe had a heap of explaining to do, and when he went over the story in his mind, he had a bad feeling that Nan probably wouldn't believe it. If someone had told him the same story, he sure as shooting wouldn't.

After puttering as long as he could, Gabe set off up Main Street, his gaze fixed on Nan's illuminated shop windows. So, she was downstairs. Working, probably. Whether she remembered the earlier bedchamber debacle or not, she'd have her hands busy. It was how she held unpleasantness at bay.

Gabe was just passing in front of the hotel when a voice called out behind him. "Valance!" a youngish male voice hollered. "Turn around."

Incredulous, Gabe froze. This was *not* supposed to happen. He'd lived through this month. He'd lived through this very night, in fact. He slowly turned to face his challenger, feeling so weary of it all that he nearly sighed.

In the squares of light cast by the street-side hotel windows, a kid stood about twenty feet away, feet spread, one hand poised over his gun holster. Gabe doubted he was much older than seventeen—tall, skinny as a well-gnawed chicken bone—and quivering with either excitement or fear. Gabe guessed it was the latter. It was scary the first time you faced a man in the street. All kinds of thoughts went through your mind, first and foremost being that if you went for your gun, the other fellow would shoot back.

Well, not this time. Gabe had only three more days left to live. He didn't really give a shit if he had to check out early, and he saw no point in taking a boy along with him. He'd died the first time regretting that he'd killed Pete Raintree, and he wasn't a man who liked making the same mistake twice, even though he'd done precisely that often enough. "Out to make a name for yourself, son?" Gabe asked.

"I ain't standin' here to talk, Valance. Draw. What's the matter? You turnin' yellow?"

Gabe nearly smiled. "Nope, I'm turning my back." He pivoted on his heel, resuming his walk toward the shop. "Go ahead. Just be sure of your aim. I don't want a slug in my kidney."

"Turn back around!" the kid yelled. "I mean it! Come back here! Or I'll kill you dead!"

Technically Gabe was already dead. And because he'd already died once, he wasn't afraid to go through it again. Pretty simple stuff, actually. Even so, he flinched when he heard the hammer of the kid's gun cock. "You ever known a back shooter who got congratulated and patted on the shoulder?" Gabe called out. "Is that the reputation you're aiming to get, son? You'll be talked about in saloons from here to Frisco, all right, but not for your bravery or your skill with a gun."

"I ain't no back shooter! I wanna face you, fair and square."

Gabe kept walking.

"You crazy or somethin'?" the boy hollered. "I gotta bead dead center on your spine!"

"Then shoot," Gabe suggested. "Either that or holster your weapon and go home. There's nothing worse than a man who talks it to death and never does anything."

Gabe angled left and gained the boardwalk. He knew then that the boy wouldn't pull the trigger. He strode purposefully to Nan's shop door, started to walk in, and then thought better of it. He angled a glance over his shoulder to be sure the kid had skedaddled. The last thing he wanted was for Nan to catch a stray bullet. When Gabe saw no one in the street, he rapped his knuckles against the glass. Watching through the door window, he saw Nan emerge from her downstairs workroom. As always, she looked beautiful, and moved across the room with precisely measured steps. She wore the same pretty blue dress that he'd yearned to tear from her body only hours ago.

He braced himself as she drew open the door, uncertain which Nan he'd be facing: the one he'd first met or the one he'd left that afternoon.

Hand still grasping the doorknob, she stared up at him for an endlessly long moment, her expression unreadable. Then, in a flat voice, she said, "Gabriel."

He wasn't sure if that pleased him or did quite the opposite. "So you remember me."

His words rattled her composure. He saw her shoulders tense and glimpsed a flash of bewilderment in her eyes. "Well, of course I remember you. It's been only a few hours since I, um, saw you."

She spun to retrace her steps to the workroom, leaving the door open wide. Over her shoulder, she said, "Your things are upstairs, right where you left them. I'm quite busy, so I'd greatly appreciate it if you'd vacate the premises with as little fuss and bother as possible."

Gabe had rehearsed what he would say if she remembered him, but now every single word eluded him. "I love you, Nan." He paused to swallow the cotton in his throat. "I know I hurt you this afternoon by taking off the way I did, but it wasn't because I don't love you and want you."

She stopped in her tracks and spun to face him. "You . . . you *love* me?" Her eyes went bright with tears. "I think you made your feelings *quite* clear this afternoon. Get your things and get out, Gabriel. I'm not interested in hearing anything more that you have to say."

Gabe closed the door and followed her into her work area. She shot him a fulminating glare. "What are you doing?" she cried. "I politely asked you to leave."

"Not so politely," he replied. "And as you can see, I'm not going to oblige you."

She folded her arms and began tapping her toe, a habit of hers when she grew agitated. Oh, how he wished in that moment that the angels had erased her memory of him. He'd hurt her in ways that might never heal. She clung to her self-control by a thread. In her eyes, he saw the supreme effort it cost her. The rigidity of her posture was also a telltale sign to someone who knew her so well.

"So say what you must and *then* leave."

There were two chairs at the table, one for Nan and one for a customer. Geneva White spent a goodly part of each morning in here, supervising the creation of her gown, which was becoming the worst eyesore Gabe had ever seen.

Gabe gestured for Nan to take a seat. She fidgeted for a moment, clearly not enthused about sitting across from him. But being the intelligent and practical woman she was, she finally gathered her skirts and perched on the seat, reminding him of a small bird prepared for quick flight. Recalling his manners, Gabe reached to remove his Stetson, then realized that he hadn't grabbed it on his way out.

He sighed as he sat down. When he braced his crossed arms on the table, Nan drew back slightly. Gabe wished . . . Well, he wasn't sure what. His not making love to her this afternoon had wounded her, but he couldn't honestly say that he'd do things differently. A woman like Nan didn't give her body lightly, and Gabe wasn't the lucky chap who had a right to accept that gift unless she knew the whole truth about him first. Only how could he explain it to her? Gabe wasn't sure where to start.

So he plunged in with, "That first morning when I came into your shop, I didn't just suddenly up and decide that marrying you was a great idea. I was sent here by two angels."

Nan rolled her eyes and puffed air into her cheeks, releasing it in a huff that said more clearly than words that she'd never heard such bunkum. "Have you been drinking?" she asked. Her tone was done to a crisp.

"It's true!" Gabe insisted.

He began to tell her the whole story, beginning with leaving an upstairs room of the brothel, seeing the boy under the staircase, and then walking farther up Main later, drawn by the candlelight in Nan's shop window. He left nothing out, not even the less-than-complimentary remarks the angels had made about his miserable failures to be a decent person. He even related all that he'd seen through the parting of the clouds as he was shown the three souls he could choose from to save: Tyke Baden, the abandoned boy, and Nan. Her expression hadn't changed from the instant he started explaining, and that expression wasn't encouraging.

"I chose to save you in exchange for being granted eternal salvation," he told her, his voice going thick. "And, yes, I picked you for all the wrong reasons. You were so damned beautiful, and I figured I might as well enjoy myself while I was down here. That's all."

Nan's gray eyes began to smolder with anger. "Is that the best explanation you could come up with during all those hours since you slammed out of here? Do you honestly expect me to *believe* all this poppycock about angels and visitations and damnation? I am *not* and never was a lost soul!"

Fury licked through Nan, and even though she abhorred physical violence, she yearned to punch Gabriel Valance right on the nose. How dared he sit there and spin a pack of lies that insulted both her faith and her intelligence? Even worse, how could he possibly expect her to believe them? She started to rise from the chair, but his voice, throbbing with urgency, made her freeze.

"Don't leave, Nan. I know it all sounds crazy. But I swear to God it's true, every word of it. Do you honestly think I couldn't come up with a better tale than this? Hell, I could dream up two dozen better stories that would be a lot easier for you to swallow."

The earnestness in his dark eyes made her feel vulnerable, and she crossed her arms over her breasts. "Then you'd better talk fast, because I certainly don't swallow this one," she snapped.

"And lie to you? Is that really what you want from me, a bunch of lies? That's one thing I can tell you, Nan. During all of this, except for a couple of white lies, I only ever lied to you by omission. As for your not being a lost soul, you're absolutely right—in a sense. I have no doubt that when you die, you'll be instantly welcomed into the presence of God. I wasn't sent to save you from living a life of sin. I was sent because you were so very lost in other ways—fearful of marriage, harboring a disgust of men, and holding yourself apart from others." His gaze, aching with appeal, held hers. "Remember asking me to teach you how to laugh? And realizing that you were so wrapped up in all the responsibilities of life that you couldn't let go and enjoy its small pleasures?"

Nan did remember that, and she hated him—*hated* him—for reminding her. He'd sung her a lovely tune, and she'd danced for him like a marionette. She'd revealed her deepest emotions and insecurities to him, and this was her reward.

He leaned closer, still holding her gaze. "You were unhappy, and you were missing out on all the joyful stuff—falling in love, getting married, raising a passel of kids with a wonderful man. You *deserve* to have all of those things, and it was my assignment to help you reach out for them."

Oh, but he was a clever liar. And he knew exactly which strings to tug. It was true that she'd always yearned for the life he described—way down deep, she'd wanted to love and be loved, to hold her own baby in her arms, to live in a real house that rang with the voices of a family. And for a brief time, she'd believed she might have all of that with this man. Now she knew that had been the height of idiocy. Gabriel Valance was not only a spinner of beautiful dreams, but also a spinner of cruel lies. He'd created that world for her, and it was all an illusion. And, oh, how she wanted to hurt him as he'd hurt her.

"So," she said softly, "you're to die in the street on Christmas morning just before dawn."

He nodded.

Nan curved her lips in a smile that she hoped sliced him clear to the bone. "Well, then, Mr. Valance, I shall make a point to attend your funeral and leave a bouquet of artificial flowers on your coffin. They'll be as real as our relationship is. Was."

He flinched as if she'd slapped him, and Nan took satisfaction in having delivered the blow. He was a liar and a stealer of hearts. He deserved no tears from her. Once he left this building—and hopefully that would occur soon—she would never allow herself to think of him again. But now pain throbbed all through her, and it made her strike again.

"You may tell those imaginary angels of yours that I will welcome having my memory erased," she went on, keeping her voice level with an enormous effort. "I'll liken it to emptying out the trash." She forced herself to look him straight in the eye. "You've told me absolutely nothing that you couldn't have somehow learned in a completely *worldly* way. I know for a fact that you hired investigators to prove that Barclay lived. You probably hired them to dig into my past as well."

"No investigators could have discovered all the things I know, Nan. *Think.* How could they have learned what happened between you and Barclay?"

He had Nan there. But she shrugged it off. "You're a clever man. You took a lucky guess and I—very helpfully, I might add—told you all the rest."

He sighed and hung his head for a moment. When he looked back up at her, she was startled to see tears glistening in his eyes. Real, or fake, like everything else he'd offered her? "All right. We'll leave it there, then. It won't really matter in the end whether you believe my story or not. But will you at least try to believe one thing?"

"What is that?" she asked, hating the quaver in her voice. God help her, but even now, knowing him for the despicable person he was, she still had feelings for him. Under the bend of her left arm, she clenched her right hand into a fist so hard that her nails cut into her flesh.

Hang on, Nan. He'll be out of here soon. You can fall apart then. But not now. Not in front of him.

"It was never my plan to fall in love with you," he said, his voice gravelly. "But I did. Head over heels, irrevocably, I'm in love with you." He pushed to his feet, his shoulders slumped with apparent weariness. "Until the angels wipe your memory clean, believe in at least that. The only reason I called a halt to what we were doing in the bedroom this afternoon—the one and *only* reason—was because I realized how much I care for you, and I couldn't make love to you with a lie between us. It was one of the requirements, a part of the tasks assigned to me by the angels—to show you how beautiful lovemaking can be—but in the end, I couldn't do that to a woman I love, not even to save my own ass."

Nan refused to be moved. "Are you finished?"

"Not quite. Where did you put the Pinkerton report?"

"I put it back on the top shelf where you had it. It's not something I want lying around where a customer might see it. My father would pay a great deal of money to learn of Laney's whereabouts."

Gabriel reached up to get the envelope and tossed it onto the table. "Put it someplace where you'll be sure to come across it after your memory is erased. I don't want you to live out the rest of your days believing you killed Barclay."

Nan couldn't look away from his dark face. His eyebrow wasn't twitching, she realized, and he'd looked her directly in the eye when he said he loved her. She remembered what he'd told Laney: that the most important thing for her to do when a man professed his love was to search deep within her heart and decide whether or not she believed him.

Nan felt as if the floor turned to water beneath her

chair. Gabriel reached for the curtain. In an instant, he would step out of this small room and then out of her life. And if his story was true, he'd die just before dawn on Christmas believing that she detested him.

"Gabriel?"

He flinched, stood with his back to her for a long moment, and then finally angled her a look over his shoulder. "What, Nan?"

"Give me something," she whispered shakily. "Just one little tidbit of information no one could possibly know about me—unless he watched me from heaven through a parting in the clouds."

His eyes searched hers. "I do have a tidbit of information no one could possibly know about you, Nan, but if I give it to you, I'll be buying your faith in me. I'm not real experienced in matters of the heart, but it seems to me that if you love me—I mean *really* and *truly* love me—you should know, way deep where reason holds no sway, that I'd never come in here and tell you a pack of lies."

Nan shot to her feet. "You're asking me to set aside all rational thought and believe a story that is *incredible*. To take a . . . a *mindless* leap of faith!"

He smiled sadly. "You're right. I guess that is what I'm asking. If you take a mindless leap of faith, where do you think you'll land? Right in my arms, that's where. If you don't feel that's a bad place to be, then leap, honey. I'll catch you."

Frozen with indecision, Nan gaped at him. And then, without even feeling herself move, she launched herself at him. True to his word, he caught her close against him. Trembling violently, Nan went up on her toes, locked both arms around his neck, and buried her face against his shirt. "Damn you! I think I hate you. No, I don't. I take it back. I think I'm losing my mind."

He laughed—a deep, rich rumble that she'd thought

never to hear again—and tightened his embrace. Then he pressed his face against her hair, swaying on his feet and taking her with him. "Thank you," he said, the words muffled.

"For what, damning you?"

Another chuckle shook his torso. "No, for believing me."

Nan's chest squeezed painfully. "I'm afraid you've suffered a head injury and have imagined everything, but I am convinced that you honestly believe all that you've told me."

"Ah, so you think my brains are rattled, do you?" He smiled against her hair. "I wish they were, Nan. I wish they were. Then I could simply work on getting better and live into old age, loving you with every fiber of my being. Sadly, that won't be the case. I have only three days left. You may not believe it, but it's true. I'm not confused. I didn't imagine anything. It happened exactly as I said. And just so you don't get it into your head to call Doc Peterson to dose me with tonic until I regain my right mind, I'll happily share that tidbit of information about you now, something that nobody on earth, unless it might be Laney, could possibly know."

Nan turned her face upward to press her nose against his neck. "I'm waiting."

"You, my sweet, beautiful, nearly *perfect* wife, have one tiny flaw. Well, not a flaw, really; I found it extremely enticing when I glimpsed it through the parted clouds."

Curiosity aroused, Nan asked, "What? What did you see?"

"A mole or a dark freckle, I couldn't tell for sure which, on your right breast. It peeked out at me over the lacy top edge of your chemise. I was so captivated that I damned near lost my balance and fell through the hole in the clouds."

Nan stiffened. No one—not even Laney, so far as she knew—had ever seen her mole. It had appeared on her breast about two years ago, and in the time since, she'd been trying, without stellar success, to teach Laney modest behavior. Parading about in one's underthings was *not* ladylike.

"Oh, dear God," she whispered. "There's no way you could know about that—unless you're a keyhole peeper."

He chuckled again. "A smart fellow like me? You're the lady who's handy with knitting needles. If I'd *dared* to press my eye to a keyhole, you probably would have stabbed me right in the pupil."

Nan giggled. But her mirth quickly faded. Gabriel had just offered her inarguable proof of . . . well, something. She still had problems believing that he'd stood on a cloud and witnessed scenes of her life. But if he hadn't, there was no way—absolutely no way in this world—that he could know about the mole. And if that much of his story was true, then did it follow that *all* of it was? And if it was—

"Oh, dear God, no!" She clung frantically to his neck. "You can't *die*. Not in three days! Not even in a year! I shan't be able to live without you!"

His mood changed swiftly with hers. "I wish I could stay with you, sweetheart. I'd give anything for that."

"What shall we do?" she cried.

"Well, my plan is to make love to you—passionately, intensely, and nonstop—before Gabriel or Michael erases all your memories of me."

He shifted to sweep her up in his arms, the move so unexpected that Nan squeaked with a start. As he carried her up the steep staircase, a horrible thought occurred to her.

"What if . . . well, what if they erase all my memories of you *while* you're making love to me?"

Gabriel missed a step, barely managed to catch his balance by pressing his shoulder against the wall, and tucked in his chin to give her a slightly horrified look.

"I reckon I'll say, 'Pardon me, ma'am. I don't know how I wound up in your bed. I'm leaving now. So please *don't* scream.'"

Nan digested that, and then they both burst out laughing.

Laughter, one of Gabriel's gifts to her. And, oh, how glorious a gift it was.

Chapter Fifteen

A s Gabriel carried her to the bedroom, Nan clung to his neck, determined to focus on the moment and not allow fear or worry to nip at the edges of her mind. Sadly, though, as much as she loved this man and hoped to please him, her thoughts drifted away from him. Oddly, she wasn't terribly nervous about engaging in the act, although her inexperience with such things did pose slightly disturbing questions she couldn't answer. What really *terrified* her was that she would soon lose him. As he gently deposited her on her feet beside the bed, left her momentarily to light the lantern, and then returned to catch her close again, all she could think was that he would leave her in only three days. It was such a short time. How could a woman let go and feel overcome with desire in her husband's arms when death hovered over him like a black specter?

Gabriel must have felt her tension. Nuzzling her ear to send shivers coursing through her, he whispered, "What is it?"

Nan squeezed her eyes shut and pressed as close to him as she could get, hoping to absorb some of his courage, or, failing that, to melt into him and cease to exist as a separate person. Oh, how she'd come to love him—his unpredictable sense of humor, his caring heart, the way his dark eyes twinkled into hers and warmed her all the way through. She wished now that she'd spent every single night in the circle of his powerful arms, enveloped by his heat. Instead she'd wasted all those opportunities. And now, in too short a while, they would be lost to her forever.

"Nan?" He tugged lightly on her lobe with his teeth. "I've got this real bad feeling that you're a hundred miles away. Are you afraid of what's about to happen between us?"

"No."

He sighed. "Well, hell. You aren't still fretting about Geneva's bright red sequins, are you?"

Nan laughed, dismayed when the sound came out as a wet choke. She tightened her arms around his neck, frustrated by her lack of height, wanting to experience the feel of him in places she couldn't quite reach. "Oh, Gabriel, I'm sorry. Sequins are the last thing on my mind."

"What, then?"

"I'm going to lose you," she pushed out, feeling as if the words had to move through a blob of cold, congealed oatmeal caught in her throat. "I can't *bear* it."

He sighed, and in one fluid motion he sat on the bed and swept her onto his lap. Reaching up to pick the pins from her hair, he said, "Life is a great big poker game, Nan. None of us really thinks of it that way, but the truth is, we all stand to lose those we love with the turn of a card, a shift of the wind, or the flutter of a leaf. And from the moment we're born, we all start to die. You'll die one day. So will Laney. Geneva is no spring chicken and will soon be wearing an awful sequined gown in heaven. That misguided woman would probably put sequins on her angel wings if she was ever fortunate enough to earn a pair."

Nan snorted, a sound that was half sob and half

laugh. Gabriel tugged a white handkerchief from his hip pocket and reached to wipe her cheeks and then her nose. Until then, Nan hadn't realized that tears were streaming in rivers down her cheeks.

"Hardly anyone knows *when* they're going to go," he whispered. "Imagine the chaos if they did. For instance, if I told you that tomorrow morning you were going to keel over dead, what would you do in the hours left to you?"

Nan gulped and held her breath for a moment to stop a sob that tried to escape. When she felt the pressure subside, she said in a rush, "I'd live every moment as if it were my last, I guess."

"Exactly," he said, grinning as he gave her nose another squeeze with the square of linen. "And that's just what I want to do—live every moment as if it's my last. I don't want to think about what will happen on Christmas morning. I just want to *live*, really live during the time I've got left." He tossed the handkerchief aside and lifted her chin slightly with his bent finger. "I know it's a tall order, but can you let go and help me do that? No tears, no dread. Let's just exist in each moment and make each one as wonderful as we can."

Nan took a deep, cleansing breath. Life offered no guarantees to anyone, and she'd be a fool to miss out on the beauty of *now*. She also knew that Gabriel needed her help in order to make the most of what time he had left.

"That," she said with a wobbly smile, "is an invitation I absolutely cannot refuse, Mr. Valance. Let's live every second as if it's our last."

He set her off his lap, stood, and stretched out a palm to her. "Dance with me?"

Nan laughed, real laughter this time. "We have no music," she said as she laid her fingers across his.

He grasped her hand, tugging her up and into his

arms. Before she could even catch her balance, he swept her into a swirl. Against her hair, he whispered, "We *do* have music. Don't you hear it?"

Nan relaxed, allowing her body to float with his, and in her heart she did hear music—not the conventional kind to be heard with the ears, but a melody all the same, precious, sweet, and only theirs. They dipped, swayed, and turned, bodies moving as one in the amber glow cast by the lamp, their shadows shifting over the walls with them in perfect unity. *Gabriel.* For Nan, he was not only the music but also the dance, and as she drifted with him through shadow and light, she thanked God for this moment and any that followed, because each would shine in her memory like a polished gem for the remainder of her life.

She wasn't sure what to expect when it came time to engage in the act, but then, as always with Gabriel, she would have been more successful at catching dust motes than trying to predict his next move. She anticipated an abrupt change in his mood and plenty of advance warning before he began to make love to her, but instead he only slowed their momentum to a mere rocking motion and kissed her, a soft, coaxing, whispery graze of his mouth over hers that delighted her senses and left her yearning for more. His mouth tasted of coffee and a masculine essence exclusively his own. Nan wished she could bottle the flavor of him and stash it in her bedside drawer, something of him that she could take out on lonely nights to savor once again. But that wasn't possible; she could count on only this moment. So she concentrated fiercely on each fraction of a second, attempting to imprint upon her memory the sound of his breathing and the rustle of his shirt, the pulse beat that thrummed into her skin from his fingertips, the feel of his palms, as thick and satiny as well-buffed leather.

Still swaying to their secret melody, he inched her back toward the wall and then pressed her against it. Cupping her cheeks in his big hands, he tipped her head slightly back to trail his lips over each of her brows, kissed her eyelids closed, traced the angle of her cheekbones, and in the process made her feel cherished. Her senses spun. Her heart began to slog. Her bones felt as if they were made of butter and slowly melting in his radiant warmth.

Gabriel. He didn't ask, and yet he didn't take. Button by button, he unfastened her dress, distracting her with kisses after each one slipped free, and soon her gown and petticoats lay in a puddle at her feet. Before she could feel embarrassed, he caught her up in his arms and carried her to the bed, where he laid her full-length on her back and then stretched out beside her. Nan momentarily regretted the lantern light, but then she grew lost in the expressions on her husband's dark face and was glad not to miss them. She saw love for her etched in every line of his chiseled features, reverence in his gaze, and adoration in the half smile that curved his firm mouth. He touched the hollow of her throat as if he were fascinated. Then he lightly traced the scallops of lace that edged the top of her chemise. He winked at her, reverting back momentarily to her mischievous, funny husband as he bent to touch his tongue to her mole.

Nan's breath snagged at the base of her throat as his hot mouth closed over the imperfection, and she learned between one heartbeat and the next that she'd only just begun to melt. Then she ceased to think at all and surrendered to the sensations of being tasted by a man who seemed bent on savoring every bend, curve, and secret place of her body. He began with the mole, then moved to the ridges of her collarbone, the slope of her shoulders, the sensitive inner side at the bend of her arms, and then spent an interminable amount of time exploring her wrists and hands. Nan's entire body tingled, and when he moved away from her to remove his gun belt and strip off his shirt, she was so limp and dazed that she felt as if she'd been sipping spirits.

She'd seen Gabriel without a shirt many times, but tonight the powerful planes of his chest, the rippling slope of his thick shoulders, and the well-muscled display of his arms seemed gilded by the lantern light. She recalled thinking once that he was beautiful, like a carving of polished teak, and how horrified she'd been to entertain such a notion. She was no longer horrified. Gabriel had a *gorgeous* upper body, every line of it sculpted as if by a master, and she had no doubt that he was just as impressive from the waist down. And he was *hers*, only hers.

When he sat to take off his boots and socks, Nan reached out to trail a fingertip down his spine, eager to feel his bare skin, a pleasure she had long denied herself. He grinned over his shoulder.

"No hurry," he said. "I've prided myself on being fast at a lot of things, but making love to you isn't going to be one of them."

Heat surged from low in Nan's belly to lick at her skin from head to toe. "You're very well practiced at it."

He turned so suddenly to brace his arms on either side of her and lean low that she blinked, the only gesture of surprise she could manage, because her body had gone heavy with languorous pleasure. "Well practiced?" His eyes twinkled with amusement. "I confess to having been with countless females, but everything I just did with you was a first for me."

Nan liked the thought that at least some of this would be something he'd done with nobody else. "No, sir." *Convince me*, her tone pleaded. "How can you have made love with countless females and experience anything new with me tonight?"

He narrowed an eye at her. "I said I'd been *with* countless females, not that I ever made love with them. That particular kind of intimacy is more . . . I don't know. . . . Quick and businesslike is probably a good way to describe it. I guess there are men who don't care if they're twentieth in line, but I wasn't one of them. I never felt emotionally touched during those encounters."

She really liked that he'd used the past tense, because she had no intention of sharing this man with anyone. From now on, whether their time together was brief or long, he would be exclusively hers.

He dipped his head to nibble on her ear, his husky voice vibrating through her as he said, "*You* are my one and only love, Nan. And most of this is as new to me as it is to you—sweet, beautiful, wondrous, and absolutely *new*." He nipped playfully at her earlobe. "Stop thinking about other females, or I'll have to start all over again."

His words eased the brief sting of jealousy that she'd felt. She hesitantly rested her hands on his bare shoulders, glorying in the vibrant and silky warmth of his skin, which had a slightly coarser texture than hers. A breathless sensation came over her, and she could have sworn her heart stopped beating as she drew her palms downward to finally feel his chest and dip her fingertips into the curly black hair there.

"Oh, Gabriel." Her voice sounded throaty and almost *sultry*, which was strange to her ears. But then, she'd never felt this way before: hot and tingly all over, with certain parts of her aching with needs she couldn't define. "Make love to me."

"Make love *with* you," he corrected in a husky whisper. "But first we need to get rid of the rest of your clothes."

Nan made fists over the coverlet beneath her as he

lifted her right leg to roll her garter and black stocking slowly down to her knee, tasting every inch of skin as it was bared. When he finally divested her of her boot and got the stocking off, she moaned as he nibbled at each of her toes and tickled the arch of her foot with feathery kisses. Her other leg and foot received the same attention before he set himself to the task of slowly—ever so slowly—tugging loose her corset strings, dipping his head occasionally to suckle her nipples through her cotton chemise. Soon the cloth became wet and cool from the air, and the tips of her breasts went as pointy and hard as metal rivets.

Gabriel's gaze went molten—and Nan felt the burn clear to her core. Oh, how she *wanted*. She wasn't sure precisely *what* she yearned for. The images she'd held in her mind of what occurred in a marriage bed had always disgusted her. But somehow, with Gabriel, *nothing* seemed distasteful.

Making love *with* him became Nan's wish when all her clothing had been discarded. She felt only a moment of shyness, but the touch of his warm hand on her bare waist blasted all such foolishness from her mind. When he lowered himself over her, she decided the tasting business could go both ways, and opened her mouth over his neck to tongue a faint bit of salt from his skin. Next she sampled his shoulder. Then she went for his chest, loving the feel of his furred flesh against her lips.

"Oh, sweet Lord," he cried, the pace of his breathing suddenly shallow and fast. "Don't. . . . I want to . . . Slow and *easy*, sweetheart. This is your first time, and I want to make it special for— Oh, *God*."

Nan ignored his protests. It seemed entirely unfair that she was now as naked as a newborn babe while he still hid behind trousers. She fumbled inexpertly with his belt buckle, wondering why he kept jerking and snapping his body taut after she dived her fingers inside his waistband to get a better grip on the dratted metal.

He suddenly whooshed out air, caught her wrists, and pinned her hands above her head, his broad chest forming a canopy of bunched muscle over hers. "My britches stay put until the time is right."

"The time is right," she informed him breathlessly.

"No." His voice was oddly thick and strained. "I've got a friend down there that loses control when I let him out of the barn."

Nan thought that was the silliest thing she'd ever heard, until Gabriel began suckling her nipples, and every thought in her head leaked out through her ears. And then she felt his hand over her center. She jerked when he fingered the flange of flesh there that she always avoided during her ablutions because it was so sensitive. *Flick, flick.* She opened her mouth to protest and all that came out was a shrill bleat. As if with a will of their own, her hips started to undulate and then pushed up to press against his hand.

Not at all sure she liked these powerful surges of sensation, Nan grabbed his wrist. But then her body decided differently, and the next thing she knew, all of her muscles seemed to spasm at once.

"Easy, sweetheart," he whispered. "Ride it out. Stop fighting it."

Nan couldn't fight it. Gabriel had taken control of her person. A tingling urgency mounted within her, and with a final push of her hips, she surrendered and felt as if she were shattering. Bright spots danced before her eyes. In the distance, she heard someone shrieking and panting, which she felt certain could not *possibly* be her. And then she felt as if she were spinning through star-studded blackness.

Gabriel held her when she returned to reality. Her

body jerked and shuddered for nearly a full minute afterward. When she could finally speak, she could think of nothing to say but, "Oh, *my*."

He turned his face against her hair, and she felt him smile. "So you liked that, did you?"

Nan felt boneless. "It *was* rather pleasant in an odd sort of way."

He chuckled and blew softly in her ear, which Nan found irksome. This marriage-bed business was quite draining, and now her whole body felt limp. She felt certain nothing could revive her at this point. She just wanted to curl against him and sleep.

Just then she felt a throbbing push against her thigh from something long, thick, hard, and silken. She had no idea *when* he'd done it, but at some point, possibly while she had been in the throes of passion, he had doffed his pants.

He shifted and rose over her, and she felt another nudge, this time close to her most private place, which had barely recovered from the last round of unaccustomed attention. For just an instant, she felt frightened. But then she focused on the man poised over her. In the wash of amber light, even though he looked primal, his black hair falling forward, the muscles of his bronze face taut with urgent need, and his eyes glazed with passion, she knew this was Gabriel, the man she loved and trusted. He clearly needed more from her, and denying him was out of the question.

She opened her legs to welcome him, and he accepted the invitation without ado. Nan gasped as his thick, hard shaft nudged into her wet passage. "Wait!" She braced the heels of her hands against his shoulders. "We've a situation."

He froze and held her gaze with feverish intensity. "A situation?"

"I fear that the fit is all wrong."

He stared down at her, and then his white teeth flashed in what she believed he meant to be a grin, but was actually more a grimace. "Nan, just hug my neck and let me worry about the fit. Okay? Everything will be fine."

Nan didn't think so. She had a small passage, and he had a very *big* friend that she now wished had been kept in the barn. "Gabriel, I—"

"Just hug my neck," he urged. "And trust me. Do you trust me?"

Nan trusted him completely, so she looped her arms around the sturdy column of his neck and clung to him for dear life as he pushed slowly inside her. She experienced an extremely unpleasant stab of pain, but it soon gave way to an odd feeling of fullness.

"Well," she said shakily, "that was simple enough." She realized that her enthusiasm for engaging in the act had swiftly waned. She'd loved all of what came before, but this part was rather uncomfortable. "Are we finished now?" she asked hopefully.

He grimaced again—another attempt at a smile, she hoped. Only he looked as if he were in severe pain. "Am I hurting you now?" he asked in a thick voice.

"It hurt badly for a bit, but now that has passed."

He drew his hips back, giving Nan the impression that he meant to depart, but then he thrust forward, impaling her again. And deep within Nan, nerve endings thrilled. "Oh, *my*!"

"Are you okay?" he asked. "Does it hurt?"

"No, but—"

That was all Nan got a chance to say before he drove into her again, setting off spirals of delight that curled through her belly. Nan felt him grip her hips, and she was glad of the guidance, because her reflexive return thrusts went slightly off center. The sensations that shot through her stole the breath from her lungs. Her head went dizzy with delight. And before she realized quite how it occurred, she was seeing stars again. *Gabriel*. He drove her upward, and then even higher, until an explosive sensation inside her made her shriek and sent her over the edge.

Later, he held her close for a long while, tenderly stroking her hair. Nan felt as if she'd died, visited heaven, and fallen back to earth with a body as limp and insubstantial as eiderdown. She drifted between wakefulness and slumber, and at some point, between blinks of her lashes, he brought a moist cloth from the water closet to bathe her lower parts. Nan, replete and too exhausted to protest, could only allow him the liberty. She didn't even care when he tossed the cloth and she heard it make a wet plop on her plank floor. Dimly, she thought that there would be time enough tomorrow to worry about the white splotch it would leave on the wax.

Gabriel rejoined her in bed, drew her snugly into his arms, and Nan fell asleep, feeling utterly content and safe.

Nan fully expected to sleep like the dead until well after dawn, but Gabriel awakened her sometime later, and when she lifted her lashes, she realized that her body was already thrumming with need of him. They began making love again, but this time Nan wished to be more of a participant. Gabriel had tasted nearly every inch of her body. Now it was her turn.

It was a heady feeling to hear the man she loved moan shakily when she trailed kisses over his belly. She felt empowered when he caught his breath and snapped his body taut at the touch of her hand on his shaft. For a brief instant, she believed that this time *she* was in control.

Gabriel disabused her of that notion by rolling her onto her back beneath him and proceeding to drive her to the brink of insanity, teasing her nipples and toying with that sensitive place between her legs.

"Gabriel, *please!*" she cried finally.

He entered her this time with one smooth and powerful thrust that set off explosions of delight. So overcome she couldn't think, let alone worry about ladylike behavior, Nan locked her legs around his hips and gloried in the journey to the pinnacle.

When they crested and sank to the other side, they lay with their limbs intertwined and slept like two exhausted children who'd played too hard all day. When Nan occasionally stirred awake, she smiled, snuggled closer to his big, hard body, and drifted happily back into the nether realms of slumber again.

Gabe woke just as dawn streaked the sky with rosy pink. They'd left the lantern burning, and its soft, familiar hiss was the only ordinary thing in a morning that was, to him, extraordinary beyond measure. He kept his face buried in Nan's golden hair, breathing deeply of its scent, which was flowery yet laced with a feminine smell exclusively her own. He'd smelled numerous heads of hair in his day, and there was something indescribably special and different about hers. Gabe figured he could be blindfolded, turned loose in a room filled with women, and find his wife without fail simply by following his nose. Oh, how he loved her. Recalling her attempt last night to halt their lovemaking, he grinned sleepily. Today he would be sure to remind her that, in the end, they'd proved to be a perfect fit.

As if she sensed that he was awake, Nan stirred and turned her head to peer at him over her shoulder. "Gabriel?"

"What other man do you lie naked with in bed?" he asked.

She ignored the question, rolling over to smile sleepily at him as she smoothed his hair back from his forehead. "Good morning," she whispered. Her cheeks turned a comely pink. "Last night was lovely."

Gabe yearned to repeat the experience, but Nan would want to freshen up before Laney came home from her overnight at Melody's. There would also be breakfast to prepare and food deliveries to make. And, like it or not, Gabe had a vigil to keep today outside Doc Peterson's office. He wasn't sure what time Rose Wilson would take her daughter to see the physician, so Gabe had to be stationed outside the waiting room prior to business hours to be sure to catch Mrs. Wilson before she escorted her child into a death chamber.

"So," Nan said, finishing with his hair and then pushing at her own, "what shall we do today? Something fun, for sure. Tonight we'll be decorating the tree, and since—" She broke off, and he glimpsed a flicker of sadness in her eyes before her smile chased it away. "Since we've only three days left, I believe I'll close the shop until after Christmas. I was thinking that we might make cookies and turn our tree trimming into a real party. What do you think?"

Gabe hated to refuse. He loved working with Nan in the kitchen, had a passion for cookies of any kind, and didn't want to miss out on the fun of making some. Except for the afternoon of their rushed wedding, when Nan had served after-school treats, he'd only ever had restaurant offerings, never homemade cookies. He could almost smell the aromatic waves of heat that would roll from Nan's oven.

"I'm sorry, honey, but I've got some business to take care of today. It may take only a couple of hours, but then again, it could take all day—until business hours are over."

"Oh." Her fair brow creased in a slight frown. "What do you have to do?"

Gabe considered keeping his own counsel about the little girl he meant to save, but when he looked deeply into Nan's beautiful eyes, he decided that there had been enough secrets between them. From this moment forward, he wanted to keep nothing from her.

"No!" Nan cried when he'd told her about the child. "You can't!" She shot to a sitting position, her expression filled with dismay. "You're not to intervene, Gabriel. You said the angels were very explicit about that. If you disregard that rule, you'll—" She gulped and pushed the hair from her face. "You'll be *damned*. They made that very clear! I know how you must feel about the little girl. Truly, I do. The thought of her dying breaks my heart, too. But it isn't your place to prevent it!"

"I'm already damned." Gabe rolled away from her to sit up in bed. Grabbing his drawers from off the floor, he quickly pulled them on. Then he stood to dress. "I wasn't supposed to breathe a word of this to you," he informed her. "When I left here yesterday, refusing to make love to you with a lie between us, I sank my boat. Then I capped it all off last night by telling you everything. It's over, Nan. At least, that part is. From here on out, how I spend the days left to me is my choice, and I choose to do some good while I'm still here."

"No!" She sprang from bed, glorious in her nakedness during her brief flight to the armoire to get her wrapper. As she drew the garment on and tied the sash, she spoke in a rush. "You've done everything they asked of you. You've *saved* me, Gabriel. You made me fall wildly in love with you. You taught me how to trust again. Now we've been intimate. Your presence in my life has wrought every change the angels requested you to make!" She shook a finger at him. "You can still attain salvation, I'm telling you! It's insane to throw that chance away."

"Nan," he tried.

She shook her head and held up her hands to silence him. "I've stated my feelings. Nothing you say shall change my mind. You can*not* put your own fate at risk to save a little girl who may die later anyway. Her heart is weak. You said so. There'll be other contagions, Gabriel. Saving her now will mostly likely be only temporary."

"Will you give me a chance to talk?" Gabe regretted his harsh tone the moment he spoke. Sighing, he finger-combed his hair, trying to gather his thoughts. "I've broken the rules, Nan. I was told in no uncertain terms that I couldn't help the boy or anyone else outside my immediate circle. I tried to pull a fast one, using you and Laney to feed the boy and dog, but the bottom line is, I connived to make it happen. The angels see and hear everything." Tapping his temple, he continued. "They even know what we think and believe. I knew when I told you and Laney about the dog and kid that it wouldn't get past them. We're all supposed to learn lessons while we're here on earth, valuable ones that make us better people. The first time around, I didn't learn, Nan. It was always about me. I guarded my own back. If someone tried to kill me, I killed him first, and I felt *justified*. Sad afterward, yes, but justified in my actions because it was either him or me. I saw bad things, *sad* things, but I never veered off-track to make any attempt to change them. It wasn't my problem, or it wasn't my place to interfere. That's how I lived my whole life!

"And now the angels have given me a second chance. It sounded to me like a really *great* chance at first, but after a month, I'm seeing that the rules the angels gave me have put me right back in the same spot. I'm supposed to ignore cold, hungry, homeless boys. I'm supposed to walk past a starving dog and do nothing. It's still me first. I'm still watching out for Gabe and nobody else."

"You shouldn't feel bad about that," Nan cried. "You are abiding by a heavenly edict!"

Gabe wished he could make her understand, but he knew he probably couldn't. "Do you believe that life is a journey, and that everybody's goal should be to learn from experience, correct their mistakes, and try to become better people along the way?"

"Yes, of course."

"I'm not becoming a better person, honey. I've tried to reach the angels, but they aren't answering. I'm on my own. And none of this seems *right* to me. Making love to you with a lie between us didn't seem right to me. Letting that dog starve to death didn't seem right to me. Ignoring that poor boy didn't seem right to me. And letting that little girl die when I have the power to stop it sure as hell doesn't seem *right* to me."

"Perhaps it isn't for you to second-guess," she said softly. "We truly shouldn't question heavenly messengers."

"Yeah?" Gabe stepped around the bed to get his guns. He bent his head and avoided his wife's gaze as he strapped them around his hips and anchored the holsters to his thighs. When he finally looked up, she stood with her arms clutched at her waist and tears swimming in her eyes. "She's such a pretty little girl, Nan, with brown hair, blue eyes, and a cute little button nose. I can't stay home to bake cookies and let her die before she's had a chance to experience life. I'll burn in hell first."

Nan stood frozen as Gabe circled around her to leave the room. At the door, he stopped with his hand on the knob. "I hate making you cry. For whatever it's worth, I'm sorry."

She whirled on him, her pale cheeks suddenly

slashed with vibrant red, her eyes flashing with anger. "Is it so much for me to ask that my husband do everything within his power during this life to be waiting for me in heaven when my time comes to pass over?"

Standing sideways to the door, Gabe gave her a long look. "That's just it, Nan. If I let that child die, I won't be in heaven. I'll be in a hell of my own making."

Chapter Sixteen

Gabriel's parting words hung in Nan's mind much like a song played on one of those newfangled phonographs, only the tune was hauntingly sad. *If I let that child die, I won't be in heaven. I'll be in a hell of my own making.* And though Nan wanted to cling to her own opinion and stop her husband from doing something so dreadfully misguided and at such a cost to himself, she also had to admit, deep in her heart, that she understood exactly what he'd been trying to tell her.

All during her morning ablutions, Nan thought about that, asking herself what she would do if she were in Gabriel's position. *What if it was Laney who was about to die?* Nan wrestled with that question, wondering if she would still ask Gabriel to stay away from the doctor's office and not intervene if her little sister's life were the one at stake. And in the end, Nan couldn't honestly say one way or the other. She adored Laney, but she also deeply loved her husband. He was a wonderful, caring, intensely thoughtful man who deserved a heavenly reward, not eternal suffering.

He was also far too young to die. Nan left the bedroom with a racing heart. Right now Gabriel was still very much alive. If he could alter events simply because he had foreknowledge of them, why couldn't Nan try to do the same? No angels had whispered in her ear, but she *did* have knowledge of what would happen to her husband just before dawn on Christmas morning.

In the kitchen, Nan decided that she and Laney could breakfast on bread and cheese. Nan had more important things to do besides cook. She took a pencil and a piece of stationery from the secretary in the sitting room and then sat at the long table to draft a letter to her sister. According to Gabriel, the angels could see and hear everything, but Nan doubted that they were watching over her just now. And she wanted to keep it that way. No word could be spoken between her and Laney that might draw attention. Not even so much as a whisper could be uttered.

Nan had just finished writing the missive and folding the paper when she heard Laney's footfalls coming up the stairs. The girl burst into the room, her cheeks as pink as the artificial tulips Nan had on a shelf downstairs. She tossed her satchel on the floor next to the door and beamed a smile at Nan.

"I had the best time, Mama! Melody's father got the family a phonograph for Christmas! He took the stage clear to Denver to buy it!" Laney spun in a circle, her skirt whirling at midcalf around her white stockings. "We danced, and we sang! It was so much fun!"

"I'm so glad you enjoyed it," Nan said with a smile. "Have you had any breakfast?"

"Melody's mother made all of us girls battered toast and eggs. We had maple syrup, too! I'm stuffed!"

Nan started to tell the child that young ladies said, "I am more than sufficiently satisfied," but all of the rules suddenly seemed trivial. "Mmm, maple syrup. I need to buy some for our table."

Laney bent to hug Nan's neck and kiss her cheek. Then she fetched her satchel and dashed to her bedroom. A few minutes later, when the child had finished unpacking and returned to the kitchen, Nan laid a finger over her lips, signaling silence, and pushed the letter across the table.

Laney frowned in bewilderment. "What?"

Nan waved her hand, signaled for silence again, and tapped the paper with her finger, gesturing for Laney to read. The girl gave her another puzzled look, but she obediently sat down and opened the letter. Nan watched the child's gray eyes shift from left to right as she assimilated the message in its entirety. When finished reading, Laney glanced toward the ceiling and then leaned toward Nan to whisper, "*Champion* idea!"

Minutes later, both Nan and Laney, garbed in their winter cloaks, left the shop. Nan's task was to visit every business along the far boardwalk of Main. Laney was to work the opposite side. Together they walked to one end of the street, where they parted company to begin their mission. Nan could only hope that her plan worked. If she dared to pray for that, the angels would surely get wind of what she and Laney were up to, and Gabriel would be lost for certain.

By eleven o'clock, Gabe had convinced himself at least a hundred times to hightail it to Nan's shop and forget his lofty intention to sacrifice himself to save a small child. It was crazy to knowingly embrace eternal damnation. It wasn't his place to intervene. One man couldn't save the whole world.

Only, every time Gabe started to abandon his post in front of Peterson's office, he couldn't quite make his feet move. He wasn't trying to save *everyone*, dammit, only one small person in a tiny Colorado town. Maybe his sacrifice today wouldn't make a hill of beans' difference, but at least he would die the second time knowing that he had tried. He didn't want to lie in the street again, with black spots veiling his vision and the breath slowly leaving his body, knowing that his passing would be considered by others to be more a blessing than a tragedy. Not that the little girl would understand the magnitude of what Gabe was doing. Hell, as far as that went, her mother wouldn't grasp it either.

But I'll know, he assured himself, *and whatever happens later, I'll feel a hell of a lot better about my time here on earth.*

When Rose Wilson rounded the corner onto Oak Street with her daughter in hand, Gabe swallowed hard a couple of times. Damned if he didn't feel nearly as scared as he had during his first shoot-out. All his instincts told him to run like a scalded dog. But he managed not to budge.

Rose Wilson gave him wary looks as she approached Peterson's office door. Fearing that she might dash inside the building to avoid him, Gabe stepped between the woman and the doorway. She jerked to a startled stop and pinned a frightened blue gaze on him. *Blue eyes, very like her daughter's.* It pleased Gabe to note the resemblance. It gave him a picture to hold in his mind of what little Charity might look like when she grew up and had babies of her own.

"Mrs. Wilson, there's—"

"I'm sorry," she interrupted. "I don't know you, sir, and you're blocking our way. My little girl has an appointment with the physician, and we're running late."

"It's an appointment you shouldn't keep," Gabe told her. "You and I haven't met, but Doc told me to wait out here to waylay you before you went inside." It was yet another lie for Gabe, who had seldom uttered falsehoods during his first try at life. *Shit.* Maybe instead of becoming a better person, he was trading one set of bad habits for another. "There's a contagion going around. It's hitting the little ones and the elderly really hard, and because of your daughter's weak heart, Doc thinks it's a bad idea for her to be exposed. He says he'll drop by your house as soon as he can. That way Charity won't be around all those people"—Gabe gestured toward the waiting room—"inside who are sick. Doc has no proof of it, but he believes that contact with sick people spreads this kind of illness."

Rose Wilson retreated a step and flicked a worried glance at the closed door. "Dr. Peterson told you this?" She looked up at Gabe. "I don't get out very much. My husband mentioned that a contagion was going around, but he never indicated that I should skip Charity's weekly exam with Dr. Peterson because of it."

Gabe was just happy that his lie had eased the woman's mind. Apparently, however much he felt that he'd changed on the inside over the last month, he still looked meaner than a snake on the outside. The little girl peered wide-eyed up at him, and he smiled down at her. She pressed her head against her mother's coat, peeked at him again, and giggled. Gabe's smile widened into a genuine grin.

"Maybe your husband didn't think about it. A write-up about the contagion was on the front page of this week's paper, a headline in bold type so it really stood out. I guess maybe you missed it?"

"We don't buy the paper," she replied.

Judging by her worn cloak and the faded hem of her dress, Gabe guessed the Wilsons couldn't spare the coin. "Well, it's lucky that Doc asked me to wait out here for you then," Gabe replied. "If you take Charity inside, he's afraid she'll come down sick with this ailment, and it's a dangerous one."

"My husband mentioned that a couple of old people died."

"More than a couple," Gabe corrected. "Even Mrs. Barker, the lady who used to own the milliner's shop, is dead."

Rose Wilson retreated another step, tugging her

daughter along with her. "I'm sorry to hear that, and thank you for the warning," she said. "It was good of you to wait out here, especially in this cold without a coat." She turned to go and then stopped. "I'm sorry. I didn't catch your name, sir."

Gabe tipped his hat. "Gabriel Valance, ma'am, and pardon me for my lack of good manners. I should have introduced myself."

She smiled shyly. "I shall tell my husband of your kindness, Mr. Valance. He stocks shelves for Mr. Red-mond at the general store. If you stop by there tomor-row, perhaps he can arrange for you to receive a small discount on a purchase."

"No need for that," Gabe assured her. "I'm pleased to have been of help."

Gabe watched as Rose Wilson scurried along the boardwalk with her daughter. He felt as if a thousand pounds had been lifted off his chest. He took a deep breath of the crisp, cold air. *What is it about women and coats?* He shook his head, wondering at the differences between males and females. Then he turned to enter the physician's waiting room.

The place was packed with sick people, standing room only. Gabe wove his way through the throng, fleetingly worried about getting sick himself, and then silently laughed at the irony. If he caught the contagion, it would have to work fast to beat the bullet he was destined for. A harried, gray-haired woman in a brown dress stood before the closed door of what Gabe guessed was the treatment room. She looked to be about Doc's age. In one hand she held a small writing board, and in the other a pencil poised over the paper. Head bent, she went over a list, scratching things out and adding at the bottom. Gabe assumed she was the doctor's wife and that she was keeping track of which patient's turn it was.

"Mrs. Peterson?"

Her gold-rimmed spectacles had slipped to the end of her nose, so when she glanced up, she stared at him myopically. "Yes?"

"My name's Gabriel Valance. I'm married to Nan over at the hat shop."

Mrs. Peterson smiled wearily. "Ah, Mr. Valance. The good doctor mentioned meeting you. He came away with a high opinion of you, I must say."

"The feeling is mutual," Gabe replied. "Listen, I didn't drop in to pester you when you're clearly so busy. I just happened to run into Rose Wilson outside. She was about to bring Charity in for her weekly appointment. Given the girl's weak heart, I didn't think Doc would want her in here with all these sick folks, so I warned Mrs. Wilson away. Doc told me that he believes illness is spread from person to person and that this sickness is hitting the little ones and the old people really hard. Charity is probably frailer than most children her age."

Mrs. Peterson winced. "Oh, dear, how *right* you are, Mr. Valance! My husband wouldn't wish for Charity to be here. She's so very fragile! I should have thought to get a message over to Rose myself, but I've been . . . well, extremely busy, and I just didn't think of it." She seemed to wilt before Gabe's eyes, like a picked flower left too long in the sun. "It's my job to keep track and make other arrangements for patients like Charity." She pressed the hand holding the pencil over her heart. "It's just that so *many* are sick. I've barely had time to think. I'm so glad you warned Rose away. If something were to happen to that precious child because I failed to . . . Well, I'd simply never forgive myself."

"Can you ask Doc to stop by the Wilson place when he has a chance?" Gabe asked.

Mrs. Peterson jotted a note to one side of the patient

list. "I certainly shall." She sent Gabe another strained smile. "It is God's work that you did out there. It settles in the chest, you know. My husband keeps telling people to stay home, or if they must go out, to wash their hands thoroughly after shopping, but very few listen. His belief about how illnesses are spread hasn't been proven, and most people think he's gone a little dotty."

Gabe left the waiting room feeling as if he were walking on air. And, he thought with wry amusement, he was one of the few people on earth who actually knew how that felt. *God's work.* As he strode along Oak Street toward Main, he grinned broadly. Maybe in hell he'd get to perch on a fire-warmed rock and wouldn't have to stand with his feet in the flames. At the corner, he stopped to pull his watch from his pocket. Not yet noon. Maybe he'd be home in time to help Nan and Laney make cookies.

As he passed the saloon, Gabe was picturing how gorgeous the tree would look tonight with lighted candles on it. He felt as excited as he imagined a small child might. *Christmas.* It was such a special time of year, and he was about to experience it firsthand. Well, not all of it. He'd miss Christmas Day. But he damned sure meant to enjoy the bits that he could.

His feet dragged to a stop in front of the brothel stairway. His chest tightened. Then he thought, *Why the hell not? In for a penny, in for a pound.* He took a sharp left and ducked under the stairs.

The boy huddled in the corner. Gabe saw that he now wore new boots, compliments of Nan, but from the ankles up, the kid was a sorry sight. He shrank into the corner formed by the two exterior walls. Nan's pretty quilts, which he'd been keeping warm with, were now even dirtier than he was.

"If you're gonna shoot me, take careful aim," the

youth said loudly. "I don't want no slug in my kidney, either."

Gabe realized that the boy had witnessed his confrontation in the street with the aspiring gunslinger. That led Gabe to wonder what other awful things he had seen. He was hiding right in the middle of the devil's playground, and what he hadn't actually witnessed, he'd probably overheard.

"I've never shot anybody who didn't try to shoot me first." Gabe sat with his back to the clapboard siding, about three feet from the kid. He said nothing for a moment, and when he did speak, he weighed his words carefully. "You know that nice lady who brings you food and bought you the boots?"

"Your wife, she said."

"That's right; she's my wife." Gabe repositioned his hat, nudging up the brim to make his face more visible. "She's a good woman with a gentle heart."

"Fussy as can be, though. She likes usin' big words and actin' fancy. I don't understand what she's talkin' about half the time."

"A really good cook, though."

The boy nodded. "True enough. I never ate meat as tender as what she puts in my sandwiches. She makes 'em so thick I can hardly open my mouth wide enough to sink my chompers into 'em."

"She doesn't want you going hungry." Gabe rubbed behind his ear. "She wants to take you in, give you a real home, and raise you like you were her own, you know. I told her absolutely not."

The kid shot Gabe a glare. "Why? You figure I'm not good enough to be around her kind?"

"Pretty much. I bet you'd squeal like a stuck pig if she told you to take a bath."

"I would not!" The boy pushed at his hair. "My

mama made me take baths regular-like, at least once every two weeks, and in between I took whore's baths."

Gabe deliberately winced. "There, you see? You talk like a guttersnipe. I was right to tell her no. She's a lady, and she's trying to raise her daughter to be one. She can't have some rough-talking kid in her home. You'd be a bad influence on Laney, for sure."

"Laney. Is that the fussy little snot with ribbons on her pigtails?"

Gabe almost grinned. "That'd be Laney, only she's not a snot. Fussy, maybe. Most females are."

"My mama wasn't."

"My mama wasn't, either. But ladies of the night, like your mama and mine, don't have much chance to be particular, do they? They lead hard lives, and it's a challenge just to keep food in their bellies." Gabe gazed out at the street, watching a couple of wagons pass by. "Somebody in this town ought to start a whore-saving place, some nice building where women like your mama could stay, and even be given money so they could leave this town and try to make a new start. That way they wouldn't feel the need to take off with some sweet-talking cowpoke and end up in a world of hurt somewhere along the trail."

"Ha." The youth shifted and hugged his bony knees. "You go on and do it, mister. All the highfalutin folks in this town would tar and feather you up, then run you out on a rail."

Gabe chuckled. "Random doesn't have any rails. I reckon they could tie my ankles to the back of a stagecoach and drag me out of town, though."

"I doubt it. They'd be afraid of gettin' shot for their trouble."

Gabe couldn't argue the point. Not many people felt inclined to take Gabe on.

"You reckon that's what happened to my ma? That she ran into a world of hurt?"

The boy's voice rang with dread, but Gabe also heard a note of resignation. The kid knew his mother would never come back. He was still clinging to a fragile hope because that was all he had. "I'm afraid so, son, though I'm sorry to think it."

"That cowpoke—he wasn't no good. He told Mama he loved her. He promised her the moon. Even said once they got settled somewhere, she could come back for me. I tried to tell her he was a lyin' bastard, but she believed him and went."

"So what do you plan to do now?" Gabe asked.

The boy rested his chin on his knees. "I haven't got past waitin' for her yet. Mama loves me. She'll come back if she can." He slanted a look at Gabe. "She's a good mother. You probably think no whore can be, but if you do, you're wrong. When she got pregnant with me, the madam where she worked told her to get rid of me before I got born or else she'd lose her job. Mama kept me and ended up on the street."

Gabe's heart gave a painful twist. "What's your name, son?"

"Christopher."

"Well, Chris, I—"

"It ain't *Chris*. You got bad hearin' or somethin'? My mother named me *Christopher*, and she held real tight to that. Said it was a proper name, one for me to be proud of."

"It's a very proper name," Gabe agreed. "It has a real important ring. Does it come with a surname?"

"Broderick. That came from my mama. She didn't know for sure who my daddy was."

"Christopher Broderick," Gabe mused aloud. "That's real fine. If I were to invite you to come home with me and spend Christmas with my family, do you think you could clean your mouth up, take a bath, suffer through a haircut, and condescend to wear some new clothes for a few days?"

Christopher favored Gabe with a disgusted look. "That your idea of doin' a good deed for Christmas? What happens after? Do I get tossed back on the street in my holey clothes to stay under this staircase again until my mama comes back?"

"That would depend on you," Gabe replied. "I won't countenance any foul language in the presence of my ladies. Absolutely *none,* and if you're inclined to pitch fits, hurting others in the process, I don't countenance that, either. And if you steal so much as a penny from my wife's cash drawer, I'll skin you alive and hang your hide over the back line to dry. Are we pretty clear on what I expect?"

"What, exactly, do you count as foul language?"

Gabe met the boy's questioning stare. "If you say 'shit,' I'll serve you some on a spoon and make you eat it. If you say 'hell,' you'll think you're there for a nasty visit. If you say 'damn,' I'll kick your behind so hard your tonsils will ache. Is that *exact* enough for you?" Gabe waited a beat. "And no calling my daughter a fussy snot, either. You can call her fussy if you're inclined, but watch out for her right hook."

Christopher grinned. "Are you really gonna take me home with you?"

"Only if you agree to my terms. And if something happens that I'm no longer around, I want your word, as Christopher Broderick, that you'll continue to abide by my rules until your mother shows up."

"Hot damn, what're we waitin' for?" The kid scrambled to his feet so fast his head came into contact with the bottom of the staircase. He barely seemed to notice. "You . . . I mean, this is for real? You mean it?"

Gabe wondered if he was about to make the worst

mistake of his life. Well, not the *worst*, maybe, but close enough to call it a first-ring bull's-eye. "We're waiting for you to give me your word."

"You got it."

"Say it."

"You've got my word as Christopher Broderick."

Gabe gave him a long, measuring stare. "Is your word as good as your name, Christopher?"

"I'll try my best to make it be."

Gabe figured that was all that could be asked of anyone. He pushed to his feet and dusted off the seat of his jeans. "We've got a heap of shopping to do, then. I can't take you home to my wife without some decent clothing for you to wear. She'll want you in the bathtub lickety-split, and what you're wearing will go in the fire. Even standing upwind of you, my nose is twitching."

"You'd stink, too, if you went as long as I have without a bath. Last rain we had, I wet a piece of sheet in a mud puddle to wash up. People around here get real upset if I borrow from their rain barrels. One man took after me with a shotgun loaded with rock salt. My ass was on fire for days."

"Ass," Gabe echoed. "There's another word I don't want you saying in front of the ladies."

"If not ass, what do ladies call it, then?"

Gabe led the way across the street toward the general store. "I don't rightly know. Now that I come to think about it, my wife pretty much pretends she isn't in possession of one."

Nan had just taken her big green mixing bowl from the cupboard when she heard the sound of boots coming up the stairs. She pasted a bright smile on her face and turned to greet her husband as the door opened, hoping that their disagreement that morning could go unmentioned and be put behind them. Arms laden with string-tied brown paper packages, Gabriel stepped into the room, wiggled his eyebrows at her, and said, "Nan, I brought home a guest."

Nan smelled the boy before she saw him. The staircase acted as a funnel, bringing the unpleasant bouquet of an unwashed body into the room in a rush. "How lovely! And who might our guest be?"

Still on the stairs two steps below, the boy peeked around Gabriel's lean hip. In the good light from the kitchen lamps, his shaggy, oily, and knotted hair was a sight to behold. "It's me, ma'am."

Nan had wished several times to bring the boy home, but Gabriel had adamantly said no. She tried to hide her surprise at her husband's sudden change of heart. Apparently, after saving the little girl, he'd decided to rescue the boy as well.

"I'm on a roll," he offered by way of explanation. Then, arms still filled with bundles, he stepped farther into the room to allow the child entry. "Nan, allow me to introduce you properly to Christopher Broderick. Christopher, this is my wife, Mrs. Valance. If she chooses to allow you the liberty, you may call her Nan."

"Oh, most certainly! Nan is fine. Please do come in, Christopher. I was about to start making Christmas cookies." She glanced at the child's hands, which clasped yet more packages to his thin chest. Not only were his fingers brown with grime, but the undersides of his nails were black. "Perhaps, um, you'd like to . . . help."

Gabriel saved the day. "He needs a good scrub first. Can you postpone cookie making to put some water on to heat?"

"The reservoir is full, and the water is piping hot. I just built up the fire to get the oven ready for baking."

Gabriel deposited the packages he carried on the ta-

ble and motioned for the boy to do the same. "He's
going to need a little extra. One tubful for washing and
another for rinsing."

Nan kept her large pots under the sink. She hurried
over to fetch them. The sooner that child got neck-deep
in water, the better. As it was, she'd have to dab vanilla
all over the house to sweeten the air. *Christopher*. What
a nice, solid name, with a ring to it that was similar to
Gabriel. Perhaps, she thought disjointedly, soiled doves
chose particularly impressive names for their children
to draw attention away from the fact that they were
bastards. *Dear God*. How had *that* word popped into
her brain? Keeping company with Gabriel had tam-
pered with her thinking, and if she wasn't cautious,
she'd soon be talking as he did, without a care in the
world for propriety.

To Gabe, the remainder of the day and that evening
ranked as the best he'd ever enjoyed. Well, if he dis-
counted last night with Nan, anyhow. Making love
with her had been purely glorious and inexplicably
sweet. He'd never in his life wanted a woman so much,
and he counted himself truly blessed to have had the
experience. If he could figure out how to do so with
two kids in the apartment, he meant to feel blessed
again before bedtime. Maybe after the children went to
sleep, he could spirit Nan downstairs and make love
with her in a hidey-hole.

For reasons beyond him, she seemed to be completely over their quarrel that morning. In fact, she appeared to be happy beyond measure, and if she had a
care in the world, she didn't reveal it. Gabe was
pleased. He didn't want the time he had left to be ruined by gloomy thoughts.

After Christopher emerged from the water closet,
transformed from a street urchin into a handsome

youngster, Nan commandeered everyone to help in the kitchen. Laney, a difficult one to predict at times, surprised Gabe by befriending the boy in a relaxed, offhanded manner, almost as if she sensed that a bunch of ado would make Christopher uncomfortable.

"Here, Christopher," she said as she handed him a bowl of dough. "You can help me roll and cut. Mama says those who don't help aren't allowed to eat." Laney smiled impishly. "Unless you want me devouring all the cookies, you'd better fold back your shirtsleeves."

Gabe would have bet a thousand dollars that Christopher had never even seen raw cookie dough, but the kid managed well enough by taking his cues from Laney. Soon he worked with the rolling pin while Laney came in behind him to industriously cut circular shapes with a floured tin can that was just the right size for sugar cookies. Nan got out flat, rectangular baking pans, and before he knew it, the wonderful smells he'd imagined that morning wafted through the kitchen, which was dusted with flour on nearly every surface. Nan, ever tidy, didn't seem to be bothered by the mess. Instead of wiping counters and fussing, she stood at the stove, stirring a pot of cocoa fudge, a treat Gabe had never tasted. He had a hunch that Christopher hadn't either.

Gabe went to stand at his wife's elbow. Leaning in close, he asked, "Have I told you today how beautiful and sweet you are?"

Her cheek dimpled. "No, I don't believe you have, Mr. Valance."

Pitching his voice to a husky, suggestive whisper, he murmured, "That's a mighty proper form of address. I hope it doesn't mean that you plan to stand on formalities all evening."

She flashed him a smile. "We've big ears about. Do you have a devious plan up your sleeve?"

"Oh, yeah."

She giggled, and her cheeks turned a pretty pink. "I'm sorry about this morning."

"No need to be. Your concerns were legitimate."

She shrugged and deepened her smile. "Yes, but so were yours. I thought about it, and I came to understand how you feel." She had paused in her stirring. In a hushed voice, she said, "Thank you so much for bringing Christopher here. It's the decent thing for us to do."

At that moment, Gabe's thoughts were far from decent. He couldn't wait to get her downstairs alone later. "Don't scorch our fudge," he warned.

After a quick supper of meat gravy over mashed potatoes, everyone joined in to help tidy the kitchen. Gabe was pleased by Christopher's eagerness to lend a hand, even though the kid had no idea what to do. When everything shone per Nan's rigid standards, Gabe went downstairs to bring up the tree, and then they gathered in the sitting room, where the small tables were now laden with treat-filled plates. They had brown-sugar brittle, squares of cocoa fudge, and two kinds of cookies, one a plain sugar cookie, the other containing nuts and brown-sugar crystals.

Lighted lanterns cast a warm golden glow over the room. Gabe stood back to admire the tree, which he'd placed in front of the window that looked over Main. "I think it's perfect just as it is. Why trim it with anything?"

Laney squeaked in dismay. "Nuh-uh. We have strings of dried berries and little ornaments Mama and I made with things from her shop. Plus we've saved candle stubs all year just for this!"

Christopher stared at the pine boughs with a rapt expression on his face. Gabe knew the feeling. It was a very special thing to have a tree inside the house. Even the smell of it was divine.

With Gabe's and Christopher's help, Nan brought two boxes of ornaments upstairs, and the tree-trimming party officially began. Laney and Christopher prepared and served mugs of hot milk cocoa, so everyone could sip and nibble as the tree was draped with strings of dried holly berries. The hot chocolate was as good as Gabriel had imagined, and judging from the rapt expression on Christopher's face when he took a sip, the kid agreed.

"Up a little," Gabe was instructed as he adorned the higher boughs with garland. Then, "No, that's not right. Down just a bit."

Tree trimming, he discovered, was an arduous and exacting task.

"You can't simply throw things on a tree," Nan said more than once. And Laney always rejoined with, "Absolutely not!"

Gabe and Christopher shared a couple of long stares, sending silent, purely male sentiments back and forth. *Fussy.* And, oh, how the ladies did fuss. From the boxes, Nan unearthed frilly little things—ribbons tied into bows, several hand-fashioned Santa Claus and angel figures, and miniature Christmas trees of beaded green felt, all of which were hung from the tree boughs with bent hairpins. Then it came time to position the candle stubs.

"How the hell are we gonna make 'em sit straight?" Christopher asked.

"Language," Gabe said softly.

Christopher flashed an apologetic look at Nan. "I'm sorry, ma'am. I plumb forgot."

Nan placed a hand on the boy's shoulder. "It may be difficult for you at first, but after a time, avoiding the use of certain words will become habit." Then, as if the slip had never occurred, Nan added, "And making the candles sit straight is easy. There's a bit of a trick to it."

The trick, as it turned out, was to light each stub, then tip the flame to melt wax onto the boughs. The blobs acted like a glue of sorts, affixing the candle to the needles.

When the tree stood finished, Gabe had to admit that all the fussing had been worth the effort. "Oh, that is pretty."

"Wait until you see it with the candles lighted!" Laney cried.

"First, we need to bring out our socks and put them on the hearth, and then you children can set out the nativity scene on the top shelf of my secretary."

"All my socks are brand-spankin'-new," Christopher blurted, his expression filled with dismay. "I'd like to wear 'em all before I use 'em for anything else. What do we need to put socks on the hearth for, anyhow?"

Laney grabbed Christopher's hand. "Your sock won't be damaged, so you can wear it all you like later. But we must put one out. Otherwise Santa Claus will have nowhere to leave us small gifts."

Gabe knew precisely what Christopher was thinking: Santa had never bothered to bring him anything before, so he wasn't likely to start now. To the boy's credit, he went with Laney and soon returned with a new sock in his hand. Laney had an older one, which was far too large for either her or Nan.

"I bought a pair of men's socks at the general store," Nan explained. "Our stockings weren't practical."

Gabe saw her point. It would take a heap of gifts to fill a full-length stocking. Before he knew it, he was rifling through his saddlebags for a sock of his own. Nan had done wash, and much like Christopher, Gabe hated to use a clean sock for such nonsense. But he didn't think his grabbing a stinky one would go over well with his wife.

"What'll we put in them?" he asked Nan a few minutes later while the kids were preoccupied with setting out the nativity scene. "I've never had a sock filled."

"Store-bought candies, toiletry items, just silly little things," she whispered back. Glancing up to catch the bewildered look on Gabe's face, she smiled and added, "It's part of the Christmas magic, Gabriel. We can even put funny things in the socks so everyone laughs on Christmas morning." Her face went suddenly taut, and shadows filled her eyes. Then, forcing her lips back into a curve, she quickly added, "Perhaps Santa will come on Christmas Eve this year."

Gabe felt as if a fist had connected with his solar plexus. Nan had just remembered that he wouldn't be around on Christmas morning, and her expression drove it home for him as well. For an instant, he felt weighed down with sadness. But when he looked at the tree, he shoved the gloom from his mind.

Nan finally lit the tree candles. Gabe stood behind her, encircled her waist with his arms, and rested his chin atop her head. "It's beautiful," he whispered. "Almost as beautiful as you are."

She sighed and relaxed her weight against him. "There's nothing more beautiful than a Christmas tree."

Gabe could have argued the point.

Laney brought out her violin, and the next half hour was spent singing Christmas carols. Gabe and Christopher didn't know the words, so they only hummed along as Nan's and Laney's sweet voices trilled in the room with, "God Rest Ye Merry Gentlemen," "The First Noel," "I Saw Three Ships," and finally "Hark! The Herald Angels Sing." After that, Laney played some other tunes, giving Gabe an opportunity to once again waltz with his wife. Looking down at her, the flickering glow of the candlelight playing over her golden hair and lovely face, he decided he hadn't been far wrong the first time he saw her. She truly was beautiful enough to be an angel.

Until Nan's upstairs workroom could be transformed into a bedchamber, Christopher had to sleep on the settee. Nan fashioned him a comfortable resting place with sheets, quilts, and a pillow.

After getting both kids tucked away for the night, Gabe sat with his wife at the kitchen table, his ears pricked for a change in Christopher's breathing to signal that he'd fallen asleep. The instant Gabe heard a snuffle, he spirited his wife downstairs.

Nan giggled in the darkness of the shop. "Gabriel, we can't engage in the act down here. We've no *bed*."

Gabe figured he could make love to Nan almost anywhere. But given her fastidious nature, he felt fairly certain she would feel more relaxed inside her work area with at least the curtain pulled for privacy. "We'll use your project table, ma'am." He grinned.

"What?" She started to protest but he caught her close, stopping the words with a kiss.

Nan's project table, once divested of stuff, served Gabriel's purpose quite well. And, Nan, though nervous about *engaging in the act* in so inappropriate a place, responded to him with gasping, quivering surrender. When it came Gabe's turn for release, his pleasure was so intense and physically draining that he wondered how he'd ever carry his limp wife back upstairs.

Chapter Seventeen

Over the next two days, Gabe could have sworn he heard a clock ticking away the minutes inside his head, and he wanted to make every single one last as long as he could. Only, somehow, in all the rush of shopping, baking, and present wrapping, the hours seemed to fly by. He couldn't recall ever having been quite so busy—or so happy. Preparing for Christmas was more fun than he expected, and he relished learning about Nan's traditions. They rented a buggy to go find pine boughs so they could make Christmas swags and drape the shop windows with greenery. Bread had to be dried to make stuffing. Surprises were hidden away. Whispers were exchanged. Last-minute dashes to the general store occurred because Nan forgot to get this or that. The entire building, both upstairs and down, was so redolent with fabulous smells from the oven that Gabe wished he could eat the air.

Gabe made use of every opportunity he got to make love to his wife. Nan, he discovered, tended to shriek when her passions peaked, and shrieking and kids didn't mix. At night in their bed, Gabe took to muffling her cries with deep kisses while he aroused her with his hands. *Whatever works.* He had so little time to make memories with her, so little time to show her how much he loved her.

He felt no fear when he considered what would occur just before dawn on Christmas morning. What
bothered him was that Nan would grieve for him. If it
were left up to him, he never would have caused her
one second of heartache. His only consolation was that
Nan would eventually get over him and move on.
When she did, she would no longer cleave only unto
herself. She wouldn't be afraid to love again, or to
marry again. By spending this month with her, he was
giving her an opportunity to see what it could be like
to live one's life to its fullest.

Oddly, by giving Nan that insight, Gabe was being
repaid a hundredfold, sort of like how Preacher Hayes
claimed it went if you tithed generously at church. His
time with Nan and the kids gave Gabe a taste of real
living. *This*, he realized, *is how it could have been for me if
I'd never picked up a gun. I could have met Nan and married
her, and we could have had children of our own.* Oh, how
Gabe wished it had happened that way. He'd never
yearned for offspring during his first try at life, but he
did now.

Late in the evening on December 23, that yearning
grew so sharp within Gabe that he whispered of it to
Nan as he drew her into his arms after they climbed
into bed. "You know what I wish?"

He felt her smile against his jaw. "Uh-oh, you're
getting the hang of this Christmas stuff. Is it a Santa
Claus wish? If so, tomorrow evening when the children write wish notes to him and put them in the fire
so the chimney smoke can carry their messages to
the North Pole, you'll have to join in."

"I don't think this is a gift that Santa can deliver," he
said softly, his voice oddly hoarse. "I wish I could make
a baby with you—a child of our very own, a part of us
both."

Nan pressed closer. "Ah." She turned her lips against

his ear. "Then plant a fertile seed in my garden, Gabriel. I shall nurture it and love it and cherish it."

Gabe wondered if he'd already sown a seed. They'd done nothing to prevent a pregnancy. "I won't be here to help you raise a child. It's a rough road to walk alone, honey."

"Not if a woman is a millionaire," she quipped. "That said, I haven't given up hope that the angels may decide you deserve to remain here. You're a wonderful man, Gabriel, a special gift in my life, and in the lives of others."

"Others?"

He felt her lips curve again. "Silly man. Did you fail to notice today how fond all the shopkeepers have become of you? Mr. Wilson at the general store has told anyone who'll listen how you saved his little girl's life! And Doc Peterson, who has seen half the town's population, has naught but good things to say of you. You're leaving a long trail of friends behind you."

Friends. Gabe had never had one. "You really think those shopkeepers *like* me?"

Nan smothered a giggle against his shoulder. "You sound rather horrified."

Gabe had to stifle a laugh himself against her silken hair, which smelled so intoxicating that he could have gotten as drunk as a lord just sniffing. "Not horrified, only baffled. Nobody has ever liked me."

She feathered kisses along the underside of his jaw. "I like you—a *lot*. And now so do other people. You're a very likable person, Gabriel Valance. Gossip runs rampant about your saving Charity Wilson and then rescuing Christopher. Your true colors have been showing."

Gabe felt her hand slip downward to his thigh. He knew an invitation when he received one. He sorely wished the children weren't sleeping in rooms so short a distance from theirs. He wanted to make love with his wife using his lips and tongue to pleasure her, but he couldn't do that if he had to be kissing her constantly to keep her from crying out.

"Nan," he asked in a husky whisper, "if I asked you to bite down hard on one of my clean socks, would you do it?"

"Why on earth would you ask me to do that?"

He traced circles below her ear with his tongue. "I want to show you how it feels to be in paradise."

Moments later, Gabe carried through on that wish, and Nan, body convulsing with pleasure, uttered only moans muffled by wool.

On Christmas Eve morning, Nan blushed every time Gabe looked her way. Over breakfast, he tried his damnedest to keep his gaze on his plate. Every time he glanced up, his wife's face turned as red as Santa's suit, and he was afraid the kids might notice. Laney, who had been released from school in honor of the holiday, and Christopher, who wouldn't be enrolled until Monday, were as sticky as honey, hovering near Nan and Gabe constantly, as if they might miss something. When the pair of them finally left to go feed the dog, he caught Nan around the waist where she stood at the sink and, while kissing her neck, murmured, "Cleaning up can wait."

"Gabriel," she protested, "we can't possibly! The children might return at any moment, and even if we finish before they get back, I'll be all mussed and—"

"Boneless," he interjected.

"I'll need to wash up. And how shall I explain that when I've already—"

"I'll bring you a wet cloth, and I'll tell the kids that you're taking a quick nap so you'll be rested for tonight's Christmas Eve festivities."

Gabe felt the resistance in her body drain away. He

lifted her into his arms, carried her into their room, deposited her on the bed, and then found the skeleton key in her armoire to lock the bedroom door from the inside. When he returned to his wife a moment later, she was unbuttoning her bodice, revealing to him that her high color ran well below her cheeks.

As he started toeing off his boots, she said, "Gabriel, I shan't enjoy . . . well, you know, the, um, activities we engaged in last night. It's broad daylight, and . . . well, even if we pull the shade, it won't be dark in here, and I just—"

Gabe, already out of his shirt, leaned down to silence her with a long, deep kiss. She sighed blissfully when he lifted his head to smile at her. "You know how to make it really dark in here?" he asked.

"No." She blinked, her expression a mixture of puzzlement and yearning. "How?"

Gabe stretched out beside her and began helping with her buttons. "Just close your eyes, sweetheart. The light will go out."

"But *you'll* still be able to see."

And he planned to enjoy the view. A few minutes later, his precious wife reached down to make fists in his hair in a halfhearted attempt to make him stop nuzzling her thighs apart. "Gabriel?" she squeaked. "I have no sock to bite. I truly think this should— Oh! *Don't* . . . Oh, *my!*"

"The kids are gone," he murmured against her.

That was all it took to send her over the edge.

Nan was dressed and perfectly coiffed again by the time she heard the children coming up the stairs. She smiled dreamily at Gabriel, who'd just straightened from putting something in the icebox. He looked so handsome, freshly shaved, with his black hair damp and just combed.

"Christmas Eve shall begin in earnest now!" Nan informed him. "We'll need to take them both out to do some last-minute shopping straightaway. The shops will close early. Because of school, they haven't been able to get gifts for anyone yet."

Just then the door flew open. Nan heard a loud thump against the stairway wall, a muffled *oomph* from Laney, and then an odd clicking sound. She turned from the sink with drippy hands suspended to see a blur of yellow barreling toward her. The next thing Nan knew, she had a huge paw on each of her shoulders, and the small of her back was pressed sharply against the counter edge.

"*Off!*" Gabriel said.

With a whine, Nan's assailant lowered his large self onto all fours. Nan stared stupidly down at the creature in her kitchen, a huge golden dog with long, shiny fur and a feathery, crescent-shaped tail that swung wildly back and forth, whacking her cupboard door one moment and Gabriel's thigh the next.

"It's Christopher's fault!" Laney stood shoulder-to-shoulder with her dark-haired partner in crime. "He says nobody should be alone on Christmas Eve, without a home and people to love him, not even a dog."

"Nuh-uh!" Christopher cried. "You can't blame it all on *me*! Ever since I came here, all you've talked about is bringin' him home with us!"

"Oh, *posh*!" Laney protested. "That isn't *all* I've talked about."

"I don't care what Gabe says; you're a fussy little snot!" Christopher nearly shouted. "It was your idea first, and now you're tryin' to get me in trouble for it. I'm not takin' all the responsibility. I'm the one here for temporary, and they could kick me out over it."

"Hey!" Gabe, holding the dog back from Nan by the scruff of its neck, gave both children a warning look.

"We will *not* raise our voices at each other in this house." He shifted his gaze to the boy. "And name-calling is unacceptable. Am I clear?"

"You're the snot!" Laney cried.

"Enough!" Gabe shouted, clearly forgetting that he'd just decreed that nobody in the house should raise his voice. "It doesn't matter whose idea it was to bring this mongrel home. The fact is that Nan said no. I have to back her on that. There's no proper yard out back for him, he'll shed all over our home and her shop, and who'll take him for exercise while you're at school? He'll have a miserable life here, shut away upstairs all day."

"Mr. Redmond has Blacky in his shop all day, every day, and *he* sells foodstuffs." Laney's eyes sparked with fiery indignation. "Why can't Jasper have a bed by Mama's shop stove?"

"Jasper?" Gabe echoed.

"Christopher says that's a famous name for a dog," Laney said. "And I like it. So that's what we call him now. Jasper."

"Well, Jasper has to go back to the lean-to," Gabe said firmly. *"Now."*

Nan finally found her voice. "Wait!" She held up a hand while she gave the dog a long, wary study. She had never owned a dog or been around them much. But this particular canine had huge, soulful brown eyes, which he used to good effect, giving her pleading looks that said more clearly than with words, *Keep me, please keep me. I'll be good. Please, please, pleeease?* And Nan was lost. "Perhaps we can work something out," she heard herself say.

"Nan, he jumped on you," Gabriel reminded her. "He has no manners. What if he knocks Geneva White on her sequined ass?"

"That word ain't allowed," Christopher informed

Gabe with a certain smugness that brought a giggle from Laney. "You said so!"

Nan saw Gabe grimace. He released the dog and straightened. "My apologies, ladies." He sent Christopher a glare. "I plumb forgot."

Nan cupped a hand over her mouth and pretended to cough in order to hide a smile. When she could keep a straight face, she bent over to beckon the dog back to her. "Come here, Jasper. Introduce yourself properly." The dog, in such a flurry to do just that, lost his footing on the waxed boards, and for a horrible moment Nan feared he might do a four-legged split. "He doesn't bite, I hope."

Jasper answered her question by worshipfully licking her outstretched hand. Nan had never in her life seen such a long, agile tongue. She felt certain the animal could clean his own ears with the tip. "Well, now," she said with a laugh. "Aren't you a dear?" Nan crouched down. Jasper started to jump up, but she stopped him with a stern, "*No!*"

The canine moved as close to her as he could get and rested his broad head on her knees, brown eyes locked adoringly on her face. Between one heartbeat and the next, Nan fell hopelessly in love. "Hmm," she mused aloud. "I seem to have a weakness for rascals and have three living with me now." To the dog, she said, "And, like your predecessors, you seem to be trainable." She sent Gabriel a teasing smile. "What do you say, husband? Can we keep him and try to work out the particulars?"

"It's *your* house," Gabriel replied. "And it'll be the fancy gowns of your highfalutin customers that he sheds on."

Nan clucked her tongue. "My highfalutin customers are not the mainstay of my business, and if Jasper runs them off, I shan't mourn the loss. That goes especially for

Geneva. No more dead canaries and no more garish sequins on a day gown." Nan discovered the joy of scratching a dog behind the ears and watching its face go droopy with pleasure. "You're a fine fellow, aren't you? Yes, you are. We'll teach you some manners, and before we know it, you'll be a courtly gentleman. Yes, you will."

Laney squealed with delight and began bouncing about in circles. Christopher, rooted in the center of her joyous circumference, pushed at his long hair and rolled his eyes. But a grin tugged at the corners of his mouth.

Deciding it was time to lay out the rules, Nan stood. "He must be brushed every *single* day."

"I'll do it!" both kids vowed simultaneously.

"And during the week, one of you must take him for a morning walk, one of you must come home during school lunch hour to take him for another run, and then he'll need to go in the evening. Always clear to the edge of town, mind you, where he can—" Nan broke off, searching for the right words. "Take care of his serious business," she settled on saying. "We can't have him making messes out front on the boardwalk."

Again, both children chimed in to volunteer. "It will grow to be a chore," Nan warned. "On snowy days, I don't wish to hear any moaning and groaning, not from either of you. Having a pet involves a lot of work, and I shall expect both of you to be responsible, caring, and Johnny-on-the-spot about seeing to his needs. If I find his water dish empty, you shall both do without supper that night, and I will *not* give in if you whine about it."

Christopher angled a mischievous look at Laney. "Hell, he may not be worth it. Maybe we should take him back to the lean-to."

"*No!*" Laney shouted.

"You're yelling!" Christopher accused loudly.

"Language!" Gabriel roared.

Nan had to stifle a laugh. Raised voices were bouncing off all her walls, and she *loved* it. At long last, she and Laney were part of a real family. They even had a dog, which in Nan's estimation made the picture absolutely complete.

During the shopping trip for the children, Nan and Gabriel split up, each of them taking a child so both youngsters could buy a gift for the absent adult and each other. Nan took Christopher with her first, and then in an hour she met Gabriel in front of the general store to switch kids. Laney's eyes were sparkling. She'd clearly had a wonderful time touring the stores with Gabriel, who had apparently stopped by Nan's shop to deposit the fruits of their labor. He reached to take the packages that Nan and Christopher held in their arms, clearly intending to drop them off at home, too.

"Guess what I got you, snot," Christopher volleyed at the girl.

Laney's cheek dimpled. When a gift was involved, she could apparently ignore being called a name. "What?" she asked.

"A great big fat cork to stuff in your mouth." Christopher danced out of the way when Laney tried to smack him.

With the children laughing and racing in circles around them, Nan and Gabriel shared a long look of wordless communication. *I love you.* And, *Isn't this wonderful?* Nan wished she could give her husband a huge hug, but such shows of affection were unacceptable in public places. So instead she tried to embrace him with her eyes. She could tell by the gleam in his that he was thinking about something far more intimate than a mere hug, and she felt heat rush up her neck to pool in her cheeks.

"Are you too hot, Mama?" Laney asked. "I could hold your coat if you want to take it off."

"Er, no, I'm fine," Nan assured her, not daring to look at Gabriel. "Christopher, you go with Gabriel. Laney, it's your turn to come with me. Where do you want to go first?"

Laney took forever to pick gifts for Gabriel and Christopher. She finally settled on a carved ivory harmonica for each of them. Nan gulped when Mr. Redmond told her the price of each instrument.

As Mr. Redmond walked away to wait on a gentleman in search of slippers for his wife, Laney said in a hushed voice, "I'll work in the shop for them, Mama. *Please?* They can learn to play music lickety-split, probably within two weeks or less, and then maybe I'll get to dance sometimes."

Nan's heart caught when she searched her little sister's expression. The child had been told Gabriel's story about the angels, and she surely understood that there was still a good chance that the substitute father she'd come to love might be gone forever by tomorrow. Nan certainly hoped that they had managed to circumvent fate, but she also realized that her scheme might not work.

"Laney, you haven't forgotten Gabriel's appointment tomorrow before dawn, have you?"

The girl's eyes went bright with tears, and her mouth quivered. "It's not going to happen that way again," she whispered fiercely. "Don't even *think* it, Mama. I love him too much! If he dies, I'll die, too!"

Nan drew her sister behind the yardage rack, where they were hidden behind upright bolts of cloth. With trembling arms, she held the child close. "Oh, darling. I know, I know, truly I do, but you mustn't talk that way. We must be strong, you and I. Gabriel needs us to be gay tonight. This is his first *real* Christmas Eve, remember, and just in case it should be his last, we must make it the most wonderful celebration *ever*. That will be our most precious gift to him, smiling even if we can barely hold back our tears."

Laney's thin shoulders jerked with sobs. Nan felt her own chest convulse, and her eyes burned with her attempt to keep them dry.

"Now, now," she whispered, patting her sister's back.

And then Nan sobbed herself. For the first time in her life, she didn't give a fig if she made a public spectacle of herself. For days, she'd kept her fear and pain at bay with bright smiles, laughter, and a deliberate, self-inflicted case of amnesia. But a person could pretend for only so long. *Gabriel*. In a matter of hours, he would leave her shop to walk to the saloon for a whiskey before he began his fated journey up Main Street.

Until now, Nan had been afraid to pray for a different ending to that stroll, but suddenly that struck her as being pure lunacy. The God she believed in and trusted wasn't vengeful, and she might as well prostrate herself in prayer for Gabriel, because there was no hiding her thoughts or her actions from Him. He knew of her scheme to save her husband's life.

Nan hooked an arm around Laney's shoulders and, with as much composure as she could muster, herded the child out of the store. Once on the boardwalk, they both burst into tears, sobbing, hiccoughing, and snorting. Nan kept her feet moving, forcing Laney to stumble along with her. At the corner, she veered them both left onto Oak, which she immediately regretted, because Doc Peterson's office lay just ahead. It was on this plank walkway that Gabriel had possibly sacrificed his soul to save a little girl's life. The thought almost took Nan to her knees.

But she kept walking, picking up her pace. She and

Laney had to regain control. If Gabriel found them like this, it would ruin his whole Christmas, and he might get to experience only half of the holiday as it was.

Nan's frenzy of walking found them at the edge of town, and still Nan kept on. She didn't stop until she and Laney were well outside the community proper and encountered a split-rail fence. There, Nan held her sister in her arms. Both of them wept until their wells ran dry.

"Oh, *dear*," Nan said as she shakily dabbed at Laney's face with a lace-edged handkerchief. "Your eyes are all red and swollen, and your nose looks as if you've had it pinched for hours by a brand-new clothespin."

Laney chuffed and shuddered. "You're a mess, too." She snatched away the handkerchief to wipe the wet droplets from Nan's cheeks and chin. "We've got to straighten up. Gabe isn't sad, Mama. We have to be brave like he is."

Nan secretly believed that Gabriel *did* feel sad, but that he somehow managed to keep his feelings buried deep within him. Nan couldn't quite grasp how he did that.

"What on *earth* will we say when he sees our faces?" Nan worried aloud.

Laney never missed a beat. "That Mr. Redmond dropped a sack of pepper at our feet, and it went *poof*, right up our noses. We went to sneezing. Got it in our eyes. It was *horrific*."

Laney sounded so convincing that Nan could almost believe it herself. "When did you become so proficient at lying?"

"When I was . . . hmm . . ." The girl dimpled a cheek. "I was about five, I think. We were in Random, because I remember our old apartment. I used to hide from you to pick my nose and eat it. And somehow you always suspected I was up to something wrong, so you'd ask what I'd been doing."

Nan reared back slightly. "Oh, *yuck!*"

Laney giggled. "Well, Mama, what was I supposed to do, tell you the truth?"

Looping her wrists over Laney's shoulders, Nan pressed her forehead against her sister's. "You should have asked for a handkerchief, goose." She sighed. "You're nearly as tall as I am. When did that happen?"

"Probably when I was hiding and picking my nose."

They both giggled. When their mirth subsided, Nan felt better, stronger for having cried, somehow. "I love you," she whispered to Laney. "No matter what may come in the morning, we'll stand together and be brave. Correct? We owe that to Gabriel."

"Will you *never* call him Gabe, Mama? It's the name he prefers."

Nan considered that for a moment. "I recall him telling me that once, but I was very upset and quickly forgot it." She chucked Laney under the chin. "I shall endeavor to address him by his preferred name for the remainder of the day. How is that?"

Laney grinned. Her face still looked awful, but there was now sincere amusement flashing in her eyes. "He'll probably check your forehead to see if you have a fever."

Laughing, they hooked elbows and retraced their steps to town. As luck would have it, Gabriel and Christopher stood in front of the general store, both of them laden with bundles and looking disgruntled. Nan felt the burn of her husband's gaze on her face and knew she must look a fright. But she kept a smile on her lips, pretended nothing untoward had occurred, and she managed to address him as Gabe three times during the brief exchange.

"What put a burr in your drawers?" he demanded.

"So far as I recall, you've never *once* called me Gabe, and now suddenly you're saying it over and over, as if it's a big word you just discovered and are trying to get your tongue wrapped around." He narrowed his eyes. "And what in the world happened? You both look as if you've been crying your eyes out."

"No!" both Nan and her sister chimed at once. Then Laney launched into her pepper tale, which Nan felt the girl managed with impressive verisimilitude.

Christopher harrumphed. "We was just in the store, lookin' for you, and I didn't smell no pepper."

"Were," Nan corrected, "and it's improper English to use a double negative."

"A double *what*?" both males asked, their voices, one deep and the other a bit higher, so perfectly harmonized that they could have been singing a duet.

"It's a nonstandard syntactic, the double negative," Nan explained. "For instance, it is incorrect to say, 'I didn't eat nothing.' The correct syntactic is to say, 'I didn't eat anything,' or, 'I ate nothing.'" She beamed a bright smile, pleased with herself for having so successfully distracted Gabriel. "I'm sure you've heard the old saying that two wrongs never make a right. Well, two negatives in the same sentence are never right, either."

A brown package poked from Christopher's jacket pocket, and he held three more to his chest. Gabriel cradled a long and narrow string-tied box in the crook of one arm, with a larger wrapped bundle tucked between his elbow and side. He shifted his hold on the box, parted his lips as if to speak, and fell silent when Nan said, "We've still some shopping to do in the general store. Have you fellows finished with all yours?"

"I have," Christopher said, sounding relieved. "I used to think I'd like shopping, when I didn't have no money to spend. Now I'm flat tired and don't wanna do it again anytime soon."

Gabriel curled his free hand over the boy's shoulder. "We'll head back to the shop. Jasper probably needs to go for a walk by now."

Nan had entirely forgotten about the new member of her household. "Oh, so true. You'd better hurry along."

A moment later, she released a relieved sigh as she and Laney entered the general store again.

"I don't think Gabe believed a word of my pepper story," Laney whispered.

Nan smiled. "Well, it is rather far-fetched, darling. But if I'm asked, I shall swear to it."

"It's a lie, and you never lie."

"I cannot lay claim to *never*. One can lie by omission, and I've done that plenty of times."

As they approached the display of harmonicas, Laney asked, "When did you lie by omission?"

"Oh, let me see." Nan fingered a particularly lovely harmonica with dark stain in the etchings. "There are many different ways to lie by omission, but I believe I first perfected the art when you were about five." She lowered her voice a notch. "I *knew* you were hiding to pick your nose. But I pretended that I didn't know, because had I known, I would have had no choice but to chastise you."

Laney flicked Nan a startled glance. Then, recovering her composure, she asked, "Why didn't you chastise me?"

Nan picked up an instrument that she quite liked. It was slightly larger than the rest, a better fit for Gabriel's big hands. "Because I had vague recollections of hiding from my nurse at about that age to do exactly the same thing."

"Oh, *yuck!*"

Nan sniggered. A squeak erupted from Laney's throat. Then they laughed until their knees went weak. Nan knew it wasn't really all that funny, but she also realized that sometimes if you didn't laugh, you could only cry.

Chapter Eighteen

Once back at the shop, Nan laid out a tall stack of yardage scraps, a roll of dark green twine, a pile of ribbon ends, and scissors on her downstairs project table so the gift wrapping could begin. Upstairs under her bed, she'd hidden small gifts that she and Gabriel had purchased to go in the children's socks. Those could wait for later. But in her armoire, she'd stashed all her main gifts for everyone, along with the things she'd chosen for her husband's sock: a comb, an ivory-handled razor, and a strop. Gabriel's big gift from her was a bright red shirt, which she'd worked on in between customers while he'd been gone for afternoon walks over the last month. To Nan, the shirt's brilliant hue was symbolic of Christmas and salvation, and she hoped he'd wear it tomorrow morning for his walk just before dawn.

Nan hid the gifts she needed to wrap in a pillowcase and spirited all of them downstairs to her workroom before she allowed anyone else to have a turn. As the primary cook, she figured she needed to go first. She'd made a nice school frock for Laney, blue with a dainty pattern of pink nosegays and darker blue eyelet ruffles, and a Sunday dress of russet satin with a pin-pleated bodice and dark umber trim. For Christopher, she'd been forced because of time constraints to purchase store-bought garments: two shirts and another pair of britches, plus some house slippers. Gabriel had gotten the boy a copy of *The Adventures of Tom Sawyer*, which Nan had promised to read aloud to the child if he hadn't yet learned his letters. Nan's husband believed that the wonderful world to be discovered in books would encourage the boy to study. Nan prayed so, but mostly she wanted Christopher to enjoy the magic of this special season. She hoped he liked the sock gifts that she and Gabriel had chosen, for she suspected that Gabriel wasn't the only one who was about to experience his first *real* Christmas. From Santa the boy would get a block-and-peg puzzle, a hair comb and pomade, a small bottle and an underarm stick of men's cologne, a hand-tooled leather coin pouch, and a colorful poke of assorted hard candies. Both children's socks would be filled to the brim.

After finishing up, Nan carried her offerings back upstairs in the pillowcase and then unveiled each gift to place it under the tree. Christopher, who'd never wrapped a present, asked Nan to teach him how, so back down to the shop she went to oversee the boy's first attempt. When he seemed comfortable with the process, she abandoned him to his own devices to stuff the first turkey she'd purchased in years. When the bird was in the oven, she peeled potatoes and covered them with salted water in a pot. Then she worked on other side dishes. The four desserts—a batch of cinnamon sticky buns, a peach cobbler, an apple pie, and a dried-fruit cake—had been prepared yesterday and the day before that.

Constantly hovering, Gabriel continuously dipped his finger in her mixings. Recalling the morning when she'd caught him and Laney tasting with their stirring spoon, Nan realized just how far she'd come in only a month. What might have raised her eyebrows before

Gabriel's arrival now only made her smile and teasingly scold. Life was about so very much more than observing rules of proper etiquette and practicing good manners. This man had taught her that. True living was about laughing, loving, and enjoying each moment. And, oh, how she did enjoy seeing Gabriel's pleasure when he snitched samples of the holiday fare.

At some point while Nan bustled about her kitchen, her husband disappeared. The dog had accompanied the children to the sitting room, where a great deal of gift probing and guessing of contents was taking place. With everything at the ready for later, when she would finish preparing the holiday meal, Nan was free until the turkey had baked to a turn. After checking all the upstairs rooms, she slipped down to her shop. Gabriel stood at a window, gazing solemnly out at the street. Now that it was midafternoon, the shops had mostly closed in honor of the holiday, and there were few people on the boardwalks.

"What is it?" Nan stepped close and touched a hand to his arm. She wondered if the reality of what he would face on the morrow had suddenly struck him. "Are you all right?"

Black hair glistening in the winter light that came through the glass, he tucked his chin to give her one of those slanted grins she'd come to love so much, only the warmth of it didn't reach his coffee-dark eyes. "Just thinking about opportunities missed."

"Such as?"

He shook his head and went back to street watching. "Remember my story about the three lost souls I could have chosen to save?" He lifted his shoulders in a frustrated shrug. "I totally forgot about the lonely old man, Tyke Byden. Or was it Bayden?"

"Baden," Nan supplied. "He's a sad case, angry at the world. He lost his whole family to influenza about fifteen years ago, or so the story goes. I didn't live in Random then. But folks say he was once a grand, lofty fellow, always jovial and friendly, a very hard worker who did well by his wife and seven children, who were all nearly grown when they died. As I recall, the younger pair of twins, both girls, were thirteen, and the older set, two boys, were eighteen. The other three kids, two girls and a boy, ranged in ages somewhere in between. I've been told that all of the Baden youngsters were handsome and trained up right." Nan sighed. "After losing his family, Mr. Baden took to drink, and now he chases away anyone who dares to darken his doorstep. His wife's name was Miriam, I believe. He must have loved her dearly, and his children as well."

"I should have rapped on his door," Gabriel said, his voice husky with regret. "Somehow I didn't think about it until now, when it's too late."

"It's not too late," Nan replied. "My goodness, our table sits six, and I've fixed enough food to feed half of Random."

"The angels told me he curses a blue streak, Nan. I can't go fetch him and bring him here to eat. Even if you are willing to put up with his language, I have to think of Laney. Besides, Tyke needs more than I can offer in a night. The angels said he needs to love and be loved again. You can't serve that up on a supper plate."

"Who says I cannot?" Nan hugged her husband's arm. "What you're saying is that Mr. Baden needs a family, and in my estimation, the feeling of family begins at a supper table."

She felt Gabriel stiffen. "He needs people who'll include him for longer than an evening." His lashes drifted down to rest like black etchings against his bronze skin. When he met Nan's gaze again, his eyes fairly ached with sadness. "From what I saw, he lives in a trash pile. The smell alone nearly took my breath away. If we invited him to our table, the stench of him would probably spoil our appetites."

"I could douse him with vanilla extract."

Gabriel laughed and shook his head.

"Gabriel, I'm willing to take him in if that will make you happy. No, forget that. I think we *should* take him in, because it's the right thing to do."

He arched an ebon brow at her. "And what, hang him on a cloak hook? You don't have sleeping room for another person upstairs."

"True, but once my workroom is emptied out, there will be room for two comfortable cots. It will be close quarters but doable. And the shelving can be used for garments and footwear. Mr. Redmond has cots in stock at the general store. He'll be closed until the day after Christmas, but you and I can empty the storage room tomorrow evening, and we can set up the cots on Saturday. Heaven knows I've plenty of quilts, and we can purchase some bed linens and pillows."

"I won't be here tomorrow night to help you empty the storage room."

Nan felt as if a fist had connected with her chest and pushed all the breath from her lungs. For her husband's sake, she managed to recover her composure quickly, though she felt certain he'd seen her flinch at his words. "Then I shall call upon Christopher and Laney to assist me. As for the cots, Mr. Wilson earns extra coin by helping customers with heavy items, and he is happy to assemble purchases for those who aren't able. He'll come right in and do the work for me."

"And where will you and I sleep tonight? We can't put Christopher on the floor and an old man on the settee. We'd have to give Baden your bed."

Nan gestured toward her downstairs workroom. "We can move the table aside and make ourselves a pallet on the floor."

"What about customers of a morning?"

"By the time the shop reopens on Monday, the sleeping arrangements will be in place."

He searched her gaze, looking a bit stupefied. "You're serious."

"Of course I'm serious, Gabriel. I'm getting the hang of this adoption business. First a boy, then a dog, and tonight a lonely old fellow who needs a family." Nan placed a palm against his cheek. "We're a bit tight on room, but we've plenty of love to go around, and feeding another mouth isn't a problem. We have a great deal of money in the bank, as I recall."

"What if Tyke Baden is an irascible, coarse, foul-mouthed old codger, and you end up sorely sorry that you ever invited him here?"

"I do not countenance coarse behavior. He'll be served a bar of soap for breakfast."

Gabriel guffawed. When his mirth subsided, he trailed a warm gaze over Nan's face. "You are a priceless gift. Do you know that? I honestly think you can take Tyke Baden on with one hand tied behind your back."

Nan dimpled a cheek at him. "Stand aside, sir, and observe me in action. If Mr. Baden needs a few reminders of how to properly comport himself, I shall be most generous with them."

Nan turned for the stairs.

"Wait! Where are you going?" Gabe called.

"Upstairs to collect the rest of our brood. If we're going calling to adopt a grandfather, we shall do it together, so the poor old fellow can see what he's getting into before he accepts the supper invitation."

Gabe wasn't any too worried about Tyke Baden's reaction to Nan and the kids. Oh, no. It was Nan and the kids' reaction to Baden that concerned him. He'd seen

Tyke through a parting in the clouds, and he wasn't exactly the grandfatherly image that Nan clearly pictured. He rushed up the stairs behind his wife and caught her three steps below the door. In the semidark, her fair skin and golden hair fairly glowed when she swung around to face him. He stood two levels below her. It was the first time in Gabe's memory that he'd been eye-to-eye with her—unless, of course, he counted when they'd been making love.

"Nan, I appreciate your generous intent, but I can't allow you to—"

"You were *wrong* about Christopher. He *is* rough at the edges, but so are diamonds before they are refined and polished. I think, considering the short amount of time he has been here, that he has fitted in beautifully."

"He still lets loose with cusswords, Nan. At the table he pokes out his elbows like a bird trying to take flight. He chews with his mouth open. I doubt he can put his own name to paper. I admit he's a lovable kid, and I don't regret bringing him home. He needed rescuing, and he's young enough to change. Tyke Baden is old and set in his ways. I can't let you—"

"*Let* me?"

Gabe was so taken aback by her sudden frosty tone that he went speechless for a moment. And while he groped for words, his diminutive wife drilled his chest with her fingertip to emphasize each utterance. "*You* do *not* rule me, Mr. Valance. Not now, not *ever*. This ring on my hand is not a deed of ownership. I am my own person, and I make my own choices. Is that *clear*?"

Gabe thought she'd made it pretty damned clear. He was just startled by her sudden assertiveness. This wasn't *his* Nan. Only how could he say that for certain? He hadn't exactly been domineering in this relationship thus far, so maybe he'd just never pushed her to a point that she'd revealed this stubborn, stiff-spined side of herself. "I never meant to imply—"

"Champion. I shall ignore your poor choice of words and pretend they were never spoken." She gathered her skirts to resume the ascent. "Come along. We've a family to collect, an old man to fetch, a turkey in the oven, and when we return, we must finish fixing our holiday supper."

Tyke Baden lived two streets over from Main on Second Street. Nan led the way, cutting behind Lizzy's Café to shorten the distance. When Jasper saw the lean-to, he let out a mournful whine.

"Don't be sad," Laney said, reaching out to pat the dog's head. "You shall never again live *there*. You're a proper fellow now and have a home!"

"He don't understand a word you say," Christopher observed.

Laney popped back, "You talk to him, too. Under your breath, mostly, but I've heard you. So don't make jest of me for doing the same."

Nan, two steps ahead of Gabriel, stopped so suddenly to whirl around that he nearly barreled right over the top of her. The light was fading suddenly. Snow clouds, blocking the sun, Gabe guessed, and in the gloaming, Nan's eyes sparkled with perturbed impatience. "Shush, the both of you! I will *not* have you bickering. It is to be a holy night for only love, laughter, and kindly exchanges. If you don't curb your tongues, I shall rap each of you on the noggin with one of my wooden spoons the moment we get home."

Gabe fleetingly wondered how kindly exchanges and head knocking went hand in hand, but he wasn't about to voice the question aloud. His spouse wasn't very tall, and she'd have a hell of a time reaching his high end with a stirring stick, but he wouldn't put it past Nan to climb on a chair to get the job done. And Gabe knew, deep down, that he'd just stand there and take the thumping.

The children stared at his wife with wide eyes. Nan turned to resume her pace. Gabe winked at the kids and fell in behind their leader again. He felt like a duckling in a queue.

In the gathering twilight, the sprawling Baden home didn't look too bad from a distance, but as they neared the dooryard, Gabe saw that the two-level residence was in horrible disrepair. The picket fence no longer sported a chip of paint, and lay on the ground in sections. Loose shingles had worked their way down the pitched roof to dangle over the edge of the eaves. The porch overhang sagged. The stoop itself had broken boards and steps that looked too rotten to bear weight. All in all, the structure reminded Gabe of a house of cards that would collapse if you breathed too hard on it.

"Nan, wait." Gabe caught his wife's arm to hold her back. "I'll go up first. If those planks are as decayed as they appear to be, you could fall through and break a leg."

"What of you?"

He gave her a significant look and moved ahead of his fine-feathered flock to try the first step. It groaned but didn't break when he put his weight on it. Flashing a palm at Nan and the kids to hold them back, he gained the porch deck and stepped gingerly this way and that to test the planks.

"All right," he said. "You can come on up. It's safe enough."

Gabe turned to the front door, which had a glass pane in the upper half. *No knocker.* He put his fist to the wood, rapping loudly several times, and then cocked his head to listen as Nan, the kids, and Jasper formed a half circle behind him. "All I hear in there is what the little boy shot at."

"What did the little boy shoot at?" Laney asked in a loud whisper.

Christopher harrumphed. "Nothin'. That's what he shot at. Don't you know *anything* normal?"

Gabe couldn't help but grin. Nan would have her hands full with that pair. Oh, how Gabe wished he'd be around to help her rap heads.

"I see a faint light," Nan said, pointing at the curtained door window. "No one would leave the house with a lamp burning."

Gabe agreed. That held particularly true for an old fellow who lived with trash piled high all around him. Talk about a tinderbox; this place was it. "Maybe he's deaf. I couldn't tell when I saw him through the clouds."

"What clouds?" Christopher asked.

"None of your beeswax," Laney retorted.

Gabe knocked again, but no one stirred within the house. "I think I'll just try the door."

It didn't surprise Gabe when the knob turned. *Unlocked.* He'd wager a big bet that half the people in Random left their homes open to intruders. As he pushed the door inward, the hinges whined in protest. Gabe was thinking that they needed some oil when Jasper tried to squeeze between him and the doorframe. "No way, fella. You probably smell garbage and hope to go foraging." Oddly, the stench Gabe had associated with Tyke Baden's home didn't drift to his nostrils. "Laney, you hold him," Gabe said, pushing the canine toward the girl. "Christopher, you stay here with Laney and Jasper while Nan and I go in. We don't want to frighten the poor old fellow."

Nan inched over the threshold behind Gabe, which felt odd, because he normally always stepped aside

while she went first. Though cast in shadow, the space
he entered appeared to be a dingy foyer, flanked on the
left side by a staircase. One door held center position
on the opposite wall, but Gabe's attention was riveted
to another portal at the end of the hallway. A thin
wedge of light shone beneath it. Nan clutched Gabe's
sleeve.

"If he's deaf and didn't hear us knocking, we mustn't
scare him. What if his heart stops?"

Gabe rotated his shoulders and tipped his head from
side to side, trying to work the tension from his muscles. "I think you should wait here, Nan. For all we
know, he may have a shotgun at the ready."

Her grasp tightened convulsively. "But what if he
shoots you?"

Gabe bent to kiss her forehead. "I don't think my
angels will allow anyone or anything to interfere with
my appointment tomorrow." He gently pried Nan's
slender fingers from his sleeve. "Stay here. All right?
I'll holler when I think it's safe."

She nodded. Gabe glanced back to see both kids
and the dog bunched together on the threshold. He
raised a hand to signal that they should wait. Then he
stepped around Nan to advance on the room ahead of
them. Picturing it in his mind, Gabe knew that it was
a small, informal sitting room just off the kitchen and
dining area. It made sense that Baden would utilize
only a portion of the large home. What point was there
in going upstairs to sleep every night when all the bedchambers on the second floor held only poignant
memories of his lost loved ones? Sadness pinched
Gabe's heart. He'd only just gotten a taste of how
grand it was to have a family. He couldn't imagine loving a woman and helping her raise seven children almost to adulthood, only to lose every last one of them,
including his wife, to illness. The pain of it must have

been inestimable, enough to take even a strong-willed man to his knees.

The hinges of this door didn't creak, which was a relief. Gabe expected to see the same room that he'd viewed through the clouds—a tiny alcove with one chair in front of the fireplace and piles of garbage along the walls. Instead a fairly tidy room greeted his searching gaze. And the nostril-searing stench he anticipated was absent.

As before, a fire burned in the brick hearth, and, ensconced in a worn green velvet parlor chair, an old man sat staring off into space. A lighted lantern perched atop a tome-laden shelf behind him, casting his face into partial shadow. Gabe froze in his tracks, for this was *not* the same fellow that the angels had shown him. This individual had a clean-shaven face. His thin gray hair, parted at one side from crown to temple, had been carefully arranged in a thin layer of strands over his bald pate and held fast with pomade. He wore a dated but clean ditto suit, a dark gray sack coat with black velvet lapels over a matching waistcoat and contrasting black trousers. At his throat, his red necktie had been double-looped and affixed to his dingy white shirt with a silver stickpin. The strong but not unpleasant scent of men's cologne filled the room.

Gabe, whose presence still hadn't been noted by the man, started to back carefully away, hoping to vanish without ever being seen. Nan had brought them to the wrong house, and if that wasn't a hell of a note, Gabe didn't know what was. How would he explain his reasons for entering this home without an invitation?

Only, just as Gabe had retreated as far as the half-opened door, he noticed a shiny streak on the old man's cheek, the still-wet path of a recently shed tear. Gabe froze. Couldn't make his feet move. And just then something caught the old man's attention. With no apparent surprise at having an unexpected caller, the fellow turned his head to study Gabe with a bright blue gaze.

"So," he said shakily, "you came after all. It took you long enough. I finally decided you were waiting for today. It's a time for good deeds, I reckon, but I'd about given up on you."

What? Gabe thought the question, but he couldn't make his voice work. How could the old man have been expecting him? At a touch on his sleeve, Gabe nearly parted company with his boots. *Nan.* She'd disregarded his order to hang back and had joined him in the sitting area.

"Happy Christmas Eve, Mr. Baden!" she said with merry good cheer. "We knocked at your door, but you mustn't have heard us."

Baden's gaze warmed slightly as he studied Nan. "I heard; I just never answer. I figured a gunslinger would come in whether I went to the door or not, and just in case it wasn't him, I had no desire to endure another visit from those addlepated church ladies." He huffed under his breath. "Not a one of them can cook worth a lick, and they pester a poor man to death with casseroles. The widows are the worst, fluttering and primping, as if I'd ever look twice." He shook his head vehemently, and a smile touched his crinkled mouth. "Don't hold a candle to my Miriam, God rest her dear soul."

Apparently Nan had gauged the situation to be safe, for she moved toward the old man. In a loud voice, she said, "We've come to invite you to spend Christmas with us in our home!"

"No need to shout. I'm not *deef*!"

"Oh!" Nan flapped a hand. "My apologies, Mr. Baden. I didn't mean to—"

Just then, Jasper shot past Gabe's leg. *No*, Gabe

thought. But before he could move, the dog leaped up to plant both gigantic front paws on Baden's bony lap.

"Jasper!" Laney cried, darting past Gabe nearly as quickly as the canine had. "No, no!"

Gabe figured Christopher would appear next, and sure enough he did, only he at least had the good sense to press his back against the wall and remain guarded until he knew it was safe. Gabe had heaps of work to do if he meant to have a family that heeded his orders— and he had little time left to effect that change.

"Jasper!" Gabe whisper-shouted. "Get the hell down!"

"Language," Christopher said from behind him.

"Not now!" Gabe told the boy. He hurried over, fully intending to drag the dog off poor Baden.

Laney futilely attempted to pull Jasper from the old man's lap. The dog, which seemed bent on making friends with every new individual he happened upon, was busily cleaning Tyke's left ear. Baden sputtered and pushed, but Jasper was a big fellow and wasn't easily discouraged.

"No, Jasper!" the girl cried. "Mind your manners!"

Nan saved the day, and the wonder of it was, she never had to so much as touch the canine. In her I-mean-business voice, which Gabe had heard her use with the kids, she said, "Jasper, *off*!"

The dog whined in protest but obeyed, dropping to all fours beside Baden's chair. Tyke Baden looked beyond Nan to skewer Gabe with an accusing blue gaze. "Your dog needs a firm hand, sir. With manners like that, he'll be knocking old ladies on their behinds and sending toddlers off the boardwalk. Large animals cannot be allowed to behave like ruffians."

"We've only had him since yesterday," Laney said. "He'll be a fine gentleman with more training. Just you wait, and you shall see! You shouldn't be so quick to judge."

"Laney!" Nan scolded.

Tyke focused on the girl for the first time. After studying her face, which had gone pink at the cheeks with indignation, he reached for his cane, which he'd propped against the brick hearth. "Well said, lass. And if you've only had him since yesterday, I'd say he's coming along at a fast clip." Using his free hand, Tyke fondled Jasper's ears and smiled. "He's a beauty, isn't he? Where'd you get him?"

A bit of the starch slipped from Laney's spine. "He was starving to death out behind Lizzy's Café."

"Ah, yes, Random's miserly restaurateur, Lizzy. She's stingy to a fault. Got it from her mother, I reckon. She ran the place first, and rumor had it that she scraped food from one customer's plate and fed it to the next poor sap who was stupid enough to eat there. Nasty business, that." He sighed. "Back to the dog. I take it you've adopted him."

"Yes, sir," Laney answered. "We've been feeding him for a while, and yesterday Christopher and I brought him home to see if Mama wouldn't allow us to keep him."

Baden leaned out to peer around the girl. "Christopher." He nailed the boy with a piercing gaze. "Come away from the wall, son, and introduce yourself properly."

Christopher moved forward to stand beside Gabe. "Merry Christmas, sir. My name is Christopher Broderick."

The old man shifted his cane into his left hand and extended his right. "I'm Tyke Baden." After a brief shake, Baden said, "It's good to meet you, Christopher. Can't recall any Brodericks around these parts, but it's a nice solid name to add to the mix."

Just then Gabe noticed a rather large satchel on the floor beside Baden's chair. He got Nan's attention and darted his eyes back and forth toward the bag. When she finally noticed it, her expression of bewilderment reflected his sentiments exactly. "Mr. Baden, how did you know we were coming?" Gabe couldn't resist asking.

"Miriam told me," the old man replied. "Long story, that, and I won't feel inclined to share it until I know all of you better."

Miriam? "Pardon me," Gabe said, "but did you say *Miriam*, meaning, um, your wife?"

"Do you have a hearing problem, son?" Baden struggled up from the chair, a dilapidated thing that had clearly seen its last good day a dozen or more years ago. When the old man gained his feet, Gabe saw that he had indeed been a big man at one time, for even now, as stooped and frail as he was, he exceeded six feet in height, meeting Gabe eye-to-eye. "You heard me right. I've been waiting for you all day. I was starting to think you weren't going to come and that I was all dressed up with nowhere to go." He smiled sadly. "Isn't right to be alone on Christmas. I've spent too many years by myself, and now I'm ready for good company!" He got a firm grip on the tortoiseshell handle of his cane and bent to pick up the satchel. "I'm ready as I'll ever be." He flicked his fingers to indicate that everyone should get moving. Leveling a stern gaze on Christopher, he said. "Turn the lamp off, son. No point in the place going up in flames."

Gabe sent Nan a befuddled glance. She merely shrugged and gave a slight lift of her hands. Tyke Baden had nearly reached the door that led to the entry hall. Christopher cut a wide berth around the old man to douse the lantern that sat on a dusty bookcase.

"Look, Laney!" the boy cried. "There must be a hundred books!"

"Help yourself, if you've a mind," Baden said. "I

can't read anymore. My eyes are failing. Books!" He harrumphed. "Aside from my whiskey jug, they were all I had to keep me company for years, and now I can't even count on them to be my friends." He hobbled past Nan, brushing against her pretty rose skirt. "You can have 'em all as far as I'm concerned, boy. Unless you'll read aloud to me, I've got no further use for them."

"Wow!" Christopher cried to Laney as he dusted off a cover. "Look, Laney, *Uncle Tom's Cabin!*"

Gabe's eyebrows rose in surprise that Christopher could apparently read.

Laney dropped to her knees before the shelf. "And *Wide, Wide World* and *The Scarlet Letter!*"

"Come along, children," Nan said. "You can come back later to have a look at the books. Right now, it's Christmas Eve, and we must hurry home to celebrate!"

"No hurry," Baden warned as he traversed the length of the foyer. "My old legs don't go fast, and I get out of breath if I try to push them."

Gabe collected the kids, who each cradled a book in their arms. Pink tongue lolling, Jasper trotted happily between them, his canine expression conveying that he was as happy as a worm in a compost heap. He'd started out with only a girl to love; then a boy had come along, and now he had five people to scratch him behind his ears. Gabe guessed that would be almost any dog's idea of paradise.

The twilight had deepened when they left the ramshackle house. With foreknowledge of the approaching weather, Gabe knew that a snowstorm was rolling in. He relieved Tyke of the satchel, which weighed enough to hold every stitch of clothing the old fellow owned. Even without a load to carry, Baden set a slow pace, and Gabe knew Nan was worried about their turkey.

"Sweetheart, why don't you and the kids hurry on

ahead?" he said. "That'll give me and Mr. Baden a chance to get acquainted."

"Are you certain?" Nan sent him a concerned look. Gabe guessed she was as bewildered by Tyke's words as he was. "I probably should check on our supper."

"Go," Gabe assured her. To Christopher, he added, "Keep our ladies safe. And don't let Jasper lift his leg on the boardwalk."

Christopher turned to walk backward. "Soon as we get home, I'll take him for a run."

Gabe nodded his approval and watched his family disappear into the gloom. He set his pace to match Tyke's. After a moment, he said, "Okay, Tyke, out with it. I'm flat flummoxed, and I don't like that a bit. How'd you know we were coming to fetch you?"

Tyke bent his head and took his time speaking. "I don't suppose you believe in ghosts, do you?"

A month ago, Gabe would have responded with an unequivocal no. Now he no longer felt certain about much of anything having to do with the hereafter. "I can't rightly say. But I do know I've never *seen* a ghost."

"Well, I never have, either, but I did smell and hear one about three weeks ago." Tyke stopped briefly to catch his breath and then struck off again. "And even then I was drunk, so maybe I only imagined it."

"Imagined what?" Gabe pressed.

"That my wife, Miriam, visited me." Tyke slanted Gabe an aggrieved glance. "Ever since my family died, I've been . . . Well, I guess I can just tell you what Miriam called me—a slovenly drunkard. That pretty much says it all. Never washed. Wore dirty clothes. Ate food from tins that Wilson over at the general store left for me on my back stoop."

"If you never left the house, how'd you get booze?" Gabe asked.

"Wilson brought me that, too. He's a kindly chap.

Not too bright, I don't think, but I never hold that against a good man."

Gabe couldn't say that he did, either. "So you had an unending supply of whiskey."

"And started chugging from the bottle first thing each morning, drank all day, and kept on into the evening until I passed out in my chair." He sighed. "I've done that for years, Mr. . . ." His voice trailed away. "I'm sorry, but in all the introductions, I never got your name."

"Valance, Gabriel Valance. I prefer to be called Gabe."

"Well, Gabe—you can call me Tyke if you want—back to my story. I never touched alcohol before I lost my family. Never had the desire. But things can change in a person's life with a shift of the wind."

Gabe knew that to be a fact.

"Call me weak, but I only held myself together long enough to get my loved ones buried and prayed over. Then I went straight to the saloon. The next morning, I woke up under one of the tables, started drinking again as soon as I could stand up, and that's the way it's mostly been ever since. On the rare occasion that I sobered up, the pain of losing my family was still there, so I dived right back into a bottle to find the numbness again."

A picture was forming in Gabe's mind. "And one night, not long ago, Miriam paid you a visit?"

Tyke stopped again. "Sorry. All I've done is sit for damned near fifteen years. Talking and walking don't mix."

Gabe didn't mind stopping. He figured this story might be better told out of Nan and the kids' earshot. He hooked his thumbs over his gun belt, cocked a hip, and waited.

Tyke met Gabe's gaze. "You a drinking man?"

"I can't say I've never gotten drunk, but I've not

made a habit of it. That doesn't mean I can't understand why another man might. Losing your wife and
children that way, and all of a sudden . . . Well, it must
have been really hard. I doubt I would have taken to
the bottle, though. I'd probably be more inclined to put
a bullet in my brain and get it over with fast."

Tyke stared off into the twilight, his eyes bright with
tears. "I thought about it, believe me. But my Miriam,
she didn't hold with suicide. Every time I got out my
pistol, I wondered if she was up there somewhere,
watching over me, and I just couldn't do it."

"So you tried to drink yourself to death instead."

Tyke nodded. "I would've kept on trying, too, if Miriam hadn't stopped me. I was sitting in front of the fire,
just like this evening, and I was well on my way to
numb. The house was quiet." Tyke dragged in a shaky
breath. "I never got used to the sound of quiet. It's
loud, you know, so loud sometimes that it hurts your
ears."

Gabe wished the old codger would get on with the
story. Then Gabe could decide if it was a bunch of poppycock or not.

"Anyway, I always kept my jug on the hearth. And
that night, just as I reached for it, it went flying. Hit the
brick, bounced off, smacked the floor, and shattered. I
thought for a second that I was so drunk I'd knocked it
over. But then, so strong I couldn't mistake it, I smelled
her rosewater, and I knew my Miriam was there."

"That's all? You smelled rosewater?" Gabe didn't
say so, but that revelation had him leaning heavily
toward saying, "Poppycock."

"No, not at all." Tyke's voice had gone thin and
quivery. "She spoke to me. I heard her talking, plain as
I hear you. She sure didn't like the garbage piles all
over her house. She was tidy, my Miriam, and she kept
that house spick-and-span. She told me it was shame-

ful, the way I lived. Then she said I had to clean myself up and leave the whiskey alone, because you were going to come fetch me."

"That's all?" Gabe wondered if it wasn't a grave mistake to take this old fellow into Nan's home. He might be a lot more addlepated than the widows he'd complained about. "She didn't give you my name or anything like that?"

"No, not a name," Tyke confessed. "She only said that two angels had told a gunslinger about me, and if I'd just straighten myself up, I might have the chance to be part of a family again." The old man searched Gabe's gaze. "You're wearing Colts. You are the gunslinger Miriam told me about, right?"

Gabe now knew how it felt to be emotionally numb, only he hadn't drunk his way to the bottom of a whiskey jug to get there.

"Mr. Valance?" Tyke looked worried. "You aren't thinking about taking me back home, are you? I've kind of got my mind set on not returning to that hellhole. You've got a nice family. I know I'm not a real relation, but I'd sure like the chance to be a grandpa." He ran a hand over his face and blinked. "Of course, maybe that position is already filled twice over. You've probably got a perfectly nice father to play that role, and your wife, too."

Still unable to collect his thoughts, Gabe took off his hat and slapped it against his leg.

"I was a good father," Tyke said. "I truly was. With all that experience, I think I can be a damned good grandpa if you'll give me half a chance. I won't tell the children about Miriam visiting me, if that's your worry. I know stories about ghosts frighten kids. Not that Miriam's visit was scary. For me, it was the best thing that's happened in years!"

"I, um . . ." Gabe swallowed hard, slapped his hat

back on, and tipped his head to gaze at the starless sky. "I don't have a father, and Nan's isn't worth having, so I'm not planning to take you back home, Tyke. Just give me a minute." After releasing a long sigh, he said, "Angels, you say?" He lowered his chin to search Baden's gaze. "Are you certain that's what Miriam told you, Tyke? It's important."

"Oh, yes, I'm certain sure. She said two angels told you about me. I know it sounds far-fetched." Tyke fell silent for a moment. "So just out of curiosity, Gabe, who *did* tell you about me?"

Gabe needed to move. "Come on, Tyke. Let's mosey home. We're having our big Christmas dinner tonight, and Nan's quite the cook. We don't want to miss out."

After they'd resumed walking, Tyke observed, "You never answered my question. Who told you about me? If I ever get a chance, I'd like to shake his hand and tell him thank you."

Gabe released a taut breath and laughed softly. "Don't be in any hurry to do that, Tyke."

"Why not?"

"Because Miriam gave it to you straight. Two angels told me about you, and in order for you to shake their hands and tell them thank you, I'm afraid you'll have to cock up your toes."

Chapter Nineteen

Christmas Eve. In all his life, Gabe had never experienced such a pleasurable evening. For the holiday meal, Nan gave him the place of honor at the head of the table, and she took her rightful position as his wife at the opposite end, affording him a wonderful view of her sparkling eyes, which looked at him with a love that brought a lump to his throat. Christopher and Laney took the two chairs at the wall side, and Tyke Baden sat to Gabe's left, where Jasper lay at his feet, clearly hoping the old fellow would share some of the bounty. The array of food took up the entire serving space, which sported platters, bowls, baskets, and small plates. The turkey held pride of place right in front of Gabe, roasted to a dark golden brown and perfuming the entire room. In Gabe's estimation, words could not describe the heavenly redolence of the stuffing, now scooped into a dish and steaming, the aromatic sweetness of hot yeast rolls fresh from the oven and brushed with butter, and the myriad side dishes, including mashed potatoes, giblet gravy, mixed vegetables, cranberry jam, and a whipped-cream salad that Nan called ambrosia, which she'd made with rehydrated fruit, nuts, and fresh apples. He'd never seen anything like this before in his life. Not once.

For the first time since his arrival, it fell to Gabe to

give thanks for the meal. Him? He wished Nan had forewarned him so he could plan some remarks, and he hoped God would understand that all he could do was his best. Since the family had grown, he asked that everyone join hands, and then, speaking straight from the heart, he expressed appreciation of the many favors bestowed on those beneath this roof, and he asked the Lord to bless the bounty on the table. While everyone chimed in with amen, Gabe sent up a private prayer of thanks. His month with Nan had been a priceless experience, teaching him so many things, not the least of which were how to pray and have faith in things he couldn't actually see or touch.

Gabe had never carved a turkey, and he was caught unprepared when he realized that the head of the household was expected to do the honors. What if he botched the job? As Gabe picked up the sharp knife and long-handled fork, Tyke, either by accident or design, muttered instructions without seeming to do so.

"That turkey's so tender the legs and wings are about to fall off. I'd get them out of the way first." Gabe removed them to an awaiting platter. Then Tyke said, "This is the moment, Nan. When Gabe cuts off an outer slice of that breast, we'll see juice spurt a bit if the white meat is moist."

And so it went until Gabe had carved the entire turkey as if he'd done it dozens of times. The razor-sharp knife cut thin, even slices, and when Jasper let out a whine, Gabe slid a small piece off the plate, hoping it looked accidental. The dog wolfed it down, gazing up at him with adoring brown eyes. Nan's lips twitched, but she didn't say a word.

When every dish on the table had been passed around, Gabe could barely wait to eat, but for some reason no one did. Christopher reached for his fork, but at once yanked his hand back when a faint thump came from beneath the table. The boy darted a startled look at Laney, who looked back at him with such faked innocence that even Nan stifled a giggle.

Obviously something was expected of him, Gabe thought, but what? He'd already blessed the meal. Had he left something out? He glanced imploringly at his wife. With a twinkle of mirth dancing in her eyes, she gestured quickly with her hand, pretending to put an invisible bite of food into her mouth.

Marveling at all the absurd rules that polite people lived by, Gabe dutifully forked a bite of turkey into his mouth, and then, as if the starting shot at the horse races had just gone off, everyone began to eat. The meal was *superb*, with a plethora—a big word Gabe loved—of tastes to please almost anyone's palate. Within fifteen minutes, Gabe had had two helpings of everything except stuffing, of which he'd had three, and he was so full that he couldn't possibly hold another morsel. Apparently Nan felt the same way, because she suggested that dessert be served later. No one disagreed, and her cheeks flushed a delicate shade of pink at the compliments showered on her about her superb cooking.

Everyone pitched in to help clean the kitchen. Christopher washed, Laney rinsed, Tyke sat on a chair by the sink to dry, Jasper patrolled among everyone in case anything was dropped after he'd wolfed down a bowl of uneaten servings, and Gabe helped Nan put stuff away. With so many hands, the mess disappeared in short order. When Nan was satisfied that all was up to snuff, the family moved to the sitting room. And they *were* a family, Gabe thought. Tyke had suggested that the children call him Pop, and they'd quickly warmed to that idea. When the old man got himself positioned on the settee, both kids sat on the patterned wool rug at his feet, begging for a story about the "olden" days.

Tyke's seamed face dissolved into a wrinkled smile

as he told a tale of his childhood, when he and a friend had taken a dislike to a neighboring apple farmer and decided to put a burlap bag filled with fresh cow manure on his porch, set it afire, knock on his door, and then run.

"We figured his house'd smell like cow sh—excuse me, ma'am—cow manure for days. So we hid in some bushes, giggling so hard our sides hurt, so we could watch that mean old farmer stomp out the flames. We pictured him with cow manure clear to his knees!"

"What happened, Pop?" Christopher demanded with alacrity. It seemed clear to Gabe that Christopher was thinking this was a prank he'd like to play on someone. "Was he mad? Did you get away clean, or did he know who did it?"

Nan shot Gabe a worried look, but he motioned for her to wait. Gabe didn't believe the man would put bad ideas into either child's head.

"Well," Tyke said slowly, to draw out the suspense, "his *wife* came to the door, and when she went to stomping, the flames licked up and caught her skirt afire."

"Oh, *no!*" Laney gasped, and put a hand over her heart.

Christopher's smile vanished, replaced by a horrified expression. "Did she burn up, Pop?"

Tyke settled a hand on the girl's golden head and fixed Christopher with a level gaze. "Of course not. My friend and I raced back to save her. We got her skirts out in record time, and she didn't even get singed. But we were both caught red-handed, and I mean that literally, because we blistered our fingers and palms putting out her skirts. Our hands hurt for days, and 'course our folks found out what we'd done. As punishment, our fathers made us not only clean that mean old farmer's stoop, but also whitewash his fence and paint his house. We worked nigh onto a month, hating every minute, but deep down we both knew we had it coming. And we learned a good lesson or two, the first being that when you play mean pranks, you may do harm to the wrong person."

"What was the other lesson you learned?" Christopher asked. A thoughtful frown creased his forehead.

Tyke chuckled and shook his head. "Well, by month's end, we discovered that the mean old farmer wasn't really so mean. In fact, we both liked him. And you could've knocked both of us over with a feather when he paid us fair wages for painting his house. By then we both felt so bad about the whole doggone thing that we tried to give it back, but he said we'd earned it. I reckon we learned from that experience to get acquainted better with a person before we judged him. And," he added meaningfully, "not to believe everything we heard about folks."

Gabe flashed a grin at Nan that held just a hint of *I told you so*.

Gabe had just joined his wife in front of the tree to help light the candles when Christopher tugged urgently on his sleeve. Gabe followed the boy into the kitchen.

His blue eyes wide, Christopher whispered, "We got no presents for Pop!"

For Gabe, it was an oh-shit! moment, but he settled for saying, "Uh-oh. Now what'll we do?"

Nan joined them just then, and when she'd been updated on the conversation, she said, "The only thing to do is share our gifts with him." She smiled at Gabe. "I got you a couple of nice things I haven't wrapped yet. They would work, if you don't mind not receiving them yourself. And I have some men's knitted socks on display downstairs. I can quickly wrap those for him."

Gabe didn't give a hang about receiving Christmas

presents, because he knew he wouldn't be around to use them. "Great plan. I'll go downstairs with you to wrap them while Laney and Christopher keep Pop occupied."

Christopher had clearly fallen in love with the old man. "I got a book under the tree. I can tell by feeling that it's a book for certain sure. I ain't sure who got it for me or what it's about, but it can go to Pop, too."

"No!" Gabe protested. "That's my present for *you*, the only special thing I got you!"

Christopher grinned. "I'll get to enjoy it all the same, because Pop can't read no more. I'll read it to him, and then he'll have no more use for it."

Gabe guessed the kid had a point. "All right. When we hand out gifts to each other, I'll give that one to Pop. But it'll mean I won't have a present for you. I'll feel bad about that."

Christopher's eyes went misty. "You already gave me the best present when you brought me home with you."

Gabe felt that tightness in his throat again. He laid a hand briefly on the boy's shoulder and turned away.

After Nan finished lighting the candles on the tree, Gabe helped her sneak gifts downstairs to her workroom. Laughing like a couple of kids, they hurriedly wrapped gifts for Pop. "This is a beautiful razor, Nan. I've never owned one with an ivory handle. Thank you for picking out something so beautiful for me."

Her cheek dimpled. "It goes to Pop now."

"Which just goes to show that it truly is the thought that counts," Gabe replied. "I'll know when he opens it that you chose it for me. Besides I'll—" He broke off. He'd almost said he'd never have a chance to use it anyway. "Such a fine gift will sure make him happy, I think," he amended.

Soon they were back upstairs. Gabe engaged Pop in

conversation, while Nan, hiding gifts in her skirts, slipped over to the tree to put the new presents beneath the boughs. Afterward, Laney got out her violin and played Christmas carols. Nan and Pop knew all the words, and this time around, Gabe and Christopher were able to chime in during the refrains.

"You play *beautifully*," Pop told Laney between songs. "This is the nicest evening, not to mention holiday, I've had since I lost my wife and kids." A moment later he was smothered by hugs from Nan and Laney. Christopher wormed an arm through feminine bodies and took the old man's hand, and Gabe grinned across their heads at him. Tyke winked at him.

Gabe thought everything about this night was beautiful. It was, hands down, the most perfect in his memory. He only wished he could be here next Christmas, and then the Christmas after that, long enough to learn the words to all the songs and be able to belt them out with confidence. It wasn't easy for him to be satisfied with only this one evening, only this one month.

Okay, it was impossible. He *wasn't* satisfied. Being grateful and being satisfied were, he was learning, a hell of a long way from each other. He truly was grateful for the time he'd been granted. But it wasn't long enough. A lifetime of this sort of happiness wouldn't be long enough.

Nan pushed all thought of what would come in the morning from her mind, determined to make this Christmas Eve wonderful in every way. As she handed out her gifts to everyone, her heart ached, but she didn't allow that to show in her expression or in her manner. *Gabriel.* Whenever he wasn't looking, she feasted her gaze on him, memorizing little details that she would be able to hold close to her heart later if she lost him. The gleam of his black hair in the candlelight as he bent his head to unwrap the harmonica Laney had gotten for him. The deep, rich sound of his laughter after he blew on the instrument and made a horrid noise. The graceful movement of his large hands, which she'd once likened to paws but now knew were capable of incredible gentleness. And the way she got lost in the dark brown depths of his eyes when he met her gaze.

"My belly tells me it's time for dessert!" he announced after everyone had opened their presents. "I've got my name on *two* of those sticky rolls, and the peach pie is all mine."

"Nuh-uh!" Christopher abandoned his harmonica to follow Gabe into the kitchen. "I ain't never tasted peach pie!"

Nan wasn't sure she could eat, but after making a sample plate for Tyke, she fixed one for herself and sat beside the old man on the settee to pretend she was nibbling.

"Thank you so much for bringing me here," he said, his voice gruff with emotion.

Earlier, Tyke had removed his sack coat, revealing the sleeves of the once white shirt he wore under his waistcoat. *Once white* were the key words. The cloth had gone yellow with age. Nan decided she would be quite busy over the coming weeks fashioning new garments for Laney and Christopher's honorary grandfather.

"I am delighted to have you here," she assured him.

"I'm thinking I need to go on home once I finish dessert. You're very kind to make me feel like part of your family, Nan, but the truth is, you don't have room for me here."

"Nonsense! Gabriel and I have worked it all out. For tonight, you shall sleep in our bed. Tomorrow evening we must empty my upstairs workroom. It is just at the end of the hall, and it's plenty large enough for two single beds. You and Christopher will have to share the space, but with all the shelving for storage, I think it will work out nicely. Don't even *think* about going back to that empty house. I won't allow it. We've all decided to keep you!"

He laughed and shook his head. "I'm not taking your bed. Until three weeks ago, I slept in a chair every night."

Nan leaned close. "Oh, *please* do take our bed. Gabriel and I are hoping for an excuse to sneak away downstairs for—" Nan broke off, not quite crediting that she was about to say such a thing. Her cheeks went fiery hot. The long-unused laugh lines at the corners of Tyke's eyes deepened, but he managed to keep a straight face. She floundered ahead. "Well, we *are* newly married, and with children in the house, we get little privacy. You understand?"

Tyke grinned around a mouthful of apple pie. After chewing and swallowing, he replied, "So my staying tonight will give you a reason to sneak out?"

"Precisely," Nan agreed. "And I shan't have to worry about Laney waking up from a bad dream, because you shall be here to comfort her."

"All right, you've twisted my arm enough," he said with a chuckle. Then his expression went serious. "I'm told that your husband must take a dangerous walk right before dawn."

Nan's heart caught. "Who told you?"

"At first I got the information by eavesdropping on a conversation between Laney and Christopher. She was explaining what Gabe had meant on my porch when he said he'd seen me through the clouds." Tyke shrugged. "Then, with some leading questions, I got the story firsthand from her."

"And you don't believe a word of it?" Nan asked tightly.

Tyke gazed at the flickering candles on the Christmas tree for a long moment. "Actually, I have good reason to believe all of it." He sent Nan a solemn glance. "But that's a story for later. I think you should herd us all off to bed to dream about Santa Claus leaving gifts in socks while you spend what remains of the night with your husband."

Nan took Tyke's advice to heart and went to her workroom to collect enough quilts to make her and Gabriel a pallet downstairs.

Nan expected the next several hours to be the most torturous of her life, but somehow Gabriel made them the most precious. After placing lighted candles in strategic places around the shop and drawing all the curtains closed, he took Nan into his arms to waltz to music they heard only in their hearts. He looked so handsome in the crimson shirt she'd made for him that merely admiring him took Nan's breath away. Oh, how she loved this man.

As they whirled slowly around the shop, Nan tilted her head back to smile up at him. "How did you do this to me, Gabriel Valance?"

His strong white teeth flashed in a crooked grin. Nan traced every line of his dark face, committing each to memory. "What exactly are you accusing me of doing to you, Mrs. Valance?"

"You stole my broken heart," she murmured, "and then you relentlessly mended all the cracks so none of the marvelous feelings you've given me can ever leak out."

"Ah, Nan." His gaze clung to hers. "Have I really filled your heart with marvelous feelings?"

"So many marvelous feelings that I've lost count."

"What about in the morning? Will you have no regrets then?"

The very thought of that broke Nan's heart all over

again, but she was determined not to spoil what might be their final evening together. He knew without words from her how shattered and utterly devastated she would be when she lost him. *Please, God, don't take him from me. Please don't.* "You have been a gift in my life, Gabriel, a perfect and precious gift. I will never regret a single moment that I've had with you."

He hunched his shoulders and gathered her close against him as he led her into yet another slow turn. "I'll never regret a single moment, either. I just wish I didn't have to leave you."

Nan squeezed her eyes closed. Pain lanced through her chest. It felt as if steel claws were shredding her heart. "Please, Gabriel, let us not speak of that just yet. I am not strong like you are, I'm afraid, and I fear I shall get weepy and cling to you with such ferocity that you won't be able to leave the shop at the designated time."

"I'm not strong," he said, his voice raspy next to her ear, the rumble of each word moving through the wall of his chest to vibrate into her body. "Truth is, I'm a coward, so afraid I'll lose control that I've chosen to pretend it won't happen instead of facing it."

"Maybe it won't," she whispered, wishing with every ounce of her being that it could be true.

His arms tightened around her with almost crushing strength. "Let's pretend this is the first night of the rest of our lives," he said firmly.

Then he swept her up into his arms and carried her to the pallet, where he reverently divested her of her clothing and made love to her. Nan allowed herself to float into paradise with him, glorying in every touch of his hands on her skin, losing herself in every deep kiss, and spinning with him through starlit blackness when their passions peaked.

Afterward, they clung to each other beneath the

quilts. Nan felt drained. At any other time, she knew she would be limp with exhaustion. But nerves and irrepressible dread kept her body taut, her heart racing, and her lungs aching with sobs she refused to release.

As if he sensed her desperation, Gabriel simply held her for a long while. Then he finally spoke. "Where is the Pinkerton report?"

"It's back on the shelf where you first hid it."

"I thought I told you to hide it someplace safe where you'll be sure to come across it? If the angels erase your memory of me, I want you to find that document and read it so you'll know a murder charge isn't hanging over your head."

"I'll find it there, because I dust the shelves once a month."

"Oh." He chuckled. "Of *course* you do. It's the perfect hiding place."

"And if those angels rob me of my memory of you, they are Satan's handymen, not God our Father's."

He drew the quilts close around them to create a cocoon of warmth.

Nan kissed him on the neck. "You've yet to give me my other gift," she said.

He arched a dark brow at her. "Pardon me?"

"The long, slender box. I saw you with it yesterday. You gave nothing shaped like that to anyone. I can only assume it was a gift for me, and you're waiting to hand it over!"

He laughed. Then his smile faded. "Ah, *that* gift. It's nothing to do with me, Nan. That one's from Santa, and when you find it tomorrow, be sure to read the letter he left for you inside the box."

Nan's chest tightened. She had never believed in Santa Claus and wasn't about to begin now. Only somehow she suddenly yearned to believe. Santa Claus was magical, and she was in frantic need of a little magic just then. "Where do you suppose Santa hid that box?"

"Out by the woodpile." There was no glimmer of laughter in his dark eyes when he met her gaze. "When the fires burn low, you or Laney or Christopher will be sure to find it. Save the letter, Nan. Keep it in a safe place. You'll have that to remember me by."

Nan couldn't bear this a moment longer. She could already feel the pain of losing him tearing through her. Robbed of the ability to speak, she sought solace in his strong arms. He made love to her again, this time with an almost frantic urgency, and afterward, as they lay with their limbs intertwined, Nan felt a tear slip down his cheek.

Or was it a tear slipping down her own? Silent heartache. Though no clock sat in her workroom, she could hear the seconds ticking past inside her mind. "What time is it now?" she asked him.

He groped for his jeans and pulled out his pocket watch. After he flipped it open, he stared at the face for several seconds. "Two," he finally told her.

The next time Nan asked, he checked his watch and whispered, "Three."

Her voice sounded thin, hollow, and unfamiliar when she said, "You must leave at four."

"Yes." That was all he said for several minutes. Then he broke the silence. "Will you do something for me, Nan?"

"Anything," she whispered. "Absolutely anything."

"When I start my walk up the street, will you stand at the window?"

Tears burned like liquid fire in her eyes. "Oh, Gabriel."

"Please, Nan. It's important to me. Last time, your sweet face . . . Well, seeing you there, my beautiful angel at the window, it helped somehow. Promise me you'll be there again so I can see you?"

Nan wanted to say that she would be out in the street, holding tight to him and walking right along with him. But she knew he would protest if she revealed that wish. Gabriel wouldn't want her out there. He'd worry about her safety, for one, and he'd also want her to be at a distance when he drew his last breath, which he believed would spare her some of the ugliness.

"I will be there; I promise," she whispered.

His arms trembled as he hugged her close. "It doesn't hurt," he told her. "If they let you remember anything, try to remember that. I felt no pain. And I'm not afraid."

Nan figured she was terrified enough for both of them. Gabriel had told her at Baden's house that nothing and nobody could interfere with the angels' plans. Was she really so foolish as to think that a woman's plot to save her husband could thwart fate?

When it came time for Gabriel to dress, Nan threw on her nightgown and wrapper so she could help fasten the buttons of his new red shirt and then smooth down his collar. Her hands shook, revealing the intensity of her emotions, but she strove to keep her eyes dry and to smile, which might possibly be her final gift to him.

He reached for his guns on the table, then stopped as he heard someone on the stairs. Laney burst into the room, and ran to him. She flung her arms around him, nearly strangling him with the intensity of her grip. Her shoulders shook, but she made no sound. Then, as suddenly as she'd appeared, she was gone. They heard her muffled sobs as she raced back up the narrow stairs.

Gabe picked up his gun belt. Nan saw him hesitate, and then he laid it back on the table.

"What?" she whispered.

"I'm not wearing them," he said hoarsely. "Not this time." His firm mouth tipped into a travesty of a grin. "No snakes out there to shoot, only a boy with more guts than brains."

That *boy* meant to kill her husband. *Pete Raintree.* Nan had grown to detest that name. She wondered where the fellow was right now. Was he already hiding in the shadows? Or had he taken a room at the hotel, where he could watch for Gabriel to step out into the street?

Gabriel tipped his hat onto his dark head. After adjusting the brim, he touched it in a final salute to her. "You're one hell of a lady, Nan Valance. The greatest honor—and pleasure—of my whole life has been to be your husband."

Nan fought for control, but her eyes filled with tears anyway. "I love you so very much. Don't go out there, Gabriel. He can't shoot you if you stay in here with me. Please don't go!"

Nan winced at the hysteria in her voice. She'd promised herself that she wouldn't do this to him. For Gabriel, walking out that door would be difficult enough without tearful pleas from her.

"I can't hide from God, Nan. Nobody can." He drew her into his arms and murmured against her hair, "This is foreordained. And tears can't save me."

"What can? Something has to! What can?" She heard herself practically screaming and managed to bite down on bubbling hysteria.

"Pray for me," he said thickly. "If anyone's prayers go directly to God's ears, I'm certain yours do. So just pray. Maybe your voice will ring through heaven with such force that the gates will swing wide-open for me this time."

Nan couldn't pray for him to go to heaven, not when

she so desperately needed him to stay here on earth. Somehow she walked with him across the shop. Somehow she stood at the door to bid him a final farewell. Somehow she didn't sob when he kissed her deeply.

"Don't say good-bye." He straightened and smiled down at her. In the flickering candlelight, he looked so beautiful to her—tall, dark, wonderful, her beloved Gabriel, the man who'd given her the priceless gift of laughter. "I can do everything else, Nan, but I don't think I can stand hearing you say that word."

She nodded, not trusting herself to speak. He turned, hesitated, and turned back to flash her one last grin. "Don't forget your present from Santa. I love you, Nan." His smile held fast. "Watch my face as I say that. I *love* you, Nan." He paused. "Are my brows twitching?"

She shook her head.

"Am I shifty eyed?"

She managed another shake.

"Do you believe that I mean it, deep in your heart?"

She couldn't speak, so she nodded. He seemed to understand.

A long look. A kiss. Another long look. Then he left the shop and closed the door softly behind him.

Sobbing, Nan ran from window to window to tear open the curtains. But by the time she could see out, Gabriel had already vanished. She ran to fetch a candle and set it on the windowsill, telling herself that she would stand there so he could see her. She'd promised, and it was a vow she meant to keep.

Clasping her hands over her heart, she trembled with trepidation. Where was he now? At the saloon? Was he just now ordering a bottle of whiskey? Was he thinking of her? Or was he thinking of the bullet that would soon be buried in his chest? Nan had never felt so helpless. How could she stand here and do nothing while some no-account killed the only man she'd ever loved?

"No," she whispered. "No, no, no! I need him. We need him. And he needs us. Oh, please, no."

Nan prayed as she'd never prayed, the words disjointed in her mind, one thought breaking short and going in circles just as another took shape. Then, as suddenly as if someone had shouted it out loud, it came to her.

God helps those who help themselves.

With a gasp, Nan bolted across the stretch of floor to her workroom archway to stare at the guns Gabriel had left on her project table.

Chapter Twenty

Everything is pretty much the same as last time, Gabe thought. Or was it? As he crossed the saloon to stand at the bar, he couldn't shake the feeling that everything was slightly off somehow. Had there been so many men inside the establishment the last time? Gabe hadn't taken a head count that first morning, but now several of the tables had a couple of fellows seated at them. *Strange.* It was just after four o'clock in the morning. Very few people were normally still drinking at this hour. They'd either passed out or they'd gone home to sleep. And to top it off, it was Christmas morning. Didn't these fellows have families?

Gabe thought of his own family—Laney, Christopher, Tyke, Jasper, and Nan. Oh, God, his precious Nan. If he'd had his druthers, he sure as hell wouldn't be standing in this saloon, about to knock back jiggers of rotgut. These men needed a couple of angels to give them a good, hard shake so they'd appreciate the people who waited for them at home.

When the barkeep came to take Gabe's order, he smiled and nodded. That was definitely different. Last time, all Gabe had gotten was a stiff, "Merry Christmas." He ordered a whole bottle, just as he had the last time, even though he knew that having it marked with his name was silly. He'd never be back to pour another measure from it.

At the end of the bar, Doc Peterson nursed a drink. This time around, Gabe didn't have to guess at the doctor's identity; he knew the man and liked him. The poor fellow's thin gray hair was in a stir, and once again his gray suit looked as if he'd slept in it. Gabe knew the physician hadn't been home recently to catch some sleep. His wife never would have let him leave the house with his necktie all crooked and escaping from the stickpin.

Gabe looked into the mirror behind the bar and met the doctor's gaze. Doc's larynx bobbed. He inclined his head in a silent greeting, which was another different thing. Either Gabe's memory was faulty, or he guessed not *every* detail could be exactly the same this time around. He'd lived this last month so differently than he had the first time, and according to Nan, he'd collected some friends along the way. Knowing that felt damned good. At least this time when Raintree shot him, Gabe wouldn't lie in the street feeling indescribably empty because no one would mourn his passing. Some people would feel a little sad when they learned of his death. And his family, he knew, would mourn him deeply.

Gabe just hoped Nan's and Laney's memories would be erased so they'd feel no grief. How would it be fair if they had to endure pain because he had failed so miserably at life the first time around that he'd needed to be sent back to take another shot at it? He had this sadness coming, but by God, they didn't deserve it.

"You doing okay, Doc?" Gabe asked. He figured it'd be rude not to speak, and if that was breaking the damned rules, what the hell? He'd already broken so many that one more would hardly matter. "I sure hope the little Wilson girl isn't sick."

Doc shook his head. "No. Thanks to you, Charity is fine." He smiled wearily. "I lost an old fellow tonight, though. The family is taking it pretty hard. In my business, you sometimes feel like a failure, and the only way to cheer up is to have a toddy."

Gabe nodded. "Just don't fall into the habit," he warned. "You've got a mighty nice lady waiting at home for you, and there's not a man alive who can save the whole world. You do your best. That's all you can do."

Doc lifted his glass. "Good luck, Gabriel. I think you're due."

Gabe frowned and knocked back the contents of his glass. *Good luck?* He couldn't recall anyone ever having wished him that. No gunman worth his salt depended on luck. He counted on his instincts, his speed, and his accuracy—which was precisely why Gabe had left his weapons lying on Nan's worktable. When he turned to face Pete Raintree, he didn't want to react reflexively and slap leather. This time around, the kid would live to walk away. Whether he deserved to or not wasn't the point.

Pouring himself one more jigger, just as he had the last time, Gabe smiled, albeit with a sting in his eyes. This time around, Christopher Broderick wasn't outside under the brothel staircase, clutching his knees and wearing a ragged coat as his only defense against the cold. And when Gabe got drilled, he wouldn't be missing an important breakfast date. *Nope.* This time the kid was safe at home, snug under a double layer of quilts on Nan's settee. Gabe hoped the boy had taken a leap of faith to believe in Santa Claus tonight and was now dreaming about a jolly old elf filling his sock with sugarplums.

It's time. Gabe wished he could ignore the seconds that ticked past in his head, but like he'd told Nan, he couldn't hide from this, and he sure as hell couldn't run from it. He drained his glass and set it back on the counter with a sharp click.

Doc stirred. "Hey, Gabriel."

This sure as hell was different. Surprised, Gabe turned toward the physician. "What's that, Doc?"

"If I never get another chance to say it, I want to say it now. Thank you for keeping Mrs. Wilson from taking her little daughter into my office this week. I don't know what led you to be in that precise spot at that exact moment, but I'll always thank God you were there and had the foresight to warn that woman away. There isn't a doubt in my mind that you saved that child's life."

Gabe held that thought close as he pushed through the bat-wing doors and stepped out into the predawn darkness. His boots thumped on the boardwalk, making crisp yet hollow sounds. His senses were so sharp that his skin prickled. He'd told Nan he wasn't afraid. But now he felt it—a cold, crawling fear that inched up his spine and turned his blood to ice. It wasn't that he was afraid of dying. What terrified him was leaving Nan alone, and knowing that he would miss all the years they could have had together.

A snowflake drifted down, startling him. He thought he heard the plank walkway across the street creak under someone's weight. Then he thought he saw movement in the thick shadows in front of the closed, dark-windowed shops.

Just nerves, he assured himself. And as he stepped out onto the street, he started to pray. *If you're listening, Lord, I still don't have the words of your prayer memorized, so all I can do is talk to you inside my head, sort of like I'd talk to a friend.* Gabe decided that sounded stupid and was glad he wasn't saying it aloud. *Nobody ever taught me to pray before I met Nan. Please watch over her for me. She's the sweetest person I've ever known. I swear, she's never had a mean thought or done a mean thing to anybody. As for me, well, I tried, but I guess you know by now that I can't follow your rules even to save my own soul.* Gabe let out a quivery breath. *I'm sorry for that, but then again, not really sorry, so I won't ask for forgiveness. Just know that I tried hard to think about things this time and do what I thought was right, even though the angels said different.* Gabe kept putting one foot in front of the other despite a faint voice at the back of his mind that kept screaming for him to dive and roll. Any second now, Pete Raintree would shout his name. *I guess that's all, Lord. Except, if you have a second to spare, I could use a big dose of courage right now. It's mighty hard to keep walking.*

Gabe searched for the candlelight that should be shining from Nan's shop window. All he saw was blackness. He took a few more steps, convinced that he wasn't seeing right. She'd promised she'd stand at the glass. So where the hell was she? Why had she doused all the wicks?

"Valance! Gabriel Valance!"

The shout was followed by a gunshot that made Gabe jerk. He closed his eyes for an instant. He hadn't been hit. Not yet. Then he slowly turned around. His hands ached to go for his guns, to shoot back and try to save himself. Only he already knew how that would end, and in a crazy way he was glad that he wasn't wearing his Colts.

A male voice barked from somewhere off to Gabe's left and nearly startled him out of his boots. "Drop it, Raintree!"

What the hell? This isn't in the script. The next instant, Gabe saw men spilling from the saloon. Who were *they*? The movement in the shadows that Gabe believed he'd only imagined moments earlier materialized into men—shopkeepers, hired help—all of them with rifles aimed at Raintree and ready to fire.

"Drop the gun, mister!" someone else shouted. "One wrong move and we'll fill you with so much lead, you'll leak like a colander!"

"You heard him!" another voice warned. "Here in Random, we watch out for our own!"

It seemed to Gabe that men shouted warnings from nearly every direction. Doc's tenor stood out from all the rest. "We folks in Random stand together, son. I don't hold with killing, but I do shoot rattlesnakes, and right now, you're looking like one to me."

Stunned, Gabe couldn't think, couldn't move. This wasn't happening. He shook his head and blinked, but nothing changed. Then his bewilderment turned to spine-chilling terror when a woman's voice, thin and shaky, shrilled from behind him.

"I've got a gun on you, too, Raintree!"

Nan? Gabe couldn't credit his ears.

"I'll shoot you dead; I promise you. If you've got a brain in your head, you'll drop that pistol to the ground!"

Oh, Lord. If Nan's hands were shaking half as badly as her voice, she'd be the one to drop her weapon, and she probably had the damn thing cocked. What the Sam Hill was she *thinking*?

Pete Raintree, as tall and gangly as Gabe remembered, staggered in a full circle, clearly too panicked to think straight. Instead of dropping his weapon, he waved it around, saying, "Are you people *crazy*? This is a shoot-out. You ain't s'posed to interfere!"

A new kind of fear filled Gabe. He couldn't let that kid die just because he was too stupid or too scared to put down the weapon. Gabe threw up his arms. "Don't shoot him! Please don't shoot him! Raintree, drop the goddamned gun! They're gonna drill your hide with holes if you don't." Gabe saw the younger man turn toward him. "Throw it down. Just throw it do—"

Gabe felt the punch of lead hit him in the chest before he heard the shot. He staggered back but didn't fall. Then, as if a metal bar struck him across the bend of his legs, he went to his knees.

"Gabriel!" Nan screamed his name. Gabe heard the terror and anguish in that cry, but damned if he could turn his head to look at her. He felt numb all over. *Go back*, he wanted to yell, but he couldn't make his vocal cords work. The darkness around him grew blacker. Bright little spots bounced in front of his eyes. Noise exploded against his eardrums, a staccato of weapon reports. "Gabriel!"

He felt her arms come around him. And for just an instant his vision cleared. *Nan, my window angel.* Only she wasn't safe inside her shop; she was on her knees beside him in the street. What if she took a bullet with his name on it?

Gabe felt himself slumping sideways, felt Nan's fingers clutching frantically at his shirt to hold him up. Then he hit the ground, shoulder first. He figured his head must have hit, too, but he was beyond registering anything. Blackness moved in. He knew how dying went. The only difference was, he didn't feel so cold this time.

Because Nan's arms were around him.

"No!" Nan screamed the word. She felt blood seeping from Gabriel's chest, hot and sticky against her hand. "No! Please, God, *no!*"

This can't be happening, she thought wildly. Nearly all the shopkeepers along Main had heeded her warning and had been waiting to protect her husband. Why, oh, *why* had Gabriel interfered, trying to save a no-account man who didn't deserve to be saved?

Don't shoot him! Gabriel had shouted. And then he'd raised his arms and walked toward Raintree, making a target of himself. *No!* She couldn't understand. Why would God take such a wonderful man when he was needed here by so many? Laney needed him. Christopher needed him. Tyke Baden needed him. Even Jasper needed him. *And so do I! He's my life, my heart, every breath I take!*

Hard male hands closed over Nan's shoulders. She vised her arms around her husband, knowing that those hands meant to take him from her. She braced against the tugs. Then she shrieked and fought, blindly lashing out. "Leave him be. Don't *touch* him! Leave us *alone!*"

But in the end, Nan's strength was no match for that of the men, and they pried her husband from her arms. Dazed, robbed of comprehension, Nan knelt on the frozen earth with snow pelting her face. One thought kept circling stupidly in her brain, something Gabriel had told her: that nothing could interfere with the plans of the angels. *I can't hide from God.*

Nan felt as if her heart were being ripped from her chest. She covered her face with her hands and began rocking back and forth. *All for naught.* All her efforts to save Gabriel's life had been futile, the silly, desperate contrivances of a frantic wife to save a man already marked for death. Only *why?* She couldn't understand it. Gabriel, so wonderful and good of heart, had been taken from her while hundreds, probably thousands of less deserving husbands still lived.

"Mama?"

Laney's voice barely penetrated the fog. It seemed as if the girl called out to her from a great distance. She felt a grip on her arm and recognized Laney's touch.

"Mama, they carried Gabe to Doc's!" Nan felt Laney give her arm a yank. "Not to the undertaker's, Mama. Do you hear me? Do you understand what I'm saying?"

Nan blinked. She was almost afraid to comprehend Laney's words. It would kill her to be given false hope. "What?" She brushed at her cheeks. "What did you say?"

Laney knelt down to look Nan in the eyes. "I don't think he's dead, Mama. I know Raintree shot him in the chest again, but it didn't kill him this time. At least, I don't think it did."

"He ain't dead." That was Christopher's voice. "At least, not yet he ain't. Dead men don't get carried to Doc's. They get took to the undertaker."

Nan's heart squeezed. Then, as the children's words sank in, hope unfurled like a bud opening to the sun.

Nan scrambled to her feet. Flanking her, both children grabbed her arms to help get her steady on her feet. *Not dead.* Nan broke into a run. Not releasing their holds on her, both kids raced along beside her. When they hit the boardwalk at the corner of Oak and Main, their bare feet made loud thumps on the icy planks.

Men crowded the waiting room. Nan scanned the familiar faces of fellow business owners, but she could ascertain nothing from their stoic expressions. Lifting her chin, she tried to push through their ranks to reach the inner door, but Mr. Redmond caught her back. "You mustn't go in there just yet! Doc's working on them both right now. It's no place for a lady."

Nan realized that she stood before these fellows in nothing but her nightgown and wrapper, which hung open with the sash drooping uselessly at her hips. *Lady?* She no longer cared to be a lady; she wanted to be Gabriel's *wife*. She planted a hand on Redmond's chest. "Let go and get out of my way! I want to see my husband!"

"Mrs. Valance, I can't allow—"

Allow. That single world set off white sparkles inside Nan's head, and no one in the room ever found out what Burke Redmond couldn't allow. Every bit of lady-like behavior Nan had ever learned fell away from her like a discarded cloak. This man was trying to prevent her from going to Gabriel. Reacting instinctively, she brought up her right knee forcefully and felt it connect. Redmond made a clogged sound, like a turkey whose feathers had been violently pulled, and released her at once, staggering against the wall. Nan spared him not a glance and stepped into the next room.

Doc glanced up from where he was working over Pete Raintree's thigh. His spectacles rode low on his bony nose. Mrs. Peterson stood slightly behind him, holding surgical implements in her hand. The patient appeared to be unconscious, whether from near death or a pad soaked in chloroform, Nan didn't know. Nor did she give a flip.

"Why on *earth* are you working on *him* when my husband needs you more?" she demanded.

Doc smiled wearily. "Don't count me as a total fool. I worked on your husband first, and all he really needed was some flushing out and stitching up. He's out cold, and he's lost some blood, but he's in no danger of dying unless infection sets in, and I don't expect that to occur. The bullet hit a harmonica in his shirt pocket. Cracked the ivory, glanced off, and went in way to the left of his heart. Missed anything vital, thank God, and basically cut a trench through his underarm before it came out the back side. He'll have a mighty sore chest and arm for a week or two, but it's not a life-threatening wound. Should heal up just fine. But this young feller's bleeding like a stuck pig."

"But—" Nan broke off to drag in a bracing breath and moisten her dry lips. "It hit Gabriel right over his heart! And I felt the blood pouring out."

"Bleeding hard is a good thing in this case. Cleans out the wound. He'll be weak from it, but a strong man like him should bounce back pretty quick." Doc inclined his head toward the other table. "Grab a chair. You can sit with him if you like. While I was stitching him up, he started to come around, so I had to put him back under. He'll probably wake up madder than a badger tangled up in a briar patch. You'd better take a load off your feet while you can, because he'll be a handful when you take him home."

"Home?" Nan said the word as if it were one she'd never heard.

"Heck, yes, *home*." Doc shook his head. "I'm not keeping him here. He'll be hurt only enough to be pesky, and I'd a whole lot rather he pester *you*."

Nan rushed over to the table where Gabriel lay covered to midchest by a white sheet. Tears stung her eyes when she saw the rise and fall of his breathing. He was *alive*. Pete Raintree's bullet had missed its mark this time. She didn't understand, but right then she didn't care. Gabriel was alive.

Taking her husband's limp hand in both of hers, Nan lifted it to her cheek. The warmth of his bent knuckles against her wet skin was the most wonderful thing she'd ever felt. Her plot to save Gabriel's life had worked!

Only, even as that thought shot through Nan's mind, she knew it wasn't true. Despite all her contrivances, Raintree's bullet had hit Gabe in the chest. The string of events leading up to that moment had all been altered because of her scheming, but even so, the ending had been exactly the same, *except* for one small detail: Gabriel had been carrying a gift of love in his shirt pocket, a small harmonica inlaid on both sides with carved ivory, given to him for Christmas by a young girl who'd come to worship the ground he walked on.

"It's a *miracle*," Nan whispered to her unaware husband. "God gave us a miracle."

Clinging to Gabriel's hand, Nan wept with joy and sent up silent prayers of thanks to a God she'd lost faith in for a short while. She would never make that mistake again. Wondrous things happened only *through* Him, and she'd been a complete goose.

Gabe jerked awake. He stared stupidly up at a cedar-plank ceiling. There was amber light, but he couldn't tell where it came from. And, oh, man, his chest hurt like hell on a rampage. That sure hadn't happened the first time around. He blinked to clear his vision. He was in a room, stretched out on his back on a hard, narrow bed. Definitely not in a shack this time, but he still saw no pearly gates.

"So, you're finally awake."

Gabe knew that voice, and it didn't belong to any angel. "Doc?" he croaked. "What the hell . . . ? Are you . . . Where am I?"

"Gabriel!" Suddenly Nan's pale face appeared above him. She looked like death warmed over as she cupped a cool hand to his cheek. "Oh, Gabriel, I thought you'd never come around."

"What are you two doing here?" Gabe demanded. Despite the pain it caused him, he pushed up on his elbow. "Are you dead, too? *Dammit.* Those angels can't get anything right! This isn't how it's supposed to go."

Doc came over to push Gabe back down onto the bed. "Don't be alarmed, Mrs. Valance. This happens sometimes after a dose of chloroform. A patient awakens agitated and a bit confused."

"I'm not confu—" Gabe broke off. *I'm not dead.* He stared hard at Nan for a moment to be sure she was real. Then he shifted his gaze to Doc and looked past the physician at Mrs. Peterson. "Sorry, ma'am. I think I forgot myself and swore."

Mrs. Peterson smiled and pushed her spectacles

back up the bridge of her nose. "No worries at all, Mr. Valance. I'm pleased as punch to see that you're rallying, just as my husband predicted."

In a daze of disbelief, Gabe listened to a summary of what had happened a few hours ago on Main. He was particularly surprised to hear that Pete Raintree had survived and now occupied the other treatment table.

"Only a flesh wound in his thigh. Luckily, I'm a fairly good shot. The missus and I used to live in California, where rattlesnakes were thick, so I got a goodly amount of practice with my pistol."

"*You* shot me?"

That was Raintree's voice, Gabe realized, and he sounded hale and hearty. Well, not hale and hearty, exactly, but definitely alive and unhappy. Maybe even insulted.

"Ah, so you're awake, too. I never time it exactly right with that blasted chloroform. I hoped you'd be out for a while longer." Doc circled his wife to return to his other patient. "Yes, it was me who shot you, and you'd better be glad of it. My pistol holds small rounds, and I hit where I aim. The bullet did some damage, I confess, but you'd be dead if any of those men had taken you down with a rifle. Instead they just shot the ground all around you to make their point."

"First you shoot me, and then you patch me up? The people in this town are plumb crazy." Raintree sat up, bunching the sheet over his groin. "Shit, I'm buck nekked and there's females in here. Where are my pants? I'm gettin' the hell out of here. It might be catchin'."

Doc gestured toward his wife. "My lovely assistant gave them a quick mend, but you'll be needing a clean pair before you leave town."

"My stuff's at the hotel." Sheet now draped around his hips, the younger man slid off the table. "Ach! *Jesus!*

That ain't no little hole you put in me, *Doc*. I'm gonna be a gimp."

"No. But you will be sore for a few weeks. It'll take some time for that thigh muscle to heal."

Raintree snatched his pants from Mrs. Peterson and hobbled into what Gabe presumed was a dressing closet. Gabe didn't envy the other man the life he would have if he didn't mend his ways, but he was jealous as hell that he wasn't the one dressing to leave.

"How long do I have to stay here?" he asked Doc.

"As soon as your head feels clear, you can go on home. It's Christmas, after all, and I think Mrs. Valance is perfectly capable of seeing to your needs, few as they will be." The physician assumed his professional mien. "Lots of fluids, plenty of rest, and *no* lifting anything over ten pounds with the injured arm for at least six weeks. You got off very lucky. It's mostly only a flesh wound, but your ribs took a hard hit, and your chest muscles were scored by the bullet. They need time to completely heal."

"My head's clear." Actually it was anything but. Gabe didn't feel woozy, just a little dizzy, but he felt an urgent need to be outside breathing fresh air. As for his head being clear, right now he was confused as hell. He was glad to see he still wore his britches, but his shirt and boots had vanished. "Where are my duds?"

Nan helped Gabe put on his boots. Then she produced one of his black shirts. "Christopher brought it over. Your Christmas shirt is ruined, I'm afraid."

Gabe's chest was wrapped, but his left arm hadn't been anchored to his side. He winced as he slipped on the shirt, then stood still while Nan buttoned it for him. Moments later, they stood outside on a snow-covered boardwalk. Old footprints were already filling with fresh flakes, Gabe noticed. He dragged in a deep breath and looked incredulously toward Main, where he'd been destined to die a second time. He was so tired his legs felt wobbly, but from someplace deep within him, a desperate energy radiated up through his belly and into his chest. He yearned to shout and laugh. Only, what if this was only temporary, and the angels could show up at any moment to fetch him?

"I'm not supposed to be here," he said softly.

Nan hugged his right arm and pressed her cheek against his sleeve. "Oh, yes, you are," she murmured. She looked up at Gabe with those beautiful silver eyes that never failed to make his heart quicken. "In fact, you are precisely where you are supposed to be, Gabriel: here with me."

"But—"

"No buts." She produced his Christmas harmonica from her cloak pocket. "There was a last-minute change of plan in heaven, I think. It was decided that you needed to remain here with all the people who need you. I wholeheartedly approve of that choice. Perhaps you are still only on loan to me, but the same holds true for everyone we love. We should take for granted not a single moment."

Gabe accepted the badly dented harmonica with his right hand, turning it this way and that. The story of what had occurred was forever chiseled in the beautiful ivory. Laney's gift to him had stopped the bullet that should have killed him. A tingling sensation worked its way up his spine. He tipped his head back to stare up at the sky. Snowflakes drifted into his eyes and melted on his cheeks. The crisp air was laced with wonderful smells coming from kitchens all over town. It was Christmas Day, and he was still alive.

Weak from blood loss and almighty sore in his chest and arm, Gabe had to walk slowly toward home and pause often. Second-story windows popped open along Main Street, and familiar faces grinned down at him and Nan.

"Merry Christmas!" was the repeated refrain. "Good to see you on your feet, Valance!"

Nan waved and returned the good wishes. Gabe had only enough strength to smile. When he felt better, he would visit every business owner to express his gratitude for their unfathomable support and loyalty during one of the darkest minutes of his life.

Pausing to rest again just across the street from Nan's shop, Gabe directed his gaze to the upstairs sitting room window. He wasn't surprised to see Tyke, Laney, and Christopher pressed in next to the tree, all waving madly at him.

"You know what just occurred to me?" Gabe whispered to Nan.

She nuzzled his arm with her cheek. "No, what?"

"I wasn't sent back to save you—or Christopher—or Tyke."

Nan leaned back slightly to search his face. "Why, then? You definitely wrought wondrous changes in my life."

Gabe closed his eyes, enjoying the fabulous sensations of the snowflakes landing on his skin and the warmth of his wife pressed to his side. "It was me. All along, I was supposed to save myself, Nan." He turned to take in her sweet, precious face. "I was the lost soul." The truth of that sank deep into Gabe's heart. "They didn't tell me that, because it was a lesson I needed to learn by myself. Those stupid mandates? No wonder I questioned the rightness of them. All along, the angels wanted me to break the rules and put myself at risk. It was a test, and I damned near failed it!"

Ah, but you didn't fail, a deep voice whispered in Gabe's ear. *You did well, Gabe. We are very pleased.*

Gabe jerked. Nan flashed him a startled look.

"It's a fine time for you to finally show up again!" Gabe said loudly.

"What?" Nan cried.

The angel Gabriel laughed softly. *God be with you, Gabe. Enjoy your life, but live it well this time. I'll give you only one last bit of advice: Always listen to your heart.*

Gabe looked down at Nan, who frowned up at him. "Did you hear that?" he asked.

"Did I hear what?"

Gabe sighed. "I figured you'd say that." He listened for a moment to be sure nothing more would be whispered; the angel Gabriel tended to be something of a chatterbox. When he heard nothing, he encircled his wife's shoulders with his uninjured arm and stepped off the boardwalk. "Come on, sweetheart. We've got a family waiting and the rest of Christmas to celebrate."

"You're going to go straight to bed, Gabriel Valance. Don't bother to argue. Burke Redmond will tell you I'm a woman to be reckoned with when I make up my mind."

"Huh? Redmond? What did you do to him?" He remembered seeing Redmond on the street just before Raintree shot him. "Hell's blazes, Nan, you didn't accidentally shoot him, did you?"

She giggled. "No, but I think he wishes I had. He tried to keep me from entering Doc's treatment room." She giggled again, louder this time. "He didn't succeed."

"So what happened?"

She told him. Gabe felt his eyes bulge.

"You actually *kneed* him? *You?*"

"Once during a poker game, you told me and Laney how to take a man down, and I followed your advice. At the time, I wore only my nightgown and wrapper, which had come untied, so all my usual concerns about ladylike behavior flew out the window. I must say, I found it rather liberating. So I suggest you obey orders. Bed rest. At least for several hours."

"Yes, ma'am!" Gabe grinned, deciding on the spot that he absolutely would *not* miss out on what remained of his first real Christmas. "Would it be possible for me to rest on the settee, propped up with pillows, so I can visit with everyone?"

"Champion idea!"

And as they walked together toward home, Gabe smiled. No heavenly mistake had been made. God had guided Gabe's hand to slip that ivory harmonica into his shirt pocket.

As they stepped onto the boardwalk in front of Nan's shop, Gabe remembered something important. "Did you ever go out back to find your Santa present?"

Nan looked blank for a moment. Then she laughed. "Good grief, no. I finally had the presence of mind to have Laney bring my clothing and shoes to the doctor's office, but the *last* thing I thought of was Christmas gifts."

"We can't have that. I have it on good authority that Santa left you something extraordinarily special."

Gabe drew her into the narrow alley that led to the back dooryard. As they closed in on the woodpile, Nan cried, "*Oh!*" Then she broke away from Gabriel to fetch the bouquet of hothouse red roses from atop a fence post, where he'd left them for her that morning. A huge pink bow with trailing ribbon held the stems together. "How on *earth* did you slip these past me?"

He chuckled. "I hid them in the alleyway." Gabe glanced at the long, slender box resting on a lower rung of the woodpile. There was no reason for Nan to read the letter inside now. Gabe would ask Christopher to fetch the container later and toss it on their sitting room fire. "The instructions say to keep them cool until they're in water. They've held up well. I'm surprised they aren't ruined from being out in the open for so many hours."

"It's thirty-eight degrees, a perfect temperature for snow, and flowers as well, I'm guessing." Nan held the blossoms to her nose and breathed in deeply of their scent. "Oh, Gabriel, roses in December. I can't believe it." She fixed him with a bedazzled gaze. "You've gone and done it now. I think Santa truly exists, and I shall expect him to bring me roses for Christmas every year for the rest of my life. They're magical."

"You'll have them, and anything else I can get for you, sweetheart."

Gabe walked closer to smell the unfurling blossoms. He started to bend down to kiss the woman who'd so completely stolen his heart. She saw him wince and stepped up on the pile of logs until their faces were level. He leaned forward, and their lips met in a featherlight kiss that went all through him.

If he could live out the rest of his days trying his damnedest to make her smile, he'd die the second time a very happy man.

Epilogue

Two and a half years later

Gabe glanced sideways at his eighteen-month-old son, who was *helping* to sandpaper the church's porch railing. The child, named Gabriel after his dad, was far too young to do chores, but he insisted on being Gabe's assistant nevertheless. Gabe tried to show him the correct way to do things, whether he understood yet or not.

Gabriel had pudgy little hands with dimples over each first knuckle. He also took his sanding assignment very seriously, bending his dark head close to the wood and frowning. It was clear to Gabe that his boy was trying to emulate him, which he found flattering. He just hoped he didn't scowl quite that fiercely while he worked.

Crouching beside the child, Gabe demonstrated with his piece of sandpaper. "Not real hard, just slowly, lightly, back and forth, back and forth. There you go. That's a fine job, Gabriel."

The child grinned up at Gabe, flashing Nan's dimple in his cheek. He was definitely a kid Gabe could never deny, with pitch-black hair, coffee brown eyes, and a complexion that loved the sun. But there was a lot of his mother in him, too. He had her perfectly bowed upper lip, and though his eyes were dark, they were shaped exactly like Nan's. Gabe was fond of telling his wife that their boy was a miraculous blend of them both, in possession of all their fine points and none of the bad. Nan always arched her fair brows and said, "Perhaps you have bad points to pass on to our children, Mr. Valance, but they shall get nary a one from me."

Nan was only teasing, of course, but Gabe completely agreed with the statement; she was as close to perfect as a woman could get. He loved her more than he ever would have believed possible.

As if his thoughts had conjured her up, he heard her calling his name. He glanced around to see her walking toward him from the house, which lay about two hundred yards away, built well back from the road where Tyke Baden's home had stood before Gabe tore it down. As it had turned out, the old man had owned an entire section of land, which stretched from Second Street, at the edge of town, into an immense acreage of rolling grassland. Pop—even Gabe called Tyke that now—had signed over the deed to Gabe and Nan two years ago, enabling Gabe to build the house he'd dreamed of during the first month of his marriage. Pop still lived with them and loved being a grandfather to Laney, Christopher, and little Gabriel. In another three months, he'd have a fourth grandchild to fuss over. Gabe had grown to think of the older man as the only father he'd ever had, and he felt certain Nan felt the same way.

Gabe swung off the porch. He didn't know how Nan pulled it off, but even large with child, she was still the most beautiful thing he'd ever clapped eyes on. Since marrying him, she'd taken to wearing dresses with modestly scooped necklines. Today she was a picture in a gown with a blue-and-white-checked bodice and sleeves trimmed with white lace, and solid blue skirts that started just below her breasts and sported a split top layer that swept gracefully back over her hips to form a stylish bustle. The garment didn't hide her pregnancy, but lent her elegance in spite of it.

"Sweetheart, why didn't you just bang on the tripod? In your condition, you shouldn't walk all the way to the church on a hot afternoon."

Glancing at the porch, Nan laid a protective hand over her swollen belly. "Gabriel, don't leave him alone up there. He may fall down the steps."

Gabe leaned back around the railing to collect little Gabriel and set him safely on the grass before walking out to meet his wife. She smiled up at him. Not for the first time, Gabe thought that he could live on Nan's smiles alone. Fortunately, she was such a fabulous cook that he'd never had to put it to a test.

"*Why* did you walk out here in the midday heat?" July in Colorado didn't bring on scorchers like Gabe had experienced in other parts of the country, but to those who'd grown accustomed to the climate, summer afternoons felt hot. He touched his hand to her moist forehead. "What was so important it couldn't wait?"

"I missed you," she said simply. "Pop is having a nap, and that big house feels empty with the kids gone."

Laney and Christopher had taken the wagon, stopped to pick up friends, and were picnicking along Random Creek, which ran through the west forty of their land. Jasper, who always shadowed the kids, was also gone and probably feasting on the fried-chicken lunch that Nan had fixed and stowed in a basket. "Let me get little Gabe, and we'll go back with you. I can't have you feeling lonely."

Nan reached up to wipe wood dust from the silver star Gabe now wore pinned to his shirt. During the last election, the townspeople had written his name in on the ballot, and Gabe had become the marshal even though he hadn't wanted the job. So far, it had worked out well. Gabe had so many people watching his back that he no longer needed to worry about upstart gun-slingers calling him out into the street for a shooting contest. Pete Raintree had blabbed far and wide that Gabriel Valance now had the equivalent of an armed battalion under his command, and only a fool would dare to challenge him.

"Let's just sit on the porch in the shade for a bit," Nan suggested. "Then you can go back to sanding. Preacher Hayes will be sorely disappointed if the rail-ing isn't painted for next Sunday's services."

Gabe had built this church with very special wor-shipers in mind, so the sign at the edge of the yard read, A CHURCH FOR SINNERS ONLY, welcoming people of all faiths, persuasions, and walks of life. Because of that, the recent Sunday services had become a huge sore point for him. He'd originally hoped this building, erected on *his* land, would be a place where people who didn't feel welcome at the other church could come to pray. Then, before he knew it, Preacher Hayes offered to do a weekly Sunday service here, and his town flock soon followed. Instead of welcoming the saloon owner, prostitutes in residence at the brothel, and the occasional stray Cheyenne Indian who had es-caped being herded off to a reservation, Gabe had to endure couples like Simon and Geneva White.

"They've got their own damn church!" Gabe had complained to Nan a few weeks ago. "Let them pre-tend to be better than everyone else in *that* church and leave mine alone."

In her ever-gentle way, Nan had pointed out that those who believed they were better than everyone else were the worst sinners of all.

"I'll get the porch painted," Gabe assured his wife as they sat together on the shady steps to watch their son toddle across the grass. "Geneva won't snag her fancy white gloves on *my* porch rail." He waited a beat. "But she might accidentally sit on a nail poking up through that pew she and Simon have staked claim to."

Nan giggled. "Did you *see* that dress she wore last Sunday? I can't believe I made it. Purple sequins on carnation pink! And the décolletage is cut so low, men's eyes pop from their sockets when she walks."

"Mine don't." Gabe nudged her with his shoulder. He'd been worrying about his wife for more than a month, and he felt that this was a perfect opportunity to talk with her about it. Since being direct was his way, he didn't prevaricate. "You're not enjoying all your absences from the shop, are you?"

Nan sighed, and Gabe knew she was considering all that they had done so she could have the time off. A year ago, she had decided that she wanted to spend more days at home, being a wife and mother. So she and Gabe had approached the young prostitute that Gabe had once consorted with at the brothel, offering her a proposal she couldn't refuse. Nan had spent the next six months training the girl in millinery and dress-making. Now Mary—Gabe still couldn't quite credit that a woman whose services he'd once rented bore his mother's name—ran the shop by herself much of the time. Nan went in to work only on Tuesday, Wednesday, and Thursday mornings from eight until noon. The arrangement had given Mary a much-needed chance to improve her lot. She made better money now than she'd ever earned in that shabby upstairs room, and she loved living in the apartment above the shop.

There had been hell to pay at first, of course. All the fine folks of Random had boycotted the shop for more than three months, the *ladies* refusing to set foot in a place where a "woman of ill repute" was employed. Fortunately Preacher Hayes had finally swayed public attitudes with several consecutive sermons about those

times when Jesus had forgiven sinners, sought them
out, and even broken bread with them. According to
Hayes, Christ had set an example for everyone to emulate, and the good people of Random seemed to be
missing the whole point, behaving toward others in
ways that Christ would not condone.

"At first, I loved having so much more time at
home," Nan finally said.

Gabe heard a big *but* hanging at the end of that sentence. He'd come to realize that Nan was a person who
seldom spoke without thinking it to death first, so instead of pressing her, he remained quiet.

"Do you want the truth?" she asked out of the blue.

Gabe chuckled. "No, I'd love to hear lies instead."

She smiled. "The *truth* is, my forward protrusion is
becoming quite large and is making me ungainly. Sometimes all the chores I *thought* would be so rewarding are
exhausting instead." She studied her palms, reminding
Gabe of the time she'd asked him if he thought she'd
been born with a serious line. "I think of all the thousands of women who have worked far harder than I do
while they were even heavier with child, and I feel—"
She broke off and sent him a stricken look. "I feel like a
lesser person, I suppose. And it's very difficult for me to
admit that, even to myself, let alone to you."

"Ah, sweetheart." Gabe curled an arm around her
shoulders. "You're *not* a lesser person. You're an *increasing* person."

She laughed and turned her face against his shirt, a
blue one that she'd made for him. It was one of Gabe's
favorites. "This is a *deep* concern, sir. I would appreciate
it if you wouldn't make jest."

"I'm not jesting. You're *definitely* increasing." Gabe's
heart clenched at the thought of her pushing herself too
hard, trying to measure up to imaginary women who'd
been able to do it *all* without a single complaint. "Why

haven't you said something to me? I'll pitch in. You don't have to do the heavy work, Nan. Make me a list, and I'll make short work of everything."

"You're already too busy tending to our livestock and crops, overseeing the construction of the new town library, being the marshal, and going to council meetings. How can you possibly find time to help me as well?" She straightened and stared toward town. "Besides, you're missing the whole point. I want to manage on my own, just as other women have done for centuries."

"That is such a load of bullshit that your wagon axle's going to break."

"*Gabriel!*"

"Well, excuse my language, but sometimes polite words don't get my message across. Other women don't have to clean homes with eight bedchambers and three water closets. A lot of the paragons you're comparing yourself to live in one-room shacks with dirt floors. Every member of the family owns, at most, two changes of clothing, so wash day is much easier, and they sure as hell don't stand over a hot iron for hours in July, pressing ruffled dresses, several shirts, and their own gowns, and also cook three large meals a day. That isn't to mention that you work at the shop three days a week and often drop in on Mary at other times to make sure all is going well."

Nan placed a fingertip over his lips, her eyes shimmering up at him.

Unable to speak clearly, Gabe said, "I'm nod finithed yet."

She laughed and dropped her hand. "You *are* finished, because, as always, you've made me feel immensely better." She slanted him a sideways glance. "So what is the answer to my problem?"

"Me!"

Nan shook her head. "This is your day off, and instead of relaxing, you've been working since sunup."

"I can resign from the school board and let the guys building the library do the job without my input. It's enough that I'm footing the bill. As for the livestock and crops, I'm not even sure I *want* to be a farmer. I'll be happy to raise a few steers, a milk cow, a couple of pigs, and some chickens. I can be highly successful at that, be the marshal, and *still* help clean, do the wash, iron clothes, and cook. Well, I'm pretty much a lousy cook, and you'll have to teach me how to do our wash and use an iron, but I can clean as good as anybody."

Her dimple flashed. "Gabriel, please don't take offense, but when you sweep, you send dirt flying three feet into the air."

"I what?"

"You sweep with all your strength. Afterward I have to dust everything in the room."

"Oh." Gabe had never considered that he might get overly enthusiastic with a broom. "Well, I'll work on it. And there's not a reason on earth why Laney and Christopher can't help more."

"They both have daily chores, and they never complain about doing them," Nan reminded him. "During summer holiday, I don't mind asking more of them, but during the school year, they need to focus on family time and their studies. And I don't want you to resign from the school board. You've brought about changes in the classroom that should have been in place years ago, and I know you want to make even more improvements. Without you pushing, none of those things will happen, and the children will suffer for it."

Gabe was a huge proponent of education, so he couldn't argue that point. "You need help around the house, though. If I'm going to keep the marshal job and remain active in the community, we have to come up with a solution. Maybe we could hire some woman to come in and lend you a hand."

Gabe jumped up to collect their son, who had decided rocks looked good to eat. He was tickling the child to distract him when he noticed a woman cutting across the back of Lizzy's lot and coming toward their place.

Returning to the porch, Gabe observed, "Some woman's coming this way. I don't know her. Do you?"

Nan narrowed her eyes. "No, I can't say that I do. I wonder what she wants."

When the woman reached the edge of the churchyard, she stopped and asked, "Can you tell me where I might find Marshal Valance?"

"You've found him." Gabe handed Nan the baby and walked out to greet their visitor. She was thin, dressed in a faded gray dress, and had dull brown hair. When he'd closed the distance to about five feet, he noticed her blue eyes and knew who she was before she said a word. Christopher had her eyes. Gabe wasn't sure how he felt about this female suddenly reappearing. For one, she'd taken a hell of a long time to do it, and second, he couldn't help but feel that Christopher was a lot better off, in a hundred different ways, now that he lived with Gabe and Nan. "How can I help you?"

The woman turned her head slightly, giving Gabe a clear look at the left side of her face. A pink scar ran from the edge of her mouth to the outside corner of her eye. Gabe had seen enough healed wounds to know that she'd been injured recently, sometime within the last year. She had another scar on her temple, paler than the one on her cheek, telling him it was older, but even so, the edges were jagged. She'd taken a blow to the head that could have killed her.

"I've been told by some shopkeepers in town that

you and your wife have taken in a homeless boy," she finally revealed.

"Yes. His name is Christopher Broderick."

The woman met Gabe's gaze straight on. He liked that about her. He saw her throat work. Then she suddenly glanced away. "I, um . . . Is he a bother to you and your missus?"

Gabe felt rather than saw Nan come to stand beside him. Then the baby tugged on his sleeve. He turned to take the child and perched him on his hip.

"Are we speaking of Christopher?" Nan asked.

The woman sent Nan an imploring look. "I'm Christopher's mama."

"Oh." Nan's voice shook just slightly. She bent her head and brushed invisible dust from her summer blue skirts. When she'd recovered from the surprise, she injected a note of pleasure into her tone. "How delightful to finally meet you!" Stepping forward, Nan extended her hand. "Christopher will be over the moon."

The woman retreated a step. "A fine lady like you . . . Well, ma'am, you don't want to be shaking hands with the likes of me." She looked past Nan at Gabe. "I came back to get my boy. I know I've been gone a very long time. Things happened, you see, and I couldn't come until now. I figured . . . Well, I had no idea fine folks like you had given him a home." Her eyes, so like her son's, went bright with tears. "That's why I asked if he's a bother to you. If he is, I'll take him back with me to Cheyenne—or someplace closer." Her shoulders lifted. "Depends on how long my money holds out. But if he ain't a bother, well . . ." She blinked and the tears spilled over onto her cheeks. "Maybe he'd be better off if I was to leave him be."

"Christopher isn't a bother," Nan said softly. "My husband and I love him as if he were our own."

The woman brushed at her cheek and smiled, her

mouth quivering at the corners. "That's good." She nodded. "That's real good." She backed away another two steps. "Will you just tell Christopher that his mama came? Tell him I'm right sorry for takin' so long and all, but I couldn't help it none. And that I'm real glad he's got himself a proper home now with good folks who love him." She stopped in her tracks for a moment. "Also tell him I love him a powerful lot, if you wouldn't mind, and that I'll write, sendin' him money by and by."

The woman spun and began walking away. Gabe stared solemnly after her. Without looking at Nan, he said, "Isn't it strange how solutions to our problems seem to appear from out of nowhere?"

Nan flicked him a bewildered look. Then the frown vanished from her brow. Her face lit up with a glowing smile. "Wait!" she cried. Placing both palms under her swollen middle, she trotted after Christopher's mother. "Mrs. Broderick, please don't leave just yet. Christopher will never forgive us if he doesn't get to see you. He loves you so very, *very* much."

The woman stopped and turned. "I ain't married, Mrs. Valance, so if you'd just call me Suzanne, I'd feel righter about it." She hugged her thin waist. "As for me seein' my boy, I don't think it'd be smart. I'd go to cryin', and he'd go to insistin' on leavin' with me." She shook her head. "I got nothin' to offer my son. With my looks goin', I don't make much money no more. It's all I can do to feed myself."

Nan rested a gentle hand on Suzanne's shoulder. "What if I were to offer you a position of employment that would pay quite well, come with room and board, and give you a daily opportunity to be with your son?"

"I'd ask where you're hidin' your angel wings."

Nan laughed and hooked arms with Suzanne Broderick. "Come along up to the house and we'll discuss the particulars over tea."

"I can't work in your house, ma'am, if that's what you're anglin' for. Folks hereabouts . . . well, they wouldn't take kindly to it, and before you could blink, they'd be actin' like you was a weevil in their flour sack."

Nan smiled and shrugged. "For a time, perhaps, but if they do, I won't give a hang. I learned from a very wonderful man that it is a huge waste of time to worry about the opinions of others, Mrs. Broderick."

"Like I said, I ain't mar—"

"It doesn't matter if you're married, dear. From this moment on, you shall be Mrs. Broderick, a widow who still mourns for her dearly departed husband."

"But that'd be a lie, and nobody'll believe it. There's men in this town who'll recognize me."

Bouncing the baby on his hip, Gabe turned to follow with his gaze the progress of his amazing wife and Christopher's mother. He grinned from ear to ear when he heard Nan say, "Not a single *one* of those men shall acknowledge that they've ever clapped eyes on you. Not in front of their wives, anyway! So you needn't worry for a second about the men. The women may be a bit of a problem if they recognize you."

"They ain't gonna recognize me. I always wore me a shawl over my head when I went out shoppin' for the few eats I could afford to get Christopher."

"Ah, so there you have it, Mrs. Broderick. Not a soul in town will recognize you. You're going to need a wedding band, but I just happen to have a spare one."

"Oh, ma'am, I can't take your weddin' band."

"Of course you can. It never meant a thing to me."

Suzanne shot Gabe a startled look over her thin shoulder. Nan, on a mission to adopt yet another family member, failed to notice. Gabe fell in well behind the two women as they covered ground toward the house. At the edge of the front dooryard, he paused, lifted his gaze to the azure sky, and winked. Gabe hadn't heard as much as a whisper from the angel Gabriel since Christmas Day well over two years ago, but he liked to think that the pesky fellow still peeked in on him every once in a while.

With only the baby to hear, Gabe said, "You told me to always listen to my heart. I'm doing that, but I have to say that if I listen to it much more, Nan and I are going to need a much bigger house."

No answer. Gabe hadn't really expected a response. He smiled, fell back into a walk, and kissed his son's forehead. The toddler grinned and said, "Dada."

Gabe missed a step. Staring incredulously at the child, he cried, "Did you just say Dada?" Gabe could scarcely believe his ears. The child had been saying *Mama* for months. He'd had no problem learning to say *Pop*. He called Laney *Neeny*. And Christopher was *Kiss*. But Gabe had only ever gotten grunts. "Say it again, Gabriel. Dada. Come on. Make your old man happy."

"Dada," Gabriel said, his toothy grin shiny with slobber. "Dada! Dada!"

"Nan!" Gabe shouted. "Wait! You've got to hear this!"